The Fabric of Honor
SELANDU TALES BOOK 1

By J. A. Komorita

The Fabric of Honor
SELANDU TALES BOOK 1

Copyright © 2024 by J.A. Komorita
All right reserved.

This is the sole work of the author, and no portion of this publication may be copied or re-published in any publication without express permission of the publisher or author.

Edited by George Verongos
Cover by George Verongos
Cover concept by J. A. Komorita
Quilts by J. A. Komorita

PAPERBACK
ISBN: 979-8-9911618-0-0

Website: jakomorita.com

In memory of my son, Keith, an unwilling and uninvited member of the 27 Club.
Love you forever, baby.

In memory of my niece, Leslie. Beautiful, multi-talented, and gone too soon.

ACKNOWLEDGMENTS

So many people to thank over the decades.

First and foremost, this book would have never been published, let alone be worthy of it, if not for the hard work, patience, and kindness of my editor, George Verongos. I can't thank you enough

To my surviving son Kyle, my daughter Elorie, and my grandson Tony, whose love and affection keep me going

To Ginny Stern, for your forever-appreciated help and unending positivity.

To Christy Lock, who leads my cheering section and gave me the impetus to find an editor.

To my mom, who fostered my love of reading, and my brother, who introduced me to science fiction.

To my very early readers, full and partial: Anne Tourney, Amy Sterling Casil, Chris Solnordal.

To my later readers of the completed first draft: Gulzar Rehman, Kristen Hardin, Elorie, and Kyle.

To all those, near and far, who gave me the strength to continue on life's journey.

And last but not least, to Paul, who puts up with me almost as much as I put up with him.

♫ What a long, hard trip it's been. ♫

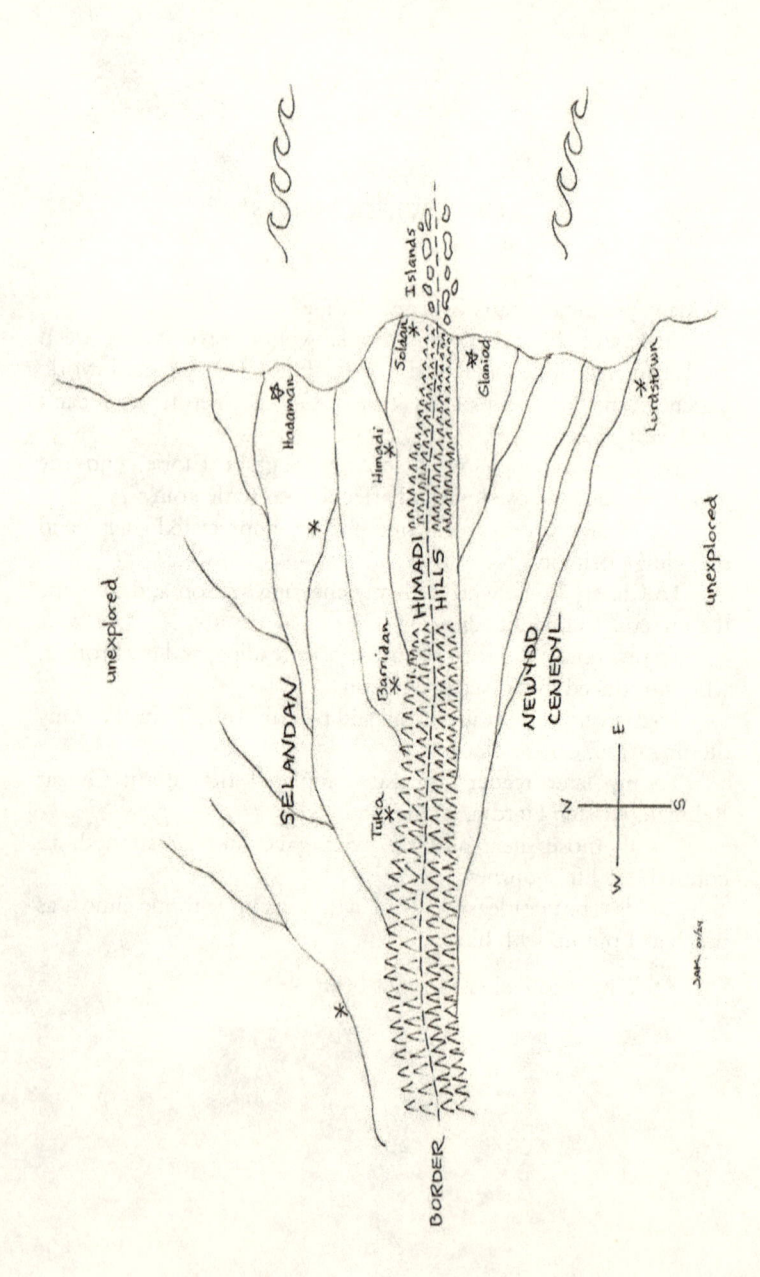

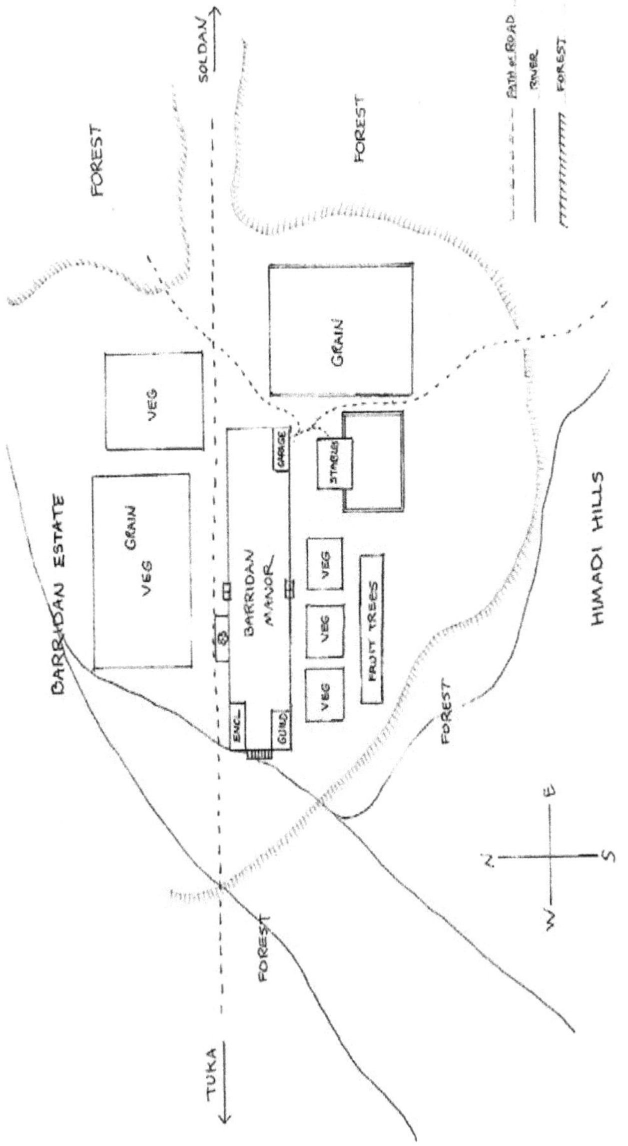
BARRIDAN ESTATE
FOREST
SOLDAN
FOREST
PATH or ROAD
RIVER
FOREST
VEG
GRAIN
VEG
GRAIN
GARAGE
STABLES
BARRIDAN MANOR
VEG
VEG
VEG
FRUIT TREES
ENCL
GUARD
HIMADI HILLS
FOREST
N
E
S
W
FOREST
TUKA
JAK 07/24

VOCABULARY

taso – leader of a Selandu House

keso – top-ranked guardian, often the taso's spouse. Makes sure the taso's orders are carried out and deals out punishments ordered by the taso.

temichi – a guardian, graduate of the Guild of Guardians in Tendiman; temichin; plural.

a'tem – honorific when formally addressing a guardian; a'tem'ai; plural.

tem'u – nickname for a guardian's partner

a'sel – honorific when addressing a non-guardian; a'sel'ai; plural.

ki'oto; ki'ono – direct translation: little man, indirect: boy; little woman, girl

te'oto; te'ono – young man; young woman; or generically, youth

a'ki'tana – little whirlwind

du – no

sai – yes

attentions – any kind of affections of the sexual type

^(text)^ – spoken Cene'l words; Cara's language

A larger Glossary can be found at the end of the book.

Cara's statement: "The invisible and the non-existent look very much alike," is a quote from Delos Banning McKown.

CONTENTS

ACKNOWLEDGMENTS i

VOCABULARY v

ONE 1

TWO 9

THREE.. 13

FOUR.. 23

FIVE.. 32

SIX 57

SEVEN.. 61

EIGHT... 75

NINE 79

TEN... 97

ELEVEN 103

TWELVE 131

THIRTEEN 143

FOURTEEN.. 151

FIFTEEN... 167

SIXTEEN.. 175

SEVENTEEN 179

EIGHTEEN... 185

NINETEEN... 197

TWENTY.. 211

TWENTY-ONE 219

TWENTY-TWO 235

TWENTY-THREE	241
TWENTY-FOUR	257
TWENTY-FIVE	259
TWENTY-SIX	267
TWENTY-SEVEN	283
TWENTY-EIGHT	309
TWENTY-NINE	323
THIRTY	343
THIRTY-ONE	365
GLOSSARY	371
TASOS AND TEMICHIN	377
AUTHOR'S BIOGRAPHY	379

We're all scared. But we can't let the fear slow us down. You have to trust yourself and follow your plan with enthusiasm and imagination and joy.

—Jack Bickham
(slightly paraphrased)

There is a writer in all of us, yeah
He knows what to say and he knows when it's done
But then there's this twenty-foot blank page
You gotta fill, darling
Or you think your life has no meaning

I cannot escape the constant equipoise
In between the mischief and control
Swinging from the pendulum of desires
In between the mischief and control

Excuses piling up like junkyards
We never want to sort through…

–Vonda Shepard

ONE

He faced an uneasy choice, this silver-haired, grey-skinned guardian. The duty offered to him would interfere with a tremendous piece of his life, his time. But the chance to guard a human was an opportunity that piqued his curiosity, professional and personal.

Strong and skilled, Rodani was a man not easily intimidated. Survival of guild training imbued one with a sense of potency bordering on arrogance. Rodani was no exception. But guard an unknown, unpredictable alien? Prevent her from offending any and every person she came in contact with? And what of his people who were adamant against her presence? It was a two-way path of danger, and he stood in the middle. On one side would be a small human woman who was generally ignorant of Selandu culture. On the other was the keso, Kusik of the heavy hand, who blatantly refused to believe a human in Barridan was a good idea.

An exceptional challenge.

And even a guardian had a private life. A severely curtailed one if he accepted this three-year, 25-hour-a-day assignment to guard a human.

Deep in inner wrestling, Rodani strode from one end to the other of the sitting room he shared with his partner. His narrow hands, well-trained hands, were clasped in the small of his back; twelve fingers waggled idly. Waist-long hair lay in a silver waterfall down his back, clipped at the neck. The vertical pupils in his deep violet eyes were wide ovals. Swept-back ears caught and identified every sound that intruded into his awareness.

Every temichi craved status, coveted the acclaim that a difficult, successful duty would produce. And above all else, one pleased the taso. Arimeso, lord of her manor house, waited on Rodani's decision. Her far-reaching visions were well known; but this—a human in the Selandu's northern lands—to some it bordered on the ridiculous. And Arimeso wanted Rodani to guard this ridiculousness.

It was an impossible job.

And yet, and yet... Rodani strolled to his bedroom window, looking down onto the south lawn and past it to the distant stables. None of the security staff aside from him could deal as capably with the frustrations and offenses a resident human would induce. His success would be a professional coupe and might earn him a place at guild headquarters—an honor no guardian would refuse.

Money rode on the human's presence, as well. Arimeso's finances came from her artisans' talents and their earning power. Teaching a human crafter respectability might be an exercise in futility, but it would relieve him of more mundane, boring duties.

Likely, there was not a bigger professional challenge he could expect to meet in the next score of years. If he lived that long.

A door slammed behind him. Serano walked through the sitting room and into the bedroom doorway. At the sight of his ruminating partner, his eyebrows creased into a V, his pupils narrowed, lips thinned to a tense line.

"You cannot be seriously considering this."

Rodani crossed his arms and regarded Serano across a divide of temperament and values. "It is an irreplaceable opportunity."

"Opportunity! The taso is living in the clouds."

Rodani squared his shoulders and lifted his chin. "You forget yourself, a'tem."

"I forget nothing," Serano said, anger and frustration leaking through his voice. "Even Kusik knows this experiment is a grave mistake. When a first refuses to support his taso's ill-thought ideas, even you should be able to see the peril."

"I see it."

"And you have decided you can survive it."

"I have a better chance than any," Rodani replied calmly.

"How can you guard what you cannot predict?" Serano marched back and forth past Rodani as he raged. "Will you lead her around in handcuffs?"

"No. I will teach her."

"And if you fail in your teachings?"

Rodani fell silent and made a tossing motion with his hand, a mild dismissive response.

"As I thought," Serano said. "And what of Kusik? He may be our superior, but you will get little support from him."

"Arimeso runs this household, not Kusik. He will do as she

says," Rodani reminded him.

Serano slapped his hand against the doorframe and turned to the side. "You gamble with both our lives."

"As senior partner, that is my choice."

"You will regret it."

Rodani stilled his body into a hunter's frozen countenance. His pupils narrowed into slits; his face blanked its expression. "And you will do the causing?" he asked softly.

Serano took a step back. "For the goddess's sake and sanity, tem'u, why?"

Rodani tilted his head. "Why do you believe I have already accepted?"

"Because I know you. You seek out the strange, not the familiar, as you should."

Rodani let a smile show for his angry partner. "Then I am well fit for this duty."

"And what if your *fit* is inadequate?" he spat back. "What if someone gets through your guard and kills her?"

"Serano, that could happen to any of us. And," Rodani continued, "if you assist me as a partner should, the danger is greatly lessened." He leaned forward. "Yes?"

Serano's pupils narrowed with rage. "You are forcing me into a duty I despise, Rodani!" He took an intimidating step closer. "The very idea of spending my days with some uncultured, untutored human leaves me with a noxious taste."

"Then brush your teeth and unclench your fists," Rodani said with equal heat, "because it is my decision to make, and I have made it."

Serano's pupils pulsed. His lips parted. A line of sharp white teeth appeared behind them. "You will lose all that you have gained." He stomped off, casting aspersions with a far-flung wave of his arm. "And you will take me down with you!"

Rodani stared mutely at his partner's departing back. The subsequent door-slam filled his ears and echoed in his head. He sighed wearily. Despite occasional flare-ups between them, he valued Serano. Curiosity and ambition might not be worth a fractured partnership, nor would constant conflict between himself and his first be easily manageable. Kusik was not known for patience, and guardian feuds within a House could tear that household apart. If Serano were right, not only would their personal consequences be devastating, but if she died under his care, it might precipitate a war between the two species. One battle already was more than enough.

Rodani took a calming breath and followed Serano out the door, down the wide stairs to the first floor, and into the confines of the taso's quarters.

Stiff in regal formality, Arimeso sat at her beautifully carved roanwood desk that gleamed darkly red with her reflection. Beside her, slit-pupiled with self-contained fury, stood Kusik.

Rodani stopped in front of his taso, clasped his hands behind his back, and bowed.

"Yes," he told her.

Arimeso leaned forward. "And you have thought this through?"

"Yes, a'Taso," he said, formal and contained as all must be when facing Barridan's leader.

Kusik shifted his stance, but anger still filled his face. "And why did you accept, a'tem?"

Rodani heard the warning. As he was trained to do, he fell back onto custom and chain of command. "Because the taso asked, a'Keso. And because I am best suited for this duty that she requires." He shifted his gaze away from danger back to Arimeso, who remained calm.

"Rodani," she began, "I am calling a meeting of my top people to relate this new venture. You and Serano will stay behind for further instructions afterwards."

"A'Taso." He bowed and left to wait in the communications room outside of her office.

At his exit, Kusik turned to face his taso, his bonded mate. "You are making the biggest mistake of your life," he said through grinding teeth.

Arimeso toyed with the cup of tea in front of her, breathing slowly. "You know I disagree, Kusik, and I tire of your obstinacy."

He stomped toward the door, then back to his desk next to hers. "I wish those humans had never fled their blasted spaceship!"

"They landed here first," she reminded him. "It is neither species' fault that some other ship attacked both of us on our way to elsewhere."

"Those two ambassadors at the government house in Hadaman should be enough," he said, staring directly at her with a hard look on his face. "You are putting yourself in danger, as well as making my duty to your safety more difficult!"

Arimeso stared right back. "I. Have. Heard. Enough."

***

An hour later, Arimeso looked out over her cadre of guardians and master crafters who resided in Barridan.

A full dozen guardians helped keep the manor house and its lands secure from both internal and external dangers. Animals, humans, and the Selandu themselves, all could be hazards to monitor, intercept, and contain or dispatch at her orders. The temichin were the first and best line of defense.

The crafters, however, were the lifeblood of her House. She and her guardians sheltered them, and they, in turn, created the objects that earned an income for everyone there.

Guarded, as always, Arimeso stood next to her guild second. Timan's clear gaze swept the meeting room for signs of ill intent, which encouraged the group to recognize this as *serious business*.

Kusik stood with his back to the exit. He wore his anger like he wore his weapons—loaded, and right at hand.

"A'tem'ai," she greeted her guardians, "a'sel'ai," and her other attendees, "I am going to invite a guest here. Of course, I have done so before, but this time will be different. This guest will be a human."

She waited for the surprised murmurs and weight shifting to settle down.

"This will cause," she warned, "some consternation among our more traditional people. I need you to be aware of this and be prepared to mitigate any disturbances. If necessary, you may call on the keso, or me, to mediate.

"The ambassadors informed me that this human woman is fluent in our language, and will be speaking it here, as none of us know hers. They described her as short, about the height of a ten-year-old to us, but they assured me that she is fully adult. She is twenty-six. She is also a crafter and will be making quilts for us to sell. She will be paid the normal rate for a median level artisan and will have a set of rooms for her own use on the second floor."

Arimeso glanced toward the front row. "This human has been assigned a pair of guardians—Rodani and Serano. One or both of them will escort her whenever she is outside of her rooms. At a minimum, they will bring her to the rest-eve dinners in the gathering room each week. If she has reason to be other places, inside or outside, her guardians will be with her.

"I expect this woman, whose name is *Cah-rah*, to behave appropriately and treat us courteously. I also," she stopped and swept her gaze over every face, "expect the same from each of you, and anyone you supervise."

Arimeso glanced at her keso, whose expression had morphed from anger to barely concealed disgust. Though it was improper for any adult Selandu to flaunt his emotions in a formal atmosphere, Arimeso declined to chide him in public, allowing him to retain the honor his status afforded him. He had already made his complaints on this venture known to her, and as was her right as taso, she had rebuffed them.

"Questions?" she asked the group.

Imal, guild third, raised his finger. The taso rolled out her own fingers in a gesture of acceptance.

"How long will this human be here, a'Taso?"

"Three years is the plan, a'tem."

Another finger rose.

"Cassig," Arimeso said.

"A'Taso," he began, looking around, "as I am the only chef in the room, will it be my duty to make sure she eats none of our food that is harmful to humans?"

"Yes."

"Then, if it would not offend, a'Taso," he added, "I should make a trip to Hadaman to confer with those chefs who feed the ambassadors during their visits."

"You will," Arimeso replied. "That can be discussed soon, to make arrangements."

Cassig bent his head in mute acceptance.

"A'Taso," Security Eleventh Naremit spoke. "When does she arrive?"

"In two months. A few weeks before harvest." She waited in silence for more questions. When there were none, she dismissed the group with a wave of her hand. "Rodani, Serano," she ordered, and left the room through a side door.

The pair, guild fifth and sixth, followed her into her private office. Kusik and Timan walked in last.

Arimeso sat at her desk covered with papers, pens, a bottle of ink, and an incense burner. Kusik took his place next to her, leaning back in his chair with a scowl.

She motioned Rodani and Serano into the seats in front of her desk. "A'tem'ai, there are a few extra pieces of information for your ears, only," she began. "This woman, the ambassadors tell me, shows more emotions than we do. She did not successfully graduate from the see-ess-see for this reason."

Serano raised a finger. "The see-ess-see?"

"It is a small school where a few humans are taught our language and culture," she told him, folding her hands on the desktop. "I believe this means that you will see emotions and expressions arise often, and for reasons we may not understand. These displays may be ignorable, or you may wish to ask for an explanation. We cannot know at this point. Although she is relatively fluent in Selandi, she will make spoken mistakes. These mistakes are to be corrected—in a mild manner, as one would a favored child."

She studied the two men in front of her. Rodani evinced polite acceptance; Serano had an aura of doubt around him.

"Her people do not believe in the goddess. Ambassador Mena'hem explained that the humans here have two or three different gods they may believe in, and some believe in none at all. They use a variety of blasphemes, many of which refer to their gods. Those without beliefs center theirs on imaginary beings in outer space. I anticipate Kimasa, using her status as high priestess, attempting to convert Cah-rah at some point in the future. You will watch these interactions carefully, with a thought toward minimizing offenses on either side. I have no knowledge to anticipate the human's reactions.

"From what I have learned in speaking with Hadaman, their notion of honor is somewhat different from ours. Instead of honor being bestowed by others, their honor is created and held internally. It seems strange to me," she admitted to the pair. "And I cannot know how this difference will affect your duties, or your interactions with her. But I suggest using caution before responding to and judging her.

"Cah-rah is the only human available with the necessary requirements," the taso continued, "that she knows our language and is a crafter. What this means to me and my House," she leaned forward and aimed her words primarily at Rodani, "is that it is important for her to be content enough to stay and to craft." The taso lifted a finger in their direction. "It will be up to you two to make sure this happens. Keep her safe, teach her our ways, rules, and courtesies, and just as importantly, make her comfortable and welcome as best as possible, so that her thoughts and energies will center on her crafting. Both of you will need patience, and it is my expectation that you will be so. Do you have questions?"

Rodani spoke. "Not at this time, a'Taso."

Serano bowed his head, a silent negative.

Arimeso waved the pair out of her office.

Once in the hallway, Serano turned to his partner with a face full of anger. "You pulled me into this fiasco, tem'u. And I am not pleased."

Rodani glanced at him with benevolent disregard. "I will assume most of the duties," he replied calmly. "And you may continue your never-ending search for your pleasures."

"With all the appealing women here? I certainly will."

TWO

The stone-built manor house at Barridan faced north with its back to a forest. It was three stories high and had a central hallway and large wings to the east and west. It had a gabled roof with a walkway encircling it, and a water wheel on the west side. Forty-seven years after the Selandu made landfall on the planet, approximately 100 Selandu crafters, a dozen guild guardians, fifteen priestesses in the Enclave, four dozen servants and helpers of various types, and a handful of administrators—and one lone human—lived and worked here.

The southwest corner was guild guardian territory and held their training facilities. A shooting range with a maze and a gymnasium for exercise and sparring. Currently in the gym, two sweaty guardians were throwing punches and insults at each other.

Rodani swung at his partner, missing his jaw by a hair's width. Serano saw an opening and grabbed him, throwing them both to the mat with a bone-jarring thump. They ended up on their sides, back to front, with Serano's arms wrapped tightly around Rodani's chest.

"You had better learn this one, tem'u," Serano whispered in his partner's swept-back ear. "You will need it to keep your human from leaving her room."

Rodani pulled extra strength from his willpower and broke free from Serano's grasp. They both spun up to a stand. Only a few feet away, Rodani grabbed his shoulders, pulled, and swept Serano off his feet. He landed on top. "And you should remember this one," Rodani shot back. "You will need it to keep a woman in your arms." He climbed off Serano and held his hands up, signifying an end to the sparring. He reached for a nearby towel and ran it over his face and neck, then readjusted the hair clip at the back of his neck. "And next time, tem'u," he continued, "keep your fingers out of my hair."

Serano smiled. "That was an accident."

Rodani gifted his partner with a gaze under lowered brows.

"Yes. Of course," he said, disbelief running through his voice.

Serano sprawled his long body in a chair against the wall, towel wrapped around his neck. "So, how is the human?"

Rodani claimed an adjacent chair. "If you spent more time with her, you would know already."

"Au, you claimed that duty, remember?" Serano replied with some humor. "Two months ago. It was yours for the taking, and it is still yours. I bow to those superior skills you boast of. So," he continued, "is she as emotional as we were told?"

Rodani tossed the question, downplaying the subject with a quick flip of his wrist—outstretched fingers that immediately folded back inward. "Her emotions flow over her face at every moment, but she has not railed at me for any reason."

"How was the ride from the coast?"

"Voluble," Rodani answered, deadpan. "It took little time for her to move from the back of the wagon to just behind our seats. Cara flooded us with questions—polite ones, generic ones. Litelon seemed eager to answer them. I allowed it; as long as he kept the benatacs under control."

"Her vocabulary?" Serano continued.

"Reasonably good. I brought her some library books to read, which should help." Rodani shifted in his seat. "There is one concern that I see." His gaze swept the room, landing on nothing in particular.

"And?" Serano asked into his silence.

Rodani drew his hands up under his chin. "She is not pleased that I lock her doors, and has complained more than once."

"Locked only from the outside, yes?"

"Yes, but I have ordered her not to leave her rooms without escort."

"And what did you say to her complaints?"

Rodani tossed this question, too. "That it was for her safety, of course. She…seemed doubtful—if I read her expression correctly. She may be more strong-willed than I first thought."

Serano turned his head in surprise. "More strong-willed than you?" he asked, eyebrow raised.

Rodani gave him the side-eye. "No. I will prevail."

"Hamman keeps an eye on her?"

"Both servants do. I cannot hover over her all day, every day."

"And their thoughts?"

"None they have voiced," Rodani said. "I have not seen Cara

have an issue with them, nor they, her. And I have cautioned both servants to be reserved in their interactions with her." He stood and brushed dirt from his pants, then reached for the door. "Have you heard any rumblings or threats about her presence here?"

Serano followed him out. "Do you mean besides Kusik?"

Rodani wiped any expression from his face, the better to conceal his thoughts in public. "I hope the taso keeps a tight rein on him."

THREE

Late summer heat lay over the room, refusing to budge to the hand-cranked fan that clattered away in the corner.

"I'll kill him," she fumed, teeth clenched. "I'll run him through with that knife in his belt, guardian or no."

Fists on her hips, Cara MacLennan brooded over his insults and a design that wouldn't come together. It was bad enough he wasn't an artisan. Serano wouldn't know a good design or quality crafting if it got shoved up his nether orifice. If he had one, that is. Alien bodies might have alien ways of achieving such things. She smacked the tabletop with the flat of her hand. Tools rattled and spun in noisy disorder.

Inspiration—that's what she needed. Something besides the flowers replaced daily in her study, something besides the humdrum landscape paintings on her walls. A moment's breeze came from the fan, cooling the back of her neck. Nice if it had been fresh air, but that was denied to her when she was alone. A vision of the large manor house's north yard scrolled through her mind. The garden might curb her resentment.

Cara crossed the room and unlocked her door. The empty hallway beckoned. She stepped out and closed the door behind her with a soft click. A little beyond it, a pair of doors faced each other. Servants and guardians. Cara had two of each assigned to her. Three weeks into a three-year stay at Arimeso Osanin's estate, she had no idea why she was so closely guarded. As it was, she was forbidden to walk unaccompanied, and the fact that she'd gotten out of her rooms without being stopped surprised her. But Cara hadn't gotten this far from home without taking a few risks in her life. She started down the stairs.

A lone Selandu male rounded the corner and started up the steps as Cara neared the bottom. His grey eyes widened in surprise at her presence in front of him, evidence enough that her solitary sojourn was unusual. But just as quickly, he masked his expression, passing in silence. Cara quickened her pace as she headed toward the heavy double doors that led outside. Guilty pleasure put a smile on her human face as she walked into the sunshine and freedom.

The garden began a hundred feet to the west, with a stone path that wound out of sight between trees and bushes. Summer sun warmed her skin. The Selandu slippers whispered against the stones under her feet. With great relish, Cara wandered through the garden, enjoying the dappled sunshine that filtered through the trees, studying the plants and flowers that grew in careful disarray. Finger-length tic'idi chirped in the grasses, and leaves whispered to one another in the clean breeze. On impulse, Cara undid the bun at her neck and fanned her hair out behind her. She shook her head, enjoying the free-falling motion of unbound locks after weeks of keeping it tightly wrapped as their culture demanded. The breeze whipped strands past her eyes and across her mouth. She stood, simply stood, in the middle of the garden walk, quietly reveling in nature's scents and sounds.

"A'Cara."

She whirled toward the deep voice. "A'Rodani," she said.

Rodani's silver hair gleamed in the sunshine; intense eyes bore into hers. He was clad in black—the color of the Guild of Guardians—making it easier to hide in shadow and conceal his tools. Rodani's gaze wandered over her unbound hair and delicate indoor clothing. He crossed his arms.

"You should not be here."

Cara's courage wavered in the shadow of her tall guardian, certain that Rodani was unused to protecting such a difficult adashi. She brought her hands around to the front of her body.

"I'm conferring with nature, a'Rodani." She frowned. "Artisans do that sometimes."

Rodani stared down from his seven-foot height. "A'Cara, you make my duty more difficult when you wander off without escort. I must know where you are."

"Why? Is something going to bite me?"

"You are naïve. You take foolish chances." His pupils narrowed into a vertical slit. "And you are being discourteous."

Cara froze momentarily in that penetrating stare. "Please forgive me. I meant no offense." She dug her hands into her pants pockets and fixed her gaze on the ground. "I occasionally fall back into humor."

"There is humor in dangerous impropriety?"

"If there's danger here, Rodani, I'm unaware of it." She lifted her chin. "And no one has told me of any."

Insects droned in the silence. Tendrils of free-falling hair tickled Cara's face. A shift of her slippers on the stone brought an answering rasp in the stillness. Voiceless audience, flowers and trees soaked up the overhead rays of sunshine in the midst of tension.

Seconds crawled by, and Cara realized Rodani was waiting for her next move. The proper action was, of course, to accept his censure and return to the manor. But she had spent the last three weeks continually trying to be proper. It was wearing thin. She turned and walked deeper into the garden. As if taking her unspoken dare, Rodani followed. In his silence, she began to relax again.

The path unfolded before her in twists and turns. Mixtures of colors blossomed in clumps from the ground like a painter's palette gone amok. A particularly soft-looking flower coaxed Cara into touching. The petals were velvety and left maroon fuzz on her fingers.

She continued along the path, mind on the patterns that nature and the Selandu gardeners had created, acutely aware of the silence in which she walked. Scents assailed her from each side of the path and from above. Peace stole into her soul as the weeks of never-ending unfamiliarities faded. She felt almost alone in this shared alien world.

Her escort close behind but momentarily forgotten, Cara stood in front of one intricately variegated red and yellow bloom, rubbing her hands absentmindedly.

Intruding, Rodani grabbed her left hand and pulled it close. "This is not normal. Yes?"

Spots.

Discolorations had started on her fingers and were spreading down her hands to the wrists. "I...it's not." She rubbed at them as if they were paint splotches to be cleaned off.

Rodani grabbed her arm and dragged her back up the path. He stopped only to pluck the flower and stuff it in a pocket before reaching for his 'com to radio ahead. Cara lagged behind, becoming uncomfortable.

"Come." Rodani pulled faster in his haste.

She started gasping for breath. From the exertion, it must be. Her arm was hurting with the strength of his grip. Her head spun. As they exited the path near the manor doors, she staggered and bent over, gasping for breath. Rodani reached down behind her knees and brought her up across his shoulder. He ran outright, hair flowing behind him. Through the doors and into the foyer, he sped, where they met the physician.

Rodani slowed. Baldar took one look at her hands and listened to her labored breathing. "Stop. Put her down."

Rodani obeyed.

Dizzy from the lack of oxygen, Cara hardly noticed the bitter taste of herbs that were pushed under her tongue, or the smoky cloud she was made to inhale. The room turned dark, and voices faded into the distance.

***

Bright light. Warm air. Cara opened her eyes. Her bleary vision focused on the nearest wall where an armoire held clothing from home, and cast-off Selandu children's clothes that ill-fit her woman's body. She blinked against the morning sun's rays.

A pocket-com crackled beside her. Cara spun under the covers at the unexpected noise.

"She is awake."

Rodani slipped the 'com back in his jacket pocket and leaned forward in the chair. Cara tucked the quilt up under her chin in modesty. She slept as most Selandu did—sans clothing. Rodani's presence in her bedroom shook her. She stared up at him suspiciously.

"Why are you here?" she asked.

"Waiting for you to wake."

"Why?"

"To alert the physician you had recovered sufficiently."

"Recovered from what?"

Rodani blinked; his pupils narrowed. "You have no memory of yesterday?"

"Yesterday?" Her eyes unfocused as thoughts followed half-remembered images. "I went outside. To the garden... You found me out there. We...spoke. I kept walking..." Cara let out a sigh. "That's all I remember."

"Nothing else?"

"Nothing. Why?"

Rodani rose from the chair. Attempting to peel back her covers to inspect her hands, he was met with a rigid grip on the quilt.

"Stop!" she told him, eyes wide.

"I merely wish to see your hands."

Confused and embarrassed, Cara carefully slipped a hand out and held it up. Rodani took it in his and studied it.

"Much improved."

To her dawning comprehension, a sprinkling of red spots could be seen on the skin, aiding her memory. "You saved my life," she concluded. Rodani looked at her distantly. "Thank you."

Still that direct and silent Selandu stare.

Rodani sat back in his chair with what looked like every intention of staying. He stretched his long legs out and crossed his booted ankles. His full dozen interlaced grey fingers rested on his abdomen; elbows splayed out on the armrests. He continued to gaze at her levelly, making no effort to hide his inspection.

Cara closed her eyes and attempted a return to sleep. But she couldn't quiet her mind. *Why is he watching me? How close a call was it? How did I get from the garden to here? He won't stop staring. Is he still angry? And I need the facilities! What is he waiting for?*

Any detail of yesterday's conversation with him was gone from her memory banks, including anything that might have provoked this vigil. Cara tried to recreate the confrontation in the garden, but there were too many gaps. She blushed at the memory of her unbound hair and improper clothing, but it was the first time she'd felt so unencumbered in weeks. She touched the back of her head to see if her hair was still down. No, someone had wrapped it while she was asleep.

Not asleep, unconscious. She must've passed out. What else had been done? Someone had undressed her, obviously. Her female servants, she hoped, with Rodani far removed.

The sound of soft-soled shoes intruded on her thoughts. They came through the hall from the servants' adjoining rooms. A pair of grey healer's guild pants appeared, thigh high to her tall bed. She turned her head to face the physician.

"Who are you?" he asked.

Dumbfounded by the question, Cara hesitated before answering. "Cara MacLennan."

"Where are you?"

"Arimeso's manor in Barridan."

"What is the date?"

Ah. Now she had it. Coherent in three spheres. "24th Sutija."

"25th," the physician said.

Well, she might have been forgiven for losing one day, given the circumstances. With no preamble and no bedside manners, Baldar checked her eyes, then pulled the quilt out of her hands and listened to her heart and lungs with a bell-shaped instrument. She tried to re-cover herself, but Baldar pushed her hands away impatiently, moving the instrument around. Evidently satisfied, he switched his attention to her hands. He inspected them closely, one at a time, as Cara tugged on the quilt.

"Any other spots?"

Having just woken up, she hadn't gotten a chance to look. "I'm unaware of any others."

Baldar gripped her upper arm and pulled her out of the bed. "Walk," he said.

Cara adjusted the quilt around her and did as she was commanded. Baldar watched her stride for stumbling and weaving, then turned to her guardian.

"Any breathing difficulties, a'tem?"

"None that I saw," Rodani replied.

"Confusion in the mind?"

"Temporary memory loss only."

Cara stood quietly as the men conferred, as if she wasn't there.

Baldar made a final turn in her direction. "You will be more cautious next time."

Cara stared at the floor. "A'Baldar."

The physician exited the room, Rodani on his heels. Cara sighed gratefully, flung the quilt on the bed, and headed for the facilities before she had a childish accident. Falita, the younger servant, greeted her reappearance with a bow. "Shower or breakfast, a'Cara?"

"Both please, Falita. Shower first."

Cara accepted the younger woman's assistance, having long ago given up insisting on privacy. It was their duty, she had been reassured on many occasions, that they do for her what she was capable of doing for herself. And they were fervent in the application of their duties.

Soon showered, dressed, and fed, Cara ambled into her workroom. The quilt design that had prompted her ill-advised garden walk still lay in pieces around the room.

It wasn't long before bootsteps in her workroom brought Cara's nose out of her work. Her guardian appeared in her doorway, a familiar envelope in hand. He stepped through and handed it to her.

"Thank you, Rodani."

Bootsteps waited, then headed back in the direction from which they'd come.

Cara opened the clasp on the outsized envelope and pulled out her latest quilt design. There was a note attached. She scanned it.

"Temi's demons!"

Bootsteps came back her direction. Swearing was not unknown among Selandu, but it was reserved for more appropriate occasions. Cara concentrated on the note.

"Problem, a'Cara?" Rodani waited just inside the room, dignified with the confidence that comes with guardian skills, hard-earned and respected.

Cara tossed the package on the tea table in front of her. "I seem to have difficulty pleasing the art council, Rodani." She waved her hand over the rejected drawing. "How can I continue to craft and contribute to the taso's household when they won't approve my designs?"

"That is the second time this design has been returned as unacceptable?"

"Third." She slumped back in her chair. "Suggestions?"

Expecting him to demur, his response surprised her. "One, make your designs simpler," he said. "It is easier to find fault in a complicated design. Two, overwhelm the council with designs. If they have too many to argue over, some may get passed by default. Three," the corners of his mouth turned up in amusement, "make them anyway."

"I can do that?" she asked, sitting straighter. "Ignore the council? What if no one buys the work because it's unapproved?"

"What is improper to one may not be to another, Cara. Conflicting opinions abound. Even the taso can have differing views from the council. In turn, the council must obey her."

In the workroom beyond, Cara's current project lay patiently on the wooden frame she'd brought from home. Afternoon sun shone through the window behind it, casting angular shadows on the floor.

"Would you ask the taso's percussion before I disregard the refusal?"

A moment of unexpected silence put her on edge.

"That would be wise, when you still substitute inappropriate words for appropriate ones," Rodani said. "The word you needed is <u>seichata</u>."

Cara's face turned pink. "I apologize for the offense."

"It was not offensive, just incorrect," he said.

"Seichata. Thank you, Rodani."

He inclined his head in acceptance of her courtesy and left the room.

Well, just in case she didn't get *seichata* for Rodani's third suggestion, she'd try his second. Cara retreated to the drawing table where she took up a pencil and pulled out a leaf of paper. She'd see how many patterns she could spit out in a day or two.

She drew an arc of thin pie slices mutating into flower petals. Pure colors melted into softer blends. Where does the eye need to travel? She made the flower petals morph into elongated leaves, curling around toward the center and expanding into the patterns that adorned the manor entrance. Muted darks for that. Keep it in the background despite its size.

A fresh piece of paper, a fresh vision—the ceiling of the foyer as seen by someone on the floor, losing consciousness. Nothing like taking a brush with death and turning it into artwork. Make the manor's inlaid granite and quartz spirals and concentric rings clearly focused toward the left center. It needed something to draw the eye to the edges and back, though, otherwise one had nothing much but a target on fabric. Good for weapons practice and nothing else.

Hmmm. Violet eyes? She grinned. *Too obvious.* Cara scratched her pencil around the border. There wasn't enough movement for the design. *Stars?* She had no star field fabric. Paint might work. Cara set it aside for later thought and stretched her muscles.

"You are well, a'Cara?" asked Hamman, as she strode into the workroom, tea tray in hand.

Startled, Cara jerked her head toward the door. Hamman was nearly as quiet as Rodani when she wished. Cultural or physical trait, it was exasperating to one as skittish as Cara.

"Yes, thank you," she replied. "And thank you for the tea." She poured a cup. It always came piping hot regardless of the ambient temperature. "How did I get back to my room yesterday? What happened?"

Hamman swept her six-fingered hands across the long drapes in her skirt. "Rodani carried you upstairs to your bed. He told me it was an allergic reaction to a misabi, and that you were in danger. He and I took turns watching you through the night."

An image of Rodani seated by her bed passed across Cara's mind's eye. She tried to blank her expression as she slipped her fingers through the teacup's handle; it was nearly too hot to hold.

"Thank you, a'Hamman."

The servant inclined her head in acceptance and turned to leave. Cara trailed Hamman into her bedroom and set the cup on her bedside table as the servant continued through the narrow corridor to her adjacent room. Cara pulled open the armoire doors and opened a storage chest. From it she brought out a bound and locked journal and a calligraphy pen, and began to write.

A knock on the door interrupted her train of thought and spun the pen out of her hand. It landed on the floor, spattering driblets of green ink on the cool stone.

"Who's there?" Cara slid off the high bed to retrieve it.

"Rodani."

"A moment, please." She slapped the journal closed and locked it, then slipped it back into the chest at the bottom of the armoire, then went into her workroom to meet him. "Please enter."

She heard a jangle of keys and the rattle of the lock.

"Arimeso wishes to see you and whatever rejected designs you still have, a'Cara."

"She'll let me do some?"

"She wishes to see them, a'Cara. To judge for herself," he clarified. It was improper to make assumptions about the taso's future actions. Everyone did as she bade. Even her human guest.

"Yes. Now?"

"Tomorrow is soon enough."

"I appreciate your efforts, Rodani. Thank you."

He gave a small bow. Duty properly performed, he turned to leave. Cara watched his long hair swing to the side with the force of his turn, then settled back to its usual straight hang from the clip.

Arimeso was willing to let her disregard the council? She'd been taught by the CSC, the Cultural Studies Center, that the high priestess—and council head—Kimasa, held a tight grip over all but the most private of decisions. Arimeso just proved the CSC wrong.

Cara spun in a circle, laughing, hugging this little success to herself. The last thing she wanted was to argue with a bunch of superstitious old women about what made a good design. She was wary of those who thought life was lived in black and white, and those who thought they had a right to dictate which was which. While reviewing history cubes, Cara had seen this type of behavior demonstrated on the home planet of her ancestors. It never ended well. And it hadn't here on their adopted planet, either.

Though the settlement Cara grew up in was relatively safe and offered rustic comforts, she was bored. That's why she became a student at the CSC. The Selandu leaders, the Council of Three, trusted no one to come north but the small cadre of CSC graduates, two of whom functioned as ambassadors.

A mountain range created a convenient dividing line, with humans in the south and Selandu in the north. Guild guardians patrolled the north side of the local hills, keeping out the riffraff and occasional human adolescents bent on undergoing their rite of passage by crossing the border. Most often, those guardians simply grabbed the offenders by the arm and marched them back across the border with not much more than some incomprehensible shouting and a cuff to the back of the head. It was a rare human who tried a second time. Most humans were either indifferent or tolerant to the Selandu. Those humans were the realists who knew that—barring genocide—neither species was going to be left sole proprietor of the planet, so every effort was made to get along, at least diplomatically.

Cara liked interesting new things, so when word came that an alien lord wanted to try hosting a human artisan in her household, Cara jumped at the chance. Being a dropout from the CSC didn't prevent her from keeping up with her language skills.

Rummaging through her cast-off pile of designs, Cara laughed at her doubters back home. She would prove herself to herself, and to anyone else who disbelieved.

FOUR

A gloomy morning dawned.

Cara shuffled from her oversized bed with the hope a shower would lift the fog from her eyes and brain.

It didn't.

Nor did the sweet breakfast tea Falita brought. It only made her heart race. The shutters that walled her from the outside world had resisted all earlier attempts to open them, with a locking mechanism that matched nothing from home.

She hauled one of the solid dinner table chairs from the study to her workroom, nestling it up against the wall. She took off her slippers and stepped up on it. It was a long reach to the lock, which rattled with her ineffectual efforts. She stopped, swore under her breath, and shook a stitch out of her shoulder. Frustrated, Cara squatted and reached for a pair of shears on her worktable. She rammed the handles into the catch from beneath. A metallic bang echoed through her quarters. She looked around for observers, but no one was in sight. She fiddled once more. The lock fell open; the shutters swung inward, then she pushed the window open.

It was, indeed, gloomy, but the warm breeze felt good on her face. And wonder of wonders, she could see outside. As opposed to her room's walls, the horizon was more than fifteen feet away. She sat backward in the chair, settling her arms on the wide stone ledge with the teacup nestled in the crook of her arm and a breeze fluttering her hair.

"A'Cara."

Damn, if those ghostly appearances just didn't make her jump, it would be routine. "Yes, Hamman. You're on early today."

Hamman bustled into the room with unusual haste. "You must not, a'Cara." She reached for the shutters; eyes wide in distress.

Cara turned her face to the side in polite refusal.

"You must not." She shooed Cara from the windowsill and closed the shutters. The troublesome lock engaged automatically.

Cara stared at it and slumped down into the chair as Hamman walked back into the bedroom. In the shadows, Falita conferred with her as she passed, then turned to follow.

Cara stared down at the designs she'd drawn yesterday, then pushed them aside. She tucked the earphones of her portable 'corder into her ears and slid a 'cording of music into the opening, then pulled a pair of fabric pieces under the sewing machine's needle and stitched.

There was more than one type of distance.

Creative reverie faded out when it came time for her meeting with Arimeso. There were two faces at her door instead of one.

"A'Cara, this is Misheiki, Security Seventh," Rodani said. "Serano and I have other duties. Misheiki will escort you."

Misheiki was a study in contrast to Rodani, with a round face and a somewhat corpulent figure made more obvious by being several inches shorter. Also different was the slight smile gracing his face, something Cara hadn't seen on her primary guardian for the first week she'd known him.

"Temi's greetings, a'Misheiki."

"A'Cara. Are you ready?"

"Yes, thank you." Cara gathered up the folder of rejected designs she'd retrieved from various scrap piles around her workroom and waited expectantly. Rodani walked across the hall. With a jingle of keys and a swift movement, he disappeared inside the rooms he shared with his guild partner.

Misheiki backpedaled out the door and turned to walk with her. The long hallways echoed with their footsteps and with the voices of other artists making their way through the manor on their individual errands.

The taso's apartments were central on the first floor and were very much off-limits to casual visitors. She knew of only one entrance for the whole of Arimeso's six-room private living area and the three adjacent offices. Just inside the area was the main guardroom for the manor, where her first-rank guardians, Kusik and Timan, held court. Cara's opinion of those guild partners was based on the reaction of her servants to the names: extreme discretion advised.

Cara entered the inner stronghold with her stomach in knots. Only once before had she met with Arimeso, the day she'd arrived at the country estate. Apprehension and cultural dissonance had left her with nothing much but blurred memories of a soft voice with a steel edge. Arimeso held Cara's life and safety in her hands. Offend her badly enough and one might garner a dire physical punishment, even a flogging. A threat could find one facing the business end of Kusik's pistol, or Rodani's. Not thoughts upon which to dwell before a meeting.

She took a deep breath.

Misheiki led her forward through the guardroom. One woman was in attendance, a guardian Cara didn't recognize. She had just enough time to wonder what rank the woman held, then was ushered around a corner, through another door, and into Arimeso's outer office.

The taso sat behind her impressive desk. As usual, Kusik, dressed in guild black, sat at her side.

A row of three chairs sat between Cara and the taso. All faced the desk. Two pairs of grey eyes stared at her as she bowed.

"A'Taso." She tried, unsuccessfully, to swallow the quaver in her voice.

Arimeso sat quietly, hands resting on her desktop. Selandu were not given to fidgeting, especially those of high rank; they had no need. "A'Cara. Be seated."

Cara slipped into a chair.

"I am pleased to see you have recovered from your misfortune in the garden," Arimeso began.

A not so hidden criticism, she thought. "Yes, a'Taso. I owe my life to Rodani's quick action."

A slight pursing of lips was all that Cara could see of Arimeso's reaction.

"It was well that he was there," the taso replied.

Cara stared at the desktop. *Ouch*. Reprimands weren't always loud. A taso had no need of shouting, either. "Yes," she whispered.

"I hear you are having trouble with the council."

Cara heaved a silent sigh of relief at the change of topic. "The council has trouble with my designs, a'Taso."

Arimeso blinked at the admission, but let it pass and held out a hand. Next to her, Kusik remained a rock, an armed and dangerous reef that would ream the bottom out of any ship going astray. Cara dared a glance in his direction. His stony gaze was glued on her face.

Arimeso slipped the designs out of the envelope and spread them on her desk. She studied each of them thoughtfully. Several minutes went by.

Cara held herself to all the stillness she could. She clasped and unclasped her hands and pulled at an escaping tendril of hair. A nervous cough escaped upon occasion. The silence continued. Finally, Arimeso folded her hands and leaned back.

"Is there any particular trio of designs you prefer?"

"Yes, a'Taso." She pointed carefully, not touching the desk or getting too close to Arimeso's august person. "This one, this one, and this."

Arimeso's gaze returned to the three Cara had chosen.

"Make them."

Her impassive face belied the words that came out of her mouth. Cara's jaw fell as she realized she'd just gotten the desired permission. Improper expression spread all over her face. "Thank you, a'Taso. Your time is appreciated, as well as your decision."

Arimeso inclined her head at the praise and intertwined long fingers. Cara stood and collected her papers with shaking hands. She stuffed them back into the envelope, disordered, then signaled her intention to leave with a low bow. A wave of Arimeso's hand gave permission to withdraw. Cara did so, hoping not to trip over her own feet in anxious exit.

She stopped in the anteroom. There was no Misheiki. Mystified, she looked around as if he might magically appear from behind a piece of furniture. The outer security office proved empty of his presence as well. The other guardian was still there and turned to face Cara, headset on her ears. "Yes?"

"Is a'Misheiki still here?"

"No. He was called away."

Away? Who would escort her? There was no one else in the room. "Thank you."

Daunted but pleased, Cara headed out the door, alone outside her rooms for only the second time. She strolled down the halls in good humor, taking advantage of the unexpected privacy, working her way back to her quarters by a different route.

Long passages went off to her left and right. Some carried voices, most were quiet. Paintings hung on walls even in these more remote places. Cara turned a corner. Voices came out of a side hall, echoing. Familiar voices. She walked down the dim hall and rounded another corner to see her two Selandu guardians at a door.

Rodani and Serano. What were they doing? She pulled back, lest they see her, waiting a few moments before starting toward the room they had just entered. Was this the errand Rodani was on?

What was down this hallway? There were many parts of the manor she'd never seen, rarely going out except to join the rest of the household on the weekly rest-eve social gatherings. Before she could finish creeping her way to the door, she heard a loud boom. Even more curious, but now a little frightened, she put her ear to the door and listened.

More bangs followed. Conversation.

Bangs and conversation? Maybe they were shooting those guns, the guns stolen from humans a score of years ago? Curiosity overcame fear of consequences. Consequences that could be quite physical in nature. Selandu discipline was often harsh; but as a guest, Cara assumed she would be spared such indignities. She turned the doorknob as slowly and quietly as she could.

Not, however, quietly enough for guild-trained ears. The door jerked open in her hands. Rodani's massive black pistol pointed at her chest. She froze. He stared at her, pupils wide.

"What are you doing?" he demanded, shifting the muzzle toward the ceiling. "Where is your escort? Why were you sneaking into this room?"

A ball of fear lodged in her throat. "Don't shoot, please."

Rodani lowered the gun. "Why...are...you...here?"

Damn if she didn't feel like a child caught with her hand in the cookie jar. "I heard booming sounds from the hall."

"You were sneaking into a room where you thought guns were being fired. Yes?"

Cara ducked her head. "I've never heard a gun being shot before."

"Foolish. You need to leave." His lips tensed into a thin line. "Escorted." He slipped his pistol into its holster. "Where is Misheiki?"

Cara stared at Rodani's booted feet, his face too full of rightful anger for her to look at. She shrugged her shoulders. "He wasn't in the guardroom when my meeting was finished. Rather than wait in ignorance, I left."

"Why was he not there?"

"I have no idea." Like someone would really tell her.

The look on Rodani's face bode ill for the missing security seventh, and probably for Cara as well. She took the silence of the moment to look into the room beyond. Gun in hand, Serano watched the confrontation. Behind him were what looked like targets. Some shaped like Selandu, outlined in various poses. Some were just concentric rings. To the left was an accordioned wall.

Cara smiled her most winning smile at Rodani. "May I try?"

His pupils widened, then narrowed to a slit. "No."

"Please?"

Rodani turned to Serano and motioned with his hands. Cara used the opportunity of his inattention to slip into the room. He spun around to face her as Serano walked out of earshot and pulled out his 'com. He muttered into it and waited.

Rodani folded his arms across his chest and stared at her. It seemed to be his favored method of intimidation. She looked at him. His gaze didn't waver. The mute contest went from chilling, to constrained, to merely a waiting game. Finally, Cara chuckled at Rodani's unchanging expression. Serano's 'com crackled with a curt answer. The guild partners looked at each other.

Rodani turned away, blank-faced, then gestured to Cara. "Go there."

Triumphant in her second victory of the day, Cara laid her envelope on the floor and went where Rodani pointed. There were parallel lines painted on the floor facing the targets. He followed and stood beside her.

"Stand here."

He removed the magazine and placed it on his belt, then handed her the pistol. The weight of it dragged at her arm. It was much heavier than she'd expected.

Rodani pointed out the parts of the gun, showed her the magazine he had stowed, how it slid into the grip, and how the bullets were loaded into the chamber. He removed the clip and the chambered bullet separately, put both into his capacious jacket pocket, then turned her toward the target. He positioned her arms, head, shoulders, and feet. Cara, trying to pay attention to what she was being shown, was acutely aware of Rodani's body behind her, his hands on her own as he helped her aim the gun.

"Sight your target and squeeze the trigger slowly."

"Keep both eyes open," Serano corrected from the side.

Rodani stepped back, and Cara did as she was instructed. The gun gave a sharp click.

She stared at the target where she had aimed the empty firearm. "Did I hit anything?"

"Did you?" Rodani replied.

Cara brought the gun up close to her face. It was half as long as her forearm, and cold. She wondered for a moment what it would be like to use it—to really kill someone. Then common sense reasserted itself. She contented herself with looking it over, trying to remember the names of the parts.

Cara tried a few more shots, pointing the gun upward and back level to re-aim, mimicking recoil she wouldn't feel without firing live ammunition. She tried some of the other targets nearby and felt a very human pang of guilt as she aimed at a Selandu-sized outline.

"Feet a little wider, Cara," Rodani said from behind her. "Shoulder width, at least."

She turned sideways to check her stance. The gun in her hands moved with her body's turn, and she heard a shout. Quickly, Cara looked around, puzzled by Serano's dodge.

"Do not point a gun at someone unless you are willing to use it!" His fists were clenched at his sides.

"It isn't even loaded."

He was shaking, thin lips were tightly pursed; his pupils were no more than vertical slits. "Never take a chance with a weapon."

Rodani came around to her side, and not incidentally between the two. "Learn the lesson," he said. "Now."

"Please forgive me, a'Serano." She looked up at Rodani. His attention was on his pistol. "May I try it loaded?"

"No," Serano said, with no allowance for his partner's seniority.

Rodani cocked his head to the side, a less intimidating gesture. "You have caused enough disturbance in us today."

It wasn't what she wanted to hear. "I meant none, I...I wished only to...."

Her guardians waited. But she exchanged her grip on the pistol for a safer one on the barrel and passed the gun back to Rodani.

He took it without comment, slipped the magazine into the grip, safetied the weapon, and slid it into its holster.

"I wish," Cara began hesitantly, "to try again sometime, under more...calm circumstances."

Rodani studied her distantly. "Possibly. Come."

He walked back to the door and opened it, waiting while she took a last look around the room. Cara's eyes swept past the accordioned wall, the targets, the ammunition cabinet, and lastly, Serano. Then she grabbed her designs and walked out the door Rodani held open for her.

"Are you still angry?" Cara ventured as they strode down the stone corridor.

"Some." Rodani's firm footfalls echoed a slow cadence against the patter of Cara's soft-soled shoes. His arms swung easily at his sides.

"Why did Misheiki leave me unescorted?"

"I will endeavor to find out."

Cara was guiltily pleased that for once, the chill in her guardian's voice was not directed at her mistakes, but at someone else's. A pair of artisans rounded the near corner, falling silent as they passed her.

"Why did you leave Arimeso's office without an escort?" Rodani continued when they would not be overheard.

"There was no one to do so."

"Toranel could have contacted me."

"The woman at the desk? I didn't know," Cara replied.

"You did not ask."

"I felt uncomfortable asking."

"Why?"

"I don't know. I have so little interaction with others, normal things still feel abnormal to me."

Rodani glanced at her thoughtfully. At her doorway, he unlocked the door for her and held it open, courtesy of a guardian to his adashi.

Cara hesitated in the face of her silent rooms. "Would you share tea?"

His gaze moved from the hallway behind Cara down to her face.

"I have duties."

Cara blanched. "Yes, of course." She walked past Rodani and into her workroom. He closed the door behind her, locked it, and left.

Cara shoved in a music 'cording, turned the volume up, and began working on her previously rejected designs. After a while, she turned off the 'corder before jumping up. The shutters opened more easily this time. She pushed the window outward and hunkered down on the sill. A breeze drifted over her, fluttering the curls that came loose from her bun. Clouds spattered the sky and left pieces of themselves behind as they traveled. The scent of late summer grasses wafted upward.

This sense of alienation was difficult. More difficult than she expected. Being a loner was nothing new to Cara, but she felt rejected. Dammit, if one of them came to her hometown, she'd seek him out. Try, at least for a while, to make them feel welcome, accepted. But that was her nature. There was no Selandu counterpart to the "monster lovers," as the opposition was wont to call the CSC members. Only Hadaman, the closest thing the Selandu had to a proper city, had any experience with humans. Pleasant experience, that is.

No aliens had ever crossed the mountains southward, ever been in her position. Therefore, it seemed, no aliens could comprehend the problems she faced. Was she ugly? Did she smell? Did they laugh and joke behind her back?

Outside, shrill voices echoed around the corner of the manor and prickled Cara's painful boredom, turning it into curiosity. A dozen or so Selandu children came into view. Two by two, they trod the grass toward her second-story window. They were animated, but constrained—orderly, where human children would likely not be. Their heads swiveled in all directions, arms pointing at various items of interest. All had their hair pulled back into clips. Buns weren't mandatory for Selandu girls until they hit puberty at about age fifteen. Maturity came a little later in this alien race, and lifespans were longer.

A solitary woman—a teacher, Cara assumed, accompanied the children. She trailed them, with a single little boy at her side. He spoke to no one, at times hanging back to closely scrutinize his surroundings, as if expecting to be quizzed later. The teacher tugged at his arm. He sped up, then looked along the upper row of windows.

And stopped.

The teacher shook his arm and said something, then followed his line of sight.

Afraid to frighten the innocent, Cara froze in the dual gaze. When more children turned toward their teacher's object of attention, Cara uncurled one set of fingers slowly, stretched them taut, then curled them back up in a gesture of good-will.

The teacher spoke sharply to her charges and hurried them along. Only the little boy turned back to watch her.

She smiled. And kept smiling as the impromptu spectators trooped off. The little boy dared enough to look at her. Study her. Gaze at her without flinching, and without threat.

Bold.

She wondered who he was.

FIVE

Cara pattered beside Rodani, straining to keep his pace as they headed down the wide hall that led to the gathering. Held weekly, it occasionally showcased recent creations by the manor's artisans.

"Have you begun one of the designs the taso approved, Cara?" he asked.

"Not yet. But I finished two approved ones."

"You must. Soon."

"Why?"

"You asserted yourself for an appeal of the craft council's decision. She rescinded it and gave you permission. Not taking advantage of her largesse would offend her."

"Mmm. Yes, I see."

The room was crowded. Heads and shoulders towered over Cara, making her feel like a child at an adults' party. Rodani dropped her off at the table with Serano and headed toward the bar.

Serano glanced up at her short frame and back down, then rose and motioned her ahead of him. She worked her way down the buffet, knowing Serano would warn her against inappropriate dishes. Most Selandu foods were digestible to humans, but certain northern continent ingredients could be fatal. She hadn't forgotten her first evening here when Garidemu, a potter, brought her a drink only to face Rodani's subsequent censure at the almost fatal mistake. Cara had never been certain if the man's choice was accidental or not, but her later attempt at soliciting information from Rodani had been coolly rebuffed. She'd not tried again.

Plate comfortably full, Cara waited for Serano to make his last choices before they returned to the table. Rodani was still at the crowded bar, awaiting his turn. She placed her plate and utensils on the table and sat. A few heads still turned her way.

Somebody stepped into her view, somebody in a skirt.

"May I sit?"

Cara looked up into narrow eyes in a narrow face. Startled at the unusual request, she turned to Serano. He opened his palm at the empty chair across from Cara. The woman put her plate and drink onto the tabletop and pulled out the chair.

"A'Cara, I am Iraimin."

"A'Iraimin." She had to be careful with the pronunciation. Glottal stops were unusual in Cara's native tongue. "I'm pleased."

"Thank you. I have seen you here for a few evenings, but never approached."

"Your work gains you esteem with each new showing, Iraimin," Serano said.

"I would hope," Iraimin said, "after such a number of years."

Cara looked at Iraimin in surprise, then at the display stands clustered in the center of the room. "You have an item on show?"

"Yes."

"Which one is yours?"

"The portrait."

"How long did it take?" Cara asked her.

"Approximately three weeks. When will we see one of your quilts?"

Cara blushed and stared at her plate. "That's the taso's decision, isn't it? What gets displayed and what doesn't?" She took a small bite. "How long have you been painting?"

"From childhood."

Rodani made it back to the table with drinks and sat adjacent to Cara. As Iraimin concentrated on her dinner, Cara nibbled, and nursed her drink.

Her guardians polished off their own drinks and turn-and-about wandered over to the bar for refills. Serano stopped at a group of three women who lingered near the food table. Animated as he rarely was around Cara, Serano talked with them, smiling occasionally and gesticulating; looking for all the world like he was flirting. He probably was. *Serano could find an interest in almost any Selandu woman, at least for a night.*

She never saw Rodani with a woman—or a man, for that matter. He seemed the solitary type. She wondered idly if he were unhappy with his life.

Cara turned back to Iraimin. "How long have you been at Barridan?"

"Five years," Iraimin said without looking up from her plate.

"Are artisans normally invited here as I was, or do they approach the taso and request a place?"

Iraimin looked up. "Some are invited. Most ask. Why?"

"Curiosity." Cara took a sip of shigeli. "Does Arimeso keep the same number of people all the time, and only bring in new people when other ones leave? Or is her household increasing?"

Iraimin glanced at Rodani.

"Asking immense quantities of questions seems to be the human way of forming or strengthening companionship, Iraimin," Rodani said.

Her curiosity stymied, Cara waited in silence. For what, she didn't know.

"How long have you been quilting, a'Cara?" Iraimin finally asked.

"Twelve years, off and on."

"Off and on?"

"I began at age fourteen to please my grandmother, but I stopped when I entered the Cultural Studies Center, a year behind Ambassador Second Andrew. When my studies ended, I began to quilt again."

"He chose you to come here because he knew you?"

"We grew up together. We were childhood companions. We played together. His family moved away when I was ten. We met again in the CSC, eight years later." The rest of the story, Cara left alone.

Iraimin finished her third drink. "Have you companions, yet, a'Cara?"

"I haven't had the opportunity. My socializing is…limited."

Serano turned his head to listen.

"For reasons of safety, of course," she added for his benefit. She had no idea how much of her conversations made its way from one guardian's swept back ears to another, and she was rightfully wary of stepping on the booted toes of those who guarded her.

"How did your path in life lead you here?" Cara asked.

Iraimin leaned back in her chair. "I have always painted," she began, slowly. "The walls of our home were my first surface, much to my parents' dismay. I graduated to paper, then to canvas as I got older, otherwise learning only what was absolutely necessary in school. I apprenticed to a local artist when I was fourteen, knowing already that I wished for a place here." She took a sip of her drink. "My parents were against the notion, but I stayed apprenticed for two years until I reached my majority. I could then do as I wished, so I immediately applied through the council."

"May I ask why your parents disapproved?"

"They felt art was not a proper vocation for one of their children. It is more important to rebuild our technology."

Cara tried to stifle an inopportune laugh. "Your parents must have talked to mine."

The painter's eyes reflected her understanding. "My first petition was refused. I tried again the next year, as the rules allow. I was accepted."

"And the future? Is your stay here lifelong?"

"Usually. We can lose our place, but only through gross impropriety, lack of buyers for the work, or if the taso decides the craft is no longer supported." Daintily she picked up a piece of cream-colored sweetmelt the bakers had made. "Each is rare. The taso is cautious in her choices." Iraimin nibbled the candy and sipped her drink thoughtfully. "Would it please you to visit me?"

Cara's eyes widened. "I'd be honored."

"Tomorrow?"

"Yes, please."

"Down the hall from you, around the corner, and first door on the right," the painter said.

Happy with the offer, Cara turned to Rodani in the hopes his imbibing had loosened his tongue. His face was devoid of expression. "And your path to the manor, Rodani?"

He regarded his empty plate and lifted his full glass. "I asked."

She laughed. "A man of many words. Were you accepted with the first petition?"

His eyes refocused on her face, pupils narrowing. "That is not an appropriate question."

Her jaw snapped shut. "No offense meant, Rodani. Forgive me."

"Forgiven."

Cara picked up her drink and rattled the ice cubes repetitively. The crowd was beginning to thin. Behind her, the ostentatious table reserved for Arimeso and her entourage sat empty and untouched; tonight, they were elsewhere.

Cara turned around, then let her gaze drift right, scanning the few still eating their dinners. She noticed an older man trying not to be caught staring at her. His chin was tucked, attention seemingly on his dinner while his eyes watched Cara. A flush crept over her face. Meeting his gaze made no difference to the duration of his stare. She thought she'd gotten used to the gawking that tested her emotional endurance during those first weeks. Incorrect again.

"Rodani."

Waiting for the question, he looked at her with the same look that came her way from the unknown man.

"There is a man over there...watching me."

"I am aware," Rodani said.

"I think he was earlier, as well."

"Of that, I am also aware."

Cara grimaced. "Are you always aware?"

"Yes. Ignore him."

Such confidence was intimidating; this quiet, unshakable surety was rare in humans. This was a composure different from bluster, or a laughing dismissal of insecurity.

Cara grimaced. Both guardians regarded her curiously. "It's difficult when I'm singled out."

Rodani lifted his glass and brought it near his lips. "By your very nature, you are singled out. Is this a new problem?"

"A room full of stares is impersonal, Rodani. One out of a crowd is unnerving."

"Do not let it cause distress. I will do a better job of your worrying than you."

Language was an inexact science. It grew tendrils into psychology, humor, culture. His last sentence was worth passing back to her instructors.

"If someone can be assigned to assume my distress, can another be assigned to assume my offenses?" she asked, mimicking his formality.

"The taso has no one to spare. It would be a burdensome duty."

Cara laughed, alone.

"I suggest an end of the evening," Rodani said.

She glanced at the tall grey people around her, and at the apprentices filling up the dish carts. "If I must." One evening a week was not enough socializing for a typical human woman—nor, for that matter, a rather atypical one like Cara. Why was she matched with an introverted guardian?

Rodani pushed his chair back. Cara followed suit. They took their leave of the pleasant Iraimin, and Serano—who was preoccupied with searching for a willing woman. Rodani saw her to her door. Cara thanked him absentmindedly and watched as he closed and locked it. She sighed with unexpected weariness and climbed into bed, falling asleep with hopes of a new friend.

***

Rest-day meant sleeping in. An early riser, Cara was not. She snuggled back under the covers in one of the first cool mornings.

What to do? What to do? Being the weekly day of rest, she was under no obligation to craft, though most artisans did, being somewhat compulsive by nature. But boredom and hunger won out over lethargy, and she crawled out. Breakfast would soon be on its way, as her servants kept close watch. A cold shower woke her up nicely and the overstuffed chair in her study invited her to sit, with a thick book for company.

After breakfast, she spent the rest of the morning reading in front of the fire. The only way to improve her Selandi vocabulary, as well as the more important nuances and idioms, was to read. Lots. It was a way to pass the time, and reading took her away from her voluntary solitary confinement.

Lunch came and went, with no signs of Rodani or Serano, and she wasn't about to keep Iraimin waiting.

"Falita?" Cara called.

Falita appeared in the doorway.

"Would you find Rodani, please, or Serano? I need to be escorted to Iraimin's."

"Yes, a'Cara." Falita disappeared into the hall.

Before Cara could even open her armoire, Hamman entered to help her. She could dress herself, preferred it, actually. But she didn't want to insult her servant by refusing her duty. At least Hamman would help her gather her hair into the compulsory bun.

Soon Falita returned and bowed, contrite. "Neither of your guardians is available right now, a'Cara."

Cara frowned and stared at the maid. "Do you know where they are?"

"No, a'Cara."

"When they'll be back?"

"No."

She returned to the study and flopped into the chair so recently vacated, beginning to fume. *What is this? He heard Iraimin make the offer. Heard me accept. He knows she's expecting me. So where is he? Why have me here at all if I can't make friends? Just to make a little more money? Surely, I don't earn enough to make a difference.* Cara got up and began to pace.

She's just down the hall. Yeah, I know I shouldn't, but all he did last time was spout vague warnings. So what, I get yelled at. And good gods of spacetime, I'm tired of these walls! I feel like a prisoner. Where is he? It's not right to keep me cooped up in here day after day.

She came to a standstill. *Fine. When he tells me again, I'll just explain.*

Unnoticed, Falita watched as Cara walked out of the workroom unescorted. She went to her room and punched a button.

"Security," was the reply.

The hallway was empty of traffic, as usual. Maybe Arimeso had stuck her in this far corner of the manor as protection or subtle insult. She walked past the door to her guardians' rooms. No sounds came from within. The cross hallway was similarly empty, and she headed farther down the corridor toward the corner that would take her to Iraimin's rooms—if she correctly remembered the directions the painter had given her. She rounded the corner and passed two men walking the other way.

"A'Cara," one said.

Cara gave the customary Selandu greeting and inclined her head, let them pass by, then turned around and stared for a moment, not knowing who they were. Soon, Iraimin's door was in view. She knocked, and the painter answered it.

"Cara." Iraimin opened the door wide.

"Thank you for the invitation," she replied. "I've been looking forward to seeing you, and your work."

Iraimin looked beyond her. "Rodani is not with you?"

"No."

"Where is he?"

"I have no idea, and neither does Falita." Cara stepped in and looked around. Paintings adorned the walls in profusion, and blank canvasses were stacked below them.

"Guardians are inscrutable," Iraimin said with a smile. "I do not know whether they are born that way or made in guild training. Would you share tea?"

Cara drew her gaze back to her host. "Forgive me, but I wouldn't recognize one that might make me ill. Thanks again for inviting me over. Sometimes I really feel alone."

Iraimin gave her a slight bow. "Maybe I can help with that."

The layout of the painter's rooms was similar to Cara's own, a central workroom with an adjacent small study and an even smaller bedroom.

Iraimin showed Cara the easel on which she worked and her preferred oils. "Quality pigments," she said. "Made by a local chemist especially for us. Portraits, Cara. Portraits are where recognition is earned." She walked around her easel and stared down at it. "This man wished to appear older and more resolute. I create what is not."

Iraimin pulled a second chair over, then sat down and gathered her tools. But before she could put brush to palette, there was a knock on the door. Her look of concentration shifted to irritation, quickly smoothing out to blankness in front of Cara.

"Excuse me." She answered the door, then stepped out into the hallway. In a few moments she was back.

"Forgive me, a'Cara. I am called to a meeting in about fifteen minutes. But I can show you a little of how I paint now. If you wish, you can return another time, and we can talk more."

"Yes, please," she said quietly. "I can draw, but I never learned to paint well. I love seeing the details, the colors, how lifelike a portrait can be."

Iraimin chose her pigments carefully. She put two or three on the bristles of her brush and dabbed it on the palette before raising the brush to the canvas. With light quick strokes she painted, working the new pigments into the existing ones. With highlight and shading, the man's jacket took on a three-dimensional quality. Iraimin moved her brush to the arm and worked on it for a while, then a few quick strokes put a pocket peeking out from underneath.

"Have you ever painted landscapes? Animals? Abstracts?" Cara asked.

Iraimin smiled. "I find landscapes boring, and abstracts are too repetitive," she replied with another brush stroke. "Unfortunately, I do not spend enough time around animals to paint them."

"Have your parents seen any of your paintings since you came here?"

This time, Iraimin didn't smile. "Once."

"I'm sorry," said Cara softly.

Iraimin waved her paintbrush in the air. "The goddess wills."

When ten minutes were up, Iraimin put down her brush and palette. "Forgive me," she told the rapt human. "I must prepare."

Cara blinked finally with the cessation of creation. "You have great skill." Iraimin's talent was evident in the work before her. Cara bowed and left the room, with the hope it wouldn't be too long before she returned. Opportunities were not to be wasted.

Cara started back the way she came, hoping to get back to her rooms with her security none the wiser. She hadn't been gone that long, after all. If all the other artists here had talent to match Iraimin's it was no wonder Arimeso's estate was so profitable. Sometimes Cara wondered if her meager skills even earned her the right to be here. A whistle escaped her lips, a tune from the music she'd brought from home.

A hand grabbed her and roughly pulled her into the cross-hall. She stumbled and shouted, fighting the grip. She looked up and found her very angry guardian with a face full of rage.

Rodani let go, grabbed her arm, and forcibly dragged her down the rest of the hall to her rooms. He opened the door with his key and shoved her inside, then slammed the door shut. She turned to face him, heart pounding, feet rooted to the stone.

"Why did you go out unescorted?" he shouted. "Again, you have disobeyed me. This makes three times, a'Cara." He shook the requisite number of fingers in her face. "Three times you have put your life in danger by walking these halls by yourself. If you cannot obey orders, I will ask the taso to send you home. Is that what you wish?" Rodani didn't shout. Selandu didn't shout. Not in all the weeks she'd been here. But he was now.

"No," was her wounded reply.

"There is no excuse for this disobedience!"

Cara looked away in deference. "You never explain the reasons for my constant guarding. And I've asked."

"You do not need explanations. You need to obey. *Do not* is all you need to understand."

Cara was silent, feeling the gravity of the moment. She had never heard Rodani sound frustrated or mad, or any Selandu for that matter.

"Maybe you cannot adjust here, after all," he said intently, pupils narrow. "I cannot protect you if I do not know where you are." He grabbed a handful of her designs off the table and waved them in her face. "If something happens to you, all this will be worthless." Rodani tossed the papers on the floor at Cara's feet.

Stung at the insult to her craft, she shouted. "Pick those up!"

Rodani's eyes widened. He let fly a slap of his hand that knocked her back against the quilting frame. It rocked and skipped across the floor under her weight.

Cara clutched at the frame and stared in shock at the familiar stranger in front of her. She ran into her bedroom and locked the door behind her. She walked toward the bedside, not knowing she'd just given a guardian a calamitous offense.

The door burst open with an echoing boom; the tremendous force of the booted foot behind it broke the wood frame. Splinters flew. Cara spun. Rodani started forward, arm raised, pupils wide, teeth bared inside a snarl. In a heartbeat, he closed on her. She grabbed the heavy brass lamp on the nightstand behind her and heaved it. Rodani batted it away like an irritating insect. It clattered on the floor, dribbling lamp oil on the stone. Cara dived for the bulky bed and clambered over it, awkward because of its height. Her foot had barely touched the floor when Rodani sped around it.

"Hamman!"

For the first time, no one answered her.

Rodani grabbed her from behind. One arm went around her shoulders, the other sought her mouth. Frantically, she twisted and turned in his grasp. He lifted her up off her feet, but his hand missed its purchase. She kicked his shins and bit down on the only available piece of flesh: the knuckle of his thumb. Hissing, Rodani set her down and shifted his hold from her shoulder to her jaw. He gripped the hinges and pressed.

Cara dug at Rodani's hands, drawing blood. But as she continued to fight, his pressure on her jaw became unbearable. She struggled wildly to free herself from the vice-like grip, keening in pain. She ground her teeth on his thumb in agony but had to let go as his strength quickly outmatched hers.

When she stopped biting, Rodani released his grip on her jaw. With a last burst of fury, Cara threw a backhand slap up at his face and turned for the door.

Before she could take a step, Rodani picked her up and threw her on the bed behind them. His shin went across her thighs with a weight that bade fair to break her legs. His wounded hand held her arms above her head, her fists in his and pressed into the pillow at the top of the bed. With his good hand, he slapped her across the cheek.

"Enough, Cara. Cease."

"Let go of me!"

"Stop," he countered, bent over her. "This has gone too far."

When Cara continued to struggle, he slapped her another time. Her head rocked to the side with the weight of the blow.

Her legs were a hopeless cause under his, but she twisted her arms frantically in an attempt to break free of his grip. The moves of protest brought another slap. Rodani's damaged hand held hers in a seemingly unbreakable lock.

"Stop hitting me!" she yelled.

"I will stop when you calm yourself."

"I'll calm myself when you stop hitting and let go!"

Deadlock.

With her own command ignored, Cara struggled again. ^Damn you!^ she shouted in her own language. She tried to pull her arms downward and rocked back and forth to dislodge his leg.

In a last-ditch attempt, Cara twisted and turned with everything she had, grunting with effort. Silent, with implacable will, Rodani held her fists and slapped once more, hard. It brought a cry of pain. Losing strength and losing heart, she stopped fighting and lay still. Tears leaked from the corners of her eyes and onto the quilt beneath her. She closed her eyes and turned her head away from the impassive face above her.

Rodani let go of her hands and lifted some weight off her thighs. Cara brought her hands down to wipe her face and massage the cheek that had repeatedly taken the sting of his palm.

Rodani moved his leg and sat on the edge of the bed. He waited quietly and took his first good look at his macerated knuckle. It was torn and bloody. A flap of skin hung from one side of it. Deep gouges adorned the top and bottom where her teeth had ground into the flesh.

Cara, leftover adrenaline pouring out from the tears that ran down her face, crawled off the bed and staggered away, head drooping.

Rodani looked up from his thumb at the movement, his back against the thick poster at the foot of the bed.

Cara shuddered, arms crossed over her chest, and spun to face him. "Never hit me, Rodani. Never hold me against my will."

"Never go outside your rooms alone," he countered. "And I will discipline your offenses as I see fit."

Command radiated from him, leaking past her weakened defenses. But she was too angry to be cowed. She kicked the fallen lamp. Metal against stone made a satisfactory racket in the corner.

"Why did you do this?" she demanded.

"You threw it at me."

Teeth bared in a hunter's grin. She pointed a rigid finger toward the bed. "This!" Finger moved past him to the workroom. "And this."

"To frighten you," he said. "I was testing you, and you failed. You repeatedly disobey me. Talking has not worked. Giving orders has not worked. I had to do something to make you stop before you were killed." Rodani turned to the servants' doorway. "Hamman."

"Killed?" Cara repeated, dazed with his admission.

Hamman appeared in quick response to the summons.

"Ice bags. Drinks."

Cara stared at her from across the room. "Why didn't you come when I called?"

Hamman glanced at Cara, then turned to Rodani, eyes wide, mute.

"I will explain."

She left.

"I commanded them both not to interfere." He dragged his attention away from his thumb and regarded her from under lowered brows. "*They* were obeying me."

"If you would talk to me, Rodani, instead of ordering me around like a child, you might be surprised at my cooperation."

"If you did not constantly disobey as a child, I would have little need for giving you orders."

"I was pushing against your orders. Against the feelings of being trapped here." Cara rubbed her face, removing the remnants of her tears in the process. "Rodani, if you ask a human to do something, likely she'll do it. Demand it of her and you'll get resistance."

"Childish."

"Not to us."

"You should do your duty regardless of how the duty is delivered, request or command." He stared down at his thumb.

"And what is your duty to me, a'Rodani?"

Her return to formality brought an alert stare. "My primary duty to you is to protect you from harm. My secondary duty is to do what is possible to help you adjust to Selandu culture—to make your stay here less troublesome."

"Then you have failed in half your duty, just as I have failed in part of mine."

Her words brought Rodani up off the bed and around to face her. "In what way?"

"You rarely talk to me, Rodani. Rarely answer any questions except in single words. You refuse information about yourself or your life here. You won't even tell me the why behind your most basic duty to me—escort. You're a blank canvas at my side. I can't interact with emptiness, Rodani. And the attempt leaves emptiness behind. My isolation hurts me."

She dared a glance in his direction, then slid to the floor. "In what way do you see yourself helping me adjust? Do you even know how? Have you asked?" Her gaze went back to the wall as she waited out the ensuing silence. Her cheek still smarted from the force of his hand, and the hinges of her lower jaw throbbed with every heartbeat.

"It is not a guardian's place to socialize with his adashi."

"Then you have a conflict of duty, a'tem, because that's something I need."

From the doorway came a rustle of clothing. Hamman entered with two ice bags and two drinks. Rodani grabbed an ice bag and a glass from Hamman's tray and handed them to Cara on the floor before tending to himself. Hamman left the room without a glance to either side.

"I understand your orders. But," Cara crossed her arms around her knees, drink in one hand and ice bag on one half of her jaw, "emotional needs don't respond well to reason." Rodani sat back down on the bed. He rested the ice bag on his mangled thumb, the other held his drink, his attention glued to her.

"I was wrong to disobey you," she continued. "I know that. But since you need my cooperation, please do me the courtesy of cooperating with me. With explanations." She looked back over to the man on her bed who was nursing a drink and a wound she'd given him. "And please don't hit me again. It's extremely offensive." She pointed to the ice bag on his hand. "It was only luck that allowed me to hurt you at all. You could kill me with a blow. Every human knows that."

Cara stretched her legs out again and took a long swallow of her drink, then adjusted the ice bag. Wearily, she stood up and moved back to the bed and sat on it, facing him. "I had no intention of dishonoring you. Nor did I mean to be dishonorable. My disobedience came from feeling offended by the constant escort. That's no excuse," she admitted. "I'm sorry."

Rodani stiffened. "Why are you offended by my escort?"

"Because I don't know why it's necessary." She looked down

at her lap. "I thought once I knew my way around, the escort would stop. It didn't. I began to wonder if people thought I would continually offend, or...or break things, like a child. But... you said 'killed.'" She lifted her head to watch him and waited with a mix of dread and anticipation.

Rodani leaned back against the bedpost and took a sip of his drink. He shifted the ice bag on his thumb. He stared into the servants' corridor, breathing shallowly. "My escort is no offense." He gazed back at her. "At least two people in this household wish to kill you, Cara, and a handful of others would be pleased for them to succeed."

Cara's mouth opened, her sore jaw dangling. "What? Why? I'm nobody. I'm not a politician or a noble."

"You are naïve. It is not what you do, it is what you are...human. You represent change, danger. They resent and fear you."

"The man last night...who was staring?"

"That is my duty. Yours is to craft."

"Why wasn't I told this at the beginning?"

"Most in the household are relatively indifferent to your presence, a'Cara. A few feel you bring luck from the goddess." He tucked his glass in the crook of a knee. "Knowing we could protect you adequately, the taso chose to keep you in ignorance. It was thought fear would interfere with your creativity." Rodani raised the ice bag and glanced at the wound beneath.

Cara sucked in a breath at the sight. "I'm so sorry."

"I am sorry to have offended you. But I do what I know. If what I did was not correct, what was?"

"What you just gave me. An explanation. Now that I know what I'm facing, I won't walk out without you. It is as simple as that."

"So simple?" He took another sip of his drink and replaced the glass in its precarious position.

"Yes." She laid her ice bag on the bed and reached across to him—hand outstretched. "Let me see."

Rodani removed the bag and held out his hand. Cara took it in hers and studied the bite mark with gruesome interest. "You should see the physician."

"I will manage."

Something in his tone brought her attention back to his face. "Too embarrassing to admit where you got it?"

Rodani swallowed without benefit of his drink.

She laughed. "If I end up with bruises on my jaw and a red cheek, we'll not be able to be seen anywhere together."

That elicited the first smile she'd seen today.

"Come here." She got off the bed.

Rodani followed her into the facilities. Cara tugged his hand under the faucet and washed his thumb, rubbing gently along the torn tissue. From the cabinet she brought out a box. She led him back to the bed, put his hand on her knee, and retrieved a tiny pair of scissors from the bandage box. Deftly she clipped the flap of skin away. She put antiseptic powder on it and a bandage then moved on to the scratches on the backs of his hands and wrists. Rodani accepted her ministrations, watching with his usual silence. Cara dabbed a bit of powder on the larger scratches, then sat and held his hand again, staring at the bandage thoughtfully. "Are we...settled on this matter?" Cara asked him. "Is the fight over, or am I still dishonored? Are you? Is there more to be done?"

To be on the short end of Selandu honor, as she now understood it; to know, after feeling so righteous, that she was partly in the wrong was an unexpected discomfort. The fight was a grim reminder of how little she really knew of the Selandu culture, and how her actions were perceived by others.

At least she'd stood up for herself. Her willingness to fight might have gained her a few status points. And she learned that Rodani could discuss things, could do other than order her around, could possibly realize she had a right to her own feelings. She hoped she'd taught him something in turn, taught him that what was right and proper for a Selandu could be extremely offensive to a human. That was a lesson difficult enough for an adaptive human to learn, much less a hide-bound guardian who knew even less about her and her culture than she knew about his.

Rodani's voice broke through her preoccupation. "Cara?"

She looked up from the bandaged hand she'd been staring at but not seeing. "Yes?"

"Are you aware of what you are doing?"

She became conscious of the motion of her hands on his, the circular massage she'd been giving his fingers and palm as she had been thinking. Gods of the wide deep, what was she doing? She'd just had a knockdown-drag-out with this man. Where was her head? She slid off the bed and backed away. "I'm sorry."

"You need not be sorry. Only aware."

The oblique reference meant something. But she didn't want to inquire. Cara resolutely kept her gaze on the far wall, wishing for a distracting view.

"As to your question," he continued, "all offense has been neutralized; all honor restored—as long as you continue to obey me."

"Thank you." She glanced at him. "And you better not hit me again."

With a rustle of the mattress and a thump of bootheels, he was gone. Cara turned back to the bed and stared at the rumpled covers. His ice bag was gone, as was the drink.

Alone again, Cara finished her drink with a convulsive gulp and clunked the empty glass on her bedside table, then tumbled into the bed with her ice bag. The room became warm with the shigeli in her bloodstream. Her head swam. Visions of might-have-beens and almost-weres flashed through her mind. She could have been murdered. The actions she'd taken pride in several minutes ago now seemed like unmitigated stupidity. She could have been raped.

Or could she? The thought had raced through her mind when Rodani threw her on the bed, but her knowledge of Selandu physiology was too scant to know the answer. And she was fervently thankful she hadn't found out the hard way. Her body ached from the bruises he'd inflicted. The one on her hip, she noted with some asperity, was going to last a while. Her arm hurt from his grip, and her jaw still throbbed. She was getting a headache.

Dinner would not be easy to chew, tonight.

Cara got up and stepped over the splintered wood of her workroom door to clean up the mess of her supplies. With methodical precision, she rearranged her pencils and tools, more from comfort in the feeling of control than from necessity. She smoothed out the designs and sketches she retrieved from the floor, sorted them carefully one by one, and tucked them into an envelope for safekeeping.

In the silence, worry began to crowd into her mind with a jumble of conflicts. Her ego versus his duty. Her hatred of violence versus his right to do as he saw fit with her disobedience. And what rights did she have here, anyway? Human rights were for humans. The Selandu held to their own, rights that the taso gave. And the reality of living with Selandu was far more restrictive than she had believed. Did she even have any right to assert any rights?

The clanking of the rickety food cart pulled her from her

thoughts. It was later than she realized. She rubbed her jaw, wincing at the pain. She hoped the manor's busy cooks wouldn't notice when her meat was returned to the kitchen uneaten. An overly laden cart met her at the study doorway as she rose in assistance. Her bruised hip complained at the effort.

"This is too much for me, Hamman."

Hamman stopped, dinner cart blocking the doorway.

"Rodani informed me he would be joining you for dinner, a'Cara," she said. "Was he in error?"

Cara thought fast. Surely not, after the fight they just had. But there was enough food on the cart for three humans.

"No. Thank you." Better to assume a mistake than ignorance.

Cara grabbed the near end of the cart and pulled it into the study. She watched Hamman, wondering if the servant could be a threat to her, as they filled the table edge to edge with food and drink. *Surely, she must know something,* thought Cara.

"Hamman?"

"Yes," replied Hamman, not looking up from her task.

"Can I ask you a question?" Cara didn't wait for a reply. "Why would anyone wish to kill me?"

Hamman straightened; eyes wide. The unflappable could be flapped after all. "A'Cara, that is not a question I can answer."

"Why not? If what Rodani says is true, then surely you've heard something."

Hamman pulled her hands behind her back. "There are duties that are mine, and duties that are not, a'Cara."

"Do you fear me?"

"No, a'Cara."

"Do you fear my people?"

Hamman regarded her with an uncomfortable expression. "We may fear their unrestrained tempers."

"But there's been only one altercation between the two species," reasoned Cara.

"So far," said Hamman, going back to setting the table.

Cara hadn't noticed Rodani slipping through the doorway. The two Selandu stared at her. A heaviness overtook Cara in the light of their inspection. She felt dirty, somehow. Uncultured, dishonorable. Someone to be kept out of the way of others for fear of contamination. She ducked her head and turned sideways to the pair. It was a courteous withdrawal that could have more than one interpretation. She preferred the ambiguity.

Hamman pulled the cart out, leaving Cara and Rodani alone. He looked the same as he had some hours earlier, except a thicker bandage around his thumb.

This should be an interesting evening. Cara put on her best face and willed herself to good humor. With exaggerated politeness, she motioned to the table.

It was the first time she'd eaten a private meal with anyone since her arrival at Barridan. The informal rest-eve gatherings didn't count. Knowing her table manners would be noticed and reported, Cara folded her hands in her lap and waited. Rodani did likewise. There was an awkward moment of silence.

"It is customary," Rodani said formally, "that absent the taso, the highest-ranking woman begins the meal."

Surprised, Cara inclined her head in mute acceptance and fumbled for the lid of the nearest covered dish. Steam rose from the bowl of spiced vegetables. Condensation dripped from the bronze cover as she held it. In turn, Rodani speared slices of meat and dropped them on his plate, along with a large piece of fresh nut bread. They rotated the dishes between them until they had availed themselves of everything. Except the meat—Cara politely bypassed it, setting the plate back down by Rodani.

"Do you dislike it?" He began to cut at the slices on his plate.

"No. I can't chew it. My jaw is too sore."

Rodani set his utensils down and watched her closely as she carefully chewed a piece of broiled yellow root. His pupils constricted in thought. "What can you eat?"

Cara considered. "Soft fruit, soft bread, cooked vegetables."

"Can you eat this?" He pointed to the nut bread.

"If I pick out the nuts."

Rodani's gaze swept the table, then he stood and went to find Hamman. Errand completed, he sat back down and made a second attempt at cutting the meat on his plate.

"How is your thumb?" Cara said.

"It is well."

As Rodani battled knife and fork, Cara smiled at his lie-that-is-courtesy. She pushed her plate aside and pulled Rodani's toward her. Gingerly, she reached out and took the knife and fork from his hands, avoiding the gaze she was certain was directed at her. Deftly, Cara cut the meat into Selandu-sized bites and passed it all back to her silent tablemate. Only then did she glance up.

Dark eyes stared at her, levelly. "Thank you."

She inclined her head again, accepting his response, and covered her mirth with another bite of vegetable. It felt guilty and good to know that she had hurt him. Cara chuckled at the absurdity of the day and then laughed outright.

"Am I so humorous?"

Cara leaned back in her chair and slid her palms along her sore jawline. "We both are. At least, I would rather laugh at our earlier tempers than…," she searched her mind for the Selandu equivalent of crying but found none, "than rain again."

"Rain is the water flowing from your eyes?"

"Yes. Selandu eyes don't rain?"

"They do not. What is more important is that you learned something from it. Did you?"

"Yes. Did you?"

That earned another flat stare. But her raised eyebrows and wry smile encouraged an answer.

"Yes," he admitted.

Cara picked the nuts out of her bread. "So, tell me of yourself, Rodani." It was a forlorn hope he would have taken her earlier request for conversation to heart.

He stopped mid-bite and glanced her way, then made a throwing-away gesture with his free hand. "There is nothing to tell."

Sure.

She tried again. "How old are you?"

Another look. "Twenty-nine."

"Not too much older than me."

"Yes."

That brought her up short. "How did you know?"

"The taso called a house meeting the week before you arrived and told us what she knew of you."

"When is your birthday?"

"17th Machika."

"Late summer. Do Selandu celebrate birthdays?"

"Children do. Adults rarely." He dished out some more vegetables onto his plate and took another slice of bread.

"Where were you born?"

"A couple of hours southeast of here."

"By foot or carriage?"

His pupils narrowed. "By carriage."

"Do you have any brothers or sisters?"

"One each."
"How old are they?"
"Thirty-one and thirty-five."
"Are you mated?"
"No."
"Children?"
"No."

The ordering of those two questions was immaterial. CSC training taught that Selandu put less importance on the institution of marriage than humans did.

"Serano isn't mated either, is he?"
"He is not."
"Do most Selandu mate later in life?"
"No. But often guardians do not become mated at all," he admitted.
"Why?"
"The duties are not conducive to long-term personal affinities."
"Oh. A personal affinity is what one has with a mate?"
"That is the polite term."

Hmm. I'm actually learning some things, she thought and smiled. *I see a tiny crack in this formidable Selandu reserve.*

Hamman reappeared with a bowl of chilled soft fruit and a plate of fresh baked bread, causing a pause in the barrage of questioning. She placed it in front of Cara and, just as quickly, disappeared.

"Thank you, Rodani." His gesture heartened her, though she was quick to suppress any extravagant extrapolations from the act. Maybe it was improper to let a dinner partner go hungry from disability. She dug into the fruit with as much zest as the pain would allow. The sweet taste of shishi flowed over her tongue and down her throat with only a twinge from the jaws.

"What did Arimeso say in her meeting about me?"

Rodani paused in thought, as if choosing his words before he spoke.

"That you were small, even for a human; child-sized to us. But she said the ambassadors had assured her you were an adult, and she gave your age. They also assured her that you were a person of good will, and you had language enough that you could communicate."

"With occasional offenses."

"Might you be mistaking *occasional* for *often*?"

"Well, not all the offenses are mine. What else did she say?"

"That you are an artisan and an invited guest here, and that we should treat you accordingly."

"And invited guests get thrown off their feet, and their faces slapped?"

Fork in hand, Rodani tensed. "Guests should not disobey their guardians and put their lives in jeopardy."

Cara took a sip of her shigeli, hoping it would help relax her; the hard ball in the pit of her stomach that had been there in the afternoon had reappeared. She sighed. "Why did Arimeso decide to bring a human here?"

Rodani pursed his lips and regarded her from across the table. "An experiment. New ideas. Possibly a goad to complacency."

"Why were you chosen to guard me?" A momentary silence started Cara thinking the question was improper.

He took a sip of his drink, called eisenico. "Arimeso also mentioned your most curious inability to keep your emotions properly hidden."

Cara slapped her palm on the table. The dishes rattled. "First you frighten me, then you hit me, then you offend me. Thank you, Rodani."

Rodani straightened in his chair and lifted his chin. His pupils narrowed. "First you disobey me, then you refuse discipline, then you hurt me."

"You hurt *me*."

"To teach you a lesson, a'Cara. To prevent worse hurts."

"There are better ways to teach."

His pupils pulsed wide. "My decision."

"Please don't teach with violence."

Rodani's lips tightened into a narrow line. Cold crept over her. "Do not give me orders," he said.

"I said, please. It was a request." She went back to the subject. "Why were you chosen to guard me?"

The corners of Rodani's mouth twitched. "My qualifications."

"Your guild skills?"

"Among others."

"Rodani, getting answers out of you is like pulling teeth."

"Pulling teeth?" His pupils widened in confusion.

She mimicked a reaching and pulling motion. "It's as difficult to get explanations out of your mouth as it would be teeth."

Rodani took a sip of his eisenico. "Few Selandu are as voluble as you."

"Few? Where are these Selandu?"

"Right now, playing in the nursery."

Her face fell. She laid her fork on the table with careful precision. "In what other ways do I act as a child, a'Rodani?"

The last of his dinner disappeared off his plate. "Did I offend you?"

"Yes."

"Forgive me. That was not my intent." He leaned back in his chair and folded his hands across his stomach.

Cara glanced at those slender fingers intertwined with knuckles a shade of grey darker than the surrounding skin; hands that could hurt…or kill. "I would appreciate an answer to my question."

"Would it not offend you further?"

"I'll try not to let it."

His face fell into distant blankness. He blinked slowly. "Your impulsiveness and disobedience. And the emotions on your face and body are those of a child. As well as your inability to hold yourself still."

She took a deep breath as those emotions rolled through her. "Most of a human's freedom of expression resides in those things, Rodani. The rest is in our speech."

"We express only what we need to convey information."

"Obviously." Cara rolled her eyes.

A small smile graced Rodani's face. Mollified, she returned the gesture. Rodani sat forward, leaned his forearms against the edge of the table, and glanced at her plate. "Are you finished?"

"Yes, thank you." She assumed he had done his duty by her earlier request for socializing and would leave.

Instead, he stood up, put his hand in his jacket pocket, and pulled out a deck of cards. "Come, I will teach you a game."

"You play games?"

"Yes."

"Do I have a choice?"

He turned to her with a quizzical expression. "Yes."

She smiled, wide and bright. "Let's play."

Rodani came away from the dinner leavings and pulled Cara's overstuffed chair to the other side of the tea table. Knowing it as her favorite seat, he motioned her into it and took his place across from it, on the couch.

"A moment, please," Cara said, before she obeyed his gesture. She went out through the workroom and into her bedroom. From a drawer, she took a small, wrapped package. She closed the drawer and retraced her steps back to the study to her accustomed seat. The package went on the table near her hand.

She glanced at his bandaged thumb. "Shall I shuffle?"

He inclined his head in acceptance and passed the cards to her.

She shuffled with some expertise, having grown up playing card games with family and friends. Cards, along with Chess and Go were some of the human recreations that had passed over the hills and become endemic in Selandan. She finished shuffling and passed the cards back. "What's the game called?"

"Tasos and Temichin. Nine cards each." Rodani fanned the cards in his hand. "Chose one. High card goes first."

Cara pulled a two, Rodani a ten. He placed the rest of the pack face down on the table, with one card turned over as the discard pile. "The object is to kill your opponent's taso with your guardian," he began. "The aces are guardians—the Temichin. If the player is a man, the taso is the king of the suit he chooses. If a woman, the queen is the taso. The other king or queen of the same color is an ally taso. The corresponding ace is the ally guardian."

He arranged the cards in his hand and continued his instructions. They took turns, picking a card from either pile, or the other's hand. He explained the strategy as the situations occurred to him during play.

Cara took a turn, and kept the card, throwing away a lower-point card.

Rodani drew her queen. "Capture. You have three turns to get her back."

Cara took a card from the deck. It was a useless ten of clubs. She kept it and tossed a four.

Rodani took another turn, hoping to capture her guardian.

Her second turn from the deck proved no better.

Rodani drew from her hand.

On her third try she drew from his hand. No good.

"Kill," Rodani said. He laid his hand on the table face up. "Temi wills, Cara. You chose the wrong suit."

"If I could read the future it wouldn't happen."

"Not even Temi can do that. Only Sela knows. Play again?"

"Yes." She reached for the cards.

Temi was the consort of Sela, their goddess. He was the demigod of duty and honor, and his duty was to protect Sela and please Her, as guardians do their taso. Austere, rational, commanding yet obedient, he embodied all the attributes a guardian wished to have.

When Cara finished and dealt the turn, she took a moment to open the foil packet and place it evenly between them. Rodani shifted his attention from the cards in his hand to the flat brown item.

"What is that?"

"Dessert."

He eyed it. "What is its taste?"

"Smooth and sweet. Will you try it?" She picked up her cards and began to organize them. "Break off a piece and let it melt on your tongue."

With second thoughts obvious on his face, Rodani put a piece in his mouth. He began the second game by picking up the discard and throwing away a three. His tongue worked around the confection, and his gaze shifted away as he considered its taste. "What is this called?"

"Chocolate."

"Shohk-lit?"

Cara jerked her head away from her cards. It was an unexpected pleasure to hear a word of her own language spoken back to her. "Close. Ch, not sh."

"Chohk-lit," was his next attempt.

"Almost. Ah, not oh."

"Chahk-lit?"

"Yes." Cara laughed. "Good."

Rodani smiled back with one of those smiles Cara rarely saw and took another piece. A larger one this time.

The play resumed. Hamman appeared with the empty dinner cart and disappeared soon after with it laden with dirty dishes.

Rodani drew another card. "Capture." He discarded an eight and placed her taso on the table.

On her second try, Cara got her ally taso, but she still lacked her guardian, having only the ally one. The other two turns were washouts.

"Kill." Rodani spread his hand on the table. "Do you wish to keep score?"

"I have paper and pencil." Both were to be found on her worktable.

"I will keep track for you," Rodani said, as Cara returned to the table.

The beginning of their third hand found Cara holding both her taso and Rodani's guardian.

"Guardian capture," she told him, placing the card on the table.

Rodani drew a seven from the deck and discarded it. That told Cara he didn't hold his taso. She had a chance. She drew another card, and grinned.

"Playing cards with me may actually teach you to hide your emotions, a'Cara."

She threw down the card. "Kill."

He watched her over the tops of his now useless cards. "You need not act so self-satisfied."

She laughed out loud. "My victories here are few and far between. I appreciate what I have."

Two drinks, two hours, and 551 more points later, Rodani called game. Cara only had 379. She leaned back in the chair and unfolded her legs. "That was quite enjoyable. Thank you."

Rodani straightened the cards and slipped them back into the box, then stood up. "I am pleased you found it so."

Cara stood up as well, a courtesy to one's departing guest. "I would play again sometime."

"Yes." He bowed slightly and Cara saw him out the door, then headed for her bed.

SIX

Shurad stared morosely at the papers on his desk. The eighth chapter of his newest book, *Death on the River Samida*, lay in front of him, and he was eager to share it with the taso. On top of it was the latest missive from his father, considered an elder among the Riverfolk. It wasn't the Selandu's fault that a battle occurred between the two species. The land south of the mountains belonged to humans. North belonged to the Selandu. *And we ran them back to where they belong*, Shurad thought with satisfaction.

But too many of his people had died, and a conflict in duty was tying his stomach in knots. Shurad's parents and their delegation were going, one last time, to Hadaman. One last time to face the Council of Three in a bid for restitution for lost lives and property. Twice before, they had pleaded their case. Twice before, they were refused.

It was a duty bound in honor. Honor to the living...and to the departed. His people felt Southern Selandu were held to a lesser honor than they, than those who had birthed, lived, and died by the river, slaughtered by humans. Honor to one's taso held sway. But the river watered their bodies, their crops, their dreams. She was a taso equal in strength to living, breathing ones. She gripped them with a force that bled to the next generation. Two score of years was not enough time to forget their loss, their stolen hearts.

His pupils went to slits, his mouth drew into a narrow slash across his face. Ink-stained fingers crumpled the letter into a wad and tossed it aside. He held himself still with an effort of control. Control the mind and one controls the body—and the choices.

At least he had that.

Shurad picked up his pen and rested his hand on a paper filled with scrawling, meandering script. The blousing sleeves of his shirt brushed the desktop, disordering papers and writing instruments. He tossed his pen, grabbed the papers, and tapped them back in order against the tabletop, and commenced with his writing.

...The essential facts have now been covered. What is left is the resolution. A resolution forty years delayed. What caused this miscarriage of justice? Several factors go into its making.

- The few survivors were wounded in mind and body. Pain degrades patience for negotiating and holding out for deserving punishments.
- The warring, dishonorable humans refused all entreaties for restitution.
- The translators were human. No Selandu could prove their translations accurate.
- Punishment of the humans, even if decided on, could not be carried out without human cooperation. This was denied.
- The humans, it was felt, no longer wanted the river lands. Therefore, there was no threat we could hang over them that would constitute a sufficient reason to make them face honorable consequences. Except war.

And we have had enough.

Shurad capped the pen with a smack of his palm. And now one resided on the estate. The same estate as he did. Nowhere was safe from both memories and current reality. He couldn't find a place at another manor. The Sagadad Estate needed no help from a writer in a household of botanists and biologists. Gedidi's engineers would put him to work writing technical manuals, a drop in status he could never abide. Hadaman's politicians would expect him to toe the political line in his work. Honor forbade him from writing what he didn't believe. The Tuka estate's miners and manufacturers would laugh at him as soft, weak. None of the smaller estates would have him, and he had no wish to go home. He'd found a modicum of happiness here, away from his people still caught in the past.

So, he stayed in Barridan. A floor and a hand of halls away from one of the hated. The goddess was testing him, no doubt. Trouble was, he could only assume what the test was. Sela wasn't talking.

There would be repercussions if his parents failed. He stood too near this human for his family not to take advantage of it.

He'd seen her a few times, an incautious, unrestrained, ill-colored, blatantly improper child. He'd stopped going to the rest-eve gatherings when it became obvious she would be a staple attendee. He shuddered in distaste of her proximity. How Rodani managed her guarding, he couldn't fathom and didn't need to. He had his honor and history to uphold. The history of the River Samida.

He was a Riverchild. It defined him, constrained him, guided his destiny. It kept him separate from most of the people here. On that note, he had more in common with Cara than he knew.

And Geseli. Bright-eyed, nearly as tall as he, sumptuously appealing, she'd acquiesced to his attentions more than a year ago and hadn't rescinded her gifts yet. Thoughts of aliens and books fled from his mind.

SEVEN

Cara shuffled to her worktable and eased herself into the chair. Incautious movements, she'd found, brought reminders of yesterday's insanity. If she didn't take an analgesic with some tea, she'd not get anything accomplished today.

Falita stepped into the doorway; her face masked of expression. "A'Cara, forgive me."

Cara looked up in surprise. "Yes?"

"The taso wishes a meeting with you and Rodani as soon as you both are ready."

Her gut clenched. Yesterday's demons were coming back to haunt her, and she had no wish to face them. How could she be so stupid as to think only her servants would be privy to yesterday's altercation? Surely Rodani would not have added to her stupidity with stupidity of his own if it were going to cause major repercussions from above.

"Falita, would Rodani have continued the fight if he thought we'd be punished?"

"I would not assume so, a'Cara, but there are no sureties."

A vague sense of nausea washed through her. She might as well kiss her life goodbye if she threw up in front of the taso. Her imagination was getting out of hand. By the time she was ready, the expected knock on the door came.

"Enter please."

Rodani stepped in and waved her out. She followed him out into the hallway. He locked the door behind them and started off.

"What are we facing? Punishment of some type?" Cara asked as she hurried to keep up with him.

He glanced down at her. "Likely not. We both received just payment for our excesses, yesterday."

"Then what will happen?"

"We do not predict a taso, Cara. You have been told that, before."

61

"I'm frightened."

"Tsss," he admonished her.

"I don't want to face an angry taso and my death."

His pupils narrowed. "That thought should have occurred to you yesterday at two o'clock."

She ducked her head.

"However, a punishment of that magnitude is not warranted by our deeds. I suggest you calm yourself." Rodani resumed his journey. With a few short strides, Cara was at his side again.

"You anticipated this meeting?"

"Yes."

They reached the wide staircase. The steps' height and width meant she took two footsteps for every stair-step. They clattered down together and headed for the central corridors, arriving at the security office door, where Cara's tension rose further. Rodani stepped up to enter first. Three people were in the room: two at the board with headphones and one at a desk, pen and paper in hand. Rodani knocked on the taso's closed door.

The intercom next to the door crackled. "Who?" came a male voice.

"Rodani and Cara," said Rodani.

"Enter."

Arimeso sat at her desk as she had the last time Cara was here. But both Kusik and Timan flanked her.

Rodani walked up behind the three chairs and stood formally, feet apart and hands clasped behind him. Slowly, Cara followed suit, mimicking his stance.

"A'sel'ai," Arimeso said quietly. "Be seated."

Rodani, face properly masked of expression, sat relaxed but alert, his focus respectfully on Arimeso. Cara couldn't keep the emotions from her face or body. Her blue eyes darted this way and that like a small veriachic trying to escape a child's capturing hands. Her breathing was shallow and quick.

"I hear of irate interactions," Arimeso began.

Cara's heart rate increased, but she knew better than to respond. She glanced down at Rodani's bandaged thumb, white against his grey skin.

"What was the nature of this disturbance?" the taso continued.

"A minor security breach, a'Taso," Rodani said.

A raised eyebrow greeted that remark. Arimeso fixed her narrowing pupils on Rodani's bandage. "A'tem, you were chosen for this duty because of your skills. Are they proving inadequate for the task?"

Cara's eyes widened at the question.

"I would not concede that point at this time, a'Taso," Rodani replied. "If I may offer an explanation?"

Arimeso opened her hand in mute acceptance.

"It was a misunderstanding, a'Taso. Each of us answered our offense with an action that, in turn, offended the other."

Arimeso turned her attention to Cara, whose heart was beating so loudly in her ears, she barely heard the taso ask, "Is that an accurate assessment, a'Cara?"

"Yes, a'Taso." The CSC taught Cara the value of fewer words. Less chance for offense that way.

Arimeso turned back to her security fifth. "Rodani, do you wish to be reassigned?"

Cara froze.

"No, a'Taso," he said.

"There would be no dishonor in the decision."

"Thank you, a'Taso, but I prefer to remain on this duty. I am the best available for it."

Cara's eyes widened further. She dared a quick glance at Kusik; his face held a grim demeanor, barely masked.

"What instruction was a'Cara lacking that caused these security breaches?"

"It was not instruction she lacked, a'Taso," he said slowly, "but the reasons behind the instruction."

Arimeso digested that one, then asked Cara, "Humans require reasons to obey orders?"

Cara swallowed convulsively. Three pairs of grey eyes fixed upon her face. She would have been less frightened in a cage facing three hungry rahkti. "Not...always, a'Taso. It depends greatly on the situation and the people involved."

Arimeso blinked slow and deliberate. "I might assume the situation and people involved here would have you obeying orders consistently and precisely."

Cara bowed her head. "A'Taso."

"And Rodani gave you the reason?"

"Yes, a'Taso."

Arimeso's pupils narrowed. Almost visibly, Cara cringed.

"Do you wish to return home, a'Cara?"

"Home?" Dismay swept across her face before she could even

attempt to repress it. Home to cooking, cleaning, washing, and outside work, all at the expense of her creative soul? "No, a'Taso," she said softly.

"A condition of your stay here was that you would obey orders...without question."

Without question? That one, I don't remember. "Yes, a'Taso."

Arimeso eyed Cara top to bottom, pupils relaxing. "A'Cara, do you wish a different guardian?"

Choice? Who could I choose? I know no one else but Serano and Misheiki. What would a "yes" do to Rodani? Offend him to the depths of his honor, probably. "No, a'Taso. I prefer Rodani."

"A'Cara, I gave assurances to your people that your safety would be provided for. If you do not cooperate in the matter, my assurances are without worth, and you cannot stay."

"Understood, a'Taso."

"Rodani, you were within your rights to discipline her, but I did not bring her here for you to start your own private River War." Arimeso tapped a curved fingernail on the desktop. "Moderation, te'oto, is the key to this experiment. Use your abilities to find alternate solutions."

"A'Taso." Rodani bowed his head out of respect.

"She has apologized sufficiently?"

"Yes, a'Taso."

"Then you will apologize to her in the manner that honor dictates." Arimeso leaned back in her chair and divided her attention between the two of them. "Is there agreement between you?"

"Yes, a'Taso," Rodani said, a split second before Cara said the same.

"Let it remain that way." Arimeso folded her hands back on her desk.

Rodani stood up and bowed to his taso. Cara echoed the bow. They exited the same way they entered and reached the corridor—both feeling relief. Cara stopped and heaved an audible sigh.

"Forgive me, Rodani," she said as she began to walk again. "Without my disobedience, you wouldn't have had to face that."

"Nor would you."

"At least some good came of yesterday."

"What good?"

She looked up at her guardian. "Exchange of information, a pleasant dinner, and Tasos and Temichin."

Rodani returned her look, then raised his bandaged hand out between them.

"It would be improper to show you the bruises you gave me, Rodani. I was limping this morning."

"A fair trade."

Rodani opened Cara's door and she stepped in and turned, giving Rodani a bow.

"You acquitted yourself adequately, Cara."

Though tall and intimidating, and an expert in hiding his emotions, Cara felt Rodani's kindness. A little something eased in her heart, a little of the guilt she felt for bringing herself and her guardian into a face-to-face censure by the taso.

"Thank you," she said.

She headed over to her worktable, expecting to hear the door shut. It did, but with bootsteps on the near side. Rodani stood in the middle of the small room, hands behind his back. His expression was a model of propriety, his gaze fixed somewhere in the vicinity of her chin.

"A'Cara, I had no wish to offend you or escalate our confrontation. How can we avoid this situation going forward?"

"Talking," she said softly.

"I knew no other way than to force my will upon you. But now I see that was not the best action."

Cara folded herself into her chair. "Forcing me will get you nowhere. And the taso can replace you as my guardian, or even send me home. It's up to us to make sure that doesn't happen."

"I must ensure your obedience—your safety."

"Coax it, don't force it. Try giving, as well as taking."

"Honor decrees obedience, regardless."

"I think we've walked this path, already, Rodani."

His gaze searched the room erratically, alighting on any number of uninteresting objects, only to flit off again. The corners of his mouth drew down. His lips parted, then met. Amused, Cara waited patiently.

"I ask your forgiveness, a'Cara."

"You have it."

He bowed and turned his back to leave.

"Rodani."

He stopped, not quite facing the door.

"What is it you fear?"

Without a word, he left the room, locking the door as always.

Cara leaned back in her chair, exhausted from the emotional tension. Her stomach growled. With a start, she realized she hadn't even had breakfast yet. At least now it would stay down.

Falita met her as she entered her bedroom. Cara plopped on the bed, which had already been made. "Breakfast?"

"Yes, a'Cara."

"Have you eaten?"

"No, a'Cara."

"If you bring breakfast for two, we can eat together."

"It is not proper, a'Cara," she replied softly.

Cara grimaced. Damn the proprieties that kept two single young women from an acceptable level of intimacy. She missed the relatively open atmosphere of human socializing.

How close had she come, these two days? Make any one of these people mad enough, and she ended up unceremoniously dumped back over the of Himadi Hills, a humiliating and costly failure. Childish, Rodani had called her behavior. Painful as it was to admit, he wasn't far wrong. This wasn't the place for human impulsiveness. She couldn't assume the freedoms enjoyed at home; freedoms guaranteed by the Newydd Cenedyl constitution. Cara's freedoms were controlled by her taso. Only now, after Cara had fought and lost, did the reality of CSC teachings on courtesy, honor, and status begin to sink in.

Should she go home, as Arimeso offered? Had the taso been hinting? Cara didn't want to leave. It looked too much like failure to leave weeks after arrival. Crawl back home with her tail between her legs? She could never face her family and friends again—let alone the envious CSC graduates she'd left behind. No. A major revamping of assumptions and actions was called for, instead. Admitting defeat was immensely premature. Cara dug deep into the strength she kept hidden, the same strength that had so surprised Rodani, and vowed to do a better job of playing by the rules. Her hope that she could coax Selandu into seeing things as humans did, died a reluctant but overdue death. She curled into her favorite overstuffed chair in an attempt to quiet a bad case of nerves.

It wasn't the clatter of the food cart that finally caught her attention. From outside the south window came a creaking noise and the clank of machinery. Cara got up and opened the shutters to look. A line of flatbed carts was heading east from the manor wall.

"What's happening, Falita?"

"Harvest, a'Cara." Falita set Cara's breakfast on the table. "That is the second crew. The first went out early this morning."

"Everyone helps?" Cara asked.

Falita closed the shutters. "Almost everyone."

"I could join them."

"The taso forbids, a'Cara."

Initial disappointment turned to relief, as Cara thought about the physical labor involved. She wasn't averse to hard work, but she preferred it to be the creative kind. "Is there any celebration that goes with it?" Her grandparents and their peers had reinstated some of the ancient Earth festivals that had lapsed during shipboard years.

"This rest-eve there will be a special dinner in the gathering room, a'Cara. The room and outside hall will be decorated, and there will be music and dancing. Some people give harvest gifts, as well."

"Harvest gifts?" She sat down at the table and began to butter a muffin.

"A gift of food one may give to another, a'Cara."

"For what reasons?"

Falita pondered for a moment. "It shows courtesy or," she hesitated, "strength of feeling between companions and family," she decided. "Or thanks, or appreciation."

Interesting. "How is the exchange done?"

"Some exchange at the dinner, a'Cara. But most do so privately, earlier in the day, or afterwards."

"Must the food be cooked?"

"No," she said. "Those who have the talent or opportunity, do so. Others give food that need not be cooked, such as fruits or nuts. Anything edible is appropriate."

"Thank you, Falita."

After breakfast, Cara went back to work on the quilt in her frame. The morning passed in stitches and snips. A knock on the door interrupted her concentration. She stopped mid-stitch.

"Who's there?" She didn't answer her own door. That rule was emphasized her first day in Barridan. She wasn't about to break it now, after yesterday's security discussions. She could only ask who it was, then either tell them to come in or go away.

"Rodani."

"Please enter."

"Last week you conveyed an interest in learning to shoot," he asked her, stepping into the room. "Have you still?"

Surprise crossed her face. Solitude had begun to pall.

"Yes."

Rodani drew a hand back toward her door in mute invitation. With an ear-to-ear grin, Cara rose from her frame and headed the way of the hand.

They took a back way down to the target room. It was empty of people, otherwise it looked the same as before. Rodani pulled out a box of shells from the supply cabinet and brought them back to Cara, with a headband that had two scooped-out thickly padded earmuffs attached. He maneuvered the band into a smaller circumference and handed it to her.

"Rodani."

He glanced up from his preparations.

"Why did Serano become so angry when I began to point an empty gun at him?"

Rodani pulled open the box of shells. "He had not checked the gun. You must always assume a gun is loaded unless its emptiness is personally verified. Caution saves lives."

Cara thought that one through. Her memory of Serano's jump and shout was still fresh. So was his angry reprimand. "But you checked it. He didn't trust you?"

Rodani glanced down at the box of shells, then over to the targets. "Trust, where weapons are concerned, is no more suitable between people as is trust between those who look to different tasos." He glanced at her. "There is too much possibility of treachery in the one or conflicting loyalty in the other. Remain cautious with unloaded weapons, so that the practice will carry through to loaded ones."

"Yes, I see."

"So," he continued. "Where do you stand?"

She moved to the spot where she'd stood before. Rodani pulled his gun out of the holster on his belt and held it out to her, business-end toward the targets ahead of them.

She'd forgotten how big it was. And how heavy. She held the weapon as if it were a bomb ready to explode. "Is it loaded?"

"How do you tell?"

She carefully pulled back the slide and peered inside. "Yes." With equal care, she let it slide closed.

"Would a guardian carry an unloaded weapon?" he teased.

Cara looked up at Rodani. The bare minimum of a grin graced

the corners of his mouth. Before Cara could return the smile, he continued with the lesson. "Width of stance?"

Cara moved her feet farther apart.

"Arm position?"

She raised her arms to the target, pistol gripped in both hands.

"Too straight."

She bent her elbows slightly.

Rodani moved behind her and laid his hands on her shoulders, squeezing them lightly. "Relax your upper body, Cara. Otherwise, you will tire more easily, and move with more difficulty. Speed and flexibility may save a life."

She tried relaxing, but it wasn't easy with him standing so close to her. She could almost feel his body heat. *You're focusing on the wrong things, fem. Buck up.*

Rodani brought his hand around near hers and held it open in mid-air.

"Squeeze slowly, and fire."

She did so. Her hands shot upward in massive recoil. In a flash, Rodani grabbed the barrel, holding it steady.

"Gods of the deep night," she whispered.

Rodani eyed the hole in the target. "Adequate. Try again." He let go the barrel and moved his hand back into a ready position.

Shoulders, arms, feet. She brought the gun up.

"Are both eyes open?"

She stopped. "No."

"You need both."

"It's difficult to aim two guns, Rodani."

"And more difficult to aim in motion without depth perception. In time, the two become one."

She re-aimed with two eyes.

"Fire."

She squeezed.

The startle reflex was less, but the anticipation was worse. A muffled boom came through the earmuffs. Again, Rodani's reflexes kept the gun under control as recoil took over.

"You tensed."

"What?"

Rodani pulled the nearest protector off Cara's ear. The band held it against her cheek.

"You tensed."

"I knew what to expect and had to hold still."

"When in training, safety comes first. Second is stance and relaxation. Third is accuracy. Try again."

Cara replaced the earmuff and took a third shot, then a fourth, and a fifth, and more.

<Click>

"It's empty?"

Rodani crossed his arms and stared down at her with narrowed pupils. "A good student does not ask questions for which the answer is easily discovered."

She took the remonstrance in the grace with which it was given and pulled back the slide. Empty. "How do I check the magazine?"

"Push this button, pull it out."

Empty.

Rodani pulled out a handful of shells and passed half to her. "Refill."

With clumsy effort, she pushed each shell into the magazine. She slid it into the grip, then shifted the gun from one hand to another, getting a feel for its weight and balance. It would take some getting used to. With a twist of her wrist, she turned it sideways to get a better look.

Rodani grabbed her hand with the gun, and forcibly turned it toward the target. He didn't let go. The pressure of his grip pinched her hand painfully. "Never forget you are holding a weapon, Cara. And always know where others are around you."

His voice was harsh in her ears, holding a hint of the anger she'd heard yesterday. She blanched and bit her lip. She hadn't realized it had been pointed at him. "Forgive me, please," she said quietly.

He was silent for a moment, deciding, possibly, whether to do so or not. Slowly, he released her hand, his stayed mid-air in readiness. "The next time you will earn the same punishment a child earns when he forgets such lessons. Safety. Stance. Accuracy. Try again." He stepped behind and to her side.

Cara worked her way through the second clip, aiming not only at the nearest target, but at the next one further back as well.

<Click>

Mindful of Rodani's threat, Cara carefully aimed the gun away from him and checked for cartridges. There were none.

Rodani's 'com went off. He pulled it out of an inner jacket pocket and flipped the switch, all in one smooth move. "Five."

"Get Jiseigin," he was told. "Andalia is having trouble."

"Have him waiting at the west gate."

"Ninety-nine."

Rodani clicked off the 'com and stuffed it back in his pocket. He took the gun from Cara, pulled out a full magazine, and shoved it into the grip.

"Come. You go back to your rooms."

Like a child let out only when company wasn't around. She grimaced. "Problem?"

"Not for us."

"For?"

Rodani glanced down at her as she tried to keep up with his stride. "Do your questions ever stop?"

"No." She let a smile accompany her impertinent remark.

"The veterinarian. There is a benatac giving birth, and his second is having trouble."

Whoa. "Where is the veterinarian?"

"In the fields."

"Why?"

"Likely to give Andalia experience."

They turned a corner.

"Can I go with you? To watch."

Rodani came to a halt in the middle of the hall and faced Cara. His arms crossed and eyes narrowed in language that she had no difficulty reading by now. "I believe you need a little more time to remember your safety lessons, first."

Cara squeezed her eyes shut and looked away, raising her hand to cover her mouth.

"I have offended you?" Rodani asked.

She nodded.

Rodani gave her a moment for silence. "Can you tell me how?"

She dropped her hand. "I'm not sure I should say."

"I am your guardian," he countered. "You are my duty. You may discuss with me whatever is important." His pupils narrowed. "I understood that as a need you expected to be met."

"Expected?"

Rodani was silent a moment. "Cara, you told me yesterday that sharing of conversation and activities was a necessary part of human life. Was I mistaken?"

Surprised, she sucked in a breath. "No. You weren't." *Gods and demons of the deep. He'd heard me, understood me. Have I won something after all?* "I've become...cautious with expectations and assumptions."

"That is wise."

***

Afternoon found her back at the quilt frame. Another empty spool of thread had found its way into the trash can. It was about time to make a list for her sister's monthly care package. Cara made a mental note to request some more chocolate bars.

With due effort, she unlocked the latch on the frame and rolled the quilt up to the next unstitched section. It was beginning to look like it would be done within the time frame she'd given Arimeso. Thank the stars for small favors. She wanted this one shown during a rest-eve. A beautiful geometric, it was one of the designs the priestesses had panned, and Arimeso had subsequently given permission to make. Echo quilting around the interweaving stars and diamonds added an extra dimension to the design without detracting from the careful color and placement Cara had given the pieces.

By the time afternoon's light was failing, her hands were cramping as badly as her back. She stretched and rose. The study and her 'corder beckoned with the opportunity for a change of pace. She went in, turned on her music, and shut the door. The sound of scraping wood against stone slipped out from under the crack in the door, followed by the thump of a musical beat.

Half an hour later and she pulled open the study door, stopping short as Rodani was standing there. In his hand was a set of envelopes. Letters, she realized, from home.

"You were occupied, so I retrieved them without notifying you."

"How many?" She reached for the precious links to a home far away in distance and difference.

"Two," Rodani replied. "That is the—"

Cara switched her attention from the letters to Rodani's face. He was fixated on something in her study. She turned to see. Her 'corder's headphones lay haphazardly on the arm of the couch. A dictionary lay open on the end table, a novel on the tea table. The bookcase was full but neat. The tiny dinner table and chairs were cleared and positioned correctly. She faced Rodani again, hoping for a better expression on him. But his arms were drawn behind him, the envelopes hidden from her. His pupils were slits. She swung her head around for a second glimpse of the study, and back to Rodani.

"You promised." It was almost a growl.

Cara sucked in a breath, stunned. "I went nowhere!"

"Why is your window open?"

"My...?" Another glance behind her proved him correct. "I was exercising," she said back into a face she had no wish to face. "I needed fresh air."

He walked into the study and closed and locked the window. "I ordered your windows locked unless I was in the room."

"Not in my hearing."

Rodani closed the shutters firmly and latched them against further tampering. "Hamman told you last week." He returned to the workroom.

"Hamman isn't you. I didn't know."

He bent his head, getting as face-to-face as seven feet could get to a smidgen past five. "Hamman's security orders are my orders."

Cara backed up. Rodani prevented the retreat with an advance of his own.

"You neglected to tell me that!"

"You neglected to listen." Rodani walked back into her bedroom. "I will withhold these," he fanned the letters through the air, "until you decide to obey me."

Infuriated, Cara grabbed her box of tools in both hands and heaved it into the empty doorway with an uncoordinated throw. Metal and wood, the tools clattered resoundingly across the stone floor. Rodani walked up to the edge of the chaos, eyes flicking from the floor at his feet to his adashi.

"I am wrongly accused!" she accused him.

"You told me you would obey my security orders. That it was a simple matter."

Cara flung her hand back toward the study. "If you had made it clear that was one of your orders, I would have obeyed it." Fists went to hips. Incredulous expression went to cold calculation. "Where is the honor in punishing me for disobedience of an order you didn't make known?"

Rodani regarded her for a moment, expressionless. "Is that what you assume? Dishonor?"

"In this type of case? Absolutely."

"Then you will add it to your list." Deep voice and narrowed pupils hinted at unspoken threats of dire punishments.

She sighed wearily and looked away, a *Yes* stuck in her throat.

Rodani tiptoed through the scattered tools and flipped the envelopes onto the top of her messy table. "Our understandings are never as complete as I would wish."

Cara rubbed her eyes with her fingertips, then pushed her fingers up into her hairline. "That is the understatement of the season."

"The shutters remain closed unless a guardian is in the room."

With a roll outward of her fingers, Cara opened her palm in unspoken acquiescence, not trusting her voice to courtesy. Rodani left through the workroom door. She grabbed the letters and turned back to the study, frankly avoiding the cleanup job still to come.

EIGHT

In the stables, Litelon dug the pitchfork into the rushes at his feet. Thin-faced, bony in adolescence, he stretched his long frame downward, silver hair clipped and tucked safely away under his tunic. He lifted a last pile of manure and tossed it into the bin by the stall entrance, then leaned back against the wooden wall in aimless regard of the narrow confines.

A boy's face appeared around the door. "You said we would ride today."

Before Litelon could answer, Domendi, the venerable stablemaster, walked into the area. "No, you will not. Not today," he said in a voice mixed with gravel. "Your attention to tasks has been weak lately." His eyes narrowed. "Mind yourself."

Litelon shut his mouth before something rude popped out, then watched as Domendi strode out. The stablemaster had a penchant for using his fists, and Litelon had earned first-hand knowledge.

Minat eyed the curved posture, the pitchfork held limply in Litelon's hand. "You deserve a break from your chores."

"Tell Domendi."

Minat pursed his lips. "I have enough chores of my own. Come. Finish. Let the wind smooth your feathers."

"I need no more bruises, Minat. I am headed in-house."

Minat sucked an audible breath into his lungs. "You face the taso?"

Litelon's pupils expanded into ovals as wide as the ones across from him. "Goddess, no. Bring me no more ill luck, please."

Minat swung the stall door impatiently. "What takes you inside?"

"The library."

The door stopped its creaky complaints. "What is there that takes you away from a ride through an autumn forest?"

Litelon averted his face.

"Your head is on sideways, lately. Why? Is it the taso's new maid?"

Litelon pulled himself away from the wall and approached his companion, brows lowered, fists at his sides.

Minat dodged backward. "It is. It is! She promised to meet you in the library. I knew it!" Litelon's look sent him out with a rush that left the door swinging on its hinges.

Litelon heaved a sigh and began dragging the pitchfork and bin to the cleaning shed at the east end of the stables. Minat would pester him. Anything not having to do with animals was an incomprehensible activity to the younger boy. Litelon was not nearly so single-minded.

He slammed the shed door and locked it, then returned to the half-sized stall that served as his own private room. A rickety cot held a lumpy mattress. A splintering shelf held most of his worldly possessions, a battered clothes trunk, in the corner, the rest. Seven steps took him to the opposite wall. Litelon stripped off his outer clothing and wiped off with the cold water. From inside the trunk, he brought out a clean shirt and pants. After a half-hearted swipe at his boots, he headed west toward the manor.

It was a long walk.

The manor inside was cool—cooler than the stables, and quite a bit less odorous. Litelon breathed deeply in an attempt to clear his head of the scent of stable sweepings. He wound his way up the center stairs to the third floor, and the small room that served as the book repository. It had a musty smell, like something old and unused since its creation half a century ago. Shelves climbed the walls, tall beyond his reach. Upholstery-frayed chairs faced each other in the center of the floor space. Litelon wandered clockwise around the walls.

Every book was of a standard size and lay horizontally in stacks on the shelves. Litelon scanned the ones at eye level first, finishing one circuit and starting another one on lower shelves.

Another circuit at waist height brought him around to the back corner, where a tiny label proclaimed *Alien Studies*.

Litelon knelt and ran a finger down the stack.

An Uneasy Peace

The Enclave Discourses on the Question of Human Honor

History of the Himadi Hills Guild Quarantine

Case Histories in the Hadaman Courts: The River People Plead for Restitution

Alien Lives and Thoughts

He tugged this last one out of the stack and sat.

Occasional sounds came and went past the library door. Voices drifted by. After a while, someone came into the room. Litelon glanced up long enough to see an artisan walk by and look at the book he was reading. He ignored the man and settled farther into the chair.

"What do you read?"

Litelon jerked his attention back to the man, who was now standing in front of him and carrying two books. Litelon lifted the cover into his view. "You are, a'sel?"

"Shurad." He glanced at the young man. "What interest do you find in that?" Shurad's eyes were slightly narrowed, his broad face constricted.

Litelon shifted in his seat, discomfited as if he had been caught in an impropriety. "We have an alien in our house, a'sel. I thought we should learn about them."

Shurad lifted his chin and regarded Litelon distantly—silent for a moment. "Perhaps it is best if we do." He turned and left.

Litelon stared at the empty doorway in confusion, pondering the enigmatic nature of artists. Talking in puzzles was anathema to the stablehand, who rode his life like he rode the benatacs he admired—fast, and in straight lines.

Shoving Shurad from his mind, Litelon continued his interrupted reading. He was past the second chapter and well into the third when a thought rode roughshod over his concentration. It was audacious. It was daring, but no more daring than his first stolen ride on a stallion. Litelon replaced the book on the shelf and strode out of the library. He headed down the hall at a rapid clip, turned the corner, and took the stairs two at a time down to the second floor.

This hall was like any other hall in the manor—stone, slightly dim, lit by lanterns, cool in the fall afternoon. But it was a dead-end hall, quiet. One few people traveled. He slowed, heart thumping behind the protective carapace that lay just under his skin. Three doors faced him as he walked forward, two on the left, one on the right. His throat tightened, shoulders tensed. He trod more lightly.

That she was guarded was well known. One of those rooms held ambulatory dangers, dangers clad in black. But which one? And were they in residence? Nothing marked the owners of those rooms. Nothing told him which one picked up laundry, and which one spat death from its innards. Adolescent rumor mills coupled with childhood stories were enough to give pause to even the bravest of trespassers. Litelon crept by the paired doors, and on toward the last one.

It sat there, a large, wooden patch in the stone. Behind it lay mystery, an adventure no one else could lay claim to. Derring-do needed no spaceships or mountains. Sometimes it needed only a twist of the wrist on a doorknob. Litelon reached the thick door, sidled up against it, and put his ear to it. No high voice came through the imperceptible cracks around the doorframe. No bubbly laughter like he'd heard on the trip from the coast. Her sky-colored human eyes flickered through his memory, causing an involuntary clenching of his fist.

Litelon drew a deep breath and raised his knuckles to the door. His muscles froze. Slit pupils spasmed. The silence fell across him in a deafening wave; a throbbing pulse traveled rhythmically through his body. He drew back his hand and tucked it under his other arm.

Slowly, Litelon let out the breath he was holding, and took a step back. Minute muscles in his ears twitched. He walked back down the hall and out toward the central staircase, stride increasing as he left the silent corridor.

At the bottom of the stairs, he broke into a run.

All through the corridors, out the south door, all across the grassy fields and into the stables, Litelon ran. The stallion Minat had saddled still stood near the back door, nose to the rushes. Litelon took a flying leap for the saddle, swung his leg up and over, and grabbed for the reins. The stallion bugled a startled protest and barreled out the door.

Minat, having postponed his own ride in the hopes Litelon would come to his senses, ran out the door shouting.

Litelon paid him no heed.

NINE

"Fire."

Three days of holding books at arm's length had made Cara's muscles better able to steady the weight of Rodani's gun. Stance and aim were coming along nicely. Accuracy, however, was another matter—as was safety.

"You must hold it still, Cara. Aim never improves, otherwise."

Cara lowered the gun. "Your pistol is heavy."

His glance slid from her face to the gun pointed at the floor. "Do you wish to end your lessons?"

"No. But a smaller gun might be easier to use."

"They are less powerful. And the range is much shorter."

"I'm not guild."

The corners of his mouth turned up. "Your capacity for understatement is improving." Rodani pulled out his 'com. "Six, Five. Six, Five."

"Six."

"Bring my Kishata to the target room."

"Ninety-nine."

Serano must have been close. By the time Rodani had exchanged the box of larger cartridges for the smaller ones and put his pistol away, Serano had arrived with the requested item, pointedly declining an invitation to stay. Rodani came back to Cara's side with the smaller pistol.

She took it from his hand, sighted carefully, and fired. There was still recoil, of course, but it was much more manageable. So was the noise. By the time she had gone through the second clip, there was a noticeable improvement.

Rodani studied the placement of her shots on the Selandu outlines. "Why do you aim for the left of center on the chest?"

"That's where the heart is in humans, Rodani. Where is yours?"

His gaze remained on the outlined targets. His face went to mask. "Why?"

Her eyes widened as he turned his whole body slowly to face her. Something primordial crawled down her spine. The hair on the back of her neck stood up. She no longer shared a room with her guardian, but with a killer. She stood still, every sense alert. If she were very, very quiet, it might lose her trail, find prey elsewhere. There was not a sound in the room.

The seconds stretched interminably, then something in him clicked—his pupils widened. He relaxed and leaned up against the waist-high wall.

Cara began to breathe. She stared back at him, not quite believing what she'd seen. It was as if there existed a dual personality inside the brain. "A'Rodani," she said quietly, "I mean you no harm."

"You may speak my language, Cara, but your thoughts and feelings are foreign. Therefore, you are unpredictable."

"Why do you allow me the lessons?"

He shifted to face her fully and brought his other elbow up, lacing his fingers across his waist. "Your firearm capabilities are those of a child. With due caution, I can protect myself quite easily."

He reached across his body for the box of cartridges on top of the wall and filled his hand. Curling his fingers over them, he held his hand out, palm down. "Reload."

Cara reloaded and turned back to the targets. *Stance and aim.* She raised her chin and took a deep breath. With its outflow, she consciously relaxed, then squeezed the trigger.

"Relaxation does help, Rodani," she said as she turned toward him. "So does lack of fear."

But she turned just a little too far.

And the muzzle wasn't quite low enough.

Rodani tore the gun from her and raised his hand as if to strike her.

"No!" She jumped back and crossed her arms in front of her face. "Arimeso said!"

His hand clenched as he lowered it. The pupils narrowed and focused intently, as if he were debating whether to obey his taso or not.

Cara let her arms fall to her sides, then took another step back as Rodani bared his teeth. He pulled the slide back with a tense jerk of his arm, revealing the metallic sheen of a shell. "There was still one in the chamber, ki'ono!" He thrust the offending weapon to his side, clenched with a force that whitened his fingertips. "Safety, first and foremost. It should always be in the front of your thoughts!"

"Forgive me, please," she said, voice shaking. His natural intensity, so often covered behind a mild manner, radiated so fiercely she could almost feel its heat.

He jammed the pistol in his jacket pocket and went to the door. "The lesson is over for the day." He opened the door and held it for her. Silently she passed through. The silence continued through the trip upstairs. Rodani opened her door, and Cara shuffled in. He closed and locked the door behind her, remaining outside.

She lay down on her bed and covered her face with her hands. Creating, she could concentrate for hours. But not for thirty minutes with a gun in her hand. No. Crafting wasn't concentration. It was a creative trance. Maybe she'd better give up on the target practice before hurting someone.

Then stubbornness kicked in. She would learn something from this incident, so she would.

The click of shoes entered the room. Cara opened her eyes. "Iraimin?"

"A'Cara," the painter said with a slight smile.

She sat up.

"You need not arise. I came to visit. Hamman said you were resting."

"No. Retreating from conflicts."

Iraimin eyed her casually. "Why?"

Cara swung her legs over the edge of the bed designed for seven-foot people. "Rodani was giving me a shooting lesson downstairs. I turned a little too far toward him with the gun pointed too close to him. He nearly hit me."

"Nearly? Guild are not usually so forgiving of safety violations."

"Hitting is offensive to me, Iraimin. And I'm ignorant of weapons."

Iraimin raised an eyebrow. "You have had no training in firearms?" She followed Cara into the study.

"We have no guardians, Iraimin, and very few guns—since your people stole them in the River War. Our offenses are usually settled with fists for men, and words for women."

"What if fists and words are inadequate?"

"Then we go in front of something like a Council of Three. They decide who's right."

Wanting a change of topic, Cara looked at Iraimin—the silver hair rolled in a bun, the grey eyes and grey skin, the slender frame. "Why does one see so little diversity among Selandu?"

Iraimin looked confused. "We are diverse."

"Where? I see identical skin color, hair color, hairstyle, similar eye color, clothing styles, height, even morals and proprieties. Only personalities seem to differ."

"That is partially true," Iraimin admitted to Cara's satisfaction. "We are a people who sit inside our molds, and there are few who have the heat to burst free. But this is a place where one may. You have not seen much of us, to make such a judgment. Especially of your guardian."

"Rodani? Why?"

Iraimin hesitated. "He has a reputation for eccentricity. He was given your duty because of it." Iraimin crossed one leg over the other. The long skirt that seemed ubiquitous to the women in the area fell in folds around her calves.

Eccentric? Sure. "In what way? He seems so," she thought a moment, "conventional. So controlled."

"Controlled, he is, Cara. All guardians are controlled. Conventional, he is not."

"Heh," she scoffed. "What are these unconventionalities?"

Iraimin glanced into Hamman's hallway. "He is both guardian and crafter. It is unusual for anyone in the Guild of Guardians to have a sideline so different from normal duties. Also, he crafts in two different mediums, wood and metal. Selandu artisans usually choose one. He crafts small items, instead of large ones. That is unusual for men. And he frequently chooses women's jewelry to craft."

Jewelry? Cara's eyes widened with interest. "What's improper about that—if it would not be offensive to answer."

Iraimin thought for a moment, as if weighing one offense against another. "Jewelry is usually worn on special occasions only," she said. "It is considered personal and should not come from someone of the opposite sex without certain assumptions associating with it."

Cara raised an eyebrow. "Then why does he continue to make women's jewelry? Or any small things?"

"He chooses to do what pleases him the most, regardless of propriety. It is a need most artisans have."

"The creative drive is powerful."

"Yes." Iraimin's eyes traveled across the room to the open door to Cara's workroom. "There is one other thing."

"And?" Not courteous, this curiosity of hers. She could only hope Iraimin understood it.

"Rodani also came here at a much younger age than most. Fourteen."

"Why?"

"He will not say."

Cara smiled, with no surprise. "Is there speculation?"

"Speculation would be improper," was Iraimin's answer, which was no answer at all. She changed the subject. "Why do you quilt?"

Cara had wondered herself why she'd stayed with quilting so long. "I chose it as my craft, partially because my capabilities in other areas are not as strong—music, for instance. I can dance, but the strongest of my senses is touch, and my design preferences lean toward the geometrics, straight and curved."

Iraimin considered. "You could be a potter."

"Too messy."

Iraimin looked out the study door into Cara's workroom, at the threads and snippets of fabric that littered the floor like leaves in the forest.

Cara laughed. "Different type of messy. And, it pleases me to think my relatives and companions might sleep under my quilts, as well as hang them on the wall."

Iraimin shifted forward to the edge of the chair. "May I see your work?"

"Of course." She slid off the chair.

"Why would someone sleeping under your quilts please you?"

"It may go back to childhood, Iraimin." Cara walked around behind her quilting frame and sat down, motioning Iraimin to a chair. "Human parents cover their children with blankets and quilts. As well as warmth, it's a sign of," she waved her hand at the lack of a Selandu term for love, "strong feelings. And it's one way to offer comfort. I can only hope my quilts give a similar feeling of comfort to those who sleep under them."

Iraimin pulled a chair up to the opposite side of the frame.

"Interesting. Do any other crafts invoke similar feelings?"

"All arts and crafts should invoke feelings, Iraimin, at least to humans. But crafts that can be utilized, like quilts, clothing, and jewelry, may invoke the most personal feelings. With one exception."

"Exception?"

"Music. From the dawn of our species, music has stirred our emotions."

"It is said you brought your own music with you."

"Yes."

"And you listen constantly."

Cara crossed her arms on the quilting frame more casually and grinned. "I thought Selandu didn't exaggerate."

"Who informed you so falsely?" the painter quipped.

"My instructors in the Cultural Studies Center."

Iraimin tilted her head to the side. "You must re-instruct them when you return."

"I'll have a lot of new material to teach by then."

"May I ask to hear some of your music?"

Cara hesitated. Selandu music was instrumental only. Why, she didn't know, but she had no wish to offend her new friend with a gross artistic impropriety.

"Most of it is vocal music. Would you prefer instrumental?"

"Vocal music?" Iraimin looked perplexed.

Cara swept her fingers up her throat. "We use our voices to help make music."

Iraimin's eyebrows raised. "We do not do that, Cara. The Enclave would object because speech is sacred. But," she hesitated, "an artist should not pass up opportunities for new experiences."

Cara smiled, picked one from the pile of 'cordings on her table, and pushed it into the portable.

"This is one of my favorites. The man's voice is exceptional." She pushed the play button. "The words are about the feelings a man has for a woman. He desires her and wishes her feelings to grow stronger. It's a common theme."

Both women listened to the music, one comprehending the lyrics, one not. To her pleasure, Cara noticed Iraimin's fingers tapping the rhythm of the song onto the quilt frame. In an effort to build companionship, Cara tapped along with it, in a counter beat against Iraimin's.

"Is there special significance to the words?"

"Yes. The words are used to generate emotions in the listener, just as the instrumental parts do."

"What emotions?"

"Any. Humor, anger, sadness, distress, dark emotions, and the desires of men and women."

"Sexual desires?"

"Yes. And emotional desires. Need, comfort."

"Do they speak boldly, or poetically?"

Cara took up her needle and began to stitch at the quilt between them.

"It depends entirely on the writer." To her knowledge, there was no word for lyrics or lyricist in the Selandu language. Or if there was one, it had been dropped from usage. "It's often difficult to discern the meaning of the words. Occasionally, they cause sadness or anger, or embarrassment."

"Why are those songs allowed?"

Surprise spread across her face. "Humans have had freedom of speech for hundreds of years, Iraimin. It's a freedom we're quite proud of."

"I begin to understand you."

Cara smiled at the tart rejoinder. At the end of the song, she waited for Iraimin's reaction.

"It is quite…loud. I have no way to judge any other aspects of it."

"You can tell me to stop. Music is extremely subjective, and people's tastes are varied."

"Why listen to music that brings unpleasant emotions?"

Cara ejected the 'cording. "Comfort in knowing others feel similar emotional pain from life."

"Are you in pain?"

Cara blinked rapidly at Iraimin's disturbingly blunt question. She swallowed. "That question," she began slowly, "needs either no answer, or one that takes three hours to answer."

"A'Cara," Iraimin began.

Cara smiled and shook her head. "You don't need to be formal with me, Iraimin. Our people, mostly, are only formal with those of high status, like the taso and keso."

The corners of Iraimin's mouth turned up, and her pupils relaxed into ovals. She tilted her head. "I thank you." She paused a moment. "Has anyone told you about Sela?"

"That's your goddess, right?"

The answer brought a larger smile. "She is. Cara, the Enclave is offering to bring you into our prayer meetings. Sela is a wonderful healer of the mind and heart, and She would welcome you.

Well, that's unexpected. Now what? She couldn't quite read the painter's expression. "Thank you, Iraimin, and thank the Enclave for me. But that's not something that interests me."

From the corner of her eye, Cara caught movement in her bedroom. Rodani stepped through the doorway.

"But if you—" Iraimin cut off her next words and stiffened imperceptibly, slipping her hands into her lap.

"Rodani." Cara wondered what he wanted, and whether he was still angry at her safety mistake.

"A'Rodani," Iraimin said. She turned to Cara. "Excuse me, please." With no further word, she got up from the chair and walked out past him. He watched her go by. Cara stared open-mouthed at Iraimin's abrupt departure and fixed a glare on Rodani.

"Why did she leave?"

"Unknown."

Her expression closed down. She jabbed the needle into the fabric with an audible *thuck* and got up. Having no desire to offend her servants by going into their quarters as Iraimin had done, she headed for her own door, reaching for the knob. Rodani approached her.

"Cara."

She stopped and turned toward him, tense in every muscle from her face to her shoulders.

"Where are you going?" The warning stare was back.

"To find the only woman in this 200-plus household who has chosen to socialize with me, Rodani."

"Unaccompanied?"

Cara tried to relax her jaw, the better to speak not spew. "Would you come with me, please?"

Rodani continued his stare. "Calm yourself, first."

Resenting the imperious command, she almost refused it. Turning her head from Rodani, she closed her eyes and breathed deeply, then again more shallowly. The knowledge that she needed his good will, and that they were probably on probation with the taso, coaxed her into calm. With a few more deep breaths, she was ready to face his intensity.

His gaze raked her up and down. Evidently satisfied with what he saw, Rodani moved to the door, opened it, and stepped out. Cara followed then immediately passed him, leading the way at a fast clip toward Iraimin's rooms. Rodani kept at her heels. Upon reaching the proper door, Cara knocked softly.

The sound of scraping came from behind the door. It opened a crack. Iraimin's face peered out. Her eyes flicked down to Cara's face, then across the hall to Rodani who was leaning against the wall, then back to Cara.

"Cara," Iraimin greeted her.

Cara clasped her hands behind her. "I want to apologize for whatever distressed you, Iraimin. I don't know what it might be."

Iraimin looked away from them both. "I would apologize as well for the offense given you."

Cara tried to smile. "A very minor one, by human standards. May I ask what happened?"

Iraimin was silent.

Cara pursed her lips and glanced away. "Forgive me for asking."

Iraimin shifted her grip on the door. Her gaze flicked back to Rodani. "I sensed disapproval."

Disapproval? She'd missed that one completely. Slowly, she spun 180° to face the vertically reclining guardian. His legs were crossed at the ankles.

"Did she sense correctly, Rodani?"

"No. Surprise only."

She turned back to Iraimin. "Will you return?"

"Possibly another time."

"Please."

The two women bowed politely. Cara turned back toward her own rooms, Rodani at her side. The door clicked shut behind them. Cara was silent until her own door came into hand. "Why were you surprised at Iraimin's presence?" She held the door open for him to come in behind her.

He remained in the hallway.

Cara stood holding the open door, perplexed. "I would assume you came in, originally, for some reason, Rodani," she said. "Will you?"

"I will return." Rodani pulled the door past her face, locking it in front of her.

She grumbled. Abrupt exits didn't used to bother her.

Cara sat back down at her neglected quilt, slid a 'cording into the player, and began to stitch. Music favorites calmed the tempers that had not quite receded from the forefront of her mind. She sang in accompaniment. Rhythm took over her mind and hands as the familiar trance stole over her. Many minutes flew by unnoticed.

The clatter of heavy metallic objects broke through to her.

Rodani walked into her bedroom from the servants' corridor and sat a toolbox on the floor. In his other hand was a strip of molding. He leaned it against the wall. Cara had wondered if her bedroom door was being left in its unhappily damaged state to remind her of her foolishness. Now she knew better. She got up and went over to Rodani as he knelt at the toolbox.

"May I help?"

He looked up at her. Funny how much less threatening he looked those few times she didn't have to stare up into the two feet of difference in their heights. Not nearly so intimidating. Visually, that is.

"No, thank you."

He opened the toolbox and rummaged inside, pulling out a small crowbar. Cara returned to her frame and divided her attention between her own hands' work and his. Rodani inserted the crowbar in between the broken molding and the doorframe. It came loose with a crack. With another placement and pressure came another crack. With another, the whole piece came loose. Rodani pulled it away from the doorframe and placed it on the floor among a new pile of wood splinters.

Cara quilted and sang. Rodani sanded old glue from the doorframe. She pulled one 'cording out and plugged in another, a dark one. When the beat filled the room, she turned it down. Rodani shot her a look.

She smiled. "It is somewhat strong."

"That would overpage a rampaging benatac."

Cara joined her voice to the song's, pretending to ignore Rodani's corner-of-the-eye attention.

Eventually, he finished sanding. He wiped the wood frame with a damp cloth and began to brush glue on the new molding. When he was finished, he picked it up carefully and set it against the doorframe. Left hand, right hand, knee, and boot held it in place up and down the frame.

Cara got up and went back over to him. "Would two more hands be of use?"

"Possibly." He moved both hands up to empty a place for her.

She put her hands on the molding, evenly spaced, and pressed on it. "How long until it sets?"

He considered a moment. "About two hours."

She shook her head and chuckled over the imprecision of her previous question. "How long do we hold it?"

"Until we tire."

This must be a game they played, this bantering of words that was a frequent occurrence in conversation. Humor, needing a common base of assumptions and prejudices, was difficult to translate across cultures. She hadn't heard a human-style joke, yet. Maybe she could use this wordplay as another opening.

"Do all humans make those sounds with their voice?" Rodani asked.

A question! A curiosity question! "Most do at one time or another, with a great range of skills. We call it singing."

"At what level are your skills?"

Two questions in a row. Up went her curiosity. "Adequate. People don't leave the room when I sing, but neither do they make requests."

"Are there more female singers than male?"

"No. They're about equal."

"Who teaches them?"

"Most have no training. They don't seek it out because they're not good enough. They sing only in private. Better singers seek training from professional singers who teach."

"Did you receive training?"

Question number five! "Some. I soon realized my natural voice wasn't strong enough to be a professional. I sing only for personal pleasure."

Rodani shifted the placement of his hands and knee on the molding. "It is a pleasure to sing?"

Her head lifted in surprise at this sixth question. "Very much so."

"Do all singers show such extremes of emotion while they sing?"

"The good ones do."

"Why?"

"Singing," she said thoughtfully, "as well as music in general, is about communication, Rodani. Communication of emotions, mostly. Or facts or stories that beget emotions." Cara shifted her palm on the molding. "To pass them along to the listeners, we feel those emotions, and then communicate them. The more pathways used, the more emotions that are passed from the musician to the audience."

"Pathways?"

"Gestures, facial expressions, body stance, words, vocal

expressions. In other words, all those things that are constrained in your culture, and relatively unconstrained in ours."

"Relatively?" he asked, eyebrow raised.

"Well," she drawled, "unconstrained may be different between you and me."

They stood in silence for a while, appendages pressed along the molding.

With nothing else to concentrate on, Cara felt Rodani's presence hover over her and wondered at his questions. Was this the beginning of the eccentricity Iraimin spoke of earlier? Was even the discussion of such improprieties considered improper? Cara ached to ask for the reasons behind his questions but didn't want to scare him away from asking more. To cover the ensuing silence, as well as to provoke, she began to sing again.

A second set of bootsteps surprised them both.

Serano walked in via the servants' quarters, following Rodani's earlier path. It was the first time he'd visited her rooms since the day she arrived, when the pair had brought her boxes and clothes chest in to be unpacked, and the trio had spent uncomfortable moments regarding one another across her belongings. Serano raked the molding up and down with his eyes and fixed his gaze on his partner. "How long will this one last, tem'u?"

Cara stared at her feet, then began to laugh. Rodani glared at Serano, then down at Cara as she raised her gaze to watch the pair's confrontation.

"I fervently hope it will last until my return home, a'Serano," she said into Rodani's silence. "I have no desire to face such rage again."

"Rage?" Serano turned to Rodani. "Rage?" And back to Cara. "I rarely see my partner in a rage."

Her lips curled. "I would trade you the experience."

Rodani removed his left hand from the top of the molding and tested its set. "You may let go now," he told her as he placed his hand back on the molding.

She did has he bade, returning to the 'corder to eject the music. "Serano," she said, turning back to the pair in her doorway, one working, one idle.

Serano turned to her in polite acknowledgement.

"Will there be dancing at the harvest dinner tomorrow?"

"Most certainly."

"Will you teach me the dance I saw a few weeks ago? Please?"

She rested her hands on the table, gauging his reaction. Her memory of the long line of dancers weaving their way between the tables had been brought back by Serano's presence in the same room as her music. He had been one of the first to join the line after the manor's musicians started the evening's entertainment.

"Which one? There were at least three we danced."

"The most popular one, please."

Serano sidled by Rodani in the doorway and entered her workroom, looking at her silent 'corder. "Music?"

"Steps first, please." She'd wanted to join the dancers when she saw them assemble but wasn't about to fumble her way through the learning process in the midst of a crowd. She stepped to Serano's side at the center of the room.

"Right foot first. Watch."

He ran through the steps slowly, then turned 90°.

"Repeat."

She mimicked his steps, holding her foot in the same position he still held.

Serano spun and stepped. Cara repeated it. They went through it again, slowly. After a third time, Cara felt comfortable trying it with music. She went back over to the table and chose a group with a lively beat and popped in a 'cording.

They began again, and Cara fell into the flow of the rhythm.

"Hands clasped behind you."

Cara smiled. "Humans have a tendency to swing their arms and clap their hands while they dance."

"That is improper. Keep your back straight, as well. Do not watch your feet. Eyes forward."

It got to be fun. When they turned left, she watched Serano's back. Not much moved except the legs, feet, a little hips, and shoulders. It was very different from human dancing, where the more that moved the better. It was decorous. Polite. Like the Selandu themselves—usually.

They danced through the song, and into another. The steps were making it into Cara's short-term memory. Serano could've left her to practice alone at that point, but he didn't. He must truly enjoy dancing. But just as Iraimin with Cara's music, she had no way to judge whether he was good at it or not.

"Rodani, do you dance?" she asked.

He was fiddling with the lock on her door. "No."

"Have you tried?"

"Yes."

Serano, however, differed. "Anyone can dance, Cara, if he is willing to relax."

"And look foolish in front of others," Rodani amended.

"No more foolish than the others in the line," Serano replied from his place in the two-person line they'd made. "He will not unclip his dignity long enough to find out differently."

As if to comment on Serano's acerbic remark, Rodani picked up a mallet and began to pound on the wood surrounding the lock.

"Rodani, would you hammer in time with the music, please? You're creating quite a distracting counterbeat," Cara joked.

Rodani rested his forearm on his knee and turned to her. "Do you wish a working lock on your door?"

"Would I be allowed to use it?"

"Yes, for proper reasons."

She returned to watching Serano's dance movements. The pleasant sight held Cara's covert fascination until another turn took it out of reach. She sighed inwardly.

It was going to be a solitary three years.

At the end of the current song, Serano stopped. In courtesy, Cara did, too.

"Adequate?"

"Yes, thank you. I appreciate the lesson. If…" Serano turned to look at her. "If I made additions to the dance, made it a little more like human dancing, would you try it?"

"Possibly," he said with a raised eyebrow. "But why would you change it?"

"Because I like dancing."

"I would consider it." Serano tilted his head and turned for the bedroom door. He walked by his crouching partner in silence, with only a tap on the shoulder in passing. Cara turned her 'corder off and ran through the steps at her own pace, trying to mimic Serano's body movements while they were fresh in her head.

Rodani stepped away from the small vises he'd put on either side of the wooden door where the lock had splintered it and rubbed at the drying glue on his fingers. He retreated to Cara's facilities. The sound of running water and splashing could be heard.

Assured now that she wouldn't forget the dance, Cara made her way around the quilt and sat back down. Rodani returned to pick up his tools and took a final look at the door.

"Was Kusik angry when he found out you'd told me of my

danger, Rodani?"

"Some." He pressed a loose splinter back into the wood.

"Was there censure for your decision?"

He eyed her from his side stance, fingers still on the door. "There are more gaps in your knowledge of proprieties."

She stopped to frame a reply. *What to say...how to say it? Formal, fem.* "I apologize for any problems between you and your superiors that I caused, a'Rodani."

He checked the splinter again. "Before your arrival, it was understood there would be unexpected conflicts and problems to be solved. We should not expect to be disturbed by these unexpected expectations."

Cara translated that one in her head not once but twice before choosing to laugh. She returned to her stitching as Rodani tested the stubborn splinter's adhesion. "Rodani." He looked over again. "Will you take me outside sometime?"

He let go the splinter and leaned against the doorframe. "Why?"

"These rooms, however nice, get boring after a while. And you won't let me walk out by myself."

His gaze flickered around the room while Cara held a hopeful breath. "The colt that was born recently," he looked over at her. "If you wish, I will ask permission for you to visit."

Cara's face brightened. "Yes, please."

Rodani pulled away from the doorframe and stood. "I will inquire." As he turned to leave, Falita padded up behind him and quietly handed him a note. He opened it and read, then turned back. "You have a package in the mailroom."

A package! From her sister, surely. It had traveled fast. The last time it took two weeks. "When you go to retrieve it, may I accompany you?"

"Yes."

Rodani passed through into her workroom, and waited by her door, expectantly. In a moment, Cara caught the cue. "Now?"

Lips curled. "Unless you wish me to delay."

She climbed back out of her seat and headed for the door. Side by side, they left.

The mailroom turned out to be not much bigger than her workroom. "A'Pasteni," Rodani said to the elderly man whose back was turned toward them. Black streaks ran through his hair, which seemed to be thinning. His face was lined with age.

Pasteni's eyes flicked rapidly from Rodani's face to Cara's in surprise, though his face was otherwise still.

"The package for a'Cara, please," Rodani's voice was coolly polite. Almost arrogant, though Cara was reluctant to hang such a negative label on a tone she couldn't quite interpret. As security fifth, Rodani was higher ranking than all but a half-dozen of Arimeso's people—and all of the artisans. Did he use it for his own advantage? For self-esteem?

Pasteni bowed in response to the guardian's request and retrieved an overly large box from a corner of the tidy room. He handed it to Rodani without comment.

"Who has had access to it since its arrival?"

Again, the mail clerk's vision flicked to Cara, then returned to rest politely on the wall behind them. "No one, a'tem."

Rodani shook the box, listening intently.

For what, Cara didn't relish imagining. With her new knowledge, she went from pleased to paranoid and began to wish she could request that Rodani open it—somewhere rather far away.

He picked it up and tucked it under his left arm, motioning Cara out of the doorway.

It seemed no great burden to Rodani, this precious package from home. She knew part of what it contained, but both previous packages had held a small surprise or two. The stone corridors echoed with their footsteps and the sounds of voices that carried around corners.

"Why did Pasteni stare at me, Rodani?"

"Likely he had not seen you before."

"I am at the gatherings every rest-eve."

"But Pasteni is not."

"Why?"

Rodani was silent for a moment, whether in contemplation of Cara or her question, or Pasteni or the answer, she didn't know. "He is elderly. And rather reclusive. One is, after all, not obliged to socialize with others."

Abruptly, Cara's thoughts veered.

Rodani had told her it was his secondary duty to help her adapt to his culture. Was he obliged to be with her? Was he resentful? What was the hidden meaning behind his words? So frustratingly often, Selandu answered a question with a statement that seemed only obliquely related to the question. Dare she ask? Ask for explicitness in a situation where implicit meant courtesy? She felt as if she were preparing to dip a finger into a pan of water to see if it was hot.

"Are you obliged to socialize with me, Rodani?"

"My duty is paramount."

Damn if it wasn't another of those answers. "I fear that means yes."

The polite look turned to confusion. "Fear?"

Cara rolled her eyes. The CSC taught not to do a word-for-word translation across the language boundary. She was getting lazy. "Rodani, I'd feel badly if you were forced to socialize with me when you might wish not to."

They headed up the wide spiral staircase and toward the hallway they shared. Rodani's lack of answer was troubling. Had she guessed right? Cara began to see the courtesy behind ignoring certain questions. Better to offend by omission than commission.

"Cara," he said, finally, "you are needlessly distressed. This duty was explained to me in full before I accepted it." With a jingle of keys in his free hand, Rodani unlocked her door, sweeping the room with his eyes before stepping back to hold it open for her. "I have private time to spend."

"You were given a choice in this duty?"

"Yes."

Cara stared at the box, again reluctant to approach it.

"Do you wish me to open it?"

She turned to him and crossed her arms, grinning. "I don't want you to be hurt, especially when the reason is my own cowardice." Resolutely, she strode forward and untied the rope, then opened the flaps.

It remained a simple box; quiet, and unassuming. Rodani turned and left the room as Cara pulled two envelopes from the top of the box's contents. She read the letters intently, fondly, then put them away and rummaged through the box. Some cool weather clothes, personal necessities, and a new book by her favorite author filled most of the box.

Ah. There, tucked in a corner, was a stack of chocolate bars.

Thank you, Elaine.

Cara pulled out six bars, setting them aside for special handling. Another corner of the box revealed two 'cordings; one by a musician she liked, and one she didn't recognize. That one had a note attached. She read it, smiling at the memory of several pleasant weeks and a bearded face with eyes so dark she could fall into them and never surface. He was a drummer and had remembered her tastes in music. She set his gifts on her worktable, next to the chocolate bars.

And in one more corner, there was a small box.

Cara lifted it out and opened it carefully. A small note was inside. *Love, Dae,* it read. She pulled the note out. Underneath was a pair of earrings, made in the interweaving spirals and knots of her ancient ancestors. "History stuff" her mom had called it, huffy in displeasure of time spent on the unnecessary or the frivolous. There was too much still to be done to make their forced inhabitancy more comfortable and safer.

History stuff and much more.

Stranded on a strange planet, bereft of their roots and ignorant of their location, her grandparents' generation had refused to part with the history cubes. Copies still existed in the ship's memory. Maps, names, countries, continents, conflicts, music, legends, heroes and madmen; many cubes had come down with humans who hungered for their past. Cara was one of them.

She picked up an earring and studied its intricacies. It was beautiful. She took out her current ones and slipped the new ones into her ears. No one in the manor had pierced ears. Maybe it was against the goddess's will to put holes where no holes grew. She chuckled.

It was absurdly easy to see others' shortcomings. Not so easy to see one's own.

TEN

Iraimin closed her door and headed toward the stairs. As she was no longer an acolyte of the goddess, she'd been surprised when Kimasa had approached her instead of a devotee still in good standing. But the opportunity to do Sela's will, to bring an alien under Her wing, was a chance she had leapt at. She missed the camaraderie she'd found in the Enclave, and the knowledge that there, she could better her people, their lives, their hearts.

The Enclave doors were closed as usual. Only if someone was expected did they stand open. But they were never locked. No one seeking the goddess's healing was prevented from entering.

Immediately inside was a desk. Behind it sat an acolyte. She knew them all.

"Adonsa," Iraimin greeted her.

The young woman placed her hands against her chest, over her heart. "Iraimin. What brings you here?"

"I would see the selaso if she is available."

"A moment." Adonsa rose and walked down past four doors to an ornate double door on the right. She tapped, stepped into the doorway, and bowed. Iraimin couldn't hear what was said, but started forward when Adonsa curled her fingers inward in a wave, signifying admittance.

They passed each other in the hall, and Iraimin walked in. Kimasa sat at her incense-laden desk. A large sun and moon motif hung on the wall behind her. Iraimin bowed deeply, reverently.

Kimasa, high priestess of the goddess Sela, waited with a serene expression and a placid demeanor that sent a wave of calm through the room. Iraimin breathed in the incense and let the calm settle her own nerves.

"Iraimin," the selaso began.

"A'Selaso, I found an opportunity to mention the goddess to Cara," she said. "I relayed your offer to her." She halted, staring at the floor in front of Kimasa's desk.

"Continue, my child. How did she react?"

"She declined, a'Selaso."

"Did she mention her own god? Or give you insight into her beliefs?"

"No, a'Selaso. I am sorrowed for my failure."

Kimasa took a pinch of incense, placed it in a ceramic bowl, and lit it. "No, Iraimin. The goddess wills that you keep trying. Her plan will become clearer as you walk the path."

Iraimin bowed. "A'Selaso, there is one other issue...."

"Yes," she prompted.

"As Cara was answering me, Rodani walked into the room. I felt—"

"What, my child?"

"I am not certain. Disapproval? Disappointment?"

Kimasa considered for a moment. "Possibly one of Temi's demons tapped your ear, attempting to stop you."

"Why would Temi send a demon to me when, as Sela's consort, he is to support Her? Not undermine Her."

"Demons sometimes have minds of their own, Iraimin. They give us the opportunity to strengthen our faith or show us our weaknesses."

Iraimin thought through the explanation. "So, I should try harder next time?"

"If you feel it appropriate."

"It is difficult to know when to press forward and when to step back."

Kimasa leaned back in her chair, unruffled by Iraimin's indecision. "The goddess will guide you," she said.

Iraimin bowed again, bolstered by the selaso's supreme confidence. "She will."

***

In a far office, Serano shifted his weight in the chair. Giving reports was never one of his preferred duties, and his discomfort proved it.

"Your considered opinion, a'tem?"

Taso and keso, Arimeso and Security First Kusik sat opposite Serano behind Arimeso's massive desk. Her expression held the distant composure Serano had come to expect over the years. The keso, well, he hadn't been the same since Arimeso's decision to invite a human into her household.

Serano was certain with whom he sided. "She is a constant challenge, a'Taso," he said.

"A danger?"

"Not purposely, a'Taso. Rodani is correct on that matter."

"He is incorrect on others?"

It was a narrow path Serano walked. Arimeso, Kusik, Rodani...all held varying opinions, all held to them with the tenacity of a sharp-clawed richu. And all could bite.

"A difference of opinion, a'Taso."

"And the challenge?"

"The human thinks differently. Constantly. And she reacts in unexpected ways, from the least situation to the most, a'Taso."

"And you cope with some difficulty?" Kusik asked on the heels of his answer.

Serano's path narrowed even further; his pupils contracted in reaction. Kusik seemed eager for an answer, one that Serano could predict. Using guild techniques, he gathered up his calm and thrust it outward, masking his emotions with years of practice. "With more difficulty than Rodani, a'Keso, but with less than many."

"Has she mentioned her people, their attitudes, their weapons?"

"No, a'Keso."

"Their willingness for war or peace?"

"No, a'Keso. She shows no interest in such topics."

"Have you discussed them?"

"No, a'Keso. Rodani believes she is already curious of guild matters and has refused to introduce the subject. He thinks she would quickly tie the two together."

"She is capable of doing so?"

"He is convinced of her intelligence, a'Keso."

"And you?" Arimeso asked.

"I reserve judgment, a'Taso. I cannot assume depth from a wide vocabulary."

"What of her honor, her allegiance to the taso?" Kusik again.

The room quieted as Serano thought. Each person sat in a chair, hands folded, bodies stilled in studious relaxation. No one took notes.

"Her allegiance seems to be directed to individual people, regardless of status or power," he told his superiors. "She considers it dishonorable to be physically punished, and honorable to fight it.

She speaks when she should be silent and is silent when speech is appropriate. She is argumentative and sees no impropriety in the fact. She is quite inappropriately curious and deflects our censures with unsubtle humor or open frustration."

"Speak to her, Serano," Arimeso ordered. "Speak of allegiance and honor. And of me."

Serano tensed inwardly, not daring to show his desire to evade the whole responsibility of communicating with the unpredictable human. "A'Taso." Diplomacy was not one of his strong suits. Another handoff to his partner seemed appropriate here.

"Other thoughts?"

"No, a'Taso."

"Continue your reports."

"There is not always information on a nightly basis."

"As you can." Arimeso waved her fingers in dismissal.

Serano rose and bowed, then left, passing Hamman in the anteroom. He made his way down past the garage to the stables. The open pens were empty. He sauntered down the corridor past the first stalls.

"A'Serano?"

He recognized the voice and waited for the body to catch up with it before he turned to face the young owner.

"A'tem," Litelon said. "I have saddled your beast."

Serano refused to answer, wordless in the face of worthless admissions. Spare time was not to be wasted.

"A'tem," the stablehand tried again. "The human. What is she like?"

Serano sighed inwardly, tired of unanswerable questions. "Why?"

"I," he fell silent momentarily. "I rode with her, on the way in from Soldan. We talked some."

"Yes, I know. Alien," he replied. Nonchalantly, dismissive, Serano turned. "Confusing." Started walking. "Offensive and talkative." Pulled open the door of the seventh stall. "Childish." It slammed behind him.

Belatedly, Litelon followed the guardian to the door. "I would wish to meet her again. Talk more with her."

Serano's voice came over the top. "May you have joy in her company, if you can get past Rodani."

"Will you help me?"

Serano stuck his head out the door. His scornful expression

made a mockery of Litelon's youth and determination. "Changing careers to alien studies? Or is she another beast for you to tether and tend?"

Litelon's pupils widened into ellipses. He backed up against the opposite door, provoking snuffles, and the scrape of claws from behind. "Calling her a beast is unworthy of your high honor, a'tem." He knew the danger in chiding a temichi but didn't want to let the insult pass.

A velvet benatac nose poked out over Serano's head as he regarded the young man. The toothy face behind the nose peered downward, the itchy chin rubbed Serano's immaculate hair on the top of his head.

"Talk to Rodani," he said. It was his standard answer, one that came in handy quite often. And it was correct. He let the door swing shut behind him.

"Litelon!" Stablemaster Domendi's voice reverberated down from the other end of the corridor.

ELEVEN

A grumble of thunder rolled across the closed shutters behind Cara's bent back. An echoing rat-a-tat brought her attention from the quilting frame to the hall door. "Who is there?"

"Rodani."

"Enter, please."

Keys rattled in the lock. Rodani opened the door and stepped in.

"Bright morn," she said.

"And to you." He crossed over to her. "The veterinarian has given permission for you to see the benatac colt, if you wish."

"Today?"

"There is time. The harvest dinner is not until late afternoon." Two envelopes lay by his hand. "Do these go to your home?"

"Yes. Rodani, do my letters get read before being sent?"

"No one here knows Cene'l."

She took another stitch in the quilt. "But the letters go by way of Hadaman."

"Not always."

"But people in Hadaman know Cene'l, yes?"

"I do not live in Hadaman, Cara." Rodani returned his gaze to the envelopes and tucked them into an inner jacket pocket. He peered over the edge of the quilt. "You should change clothes."

It was an accurate observation. Playing in stables required a certain lack of refined dress. She rose and excused herself, then shut the bedroom door behind her. In a few moments, she returned dressed in an old heavy-duty pair of pants she'd yet made use of. A bulky sweatshirt covered her other half. On it was painted the logo of the CSC, and an outline drawing of the two continents and mountain range that separated them. The caricature of a tall, imposing Selandu male, arms crossed, stood on the northwest side of the Hills of Himadi. Southeast across the hills, a human with field glasses held to her eyes peered back.

Cara walked up to Rodani and turned off her 'corder, then stood with her hands clasped behind her.

"What does it say?"

"Newydd Cenedyl Cultural Studies Center."

"Is that how humans see us?"

She ducked her head. "It's how we students and graduates see the CSC. Only the ambassadors ever get a close look."

"Until you."

"Yes." Cara ran her finger across the tabletop, dislodging a few pencils that sat in the way. "I was the recipient of quite a bit of envy, as well as anger, when I was chosen."

"Why?"

"They felt I was unqualified. Unsuitable."

"Were there any artisans among those who graduated from this see-ess-see?"

"Not that Andrew and I were aware of. Most art and CSC requirements seem to be mutually exclusive talents."

"Then you were properly chosen and have no need for distress at the fact. Yes?"

She nodded.

"The colt is waiting."

They left the room, heading for the garage. It was full of vehicles this time, but Rodani picked one out-of-the-way carriage. Since humans built the few that exist, she wondered if there was something special about it. It looked unimposing, except for the darkened windows.

"Center seat," he told her.

Cara stood at the side door as Rodani unlocked it. They clambered in together. Rodani started the engine and took off slowly, mindful of the crowded garage and the possibility of inattentive people.

Outside the garage was a cloudy fall day. Cara rested her eyes on the distant horizon, so different from the close-up work that filled her hours. The trees were beginning to turn color; their leaves flickered in the cool wind. "Are you ready for a rematch?"

"Always." Rodani wheeled the vehicle around a sharp curve.

She'd finally won a game of Tasos and Temichin for the first time since they started playing two weeks earlier and was eager to test her skill again. "What else do you do in your spare time?"

"Practice. Craft."

A series of potholes bounced the carriage and its occupants as they headed for the stables.

"What—"

Another jolt took Cara's words from her. She grabbed the door handle and the seat in front of her. "What are you working on?"

"A commission."

Now what kind of culture makes me ask three questions where one might do? she thought, frustrated. "What's the commission?"

Silence.

The drive continued. Stables showed in the distance. Cara leaned forward and crossed her forearms on the seat in front of her.

"Rodani?"

"Yes."

"Why is my question inappropriate? Are we not both crafters?"

Rodani slowed the carriage to take the turnoff to the stables. "We are."

"I mean no offense."

Silence.

Iraimin's earlier comments about his reputation as an eccentric ran through her mind. "In my country, we're allowed to indulge in as many professions as we wish." The carriage swayed along the gravel road. "Some people may have two or three things they excel at. It's considered lucky to be such a person."

"There are no guardians in Newydd Cenedyl."

"That makes a difference?"

"The ability to be a guardian is given by the goddess at her consort's wishes," Rodani told her. "Temi chooses, Sela grants. The guild trains and hones those abilities. One should live and die as a guardian, not intermixing other professions in with it."

"Why?"

"Diluting our time with other professional activities risks losing the skills we need to survive."

"The time you spend crafting, the guild would prefer you spend practicing?"

"Essentially."

The carriage pulled up to the stable. Cara got out.

The stable doors were open to the autumn weather. The wall was laden with riding accouterments, the scent of benatac permeated the damp air, and wisps of rushes littered the stone floor. A woman appeared, leading a colt. Andalia, she was called, the veterinary second. She brought the colt into the pen and closed the gate behind it. It trotted to the water trough and stretched, sticking its nose into it. Only a week old, it was ungainly but sturdy, on its way to being massive.

Cara looked back at Rodani for permission. He waved his fingers. She opened the nearer gate and walked slowly toward the colt. Behind her, Andalia approached Rodani.

Cara neared the skittish colt. It took off back toward the gate it had come in, dripping water from its whiskery muzzle. Cara changed direction to head it off. It twirled and scampered back toward the trough. She took after it in a run.

"Will she harm it?" the veterinarian second asked.

"Unlikely." Rodani leaned on the gate. "The opposite might occur. Physically, she is quite weak."

Mindful that Rodani might wish her within reaching distance, Cara sat down in the dry rushes near him. Ignoring the colt, she began running her fingers through the rushes and letting her nails drag across the cold stone.

The colt stood still in the far corner, watching, listening. When the whistling began, it was too much for the colt to ignore. It tottered toward the sounds.

Cara continued whistling and picked up some rushes, then dribbled them back onto the floor. The colt edged closer, snuffling the scent. Soon he was within touching distance. The colt came up beside her and snuffled at her neck.

She grabbed a few rushes and held them under the colt's nose. He sniffed them. Mobile lips curved around the loose ends. A black tongue wrapped the rushes in a sloppy embrace. Cara held on long enough to get her other hand on the colt's neck, then let go of the rushes. He startled with the touch.

The coat was softer than she expected; smooth, rippling over the still prominent ribs of the infant benatac. She looked more closely at his face as he chewed. Wide black eyes were set far apart on his head. His rounded ears were adorned with long wiry hairs that stood upright from the tips. The teeth were white, and surprisingly sharp. The long incisors already showed promise of weapons that matched his species' temperament. Gently, she touched one as her fingers brushed by his flattened nose.

<Thump>

She was on her side. The colt snuffled in her face, leaving a dribble of saliva on her cheek, then lowered his head between her legs. Cara laughed and tried to push him away. But pressure on his nose made him nuzzle harder. She found herself on the losing end of a push-of-war. She stood and bent over to brush the rushes from her pants.

"A'Cara," Andalia said.

Cara turned to the woman, anticipating further humor at her expense.

"Give this to him." She held a benatac-sized food pellet.

"Thank you." She held the pellet high up for the colt to reach. He craned his neck in an attempt at the noisome treat. Cara lifted it just out of reach.

It reared a little. Cara raised and lowered the treat in enticement. "Jump."

Another attempt.

"Jump."

With a heave, the forty-pound colt planted its front hooves on Cara's chest.

Down they went. The pellet flew from Cara's hand, backward toward the gate. As more laughter erupted, she rolled over and lunged for the pellet at the same time as the colt.

He won.

Cara sat back on her heels and pulled rushes from her hair. The colt ambled over, snuffled her hands, and licked her fingers. As Cara petted the smooth hide and rubbed the soft inner ears, a squeal erupted from down the corridor. She spun up to her knees, startling the colt. Rodani stiffened and put a hand on the gate.

Andalia faced the stalls, eyes wide, tense. An adult benatac lunged at its reins and pawed the air. "Rodani. Onana."

Mama.

Expression serious, he opened the gate, holding out his hand. "Cara."

Cara rose from her place in front of the colt and allowed her guardian to draw her out of the enclosure. Lightning lit the stable doorway as an immediate crack of thunder startled her. The benatac screamed and snorted, pulling against the reins that Litelon held. Clawed, padded feet thumped and clattered against the stone. Cara took one look at the exposed teeth. Once was enough.

Andalia backed away. "Out."

Rodani ran, nearly pulling Cara off her feet in the process. They beat a headlong retreat in the face of an enraged ton of muscle and bone. The sight of strangers running from her offspring goaded Mama into action. She ripped the reins from Litelon's hands and charged, snorting, thundering down the short row of stalls. A chorus of shouts erupted behind her.

Andalia dived across the path, hitting the dirt in a roll, and coming up ready to climb the safety holds that lined the stable walls. Rodani reached the carriage side door and yanked it open. With a wrench to Cara's shoulder, he hauled her up before him and pushed her inside. Cara scrambled for the driver's seat as Rodani jumped in behind her. He gave a massive heave to the door to close it. The benatac's squeal nearly deafened them as Cara started the engine.

<THUMP>

The carriage rocked. The benatac had stuck her jaw in the door, keeping it open. Rodani jammed his foot against the door handle to keep her deadly teeth outside. One tooth snapped off. She withdrew, and Rodani slammed the door shut with his boot. "Go!"

Off went the brake. The carriage shot backwards in the path, fishtailing. Rodani swayed, trying to keep to his feet. Gravel spit out from under the wheels. They took off down the lane. Rodani turned to watch behind them.

A handful of Selandu raced out onto the road. The mama benatac ran behind the carriage as best she could. But as the vehicle's speed outstripped hers, she gave up on the chase and stood in the middle of the pathway, panting.

Only then did Rodani turn back to Cara. "By Chendal's eyes! Go around the turn, then pull over."

"I can drive." She gripped the steering wheel fiercely, arms locked to keep her pulled forward enough to see over the wheel.

"Go around the turn," he said slowly, "then pull over."

The turn appeared. Raindrops splattered the windshield randomly. Cara stopped next to the grass. She shifted the carriage into park, and they switched seats.

"Are you hurt?"

"No." He started driving.

The carriage swayed and settled. "I never wished this to happen. I should apologize to the stable manager and Jiseigin. Will they accept it?"

"You had permission to be where you were, Cara. You did nothing wrong. You need not apologize."

"I feel distress over her fear and pain."

"And your fear?"

"She was defending her baby."

"No matter," he told her. "Litelon should apologize. He made the greatest error by bringing her out, knowing you were still in the pen." One last turn brought them into sight of the manor. "I will discuss it with his superior."

"Is that necessary?"

"He put both our lives in jeopardy. Should he not be informed of the gravity of his misjudgment?"

Cara rested her forearms against the seat in front of her. "I'd assume he's already aware."

Rodani shot her a glance from the wheel. "Is that humor?"

"Partially." She paused. "Rodani."

"Yes."

"Was this accident on purpose?"

Eyes went back to the road. "Though your vocabulary growth is slow, Cara, your humor is maturing rapidly."

Forked by another conversational redirection. *Because it was a security question*, she assumed.

It was a close call. His reflexes and quick thinking had saved them both from severe injury or death. What would she have done had Rodani not been there?

He took the last turn through the doors and into the manor garage.

"Thank you," Cara said.

He pulled the carriage back into its assigned spot and shut off the engine, then turned to face her. "Is it human courtesy to thank me for doing my duty?"

"Sometimes. Especially when you save my life." She stared at him. Gods, his eyes were beautiful. They were motionless, reflective, almost glowing.

Back in her room, she wondered. How far would he go to protect her? Would he die for her safety? She was no one, just a lone human many miles from home, bereft of friends and family, clinging to what companionship she could wrest from a man who had no conception of the word *friend*. It still seemed strange to have him at hand, someone so capable and duty-bound to protect her.

It would be ego enhancing if it weren't so...stifling. How she wanted to just get up and walk outside. By herself. Without fear. But his duty had been commanded from the highest authority around. Because someone didn't want her here. Someone who was afraid of her.

Rows of books sheltered in the bookcase in her study. Some of them she'd even managed to read. But Selandu minds were still opaque. Rodani thought her requests of him strange. A desire to learn to shoot while living in a household where she never went out unescorted, a longing for this aloof, quiet man to share his thoughts with her to make her life less lonely, a desire to indulge her curiosity in areas she wasn't expected to have any, a need to have her laughter and tears accepted, if not understood.

She wanted back out there. Wanted outside these walls. Wanted a thousand coins in her satchel and an open road in front of her. She wondered idly how far she would get if she escaped.

Escaped? Odd slip of a neuron. She wasn't a prisoner. Not really. Just felt like one sometimes. The drop from her second-story window was a long one. The stairs would be a better idea if it got that bad. A change of clothes or two. Raid food from the kitchens? Where might she go? Going down the road in either direction would expose her, and she would be seen. Into the woods? Rodani would probably hunt for her. Serano, too. He was the tracker. *Would Rodani feel dishonored for "losing" me?* She wondered. *Be punished?*

With that last thought ending her ruminations, she headed to the shower to remove the benatac odor and the spice of damp rushes.

***

Centuries of traditions went into the harvest celebration, which was carried into space where hydroponic harvests existed. Traditional foods that were served at no other time in the year had been recreated as best as possible or created anew. Ciders and punches from the final fruit harvest, meats with special holiday sauces, harvest decorations, and holiday music; all went into the festivities. It was all there.

And the harvest gifts.

"Thank you, Falita. I need three mail pouches. Would you find them?"

Questions remained unspoken. "Yes, a'Cara."

Cara retreated to her haven in the study, determined to spend one day without her daily craft and refusing to feel guilty about it. She pulled her best calligraphy pen out from its resting place and tested the nib against a piece of paper. Scratchy, it ran in fits and starts. Cara washed it, then tested it again.

Better.

She sat back down in her comfy chair, pen in hand, and not

without a pause to wonder if it smelled of benatac as well. Suspicious, not wanting another shower, she turned and sniffed the woven fabric of the chair. A faint scent clung to it. She grimaced and moved to the couch, propping her feet onto the low tea table. The patter of a light rain on the window behind her lulled her mind into restful respite. Her eyes closed.

Then the sound of slippers intruded. Quickly, they neared sufficiently for Cara to feel obliged to open her eyes. Falita held out two pouches.

"Hamman is searching for another one, a'Cara. Here is the correspondence paper. I have put a small stack of it on your table for you."

"Thank you, Falita." She tapped the pen again.

The first letter went to the Stablemaster Domendi, with profuse apologies for the disruption of his staff and animals. The second went to Veterinarian Jiseigin with regrets for causing the new mother stress, and for putting Andalia in danger. The third went to Andalia.

The first two went into their cases. Each lid closed with a whisper of animal hide. Cara could only hope any offenses she'd committed would be alleviated with her missives. The third she set aside for Falita's return, then she drew a book from the bookcase, attempting to lose herself for the remaining hours until the harvest dinner.

There was a tap on the doorframe.

Cara jerked her head up at the soft sound to face Hamman. "Forgive me. Is it time?"

"Yes, a'Cara. Do you wish to wear something from home? Or from here?"

"From home, thank you." Cara tore a piece of paper from the sketchpad on the end table and marked her place in the book, before slipping it back into its place in the bookcase. A distant rumble of thunder rolled through her awareness.

Hamman reached into a voluminous pocket in her skirt and pulled out a mail pouch.

"Falita said you requested this, a'Cara."

"Yes, thank you." Cara leaned down and placed it on the tea table next to the others. She folded the apology to Andalia, slipped it into the third case and passed the pouches to the waiting servant. Cara followed Hamman into the bedroom, stopping at the armoire to pull out a grey leather skirt and jacket. A silver satiny blouse joined it on the bed.

She was halfway dressed before Hamman returned to assist; it was a gentle reminder to the servant that she needed no help. She wore the silver interlocking spiral earrings her father had sent her; they dangled, nestling against her neck.

Cara stepped in front of the mirror. "Well enough?"

Hamman's face folded into reserve. "Yes, a'Cara."

In due time, Rodani arrived to escort her. Though he averted his eyes, Cara saw his pupils widen, and felt more than a hint of satisfaction at the involuntary compliment.

Assumed compliment.

He wore a black jacket with blue and green trim, tapered from broad shoulders to slim hips. The pants were a match, complete with blue and green trim around the ankles. His shirt was grey. The black boots looked new.

Cara grabbed her satchel from the table. "You look handsome."

"Thank you." With ever-present courtesy, he opened the door for her to exit her rooms.

The curved staircase sported cloth ribbons wrapped around the banisters. Blue and green streamers hung from the ceiling in the main hall. Baskets of fruits, vegetables, and nuts lay on the display tables, temporarily displacing the artwork that normally graced Arimeso's abode. Different tapestries hung at intervals along the walls, showing autumn scenes.

Inside the gathering room, confetti lay strewn on the floor in a profuse medley of golds, oranges, reds, and browns. More confetti gracefully littered the seven-candle centerpiece that adorned each tabletop. The food tables along the far wall almost bowed under the weight of the harvest bounty.

Rodani and Cara walked to their usual table in the near corner where the taso's guardians congregated. He was quiet, studying their surroundings. Selandu milled about, grey and silver. Dark and pastel colors filled the room, but very few brights. Small clusters of people stood and chatted in sotto voce. Rodani studied some from his side-view vantage, others he seemed to ignore. Some, in turn, watched them.

More of the security staff arrived around them, settling into chairs before or after the obligatory trip to the bar. Serano trailed in after the fourth rank guild pair, two men who sat themselves beyond the taso's table. Arimeso, Kusik, and Timan held court at the head table.

Serano joined his partner and their adashi, avowing he would hold the table for them while they ran the bar line. The food line was short, so far.

Cara and Rodani chose their drinks, then returned to their table where Serano now sat. They had just gotten settled when one other man stepped up to the table. This one, Cara recognized.

"A'Cara." Straight and formal, he stood with hands behind his back.

"A'Misheiki."

"I have been away from the estate, a'Cara. It is necessary for me to apologize for my error in our first meeting. I should never have left you to walk back from your rooms alone." His eyes were fixed on the drink in her hand.

"It caused no problem, A'Misheiki," she replied formally.

"Only by the grace of the goddess, a'Cara, not from my duty."

Well, that was true. If something had happened to her, he'd have been grass in the great desert.

"There's no offense between us." She needed no more enemies here, especially one on the security staff. Holding grudges was not an option. Besides, it had turned out all right. Her missteps and his had taken her on a better path.

Marginally.

From the corner of her eye yet another body neared the table.

"Rest assured a'Cara, that I will not so dishonor myself and my guild, again."

Cara could only incline her head in response to his contrition. Misheiki bowed in return and left as quietly as he had arrived. Cara turned to see their next visitor and stared.

"Iraimin, your hair is beautiful!"

It was. She had woven gold and orange ribbons through the bun and placed tiny flowers through the strands on her head. A golden cloth was tied behind the bun and draped down onto her shoulders.

"Please join us," Cara continued.

Iraimin glanced over to Rodani and back to Cara, then put her glass down in front of her and took the seat that was offered. "Thank you."

That glance. Was it in reference to her leaving Cara's room so precipitously a hand of days ago? She had seemed quite disturbed over Rodani's entrance, even as Cara had been totally oblivious. Or possibly, Cara thought with dismay, there was something deeper going on. She felt a pang at the thought of Iraimin and Rodani being involved. Despite it being none of her business, a surge of jealousy reared its head, surprising in its intensity. Cara stole a glance at both of them as Iraimin settled in. Rodani acted supremely unconcerned, which was, Cara remembered, easy for a Selandu.

Hand signals erupted from the vicinity of Serano's chest. Cara watched the display of gestures and rapidly flickering fingers that made up the silent guild language. For a moment she considered explaining how rude that was to humans, but resisted the impulse. Instead, she turned back to Rodani and watched the reply. In a moment, the attention of both men was back on their plates, with Cara none the wiser for their discussion.

The gathering room was full. More crowded, even, than it normally was. Children of many ages sat with their parents and grandparents—if the amount of dark strands in their hair that signaled advanced age was any indication—at the far ends of the room. Their shrill voices could be heard over the muted tones of their elders.

Ahead of her was a baby asleep on her father's shoulder. She was tiny, with a mop of silver standing up from her head. One fist was clenched to her mouth. It was the first baby Cara had seen. She had an overpowering urge to go over and ask to hold her.

Yeah, right. "Yes, alien person, you may hold my firstborn." Heh. Better stick to benatac colts.

A clatter near the doors heralded the arrival of the night's musicians. Two people rolled out the drums: tall, medium, small, and tiny barrel-shaped ones, set in a row along the edge of the dais. Rhythm was one of the most important aspects of Selandu music. A variety of stringed instruments were pulled out of carrying cases. Pipes were set out in another corner. One woman held an intricately wound brass instrument and placed it carefully on a small stand.

Soon, the lights dimmed. In from the far door walked a solitary figure. Parents stilled their children's noise. The room quieted. The figure, regal in bearing, was clad in gold, hair flowing quite improperly unbound. She, as it came to be obvious, approached the musician's dais. Two other women followed her. One held a tall triad candelabra in an elaborate gold stand with unlit candles. The other held a bowl of some kind on a shimmering silver pillow cradled in her hands.

"Who is that?" Cara asked softly.

Rodani's were the only eyes in the room not riveted on the woman. His adashi's safety was still his primary focus. "Kimasa," he whispered.

"Who is she?"

"The high priestess—the selaso."

Kimasa took the bowl from her assistant and placed it on the dais with careful deliberation. The second assistant held out the candelabra for Kimasa, who took it and set it on the floor past the bowl. She placed the pillow near her feet before the bowl, then knelt on it. The assistants fell in behind her, standing one on each side, formal in their dignity.

Kimasa reached out and held her hand over the first candle, a yellow one. She became still as stone, chin raised, eyes closed. If it were possible for the room to become quieter, it did. No one breathed. No one moved, except Rodani, whose eyes never stopped their intense flickering, ever alert to danger.

A tiny flame shot up from the previously unlit candle wick. Everyone in the room, Cara included, exhaled at the magic on display. Kimasa moved her other hand to an identical position over the purple candle, withdrawing her right one. The silence resumed, as did the ritual. She repeated her feat, then brought both hands over the center black candle. As the crowd watched intently, the wick spat into flame. Room lights dimmed to a merest hint.

Drumming began slowly, building up from a trembling whisper to steady thrumming, to a pounding five-count cadence that raised the hackles on the back of Cara's neck. The table shook in empathy. Kimasa raised up, stood in the center of the platform, silver-born, gold-clad. Emissary of the goddess, she gathered up her people's concentration and, with arms raised, flung it upward toward the sky. Liquid candlelight spilled down the folds of her robes and reflected in every eye. A collective ambience flowed, tying Kimasa and her rapt audience in a web of timelessness. The beat held steady the strands of that web, then began to vary in intricate traceries of tone and cadence. Flawlessly timed, the drumming reverberated throughout the vast hall and into Cara's bones.

Cara closed her eyes and felt every drumbeat in her body and brain. It filled her to capacity, stirring something primal in the depths of her being. It flowed up her spine and curled the hair on her head. The decorated hall and its grey inhabitants faded from memory. The manor went away. Mother earth enveloped her in loam and sea spray. Cara felt cradled in the venerable womb, mother's heartbeat overtaking her own and bringing it into sync with the power of creation.

Slowly, the drumming died down to a whisper, and Cara returned to the world, opening her eyes.

Rodani was staring at her.

As was Iraimin.

She curled inward, wrapping her arms across her chest protectively, and returned her attention to the platform. Kimasa left the dais in the near darkness, making her slow, stately way toward Arimeso and, incidentally, toward Cara. To Cara's disbelief, Arimeso stood as Kimasa reached her. Leader to leader, the two women met. Kimasa held out her palms, and Arimeso placed her hands under them, raised them, and lowered her face to the fingers in a bow. She straightened again. Their eyes met. Arimeso reseated herself, and Kimasa moved to Kusik. He repeated the bow, meeting the priestess's eyes for only a second. Timan followed suit.

Kimasa went in turn to the nearby tables where the guardians held seats for the celebration. When she came to Rodani's table, he rose to greet her, bowing over the opened palms as the others had done. But when he straightened, he looked boldly into her eyes before sitting. Iraimin took her turn, then Serano. Then Cara.

She was secretly pleased, not only for the courtesy to the solitary alien on the continent, but for another reason. Cara followed the by now standard procedure, bowing over the priestess's hands. But she kept her eyes modestly downcast. Kimasa left for the outer arc of tables, populated by ordinary house members.

"Did you enjoy the ritual?" Iraimin asked.

"It was unusual," Cara answered, "though it didn't mean much to me. But the drumming was..." She searched her mental dictionary. "Stunning. Powerful," she said, her eyes unfocused in clouded thought. "If I never hear such rhythms again, I'll be the poorer for it."

"You felt the goddess. She was here," Iraimin explained.

"You believe the priestess brought Her?"

"Yes."

Right, Cara thought.

As the emissary worked her way around to the farther tables, those in the nearest ones headed for the food tables.

"Come," Rodani said.

Each took an outsized plate and walked the food line, Iraimin behind them. Rodani showed Cara the traditional foods, plus others she may not have tried. She took a little of each. Plates laden, they returned to their table, leaving the way clear for Serano to take his turn. Time passed in talk of inconsequentialities. All went back for seconds on food and drink. Cara and Iraimin discussed their respective work. Rodani and Serano remained conspicuously silent on theirs.

"Serano, did Rodani tell you of our rather close call today?" Cara asked during a lull.

Serano looked over to her from his search of the gathering room, then glanced across at his partner. "No."

"We went out to visit the benatac colt this morning. Its mother got rather disturbed at me being near her baby and chased us."

"Obviously, she did not catch you."

"It was close. She left a tooth behind as a souvenir."

Serano eyed Rodani across the table, pupils oval and mouth pursed. "Close?"

Cara's face began to burn. "She was...very fast. Frightening," she said with emphasis. "If Rodani hadn't been so watchful and quick, I wouldn't have survived."

Serano's attention returned to her, grin still intact.

"I owe him my life," she added.

"That is his duty."

"It's still appreciated." Cara stated as the strains of a slow melody began from the musicians' dais. The music provided a chance for redirection. She hadn't meant to cast aspersions on Rodani's protective abilities. It just came out that way. It was a difficult way to live.

Rodani tipped his glass to finish his drink, then set it down. "Another?"

She'd had two but didn't really feel them. One more might not hurt. "Yes, thank you."

"Iraimin?"

"Please."

Listening to the music, Cara began to drum her fingers lightly on the table, keeping time with it.

Rodani rose and went back to the bar, returning in a few minutes with three drinks. Serano grabbed his empty glass and stood as his partner sat.

"You're not dancing?" Cara asked him.

"That is not dance music. It is traditional harvest dinner music. Dancing comes afterwards."

Rodani pushed his plate aside as Iraimin and Cara had already done. Serano picked up a few sweets still sticking to his plate and renewed his drink at the bar. The others sipped their drinks in companionable silence.

People were pushing back their chairs, crossing legs and ankles, removing jackets or vests—displaying an unusual amount of casualness for a public place. The food table looked as if it had been ransacked; the bartender had been replaced by a cohort. Kitchen hands were making the rounds with food carts, gathering up dirty dishes. Another roamed the tables, enticing the not-quite-full to sample items from the dessert cart.

Cara figured she'd better beat them to the punch. She reached into her other pocket and pulled out a small package she'd carefully wrapped earlier. Without fanfare, she sat it on the table next to Rodani's left hand.

In mid-sip, he pulled the glass from his lips and stared down at the package. Slowly, he set the glass down and glanced over at Cara, then at Serano, then back at the package. With his left hand, he pulled at the ribbon. The bow collapsed onto the table. He tugged carefully at the edge of the cloth wrapper. It fell away. Inside was a stack of a half-dozen chocolate bars, the kind she'd offered him on the nights they played cards. Rodani picked up the top one with the tips of his fingers and turned it over in his palm.

"Thank you," he said quietly.

Black pupils were round as the face of the full moon. Only a thin ring of violet could be seen. The rest of him was still except for his gaze, which flickered from Cara to her gift and back again. Cara's stomach roiled. She didn't expect effusive gratitude. But she couldn't interpret his reaction. Rounded pupils meant disturbance of equanimity. Pleased? Annoyed? Embarrassed?

Rodani slit open the chocolate's outer wrapper and placed it to the side. He folded back the inner wrapper, then put the bar on the table between the four of them.

Iraimin leaned forward. "What is it?"

"Dessert. *Chock-lit*, if I recall." Rodani broke off some pieces and put one in his mouth.

"You have a good memory," Cara told him as she nabbed a piece for herself. "You saved me the task of reminding you." Iraimin tried a piece, somewhat reluctantly; then broke into a smile.

Serano declined.

"Is it traditional for your harvest dinners, Cara?" Iraimin asked.

"Being centuries old, it is. But not exclusive to any time or place."

"Centuries?"

"Yes. My grandparents told me it came with their parents on the ship." She reached for another piece.

"Came with them?" Iraimin asked, incredulous.

Belatedly, Cara thought it through, then began to laugh. She picked up an unopened bar and waved it in the air. "These are not centuries old, Iraimin. The recipe came with them, and seeds from the plants it comes from. Chocolate does, however, last a while. Months, if kept in airtight wrappings."

She put the bar back on the stack just in time to see the last of another guild gesture from Rodani.

Serano slipped a forearm onto the table and leaned in her direction. "May I ask?"

"Ask?"

"Why the gift?"

Hmmm. It was obvious to Cara. But not obvious elsewhere, obviously. What had the men said to each other? "He's saved my life, Serano. He's also chosen to socialize with me sometimes, which alleviates some of my distress."

"Distress?"

That one came from Iraimin.

"From having no family or other human companions here."

There was no comment. Possibly they were digesting her admission, as Rodani had done after their fight. Probably neither Iraimin nor Serano had ever put themselves in her place. Most Selandu were insular, staying near where they were born. What little the humans knew about the rest of the people who shared their world came from the CSC ambassadors. And their information, of course, came from the Council of Three, who told them only what they wished the humans to hear. Selandu were as chary with specifics about their race as they were with their possessions. Knowledge was valued trade goods.

"Rodani," Cara said quietly, glancing over her right shoulder. "Are the, ah, nearby facilities available to me, or is it a security risk?"

Rodani looked out over her head at the surrounding security staff. Several men and a few women sat nearby, dressed in blacks and greys. "There is a way."

119

He walked to a nearby table where four guardians were having a lively discussion on who-knew-what, stepped up to the lone woman and spoke quietly to her. She answered and followed Rodani back.

"A'Cara, a'Toranel."

The two women bowed. Cara recognized the woman who had been in the security room when Cara had walked out alone. Toranel followed her to the far side of the hall, behind the musicians. Rodani turned sideways in his seat to follow their progress; at least until they were behind doors he dare not pass without a life or death emergency.

In more time than a man would take, but less time than Rodani expected, they returned. Almost no one gave the diminutive human more than a discreet once-over, though the way her clothes clung to her body instead of draping in more modest ways might have caused more looks. How Hamman could have let her dress so inappropriately was beyond him.

It was almost indecent.

A muted rumble made its way through the manor walls, as if agreeing with the guardian's critical thoughts. Though, he thought, she did look—

A fierce thunderclap interrupted both Rodani's train of thought and the power cells to the hall's lights, plunging them into sudden darkness. Rising half out of the chair, he pulled his gun. But the lights flickered once, twice, and then remained lit. He checked Cara's whereabouts and Toranel's presence behind her before he replaced the pistol. Toranel's gun was out. Slowly, he relaxed.

As did everyone else in the hall. Scattered smiles could be seen around the room. Children who had headed for their parents' laps were coaxed to act bravely and return to their own seats. Kusik and Timan, on their feet and on their guard next to Arimeso, sat down.

Cara returned to her seat with a thank-you to Toranel and a sigh of relief. "It's well the light returned, or Toranel would have needed to lead me back to the table like a blind borundi on a leash."

He'd forgotten. Goddess and consort, Rodani had forgotten in the duty to rush to her side that she would be effectively sightless in the dark. Silently, he chided himself for his lapse. At least if he were guarding a Selandu he could make adequate assumptions of the adashi's capabilities. But he was not guarding one of his own, a fact he'd temporarily lost track of in the momentary shock.

"You cannot see in the dark, Cara?" Iraimin asked.

"We can see, but given the same amount of light, we don't see nearly as well as you. It would have been interesting to see the room." She brought out a small pad of paper and pencil from her pocket and began to sketch. Serano looked at her in confusion as she ignored her dinner companions for a time. But Iraimin and Rodani, artisans both, knew the state of mind she had just drifted into. They exchanged glances. Thunder continued to make the presence of the storm known to the people safely tucked inside the manor. Three sheets of paper later, Cara set her pencil on the table and rested her hand on her empty glass.

"Another shigeli, a'Cara?" asked Serano. His glass was empty, as well.

"Yes, thank you." She stared at the last of her sketches. There was a moment of silence, then Serano reached across her and took the glass from her hand. She startled in recognition of her impropriety.

"I'm sorry."

He tossed her apology away with the hand gesture and walked back toward the bar.

Rodani leaned toward her. "Cara," he said softly, "would it be improper to ask to see your earrings?"

What? Selandu men weren't supposed to be interested in women's jewelry. Iraimin had told her so. It was inappropriate, except under certain circumstances. And those circumstances decidedly did not exist between her and Rodani. Eccentricities?

Cara pulled out both earrings and laid them on Rodani's palm. One he put on the table in front of him, the other he kept in his hand to study. Intently. His pupils went from ovals to narrow slits. His lips thinned; feathery eyebrows moved with the tension in his eyes. He picked up the other earring and held them side by side, comparing the intricate interweaving curves. He put the second one down again and patted a pocket.

"I incorrectly assumed my notebook would not be needed tonight."

Cara grinned. "As long as I have mine, yours isn't needed, Rodani. Humans consider it a point of honor to share." She passed the pad and pencil to him. Serano returned with her drink, as well as a plate of sweet nibblets. "Thank you."

Now that his partner had returned to the table, Rodani gestured to him, then picked up the pencil. Slowly and with great attention to detail, he drew the earring. Curve by curve, section by section, he reproduced the design in his hand onto the paper on the table before him.

Cara leaned toward him to watch the activity. Chin in hand, her dark head and Rodani's silver one bent over his hands as he worked. Their close proximity went unnoticed by them for the duration, as did the silence surrounding them. But not by others.

Task completed, Rodani leaned back to study the sketch from a distance. Nearby eyes that had been drawn to the unusual scene between human and Selandu went back to their own business.

"Good," she judged. "Not even one erasure." She liked what she saw in this first glimpse of his other side.

"Accurate, at least."

"But that's expected of a guardian. Yes?"

He tore off the page and passed the pad and pencil back to her, then returned the earrings as well. Somewhat reluctantly, it seemed to Cara. He eyed her as she slipped the earrings back in. "And what does one expect from a quilter?"

She gnawed on her lip while an appropriate answer bubbled to the surface of her thoughts. Rodani folded his paper and tucked it into an inner pocket, then reached for his drink. The musicians switched from the slower rhythms they'd been playing to a faster one.

"The same as from any Selandu artisan, plus stronger emotions—that are less well controlled."

"Goddess, protect us." Serano got up and gestured an empty palm to Cara. "Will you dance?"

Cara's eyes widened at the invitation, and her smile stretched from ear to ear. She looked out over the crowd. Sure enough, a line was already beginning to form.

Cara and Serano joined the line near the musicians' dais. It took a second or two for her memory of the steps to kick in again, but soon Cara fell into the rhythm of the dance. She kept time with the others, hands behind her back, chin up. Acutely aware she was again the object of visual attention, Cara focused on the tapestries and paintings that decorated the far wall.

The melody was a pitter-patter of notes and a twinkling of harmony behind it, supported by the intricate drumming she'd come to appreciate over the weeks. As she turned from side to front to side, she tried to watch Serano's body motions, the better to mimic them.

But she stumbled. *Not too much watching. Mind on the footsteps, please.*

After two songs, the line was long enough that another formed behind the first, dancing a different step. People from the first line joined the second. Gradually, Cara lost her self-consciousness as the pleasure of the dance and the rhythms in her ears took over. Beside her, Serano never wavered. Occasionally, Cara caught sight of Rodani at their table, through the seated crowd. Twice, he was watching; once, his back was toward her, talking to Iraimin. Cara felt another pang of jealousy, then berated it back into nothingness.

After six songs, Cara had had enough. High heels were not conducive to long stretches of dancing, and she was thirsty. She whispered a thank-you to Serano and wended her way back through the spectators to Rodani and Iraimin.

Rodani tracked her progress. Iraimin inspected the label on the bar of Cene'l chocolate, which was almost gone. Cara took one of the last pieces and set it by her glass, then took a rather long drink.

"Did Serano teach you to dance, Cara?" the painter asked.

"Would you believe Rodani taught me?"

"No." A hint of a grin showed on her face.

Cara smiled in return. "Serano taught me the one step. I may ask for a second lesson. There is more than one dance being danced out there." She turned to watch the two lines of dancers, now beginning to form a third. Cara studied the new and nearest line, trying to follow the complicated steps from a distance. More thunder rumbled in from outside, causing a few heads to raise and look, as if they could magically make the walls transparent.

"You enjoy dancing?" Iraimin asked her.

"Yes," she said. "I dance at home, too."

The food tables were entirely empty now, having been cleared by kitchen staff. The bar was still on idle; Cara could see the original barkeep in the second line of dancers.

The musicians took a well-deserved rest. The lines of dancers broke up and returned to their seats, most by way of the bar. Serano returned and finished his drink, then went to get himself and Iraimin a refill.

"You did well, Cara," Serano noted above the rumble of thunder.

"Thank you, though I'm certain to have stood out amongst the others like a beacon in a storm."

"In that clothing, most certainly."

Cara looked down at her attire as if noticing it for the first time.

She'd loved the look of it since seeing it hanging on the rack at Moran's, down the street from her parents' house. And she was proud of her ability to wear it well. "Is something wrong with it?"

"It is not something a proper Selandu woman would wear."

Cara ran her fingers up and down the outsides of her glass. It was cool. Moisture had formed, dried, and reformed on it, leaving rivulets of condensation down the sides. Her fingertips erased them.

"I never claimed to be a Selandu woman, Serano."

"But you are judged by their standards."

"And found lacking, obviously."

"By some," Rodani said from her other side. "Others will make allowances for your differences."

Cara leaned back in her chair, staring at her glass of shigeli. It was nearly empty. Methodically, she pulled her fingers down the side of the glass. Designs etched into the glass produced pleasurable sensations in her sensitive fingertips.

She was heartily embarrassed and angry with herself for not deliberating on the fact of Selandu women's loose, flowing clothing and, moreover, what might be inferred from her own. Cara finished the last of her shigeli.

More guild gestures flickered and waved just at the edge of her vision. She turned to watch the hands but refused to look at their owners. They stopped, then started, then stopped again. She raised her head and stared idly out into the crowd. It was beginning to thin.

The original bartender was back behind the bar, doing a brisk business again. Infrequent eruptions of laughter rose up. Selandu were not copious laughers, though an incongruous situation or slip of the tongue could cause it. They preferred to show pleasure with smiles and eye movements. Consummate silent communicators, they prided themselves on maximum expression with the minimum of voice and bodily movements. Economy of expression, economy of movement. It created their grace. Muscle and bone worked together with the same harmony as the strains of music that had enveloped them earlier. They were a pleasure to watch.

"Another drink, Cara?" Rodani asked.

She eyed the empty glass dispassionately. "No, thank you."

She'd lost track. Three? Four? Five? Rodani would know, of course.

"Do you tire?"

"A little," she admitted. Serano's last comment had diminished her pleasure in the holiday gathering.

"We may leave if you wish."

Was that a reference to her clothing? Or to her sudden disquiet? "Should I?"

Rodani tossed the question. "Not necessarily."

"You might want the rest of the evening for your own." If he and Iraimin were involved, he might wish Cara back in her room before the celebration ended. It wasn't fair to him, otherwise.

"I cannot return if I take you to your room. And I will not ask someone else to interrupt a holiday to guard you while I continue to socialize."

"Why?"

"If I am seen escorting you out, then returning without you, it is obvious to all that you are alone and unguarded. That must not happen."

Her eyes went wide, and her expression fell into sadness. Gods and demons! Had it been that way from the beginning? He'd given up so much. "Forgive me. I had no idea."

Rodani crossed his arms on the table near his chest; fingers draped over the sleeves in casual grace. "It is a constraint a guardian must live with. It does not disturb me as it seems to disturb you. Have we offended?"

"No."

"May I ask, then, what is the cause for what resides on your face?"

Cara shrugged. "Being different, Rodani. To offend when I mean only good; to scandalize when I seek only a compliment." She bent her head. "To be reminded of how difficult your duty to me is."

"Do not assume too much," Rodani told her.

Three faces stared down at Cara, harboring alien minds and judgments. She didn't want to think of what they kept between their teeth, what lurked behind the cat's eyes. If her pupils could've widened, they'd have been saucers. In a flash, she saw herself as they saw her: childlike, alien, face awash in unrestrained emotion, dressed indecently in total disregard for cultural proprieties; blithely going about her business in their company as if nothing were amiss. She felt as if the floor had given way.

Iraimin leaned forward. "Is honor the same between humans and Selandu?"

Now where in the Kemindi Desert did that come from?

Cara put her chin on her fist and stared toward the dance area, trying to slow her breathing. "That answer would take much more discussing between Rodani and me than we have had an opportunity to do." She took a sip of watery shigeli. Faster than the dancing, tension had dried her mouth. "There may be areas of overlap. But considering the amount of difference elsewhere, I would also assume differences in honor."

Serano spun his drink in his hand. Clear liquor slid up the sides of the glass, threatening to wet on his fingers. "That could make for an interesting evening's discussion."

It certainly could.

"Can differing honors be discussed calmly?" Cara asked.

"Among allies of good will, yes," Serano said.

"Who ultimately decides what's honorable and what isn't?" she asked him.

"That varies widely. If two or more people have a confrontation over honor or offense, then they decide themselves how best to answer it. Sometimes it is by duel, sometimes assassination, sometimes by arbitration."

"Who arbitrates?"

"The local priestesses, or the taso if she holds the allegiance of both people, and if no one involved is a guild guardian." Serano leaned back. "If one or more is a guardian, then guild seniors send a representative to the arbitration for judgment. If both or all involved are guild, and they still wish arbitration, they may go to guild headquarters in Tendiman."

So, it's not always shoot first, Cara thought. The CSC has been misinformed again or left behind the times. "The CSC taught us that anyone could shoot anyone else."

"In theory, yes. In practice, there are cultural constraints upon one's actions. Rumor on our side of the hills says humans have no cultural constraints against fighting, and no honor in the act," Serano replied.

"Don't judge our race by the River Samida War, please. Ask your partner how I fight, and how I act afterwards."

"The goddess protects you," Iraimin added.

"Rodani protects me."

Iraimin set her glass down. "Sela is behind Rodani's protection."

"I see evidence of Rodani's guarding. I see nothing of Sela,"

Cara countered the assertion.

"The goddess works invisibly."

"The invisible and the non-existent look very much alike."

"She has Her hand on you, nonetheless."

"If I am to have a hand on me, Iraimin," Cara replied flippantly, "I would prefer a hand I can feel."

Again, there was silence. Then Serano began to grin, which caused Rodani to crack a smile. Cara looked off into the crowd, a safer bet for the moment than eyeing anyone around her. The musicians returned to their stage and began a quiet tune.

"But you felt Her," the painter continued.

"I felt great emotions and great pleasure from the drumming. Not a goddess."

"She does not speak with words."

"Then I won't be able to hear Her."

"You will…if you listen with your heart."

"Iraimin, my heart isn't a brain. And if I listen with my head, with the part of me made for thinking and hearing, I hear only assumptions sprung from my own needs. That's nothing on which to base a faith."

Iraimin pursed her lips and shifted to a more comfortable position in her chair, leaning back into relaxation. "Do human men and women feel about each other in the same way as we do?"

Now that, dear Iraimin, was a 180° turn in the conversation.

Some things were known. Selandu mated and had children who were a genetic combination of the two. But feelings? Those were too complex and hidden for the two species to delve into together, and with no interspecies couples to do the delving. So far, that is. Both species were too busy planning to rebuild their technology to make rockets before their unknown, unpredictable attackers started hitting planets as well as ships. Maybe there wasn't time to care about biology, let alone the psychology of emotions.

"I don't have that knowledge," Cara said. "How do Selandu men and women feel about each other?"

Iraimin's face went to mask. Her pupils dilated to full, and her short fingernails clipped on the side of her glass. "I am not the proper one to answer that."

Cara had never seen any Selandu drum fingers in agitation. She was single, Cara guessed. Maybe she'd had a series of failed relationships. Maybe a nasty divorce. She glanced at her guardians, but they gave no sign or explanation. "Forgive me for disturbing you, Iraimin."

"I am well." But her eyes betrayed the lie-that-is-courtesy.

"My question was well meant. It's impossible to make a comparison without information."

Rodani shifted to a more comfortable position and brought an ankle up over the other knee. His fingers grasped the edges of his napkin along its embroidered edge. His pupils were relaxed at half-width. Iraimin's discomfiture had evidently not affected him. "Are you of the Guild of Scientists, Cara?" he asked.

"No. We have no guilds as you know them. But every human is given basic training in science and rational thought."

His pupils narrowed, and a corner of his mouth turned up. "Rational thought?"

Exasperated, Cara turned in her chair and put a fist on her hip. "Rodani, if you were human, I would be tempted to make you wear your drink."

Rodani's eyes flickered from Cara to his drink to his shirt and back. "That would be a major offense."

She grinned at him. The place was clearing out. More than half the tables were empty of people, though not of dirty dishes. Kitchen staff still made their rounds. The bar was still active. Cara looked around behind her, to the left, then back to the right.

"Problem?"

"I meant to impose upon a'Toranel again, but she seems to have left."

"Do you wish to return to your rooms?"

"I'm enjoying the company, Rodani, but I have to visit one facility or another. If leaving doesn't disturb you unduly."

Rodani blinked. His pupils pulsed. "Was my explanation unclear?"

"No. It seemed clear. Occasional reassurances help." Cara stood up. The room swam. She made a convulsive grab for the table edge, and the room settled into mild sloshing.

Rodani grabbed her arm. "Are you well?"

"Yes, forgive me. A little too much shigeli."

"Can you walk?" he asked, raking her up and down with his eyes.

"Yes." She let go of the table and grabbed her satchel, then turned—a little more carefully than normal.

Rodani followed closely at her elbow.

Shoulder.

Cara wove her way through the obstacle tables, then headed into the open area in front of the double doors. The hallway alternately shrank and expanded with the shigeli slosh as she neared the curving stairs.

"What do people do after harvest dinner, Rodani?"

He stopped at the base of the stairs and studied her again. "I suggest bed for you. If your coordination is similar to mine in this state, you will be taking out all tonight's stitches, tomorrow."

She started to giggle, then laugh, then got moving again when her bladder protested. With the help of the banister on one side and Rodani on the other, she made it to the second floor without mishap. Only a little more; there was her door.

He checked it, unlocked it, and looked around before bringing Cara in. Hand still on her arm, he led her to her bedroom and called for Hamman.

Then Falita.

No one was home next door.

Rodani looked at her, pupils wide. She tugged herself free and put her hands on his arm, turning him around.

"I can manage, Rodani. Thank you." She gave him a push.

When Hamman peered in later that night, all she saw was a tousled head of dark hair and clothes strewn all over the floor.

TWELVE

Waking, Cara turned over and glanced at the timepiece. Someone had blurred the numbers. She crawled to the edge of the bed and sat until the room began to behave. Unfortunately, neither her stomach nor her temples seemed likely to follow. The toilet was a long way away, but she made it, then crawled back into bed.

Never again. Overindulgence was for teens. The shigeli had become an unwelcome guest in her mouth overnight and was in the process of setting up residence. She sighed and curled into her pillows for comfort.

Harvest-after was a rest-day. So were the solstice-afters, and equinox-afters. Winter solstice was a time of prayer. Spring equinox was the Selandu New Year, with gift-giving, and an amateur night for a house full of artisans who might dabble in a second or third artistic area. It was the best celebration of their year, Rodani had told her, the only time when his reserved people allowed themselves an evening of public improprieties. Somehow she couldn't picture it. Serano, maybe. Rodani? Iraimin? Hamman? She chuckled at the image of staid, middle-aged Hamman behaving in the outrageous manner Cara's human friends indulged in at the least excuse.

She slipped her robe on and made another trip to the toilet, then came back to the bed. But she sat on the edge and curled her feet underneath her in an attempt to decide whether to stay up or not, and what to do if she did.

There was no radio in her room. The taso hadn't seen fit to provide her with one, despite the insights she could have gained. It might have improved her pronunciation as well, if not vocabulary. Some soft music might do. Maybe some design work. It would be nice to go somewhere, but her last request for an outing nearly got her and her guardian killed.

Footsteps behind her interrupted her indecision. Cara turned. "Falita."

"A'Cara. Did you have a pleasant time?"
Cara smiled wide. "Yes."
"We saw you dance."
"We? Where were you?"
"In a far corner."
"With whom?"
"Relatives. Companions."
"Companions?" Cara teased.

Falita turned her head. Cara didn't press the matter, though she dearly wanted to.

"Rodani checked on you this morning," Falita said. "Are you well?"

"I've been better, but I'll recover from my foolishness."

She showered, then headed for the armoire, but Falita beat her to it. Cara accepted the help with resigned humor, then curled up in her chair in the study. She managed breakfast, carefully, then wished again there was somewhere she could go.

Autumn was beginning to transform the view outside the window. Reds, golds, and oranges decorated the seasonal trees in the distance. Breezes fluttered the doomed foliage, hastening their mass demise. The sky was brilliant blue with just a scattering of feathery clouds, reward for yesterday's disruptive storm. Cara wished Rodani would come over so she could open the windows for a breeze. They had re-discussed the subject, Rodani deciding, with much complaining from Cara, that shutters could be opened but not the windows beyond them. Second story or not, there were ways for entrance to be gained, and unless Rodani or Serano were in evidence, the windows stayed shut.

A map would have been nice. See what existed around there. Towns, farms, forests, roads, rivers. But humans were allowed only the most cursory of maps handed out from Hadaman. Maps held information, and as well, the lay of the land was a security concern. Only the high-resolution scanners on the ship above could obtain detailed geographical information.

Cara pressed her face and hands against the glass. Cold seeped through to her nose, forehead, and fingertips. She crossed her arms and leaned a shoulder into the curtains, minimizing the angle of view. Long-term exposure at the window was also prohibited.

A flock of birds flew across the sky, heading for warmer weather. Gesabi birds, with their outsized wings and pouched beaks, roosted on Newydd Cenedyl's east shore cliffs every winter.

There they mated and nested, rooting young fledglings out of the nests each spring. Many a family took a cool winter outing to the limestone cliffs to watch their antics. She growled to herself and slapped the stone sill. Homesickness was something she couldn't afford to fall prey to. Given her wanderlust, Cara thought she was immune.

One more mistaken assumption to her credit.

Someone crossed her workroom and stopped near the study door. Rodani, likely, considering the heavy tread. Cara turned from the window as he walked into her study.

"You are too exposed."

She leaned back on the shutters. "It's clear all the way to the forest."

He walked to the window that held her melancholy fascination. "Yes, a clear line of sight."

"For me to see anyone out there."

"Are you paying attention, or dreaming?"

She sighed and grinned with a shake of her head. "You win."

"I had better."

"Always?"

He cocked an eyebrow. "Always in matters of your security. Is it necessary to re-discuss it?"

"No."

"I am to be assured?"

Cara sighed hugely in mock exasperation. "Consult the Enclave's oracles, Rodani. They see the future. Let the priestesses tell you whether I'll disobey."

He relaxed his stance. "If they gave me anything but vague assurances and admonitions, I would be consulting them daily over my duty to you."

No *why* was necessary. Instead, Cara shared the humor he found in their mutual situation, unusual allies in a war against their own ignorance and prejudices.

"I came to inquire if you had recovered from your overindulgence of yesterday."

"Partly."

"What caught your interest outside?"

"Colors. Desire for open vistas and cool wind. Memories." She turned back to the window. "Is there anywhere we may go?"

"I came in to—" he began, then his pocket 'com went off. His eyes drifted to the ceiling as he pulled it out. "Five."

The 'com crackled. "Answer?"

"We were delayed. Hold." He fingered a switch. "Serano and I are going for outdoor target practice. By your expression, it seems you may wish to join us."

Her eyes lit; she woke up again. "Yes."

"Change."

She laughed, anticipating companionship, cool breezes, and blue skies. She obeyed quickly while Rodani relayed their affirmation to Serano. The pair met him at the dark-windowed carriage. Guardians got into the front seats, the lone human in the middle.

"Where are we going?" she asked.

"East," Rodani said.

"To the fields?"

"Past them."

Several pair of grey eyes watched their exit while Serano started the carriage and pulled it out of the garage. He took the same track toward the stables but passed by them. Cara stared through the windows for the time she could keep her impatient longing in check, then reached for the window crank. It thumped up against some inner securing mechanism and remained stubbornly motionless. Rodani turned at the sound.

"The windows do not open."

"Obviously. Why?"

"Security."

Distant foliage and empty fields passed behind Rodani's head and shoulders as he faced her. His body bounced and swayed with the road's uneven surface. Serano kept his attention forward, hands in slow motion on the steering wheel.

"What happens if we have an accident? Everyone is unconscious, and no one can get inside to rescue us?" She rapped on the window with her knuckles. "Is this glass even breakable?"

Rodani's gaze lingered on her just long enough for Cara to recognize a reproach. "The chance of that situation's occurrence is much less than intended ones." He returned to a forward view, seeming intent upon the lands that surrounded Barridan as if expecting ambush from the midst of recently harvested fields.

Cara contented herself with a 360° view interrupted only by wood, black upholstery, and silver hair. Trees began to interrupt her long-distance line of sight. She fingered the seat cushion behind her knees, wishing either her feet would touch the floor, or one was allowed to bring shoes up on the fabric.

"How many boxes did you bring?" Rodani asked his partner.

"Four and one."

"Was Bergami cooperative?"

"Yes." Serano eyed Rodani for the moment he allowed his attention to leave the curving road. "Was Mitanan?"

Rodani turned back to the open land outside his window.

Serano laughed. "You need a new approach, tem'u, or unexplored fields."

Who's Mitanan? A woman? Is this Rodani's love interest? Cara rocked her head back onto the seat, eyes wide, suddenly certain that Rodani would have a few restrained words with Serano the first time she was out of hearing distance. Fleetingly, she felt sorry for the too quiet, too dutiful guardian who kept her safe; then the irrational jealousy she had felt during yesterday's dinner made another appearance. But she felt no such envy with Serano's more open search for attentions.

The trees outside the carriage grew as thick as the silence inside. As they bounced down the rough winding road, a narrow strip of sunlight paved the vehicle's way. Occasionally, a side road would make its appearance in an arched opening between the trees. One of them, unmarked as all the rest, became their next turn. Serano fought the steering wheel in earnest as the smoother road turned to rocks. Cara and Rodani held on to whatever was available as support against the increasing jolts.

He pulled off the road into a vehicle-sized open area. They got out, and Serano opened the hind door. In the trunk were three boxes of fruit and some gear. Rodani pulled out a massively oversized yellow jacket, handing it to Cara.

"Put it on."

At least no one could mistake her for a target.

Each guardian took a box of fruit and balanced it on his shoulder. The smaller one went to Cara. They entered the woods, following a path only Serano could easily read until it widened into something recognizable. A few courageous birds cawed their protests from unseen perches above the walkers. Life in all its bounty invaded Cara's senses; her mind opened wider to the beauty to be found. Forest vision, twittering birds, the scent of autumn's decay, the touch of a breeze on her face. Feedback brought her to a virtual standstill on the path as she soaked into every pore what she had longed for and glimpsed in her garden walk of weeks ago.

"Cara?" Rodani queried the blockage on his path. Serano turned and waited.

"Do you feel it?" she said.

"Feel?"

"Life. The world turning under your feet. The universe unseen overhead." Could she convey some sense of her inner visions to the practical, no-nonsense guardian behind her?

"You feel the goddess. She touches you."

Cara turned to face Serano. "That's how you interpret it?"

"That is how we know Her. At these times, She speaks the loudest."

"When it's quiet?"

"When we are closest to the world as She birthed it, not as we have refashioned it."

This was an aspect of Serano Cara hadn't seen before. A facet that had been hidden now sparkled in autumn sunshine, begging her to search further through his reflective eyes and mind. "I'm beginning to understand."

"So, you believe now?" Serano asked.

"No."

The trail terminated in a clearing to their right. Rodani and Serano unload the boxes. Serano hid some melons in deadfall at the end of the clearing and on some nearer fallen logs. Rodani put some of the smaller beiregi on tree branches and in the midst of shrubbery further back. He took out the Kishata and unloaded it, then handed it to Cara with the clip separate.

"Load it."

With less difficulty than in the beginning of her training, she loaded the gun, revealing the beginnings of smooth confidence. Serano came back from the target setup and watched her, then moved around behind her.

"Remember," Rodani said, handing her the ear protectors, "at this longer range, the pistol will shoot low. Aim it slightly higher than what you might assume would be accurate."

She adjusted her stance to what he had taught and aimed, remembering at the last moment to keep both eyes open. She pulled the trigger. The familiar boom seeped inside her ear protectors, and the recoil shook her hands. She lowered the gun and studied her shot. The melon sagged on one side.

Sighting slightly higher than the center of the mutilated melon, she squeezed the trigger slowly. The gun boomed again. Now the melon was nothing but juice and rind. She smiled, then sighted the other melons in turn, trying to disintegrate each in one shot. With some respectable measure of success, she liquidated them. In turn, she moved on to the beiregi, not much bigger than her fist. She sighted the first one carefully...and fired.

Clean miss.

Rodani bent over her shoulder to see where she was aiming, then leaned back. Another shot. She moved closer, with Rodani following her in. She re-aimed and fired once, twice, three times. The beiregi remained stubbornly whole. Dammit, it was right there in front of her. And her arms were getting tired. Cara planted her feet farther apart and held the gun tightly. She pressed the trigger repeatedly, giving in to a fit of emotion that welled up from her limbic system. The beiregi disintegrated.

With quiet deliberation, she safetied the pistol, and handed it back to Rodani, properly. He was wearing a grin.

He didn't ask.

Maybe he assumed.

Maybe correctly.

"Finished?" he asked.

"Yes, thank you. For today." Cara moved behind the men and found a rock on which to sit, prepared to watch their practice.

They took their turns side by side, facing the forest, alternating shots. In short order, all the rest of the targets they'd brought with them were gone.

Rodani relaxed his guard. From some fastness inside his sleeve, he pulled out three lengths of metal that glittered in the sunlight. He twisted his feet in the dirt for purchase. The glittering metal revealed itself as knives. Rodani shifted his shoulders and settled into a stance.

<Thunk>

The flash revealed itself in retrospect as a knife throw. Only by following the line of motion did Cara know where to look. His knife protruded from a tree trunk twenty feet away.

<Thunk>

Another hilt extended from the sepia bark, next to its partner.

<Thunk>

The duo became a trio.

Rodani walked up to the tree and yanked on each of the knives in turn, stacking them in his right hand. He came back to Cara's vicinity, then tucked one knife back in his sleeve and turned his back to the tree. He stared out over the path, body stilled. A constriction washed over his face. Lips thinned, a tension at the corners of his eyes and mouth that hadn't been there previously. He spun on the ball of one foot, planting the other one behind him for balance. Twin overhand throws sent the knives deep into the tree. The tension melted from Rodani's face as he studied his accuracy. Three times more, he repeated the throws. Three times more, emotion overcame his normal hidden expression. He slid the knives back into their sheaths.

"That was quite a demonstration," Cara told him.

He glanced at her, then turned back to Serano, and the clearing.

"Rodani," Cara said, following him. "When you were throwing your knives, who were you killing?"

He stopped in his tracks, eyebrows lifted, pupils spread wide. She pulled her hands behind her back in deference but stood her ground, waiting for an answer that probably wouldn't come. He wasn't threatening. Wasn't intimidating. He was—what? Shocked? Frightened, she couldn't credit. Disbelieving? Her crass question could've provoked his temper. She waited.

"What did you see?" he asked suspiciously.

Cara dug at the dirt with begrimed shoes. "I can only interpret through my own humanity."

"And?"

There was a measure of control in his face again, determination in the tone of his voice. She swallowed a lump in her throat. "I saw...."

Rodani crossed his arms; his pupils narrowed. "You saw what?"

She had to look away from his expression. "Loathing. Revulsion." She stared at the ground between them. "As if the tree you were aiming at were not a tree, but a person."

Whatever he might have said stayed inside him as he studied her, "Are you ready to return?"

"No," she admitted. "Is there anywhere else we can go?"

"Where?"

"It doesn't matter. Just—outside."

Serano waved his arm. "There is a forest to explore."

Well, she seemed to be adequately protected against dangers. "Anywhere?"

"Anywhere you do not hear a 'No.'"

She took off farther down the path, Serano behind her and

Rodani following. The breeze waned and sunlight faded as they wound their way deeper. Cara's conscious mind wandered in and out of *now*, thoughts trading places with a pleasant cognitive void.

They continued along the path, Serano now side by side with Cara, pointing out some of nature's curiosities. The foliage made patterns of darks, mediums, and lights, vertical striped trunks, and arcs of curling vines. An occasional diagonal of a fallen tree slashed across the ever-changing view. Cara sauntered down a side path that branched off. It was narrow, forcing Serano to fall behind her again. Brought back to the world for a moment, Cara craned her neck to see around him. Rodani was still there, watchful.

Serano put a hand on her ill-colored jacket. "I will go first."

"Why?" She stepped aside to let him pass.

"There is a stream ahead. Animals congregate along it." He led the way slowly. His gaze swept the area from side to side. Soon, Cara could hear running water. As the stream came into view, both guardians checked the area.

"Is there a way across?" Cara asked them.

"Stones over there." Rodani pointed into the stream.

And there were. Quite far apart from each other. Cara was doubtful, given the length of her stride. But she willed herself to try. She went over to the first stone and stepped on it, somewhat precarious in her balance. The next one was manageable, barely; she flailed her arms in an effort to avoid a cold bath and colder walk back. The third stone proved impossible to reach.

She turned. Rodani was on the stone behind her. "It's too far away. And I won't swim in this cold."

Rodani looked beyond her, then stepped forward—straight into her. The rock wouldn't hold all four feet, especially when two were Selandu. Cara began to fall backwards and grabbed for his jacket. Rodani picked her up and sat her on his hip like a child. She gasped and wrapped her arms round him.

"Hold still."

She froze. It wouldn't do for her to dump them both into the stream. Behind them, Serano's amused expression took away neither the tingling where Rodani's hands held her, nor the painful jab in her thigh from something on his weapons belt as he jumped from stone to stone.

They reached the opposite shore in a matter of seconds, Cara dry—and flustered. Rodani stood her on the ground and let go, then fussed with his jacket. Before Serano joined them, Cara had time only to regret the stream wasn't wider. She thanked Rodani somewhat shakily and continued on the path. She thrust her hands into the ugly jacket pockets. With some effort, she focused on the plant life before her as opposed to his touch.

As they made their way beyond the stream, a pungent scent began to tickle her nose, then her memories. She looked around for anything familiar, but her botanical knowledge was far too scant for recognition. The further they walked, the stronger the scent. Finally, she turned to Serano, who had again taken his place behind her.

"What's that smell?"

"A type of plant called tanam," he said. "You dislike it?"

"No. What does it look like?"

"You will see."

No lie, that. Before long, there was a thinning to the trees and a great expanse of feathery blue-green fronds, all of uniform height. Cara stepped to the nearer edge, then shied back as rustlings and squeakings erupted from nearby wavering fronds.

"What are those?" she asked.

"Kumirin, most likely," Serano said.

"What are kumirin?"

"Soft furry four-legged animals, about this long," he held his hands a foot apart. "They eat the tanam."

"Soft and furry?"

"And tasty."

Neither man held any expression she could read. Serious, or a tease? Cara shrugged her shoulders. She started off again, running her free hand over passing fronds and startling the tasty kumirin. The trio passed in and out of sunlight as the path began to arc back west. Serano snagged several small reddish fruits from the vines above their heads.

"You like those?" asked Cara.

"Someone else does." He stuffed an overfull pocket with some effort.

"What's her name?"

Serano glared at her. She caught the ghost of a grin from Rodani behind him.

"Katu," he admitted.

"Pleasant sounding name. I hope she appreciates your thoughtfulness."

Serano planted his feet and crossed his arms over bulging

pockets, face fixed, and pupils constricted.

Cara let a smile spread over her face.

Eventually the stream made its noisy reappearance. This time the crossing rocks were comfortably closer in distance, though smaller in size. Cara stripped off her shoes and socks, trusting more to the soles of her feet than the soles of her shoes. She crossed without mishap but with a quick pang at the memory of Rodani's hands, then redressed her feet. The men followed behind. The rest of the trip through the woods was uneventful. Then they faced an open view.

Rodani peered out and beckoned to Cara. They moved on, just outside of the line of trees—leaving Serano to walk nearer the road. They remained undisturbed as they rounded the bend in the road and came within sight of the carriage. Serano went around the back as Rodani and Cara, chatting amiably, angled their stroll toward the side doors. Gratefully, Cara stripped off the cumbersome jacket and tossed it onto the vehicle seat. They took off.

The outing had been both a pleasure and a disturbance to her equanimity. The memory of Rodani's touch as he carried her across the stream sent warmth through her body.

No. This just won't do. It was ridiculous, unthinkable. She shut it down.

Reluctantly.

With a sigh, Cara relaxed into the seatback. They left the forest interior and headed back toward civilization.

The manor materialized out of the distance. The black square marking the entrance to the garage grew from a speck, to a square, to a gaping maw.

THIRTEEN

Serano stood in front of Kusik in his office.

"Report," the keso snapped at him.

"Cara was pleased to be outside, a'Keso. She did not act in any overtly inappropriate manner, though she did tease me once."

"What did she speak of? What did you do?"

Serano willed his twitching ears to a calmer state and took a deep breath. "I showed her our land. The trees that grow here and the animals that inhabit it."

"Was she a burden to your skills or temperament?"

"No more than would be expected, a'Keso."

"Was she childish? Frightened?"

"I saw no particular fear in her, a'Keso. Caution, yes. Curiosity," he raised an eyebrow, "quite strong."

"Did she mention anything of her own lands, her people?"

"No, a'Keso."

"None?" Kusik asked in a skeptical tone.

"None, a'Keso."

"And Rodani?"

Serano considered the question. "Quiet for the most part. He let me instruct her on the nature we saw. When we arrived at the stream, he carried her across."

Kusik's expression morphed into anger. "Why?" he growled.

"The steppingstones were too far apart for her to walk them."

And the keso's anger turned to disgust. "Nothing else?"

"To the best of my knowledge, a'Keso. Rodani may have better answers."

Kusik leaned forward with a fire that burned in his eyes. "I do not trust your partner. Not for this."

Questions flew through Serano's mind. "May I ask, a'Keso?"

"He is too tightly bound to this ridiculous venture, and to the taso." He sat back. "Keep trying, Serano. I need whatever information you can glean from her on important," he emphasized, "information. Not the ramblings of a half-witted crafter."

"She may not have any, a'Keso."

"Wit? That I believe. I want her *gone*, a'tem, and I cannot do it from a desk."

Serano bowed in submission tinged with doubt, and with a wave of his superior's hand, left the room.

***

Cool morning mist hung in the air as the stallion thumped down the road. Litelon adjusted his position in the seat and retrieved a bottle from his saddlebag. "Da!" he commanded. The stallion stopped. Litelon took a long drink and stared out at the sunrise.

Alone.

No apprentices, stablemasters, siblings, groomers. He took a deep breath and let it out slowly, enjoying the cool air as it passed through his lungs. Droplets of mist clung to his hair and clothes.

The sun lay just above the horizon. Wisps of clouds trailed overhead. The air was redolent of never-die trees and papani bushes, whose sweet scent reminded Litelon of his mother's holiday cooking.

The stallion stomped his forefeet, turned his head, and snuffled Litelon's pant leg. Litelon gave him an absentminded rub along the jaw, while avoiding the deadly incisors.

"Hu!"

The stallion broke into a trot, clawed feet padding against the path. The leather saddle creaked with Litelon's weight, and his pants rubbed against the beast's side. He touched the saddle.

It was a little large for one as slender as he, but too small for two. Imagination put a pale, curvaceous alien body in front of him, and drew her back against him. Something stirred deep within. He tightened his grip on the reins, sending an unintended signal to the stallion, who sped up. Litelon leaned forward and spurred the benatac into racing speed. The path turned into a blur beneath them. Wind brushed his face, a cool, constant caress. It wasn't the one he wanted. Silver hair fluttered against his back; his thighs tensed with the effort to keep his seat as he rocked to the stallion's pounding gait. Trees passed by in rapid succession.

Litelon hauled on the reins, aiming the benatac at a break in the forest wall. Youth and beast whipped between bare branches that caught, cut, and stung. Overconfident bushes crowded the narrow path, earning a multitude of snapped twigs. Litelon tightened his jaw and narrowed his eyes against injury, letting the stallion take whatever path presented itself. They slowed.

One fallen log lay across the path. Litelon turned the benatac onto a side path and up to the edge of a wide stream, then slid off the saddle. He wiped the sweat from the beast's hide. It drank deeply, then dribbled water and saliva over his pants.

"Must you?" he asked.

"Of course."

Litelon jumped as if he'd been snapped by a whip. A booted man stood in the running water half hidden by foliage. In one hand was a net; the other held a long-handled tickler, enticement to the fish as it dragged the surface of the stream.

"A'Shurad," Litelon said.

"And have you finished the book?" he asked, discourteous in the absence of address.

"Book?"

"*Alien Lives and Thoughts*, a'sel." Shurad's mouth turned down in overt disapproval.

"Ah, yes." He shuffled his feet. "I have. Do you fish here?"

"No. I am cooling my feet after a long race."

Litelon's pupils narrowed; his face tensed. He turned his back on the older man, yanked the stallion's reins, and slid a foot into the stirrup.

"Litelon."

Knee at his chest, he looked over his shoulder.

Shurad walked up on the bank and laid his tools on a rock. "What is your interest in the aliens?"

"Curiosity."

"Curiosity," he repeated, as if disbelieving the simplistic answer. "In regard to what?"

Litelon pulled his foot out of the stirrup. "To the aliens. To Cara."

"To Cara," he said slowly, sitting down on the rock. "To a child-sized alien female with no sense of honor or propriety."

"I refuse to believe that."

"Believe what you will." Shurad leaned his elbows on his knees. "Your family was not nearly decimated by her people."

"You do yourself no honor to damn her for something she had

no part in."

"You do not understand."

"You are quite correct. And I would prefer you not try to convince me."

"You have made up your mind about her."

Litelon turned his head aside in polite refusal, but his pupils pulsed with desire.

Shurad froze. "What nonsense do you hold in your head, te'oto?"

The stream gurgled at Litelon's feet, muttering remonstrations. "A man may dream."

"A boy dreams. A man beholds reality." Shurad interlaced his fingers and let them droop between his knees. "Reality precludes aliens, especially in such ways as you are thinking."

"This is fact or supposition?"

"Logic."

Litelon mounted the stallion. "You know no more than I."

"Then find out. I would be interested in the answer."

"Why? You hold a similar interest?"

Shurad stood. The tickler rolled off the rock. "You dishonor me?"

Litelon swallowed a trickle of fear. "I should wish to know your interest in her."

"She holds answers."

"Answers?" There was no mistaking the confusion in the young man's voice, or the disbelief.

"To the war," Shurad spat. "To the deaths. To the dishonor." He bent down and retrieved the tickler. "She is the closest I will ever be to the answers."

"Answers have been given, a'sel. For longer than she has been alive. Or me."

"Inadequate answers."

"And a young human crafter holds better ones?"

Shurad tapped his pole on the rock. "Politicians give political answers. I do not trust them."

"And you trust Cara?"

The two men locked eyes, the young and the not-so-young, the hungry and the hurting.

Shurad blinked first. "Yes."

Litelon turned the beast carefully in the narrow confines of the clearing. "Unlikely." He snapped his opinion into the reins. "Hu!"

The stallion cantered off.

***

Afternoon rain beat a monotonous lullaby on the study's window—locked window. Cara stretched her legs. Even easy chairs get uncomfortable over the long sail. She put her book down, tired of shuttling between its pages and the dictionary that rested wide-open on the end table next to her. The list was growing.

She sighed wearily, empty stomach beginning to complain. Hamman had brought her a new warm cereal that morning. It was improper, the servant had told her, to have cold foods on cold mornings. But Cara would have to add another impropriety to her tally sheet. The hot cereal had gone down like glue.

The rain beat harder, drumming interrupted by a crack of lightning that set off her reflexes. Thunder rumbled across her senses and sent a tremor through the stone floor.

<Splat>

She rifled through the stack of 'cordings on the music shelf.

<Splat splat>

She cocked her head. There. In the corner. A tiny puddle, widening into something worthy of notice.

<Splat>

It landed right in front of the bookcase. She felt the spines of a few of the books Rodani had lent her. *Damp? Maybe.*

Leaky walls were endemic to Newydd Cenedyl. Something about the local softwoods. A towel would do for this one, temporarily. She turned on her errand, then turned back. Stone? How in the deep night could stone leak? She peered up into the shadowed corner. A line of water dribbled out from the corner and onto a bump on the wall.

<Splat>

She headed for the bedroom. "Hamman?"

The narrow corridor remained empty.

"Hamman?"

"A moment, a'Cara." The servant's voice echoed down the hallway.

Cara's eyes swept her bedroom ceiling for water stains, but the view remained pristine.

"A'Cara?" Hamman appeared at the far doorway, silhouett

against the soft light that trickled around her.

"My ceiling is leaking." Cara pointed the other way.

Hamman followed Cara through the doors and into her study. The leak was evident, both visually and audibly. Hamman pursed her lips and shot a critical look at the beginnings of a mess.

"Pull the books from the bookcase, please. I will return." She went back through the bedroom, disappearing into the corridor.

Cara pulled the books from the top shelf of the corner bookcase and piled them up on the tables. The second shelf joined the first. When she pulled a group off the third shelf, something caught. A handful of books tumbled to the floor. Cara scrabbled for them, hoping nothing was bent or wet. She felt around on the shelf and found a wire. A series of tugs stretched it outward into the light for inspection. A simple wire, with some small contraption on one end.

Dazed, Cara let it drop. It swung pathetically, like a dead vine from a tree. She sat down. A knot grew in her stomach, hard and nauseating. She began to burn.

A microphone. It had to be. What other reason for hiding a wire where she'd ordinarily never find it? Rodani's doing? Damn him! She yanked on the offending wire. More of it came out, still attached. She wrapped it around her hand and pulled until it slid out. Metallic clanks erupted from her bedroom. She stuffed the wire in her pocket as her servant reappeared with towels and a bucket. Cara pulled out the rest of the books while Hamman made temporary repairs.

Cara tried to return to her reading when Hamman left. But the bulge in her pocket prevented any other thoughts from intruding.

<Clunk>

The pail rattled.

Did she deserve to be monitored? It should be obvious to Rodani by now that she was harmless. The lack of trust hurt, though the reasoning parts of her brain understood. Confront him? Better, maybe, to let him remain in ignorance; it was less likely the wire would be noticed and replaced.

Fat chance.

<Clunk>

She stuck her hand in her pocket and fingered the wire, wondering what kinds of things she had said out loud. Who listened? Who, for all the gods' sakes, translated? No one in the manor claimed to know Cene'l. They were too far away from

Hadaman for such a skill to be necessary. Did they send them to the capital? Did Andrew translate her daily mutterings for the guild and CSC to peruse?

<Clunk>

Cara let go of the wire and heaved herself out of the chair. She went to the facilities for a washrag, then arranged it on the bottom of the pail. A drop fell on the top of her head as she studied the arrangement. She brushed it off with less than a thought and waited for the next one.

<Pttt>

Fists on her hips, Cara sighed and stared down into the tin bucket.

"Problem?"

She jumped, then spun, eyes wide. "Will you please refrain?"

Rodani's expression softened in the face of her ire. "Even your inattention to surroundings teaches me, Cara."

"What do you think it teaches you, Rodani? That my people are easy targets?"

"No." He peeled himself off the doorframe and walked over to her, peering into the bucket. "The noise disturbs you?"

"When I'm thinking or studying, yes."

He glanced back at the two open books near her favorite seat. "What do you study?"

"Vocabulary."

"I thought I had detected improvement."

"The thought cheers me. It's not wasted effort." She looked up at the crying ceiling. "Is it fixable?"

"Yes. But yours is not the only room with water problems. Someone will be along later."

Cara sucked in an angry breath. "To fix the wire, as well as the leak?"

The relaxation she'd seen in his body disappeared.

"Wire?"

She pulled it out of her pocket and thrust it at him. Loops and coils dangled from her fist. He held out his palm. Cara surrendered it with undisguised revulsion. "Is this necessary?"

Rodani held it up for extended scrutiny. He twisted the wire and prodded the tip. "Where did you find this?"

"As if you don't know."

He turned his inspection on her, pupils narrowed into slits. "Where did you find this?" he asked slowly.

She replied in the same slow cadence. "In the bookcase."

Rodani motioned with his hand. "Where?"

Cara showed him. He stuffed the wire in a pocket and pulled a tiny light from his weapons belt, then crouched down in front of the shelves. The light snaked its way from one corner of the shelf to another, illuminating bits and pieces of nothing that Cara could see, bent as she was over Rodani's broad shoulder.

It was difficult to credit his reaction. Rodani was too sharp, too thorough. But here he was, rear in the air, trying to puzzle out what Cara didn't even want to think about.

The food cart rumbled in from the bedroom, followed by Falita. She pushed it into the study doorway. But at the sight of the overly full table, she pulled it to a stop.

"I can eat on my worktable."

"It is not proper, a'Cara."

"It doesn't matter to me." Cara shoved tools and papers away from the near edge of her table. To Falita, she said "Can I ask for something different from the cooks?"

"Yes, a'Cara."

"Would you ask them to give me fruits and bread, or meat and bread for breakfast instead of warm cereal?"

Falita took her eyes off her duties long enough to regard Cara and her request. Rodani passed by the two women at a rapid clip.

"Rodani!"

He ignored Cara's call.

"I will tell them, a'Cara," said Falita.

She gave up on her uncommunicative guardian and turned to the younger woman. "Have you eaten?"

Falita's arm stopped its forward motion, then resumed it. A bowl of soup now sat steaming in front of Cara's nose. "No, a'Cara."

"I wish you could share a meal with me."

Falita wouldn't meet her eyes, just lay the other dishes on the worktable. "Forgive me, a'Cara."

FOURTEEN

Things were better than before, but she missed her home and her freedom, missed the unspoken understandings that two friends can share with a glance. Not one thing here could be taken upon assumption. A glance might mean anger or come-on, and she wouldn't know. Like her own language, a word could easily mean something in one situation and something completely different in another—and she might not even notice.

Filtered afternoon sunlight lay warm in the workroom, edging over the quilt and onto Cara's busy hands. Stitches appeared in rapid succession, outlining the shape of the leaf it surrounded and enhanced. The intricately appliqued wall hanging bounced under the pressure of the needle. The smell of fabric dyes wafted over from the shelf, courtesy of a recent and unexpected package from one of her younger sisters. Cara had not been completely forgotten in this out-of-the-way, out-of-this-world alien abode. She clicked her way to another singable song on the 'corder.

Someone knocked on the hallway door. She glanced up. Inattentive to an unfinished stitch, she poked the needle into her fingertip, and gasped. She drew her hand out from under the quilt. A bead of blood welled up from the puncture.

"Who's there?"

"Litelon, a'Cara."

Cara sucked in a deep breath. Such an ordinary activity as a visitor at her door made her stomach drop. It wasn't allowed. Rodani had said so. Iraimin always came in through the servants' quarters. She was allowed. Litelon showed up at her door, unannounced. Worse, Rodani had said nothing about the possibility. Cara swallowed heavily; her hand rubbed nervously at the needle-pricked finger.

"What do you need, Litelon?"

There was a silence on the other side, as if he were digesting the unusual reply.

"To speak with you."

Cara left her chair at the frame and tiptoed over to the door. Litelon wasn't on her extremely short list of approved visitors but was waiting patiently for entrance to her private rooms. Courage was simpler when she had an armed guardian at her side.

"Forgive me, a'Litelon. I can't. Rodani said all visits must be cleared through him, first. Please don't be offended." Probably this was nothing to worry about. But she didn't want to see Rodani's reaction if she let Litelon in.

"It is a fine morning. I have been out riding already. Will you ride with me?"

One of those beasts? Cara shivered at the memory. "You must talk to Rodani." No way he'd say yes. This was an easy refusal, a cowardly one.

Shoes scraped against the hallway's stone floor. "Where might he be?"

"Uh, I don't know. Likely the security office will."

"Do you expect him? I would be pleased to wait with you."

The kid didn't know the meaning of no. Human bluntness might be in order here, though she hated to resort to it. Something about the boy pulled her heartstrings. "I can't allow it, Litelon."

"There is a great deal of curiosity surrounding you, a'Cara."

She gaped like a fish out of water at his admission. *What the heck was he getting at? A warning?* "Is there a problem?"

"No. If I talked to you, I could satisfy others' curiosity, and save you the interruptions."

"And you would get what in return?"

Silence.

Cara bit her lip to keep the smile from her voice. "Talk to Rodani, Litelon."

"Thank you, a'Cara. I will try."

The footsteps moved down the hall.

Did Litelon not know her situation? No one boldly knocked on her door and asked for admittance, let alone a bedamned date! He'd talked to her only on the ride from Soldan. Hardly a basis upon which to request an invitation to her quarters. If he were human, she'd be suspicious.

Distracted, Cara rubbed at her sore finger and went into the facilities for a bandage. But it felt strange to work with. She couldn't feel the needle tip enough to control it until it punctured the bandage and added wound to wound. She gave up and grabbed a pad and pencil instead, shoving thoughts of Litelon aside to concentrate on her next commission.

Afternoon sunlight fell towards dusk. Having promised herself an evening doing nothing but what she pleased, Cara tossed her tools on the table and headed for the study with her 'corder. But the sight of the empty bookcase and stacked tables reminded her there was no proper place for the items under her arms. She plopped them on the tea table along with the rest and flipped through the 'cordings. If someone was listening, she was going to give them an earful.

The door to the hall opened, and a clunk and clatter entered the room. Rodani strode into the study, two men behind him; one taller, one shorter, both dressed in heavy brown clothes and well-worn boots. Both eyed her with misgiving as Rodani stepped to her side and crossed his arms. Mind on business, he seemed to be telling them. Reluctantly, they turned their backs to her and set to work.

"You will have dinner in my quarters, tonight, Cara."

Cara pivoted toward him at the unexpected invitation. "Thank you."

"Not necessary. It is inappropriate for you to eat in the midst of dust and noise if another option is available."

"I appreciate it."

He waved his hand toward the bedroom. "Do what is needed. I will wait."

She did what was needed, then Rodani escorted her across the hall and into the rooms he shared with Serano.

To her immediate left was a radio nestled in a set of shelves along the wall. In the corner of the sitting room was a dinner table with four chairs, and a bookcase filled with books save for the top shelf, which held a variety of items; Cara wanted a closer look. On the wall opposite was a long table. Small bottles, bowls, and other less recognizable items sat orderly on the tabletop. On the near wall, a half-closed door revealed a neatly made bed. On the far wall was a door to another bedroom. It stood wide-open, a bed, and dresser in plain view, and a door to the facilities partially hidden. There was no sign of Serano.

Cara strolled to a bookcase. "Whose are these?" The shelf held an assortment of small items made of wood and metal.

"Mine."

"Someone here made them?"

"One lone guardian/artisan."

The statement sank in. "You made them?"

"Yes." Quiet. He was very quiet.

"May I?" she asked warily, hand outstretched but not too close. Most artisans didn't want their work fingered by just anyone. Too much effort went into the creation for it to be marred by incautious handling.

"Yes."

Two pictures framed in carved berelwood stood at one end of the shelf. A different woman stared out from each. One painting seemed old, faded, and blotched in one corner, the other was a side view of a young woman aiming a pistol at a distant target. Next to them, a set of three boxes in ascending sizes sat in the middle of the shelf. Cara picked up the smallest. Each mitered corner was a perfect match on base and lid. She turned it around in a circle. Designs had been burned into the sides and lid top, ornate curves that twisted and twined. Carefully, she brushed a fingertip around the perfect corners and over the reliefs, then put it back in its place on the shelf.

Next was a rectangular silver belt buckle. It was made of thick wire that had been braided and then pounded flat. No mean feat, that, to get wire flattened into a regularized shape without lumps or bumps or misshapen edges. The buckle's polished surface shone bright in the overhead lantern. A small pin, also silver, as much of Selandu jewelry seemed to be, rested next to the buckle. It was round and crisscrossed over the top with an intricate interlacing of almost hair-thin wire. Around the edge was another pattern, embossed with curlicues. It was quite dainty.

Last were two beautiful rose-gold flowers, each in a separate stand, long copper stems coiled around each other in a graceful embrace. The petals of both flowers lay open, creating a small resting spot for something. Cara lifted them reverently, twisting her hands to part them.

The door behind them opened and closed. It was Serano. When Rodani looked his way, he gestured in the guild language. Rodani inclined his head.

"What are they?"

Rodani turned back to face her. "Candleholders."

"They're beautiful, Rodani. Do you use them?"

"No."

"Why?"

He hesitated. "They were meant to be a gift. Then the gift became...irrelevant. I kept them."

She looked up at him from the corner of her eye. "And there has been no one since who deserved such a magnificent gift?"

Rodani avoided her question with the same reserve with which he avoided her eyes. Cara placed the candleholders back on the shelf carefully, intertwining them and turning them to the same angle as she found them.

"Rodani awards such gifts charily, Cara." She turned from the bookcase to face Serano. "I, however, have learned that the best way to entice a woman is to first present her with what gifts I can procure."

Cara broke into embarrassed laughter at his admittance of a seduction technique. Rodani regarded them both blandly and walked over to the dinner table. He poured himself a drink.

"At the moment, Cara, there is no ice. A servant will bring some." He took a delicate sip of the eisenico and stared into its amber depths.

Rodani turned on the radio and settled onto the couch, inviting Cara to sit on the other end. Serano sat on a carved wooden chair with embroidered seat cushions, as a woman's voice came through the radio. A radio for their private use was a strong indicator of the status of her guardians. Only about a dozen sets existed in the whole manor, four or more of which sat in various game rooms or conversation rooms scattered over the manor's three-story expanse.

"...for the third year in a row," said the woman on the radio, "the drought has caused the people of Diregi Valley to cluster together for support under the eaves of Taso Ushando. This increase in status has given him a higher platform from which he can espouse his opposition to human presence on the world."

"The goddess will not countenance the sharing of this planet any longer," Ushando shouted through the speakers. "She has shown Her displeasure by withholding Her life-giving moisture from us. We must," his voice strengthened, "cleanse our new world of the presence of these dishonorable humans. The goddess has spoken."

The voice switched back to the newscaster.

Shaken, Cara turned to Rodani. "We were here first! Why isn't the drought a sign from the goddess that his attitude is the wrong one? Otherwise, the goddess would be sending the drought to

Barridan or Hadaman. Or to Newydd Cenedyl!"

"Minds such as his do not feed on reasoning, Cara," Rodani said. "His open disgust is unusual among our race. His is a small minority. Keep it in your saddlebag, but do not let it interfere with your journey."

"He's frightening."

"That is his intention," Serano said.

"Does he have the means to attack us?"

Rodani took a sip of eisenico. "There are two reasons that the guild guards the Himadi Hills. One is humans."

"They could come by the river."

"We would not be caught off guard."

"Tsss." Serano let off a spate of hand motions. Rodani read them but declined to reply, preferring to turn his attention back to the news broadcast.

"On the technology trail," the newscaster went on, "The second round of discussions with the ambassadors has ended. Agreement has been made for the two species to join their knowledge and technology to increase chances of a successful return to space." The shuffling of papers came through the set. "The site for the new manor is the Himadi Plateau. Ground has already been broken in anticipation of the accord.

"Upon its completion," she continued, "the manor will be the first ever household of both Selandu and humans."

Cara leaned back. "Maybe I'm an experiment of another kind, as well." She shifted her head to each side. Both guardians were looking at her. "Am I?"

"Possibly," Rodani admitted.

"Who'll rule the manor? Who'll guard it? Who'll settle differences of honor and offense?"

"It had better be Selandu."

"Why, Serano?"

He refused to look at her.

"Why? Because we have no honor? Because we lie, cheat, or steal?" Cara leaned toward him. "Because we don't think of consequences? Because we're incapable of reasoning? Why?"

Serano took a sip of his drink, gaze deliberately fixed on the radio set.

"Am I so terrible?" She glanced over at Rodani, who was watching her, then back to Serano. "Does my very breathing offend you? The blink of my eyes? My inquiries into your well-being?"

He glared at her. "You talk too much."

Cara burst out laughing. "If that's my only fault, a'Serano, I wear it proudly."

"It is not."

She sobered. The knot that had tied itself in her stomach at the sight of the wire reappeared. "I request a measure of your time, a'tem. Please write down all the ways I offend you, and I will write down all the ways you offend me." A wave of her hand belied the seriousness of the offer. "Then we will exchange them, find solutions, and pass them on to Hadaman and the CSC. We'll be doing both species a favor."

Serano looked at her from the corner of his eye. That look crawled down her spine and flexed claws into the knot in her stomach. "You toy with the guild at your peril," he said.

"I'm not toying with you, Serano. The offenses go both ways." She pointed a dire finger toward the radio. "And the sooner those in charge of the new manor know it, the better." Her crossed arms and direct stare dared him to contradict her.

He threw her an angry look and walked out.

Soon a rattling tray stopped outside the door. Rodani tugged Cara out of the line of sight before opening it. He turned off the radio and waited near the table to inspect dinner. He eyed each dish critically as the servant passed it by him on the way to the tabletop. "A'tem," he said, bowed into his scrutiny, then retreated with the clattering cart.

Rodani motioned Cara to a seat, the one that put her back to the corridor wall. It offered just a touch of protection from the door via the shelf that held the radio.

She remained silent, waiting to see if Rodani would begin a conversation. Invariably, in the past, she had been the one to start talking, vocal human female that she was. A bit stung by the room's emotional residue, she picked at the food on her plate.

"No more questions?" Rodani finally asked.

Cara laid down her fork and rubbed one eye. "I'm leery of more tempers."

Rodani sliced off a piece of meat and inspected at it on the end of his fork. "You would do better," he said, refocusing on her, "to be more circumspect in your conversations."

Cara smacked her forehead against her palms. *Like right now, fem. Patience.* "That means I have to worry about every single statement that comes out of my mouth. For everyone," she continued, her vision locked on her plate, "from the taso down to Falita and Litelon."

"Begin with Serano, Cara. Of the people you are around most often, he is the least patient."

"Alright."

"Do I need to reinforce your courtesies with Arimeso and Kusik?"

That brought her head up out of her hands. "No! I'm so afraid of them that it's hard to say anything at all to them."

"Then that is fortunate." Rodani gestured to her food, which was growing cold. "Eat."

Cara pursed her lips tightly.

"Please," he added.

She picked up her fork and stabbed a vegetable. The meal finished in silence.

Serano walked back in and disappeared into his bedroom. Rodani pushed the dishes aside, took a set of cards from some place in his room, and sat back down at the table. "Play?"

She nodded, a gesture she knew he understood.

"Red or black?"

"Red."

He dealt. Cara started out well, then quickly fell to Rodani's experience. One loss led to another.

"Kill," he said for the third time in several minutes.

"I don't know why I bother to play, Rodani. Do you know any games I have a chance of winning?" She tossed her cards on the table in forfeit.

Rodani gathered up the cards and shuffled. "Competitive quilting?"

Cara leaned back in her chair. Having finally pushed Serano's insults from her mind, she laughed softly, watching the intricate motion of Rodani's hands. "I'm pleased to see your thumb healed. You seem to use it without difficulty."

"Generally." Another shuffle, another tap on the table. "But it aches when it rains." He raised an accusatory eyebrow to her.

"You always wished to know when a storm was coming, did you not?"

"We did manage to manufacture barometers without you."

They were interrupted by Serano exiting his bedroom. He thumped a box of glass bottles on the far table that clinked against each other. Then he set out a conglomeration of apparatuses worthy of an apothecary shop. His movements held Cara's attention until Rodani dealt another hand. The play went as usual.

"Kill," he said.

Cara laid her forehead on her arm in dramatic repose, then tossed her now useless cards onto the table. Frustration gave her wrist a flip that sent two of them past Rodani and onto the floor. She raised her head at the click of the cards against stone.

Pointedly, Rodani looked over the edge of the table and onto the floor.

"Forgive me. I'll get them."

"No." He retrieved them with a quick swipe of his hand.

Cara stood up, stretched, and wandered over to Serano. He was grinding leaves with a mortar and pestle. Filtering cloths and a kettle of hot water sat nearby. An opportune moment presented itself when the grinding stopped and Serano put down the tools.

"May I ask?"

He glanced her way with a look that said she was not quite forgiven. "It is a concoction I make for some of the artisans here." He tapped the mortar gently, poured the ground leaves into a container, then reached for a few more whole ones. The grinding resumed.

"What does it do?"

"It affects the senses. Gives visions of the goddess, some say. Enhances creativity, others say."

"Is it true?"

"The effects of the plant are standard, the interpretations limitless."

"Do you take it?"

"I have tried it. But not being an artist, I have no creativity to enhance. I make it because I have the skills to do so and earn a small income from it." He poured steaming water into the container.

Cara turned to Rodani, who was still at the table watching their exchange. "Have you tried it?" she asked him.

"Yes."

"Often?"

"A time or two."

"What's it like?"

"Interesting. Confusing. Not something to do often," Rodani cautioned.

She spun back to Serano. "May I try it?"

He poured the littered water through a cloth. "Cara, this is not a drink to imbibe and forget about. It may be poisonous. To my knowledge, it has not been tested on humans."

"Is there a way to find out? Without killing me, I mean?"

"Possibly."

She waited while he made another filtering pass through a different cloth.

"Do you wish to take the chance?" he asked.

"Do you have any idea of the level of danger?"

"With just a touch on the lip this time, probably low. If it has no ill effects, next week we would try a drop on the tongue. If that proves harmless, you may try a low dose the week after." He leaned back in the chair and studied her. "This is at your own risk, Cara," he said with some heat, "not mine, not Rodani's. Yours."

"Alright."

Serano touched the now filtered liquid with a fingertip. Carefully, he rubbed the excess off on the side of the container, then touched her bottom lip. "Do not lick your lips. Tell me if you feel any tingling, numbness, burning, or nausea."

Cara grimaced at the litany of symptoms, then nodded.

She remained nearby as Serano went back to his decoction. He filtered a third time into a measuring cup and separated the liquid into the small bottles. She concentrated on not licking her lips—an unexpectedly difficult effort just because it was forbidden.

He poured the last dose and capped it. "Any effects?"

"No." She turned to Rodani and smiled. "Will you avenge me if it kills me?"

Before he could reply, Serano launched from his chair and slapped her across the face. She hit the wall and sagged to the floor.

Rodani stood up and started forward. "Serano!"

Cara climbed unsteadily to her feet to face the two men.

"Cara—" Rodani began as he moved closer.

"I wish," she said furiously, interrupting whatever remonstrance he had in mind, "that you two would spend a year with people nine feet tall and 500 pounds who could kill you with a blow, and who don't even allow you to apologize before they hit!" She pounded the wall behind her in rage, looking from one to the other. "You might see what it's like to be me!"

She stomped to the door and grabbed the handle, slammed the door against the wall, then slammed it behind her with another pull. She sought her bed and curled into it, carefully nursing an emotional sting as sharp as the physical one Serano had dealt. Her right temple had become a kettledrum. She crawled back to the edge of the mattress and sat up.

"Hamman?"

Her senior maid appeared in the bedroom doorway.

"An ice bag, please."

Hamman moved toward her. "Are you in pain, a'Cara?"

"Some."

A Selandu did not exaggerate injuries to gain sympathy. Her actions would garner none, anyway. Hamman left the room quickly. Cara lay back down. Resting her arm across her eyebrows and the bridge of her nose, she closed her eyes and tried to will the pain away.

It wouldn't cooperate.

Whatever she said to offend him, he hadn't given her a chance to realize her error, let alone a chance to apologize. She thought she'd made her point with Arimeso.

Guess not.

When Hamman returned, Cara took the ice bag into the study, put on some of her favorite music, and journeyed inward for solace. Tears leaked from the corners of her eyes. Her voice throbbed with intensity, releasing the humiliation and frustration. In the silence between songs, she heard the scrape of booted feet. Rivaling Serano's speed, she spiraled up on her feet to face her uninvited visitors.

Cara moved back from them, putting the couch between her body and theirs, waiting to see what they would do. Rodani flicked an eyebrow at her wary move, the action of an animal trapped and needing an escape. With arms and ankles crossed, Serano leaned his shoulder against the doorframe in silent study of her response to their presence.

"Cara..." Rodani began.

"Yes, yes. I offended. I'm sorry. I anticipated neither the interpretation of my words, nor the intensity of the reaction." She managed a momentary glance at Serano. "I apologize."

"As do I."

She looked up sharply. Maybe Arimeso did understand.

"One still unfamiliar with our culture should have the chance to redress offenses before punishment is meted out," Serano said.

"It would be appreciated. I rarely mean to offend."

"Rodani says violence is very offensive to you."

"Yes."

"Are you sure you wish to remain here?"

"Am I in danger from you two, a'tem'ai?"

Rodani shifted in the doorway. "Such questions."

"Only by the taso's orders," Serano said. "I suggest you not offend her, even accidentally."

"I know," she answered him with a glance at Rodani. "We discussed that. I'd appreciate any assistance in avoiding it."

"Judging from today," Rodani replied, "by the time we could help, the offense would already have occurred. I had no chance to stop your offense to Serano."

"Yes." Tension put a quiver in her voice. "Fortunately, I have no wish to offer humor to the taso."

Serano unlocked his arms and stood straighter. "You have learned some discretion."

Cara's eyes began to water. "Serano," she said, "I was trying to make a joke of my fear. Does that make sense?"

"Why did you wish to try the herb if you were frightened?"

"If I never did anything fearful, I wouldn't be here. And neither would the ambassadors."

Silence greeted her admission, and her emotions.

Rodani waved Serano out. He retreated quickly, as if in a hurry to escape his adashi. Cara turned sideways and brought her arms across her chest, then curled up on the couch in an ineffectual attempt to rebuild her walls.

Rodani left his place by the door and sat down next to her. "You have apologized. So has Serano. Is something still wrong?"

"I need something that can't be found here, Rodani. Something human."

He rubbed his palms on the top of his pant legs. "What is your need?"

"A friend."

"What is *friend*?"

A try might be useless, but worth an attempt. She sighed and considered her answer.

"A friend is like a companion, but maybe more," she started. "A friend can be male or female, young or old, smart or stupid; those things matter little. A friend wishes you well, shares interests, listens without criticism—unless it's requested—and shares confidences. A friend spends time with you and helps when you need it because it pleases both of you, not because it's expected.

Friendship isn't about duty. It's about two or more people sharing their time, interests, and good will with each other."

Rodani's pupils expanded. "I have attempted. It seems I have failed. Again."

"No! I mean...." *Good gods and all the oceans of space. What have I done?* "I can't... It's... You may never know how much I appreciate what you've done. I don't have the words."

"Obviously."

She squeezed her eyes shut against a confrontation she never wanted to start. "But you do it out of duty."

"Does our duty displease you?" he asked quietly.

Cara leaned forward, elbows on her knees. To make such a proud man feel his duty to her life was unappreciated—his thoughts went off 90° from the way she was trying to lead him, into territory where offenses ran rampant.

"No, Rodani. That's not what I meant. Please don't think that." A few deep breaths made her momentarily more calm. She sat up. "I've been given courtesy from nearly everyone, and patience from most. My security and physical needs are well attended to. The people assigned to me deserve all honor and respect. It's the needs of the mind and heart that aren't met. And that's no one's fault."

"I will do what I can, but you must tell me." Rodani leaned back and put his arm over the couch and stared at her unblinking. "What would a friend do for someone in distress?"

She shrugged. "Hold her, perhaps rub her back or head, let her talk or rain or be silent as necessary. Possibly offer advice." She stopped. Meeting his gaze was impossible; watching the rest of him for some reaction was possible—barely.

Rodani uncurled his fingers and opened his palms, a nearly universal gesture of acceptance. Supremely aware of him as a male but trying to ignore the fact, Cara leaned against his chest. He slipped one hand under the bun at her neck; with the other, he cupped her shoulder, arm draped across her back.

His heart beat rhythmically under her ear, his arms a comforting weight. His breaths ruffled the loose curls on the top of her head. She lay there unmoving, wrapped in alien scents, warmth from the fire on one side, Rodani's body on the other.

"Does this truly help?" he asked.

"Yes. Thank you." His chest muffled her words.

"How does it help?"

"Humans are a touch-oriented people, Rodani. A touch, a hug calms us, comforts us. It makes us feel that someone wishes us well."

"Does this touching make you less emotionally reactive?"

She chuckled into his shirt. "Usually, yes."

A handful of minutes went by. Cara could feel the rise and fall of Rodani's chest as he breathed, and the weight of his arms around her. Not wishing to leave the comfort but also not wishing to cause a greater problem, she sat up. With her movement, Rodani released her.

"Thank you. That was much appreciated."

"It is well to know something that will calm you."

"Are my emotions that disturbing to you?"

"They are very strong."

"Meaning 'yes'?"

He glanced away.

"Forgive me. That was improper." One did not take a polite sidestep of an answer, make it blatant, and throw it back at the speaker. "Tonight seems to be a night for offensive comments."

"Is that different from any other night?"

The comment earned him a look of which he was normally on the giving end. "Is that offense, or humor?"

"Humor, of course," he said. "We rarely seek revenge for an offense that has been apologized for."

"Gods. Spare me from a guardian's revenge. You know, you ran the risk of disturbing me again with your humor, as Serano's temper did."

"Then you would need another embrace, would you not?"

She couldn't help but laugh, but couldn't look at him, either. This was getting entirely too personal. And, of course, it was her doing. She had no one to blame but herself if it went out of control. She sat demurely, hands in her lap, wondering what the best way to say goodnight was.

"You seem calm, now."

"Yes. Thank you. Thank you for talking with me, and for the hug."

Fortunately, the hint translated. He rose from her side and headed for the study doorway. It was good he was honorable, considering Cara's level of naïveté.

"Safe night," she said.

A tilt of the head was his reply.

***

Shurad stomped out of the third-floor festive room in the middle of the news broadcast about Himadi House. Only a few heads turned. He fumed all the way back to his rooms. Never so crass as to slam a door, he closed it behind him, then unlatched the shutters. Night sky and stars greeted him.

"Fools!" he shouted to the sky. They were all fools. Were memories so short? How many would die in this attempt to force two incompatible species to work together? He had to warn them. Someone should go to Hadaman. Someone who knew what the stakes were, what the consequences would be.

But no, his parents had not written him, therefore they had not yet returned from the capital. They could argue as eloquently in person as he could on paper. Surely, the council would listen. Surely, this mad scheme would be terminated before more deaths haunted his people.

There would never be another River War. Never be another cohabitation. Once was enough. Shurad knew he was no soldier, no guardian. But like all the river's children, he would do what he could to prevent another massacre.

Arm on the windowsill, he clenched his fist in frustration.

Space was not that important. They could go nowhere for decades, even a century or more. The aliens that had blasted his parents from the sky made sure of that fact. The holes in the engines attested to it. More important was consolidating their hold on their continent to prevent further human incursions. The guild quarantine at the border was not enough. The Himadi mountain range was too long, the forests too thick to track every five-fingered alien attempting to break through.

Guard what you have. Secure what is yours before grasping for the next prize. And nothing was secure where those humans skulked. It wasn't the time for deadly social experiments. Too many other things demanded his people's attention; too many petitions to the goddess had yet to be answered.

A knock on the door broke into his restive reverie.

"Enter."

Garidemu walked in.

"Sel'u," Shurad said from the window.

"I need not ask what disturbed you."

Shurad turned back to the autumn chill and the smell of never-die trees that rode the north wind. "You need not."

"It will fail."

"After how many deaths?"

"At least there is more at stake than water rights."

Shurad looked over his shoulder as his companion strolled closer. "You mock me?"

"No, sel'u. But you should stop living in the past."

"I have enough shoulds in my life."

"That you do." Garidemu leaned against the shutters. They thumped the wall. "Come. End your brooding. There is a new bar in town."

"You have yet to drown your troubles, despite years of practice," Shurad said. "Am I to imitate your failures with women?"

The potter pursed his lips and slid one hand down a hip pocket. "No. My successes."

"My bond with Geseli is the only success I need," Shurad told him. "You seem to be in competition with Serano."

Garidemu's pupils pulsed. He waved off his companion's prurient comment. "Serano has guild status to assist in garnering female attentions."

"No matter," Shurad countered. "I leave sniffing other women's trails to your sensitive nose. I have my quarry in sight and nearly in hand."

"Geseli does not wear your clip."

"She will."

"Is that your final word on tonight?"

Shurad left the window and removed a large coin from his personal lockbox. "No. I have an idea."

"About what?" Garidemu asked.

"Dispatching that human."

They walked out together.

FIFTEEN

Cara returned her attention to the quilt in front of her.

The open portion of her work lay out before her, one end rolled up next to her waist, the other beyond her hands. Her busy fingers took a break to click past an ill-favored song on the portable 'corder and readjust the headphones against her ears.

It was peaceful, this mixture of music by ear and craft by hands. Cara stitched her way around a particularly intricate geometric figure and sang along with the female vocalist, whose powerful voice filled her ears. The passage of song through her ears and voice coincided with the passage of thread through the needle in her fingers. Time passed unnoticed and unbroken.

A pattern of five knocks peppered the door. Cara jumped, heart thudding in her chest, then she recognized the cadence.

"Who is there?"

"Rodani."

She took an audible breath and let it out. "Please enter."

Rodani stepped through the door and stopped just inside.

"Bright morn," she greeted him politely from the other side of her table.

He eased himself into the adjacent chair with a grace she envied. *Mind on your quilting, fem.* "What will you do today?" she asked.

"I spent time thinking about what you said last night," he began. "A friend shares his interests with another?"

"Among other things, yes."

"I would ask something."

"You can always ask, Rodani."

There was another hesitation; a short one, accompanied by a subtle shift in posture and aversion of the eyes. Cara recognized the body language. "Lay your cards on the table," she told him.

They shared a grin at the shared colloquialism.

"Would you teach me to use my voice as you do?"

Her hands stopped scribbling. Selandu don't sing, Iraimin had told her. There was no vocal music to be found.

"I'm neither professional singer nor teacher, Rodani, but I can try. May I ask?"

"Many things are improper that need not be." His eyes focused into the distance, as if in contemplation.

"Yes. My music is all in Cene'l. But I can translate the words so you will know what you're singing and turn down the original vocals so you can sing over top of them. Would that please you?"

"Yes."

"Well, sit down in front of the 'corder and find some songs to sing with." She stood up from her quilt and went into the study. Rodani followed.

"Have you sung to yourself before?" she asked.

"Not with words. There are no songs like that. Without words, yes."

"Good. Choose songs you think will be in your voice's range."

She left him to listen and went back to her calculations. Eventually, he returned to her side.

"Found some?"

"Yes," he said, eyes downcast like a courteous child asking for candy.

They went back to the study. Cara motioned Rodani to take a seat across from her on the floor. He knelt, feet underneath his rear, and watched her intently.

"First, breathe correctly," she said. "Too many people sing with too little air. Proper posture is important, too, which you already have. Sit or stand straight." She imitated her words, taking a deep breath. "Otherwise, there is not enough room in the lungs. Don't sing all the air out of your lungs, either; the voice gets weak. Take breaths often enough that you keep your lungs at least half full."

"How do I know?"

"By the tone of your voice—how much power you still have in it. The knowledge comes with practice. Which song first?"

He picked up a 'cording. "This one. The fifth."

Cara took it. "Good song. I'll phoneticize it, you listen and think about how you'd sing it and when you might draw breaths."

It took a few times through the 'cording before she got the words down for him. By then, he had a general idea of how he wanted to go about it. She turned the vocals to half-volume, leaving the instrumentals on full. His first try was tentative, that was expected, but his voice was clear and deep. She prompted him to breathe when he got low on air but left the rest for a time.

"Good. Now do more. Have you ever put a piece of hot food in your mouth, then dropped your jaw and tongue and breathed around it while it cooled?"

He blinked and pursed his lips. "Yes." Then grinned.

"Open your mouth and throat more," she said. "You pull your tongue down and back to make more room for the air to go through. It gives more volume to your voice. Try it."

She reset the song back to its beginning, and Rodani made another attempt.

It made a difference in the quality. When he finished the song for the fourth time, she had to compliment him. "That—was wonderful." He looked away, pale with embarrassment.

"Try again, unless you need a break," she continued.

"No break."

"Remember three things: keep air in your lungs, keep your jaws and throat open, and keep your tongue down." She reset the song and listened. He sang through to the end without stopping, then waited for her response.

She stared open-mouthed. The tone and timbre of his voice were incredible; he was a natural. How he managed to keep this ability unused for almost thirty years mystified her. No wonder he was willing to face laughter or disdain in order to learn. A desire to sing was difficult to deny. And he was oceans and mountains better at it than she was.

"There's only one more thing I can teach you," she said. "And this will be the most difficult."

He composed his face.

"You have to put emotion into the song, Rodani," she said carefully. "You have to feel the emotions the song is describing and pour those emotions out through your voice." She smiled at his skeptical expression. "I'll sing this time. The quality of my voice is not as good as yours, but I can pour on the emotion like no one you've known before."

"That is certain," he said wryly

"Listen to the strength of my emotions."

The opening bars came through the speakers. It was soft at the beginning; quietly sad. She thought about the man singing the song and how she would feel in his place, feeling the loss of the woman he loved. Stronger in the middle verses, she increased the strength of her voice and the depth of her imagined pain. As the last verse started, she remembered some of the men in her own life who had come and gone and pushed those memories out through her voice. A few tears came unbidden as she put her heart and soul into the last stanzas.

As the song died out, she opened her eyes.

Rodani was watching her, pupils wide. "You are raining."

She laughed through her tears and wiped them from her face. "I felt the emotions of the song. I felt the pain and loss that the song is referring to."

He sat in silence for a minute.

She shifted on the hard floor. "Have you ever…" Gods. What was the Selandi word for love? How should she word it? "…felt strongly for a woman, only to have the affinity end painfully?"

He looked off in the distance, and back into time. "Yes."

"Then what you have to do is put yourself back there and relive the feelings you had at that time. Let those feelings come through your voice. It may be difficult for you. But it's just you and me in the room." She tapped his thigh gently. "I won't laugh, and you won't dishonor yourself. Will you try?"

She let him consider it. His thoughts went away somewhere. She watched him depart, then return, all without leaving the room.

"Yes."

She pressed reset. "Quietly at first. Build up in the middle, then pour out your pain to me at the end."

He began as she told him, quietly, but he didn't change in the middle verses. She stopped him.

"Try this," she told him. "Take deeper breaths and force the words out. Put *power* in your voice. *Pain* in your voice. Keep your thoughts clearly on those memories. Feel them all over again."

"Recreate the pain?"

"Yes."

She hit reset then play.

He went over the easy part, then continued into the middle with more emphasis in his voice.

"Yes. Force the words out."

His eyes narrowed. Tension filled his face.

"Strongly now. You're hurting. Rage at the world."

His voice filled her study as the last verse of the song came and went. The wordless finale became the backdrop as Cara and Rodani stared at each other.

"Good gods and Temi's demons," she said, grinning.

He looked away. She shut off the music.

"Cara."

"Yes?"

"What is done with the reawakened memories?"

Good question. It threw her off balance. "Keep them tucked away for the next time you sing?"

His pupils expanded and contracted again. A slow blink interrupted her view of them. "Last night when you sang, was it your pain or the song's pain you were feeling?"

"Mine, mostly."

"You felt so much pain from one slap?"

"No. I felt pain, but it awakened memories. The offenses I've given you, and your hitting me came back in at the same time. All my mistakes and the anger they've generated became overwhelming."

Rodani leaned forward, almost uncomfortably close. "I am not quite so sorry you offended Serano yesterday."

She smiled. A companionable silence surrounded them.

His reserve was returning as the emotions he'd shown with his singing were tucked safely away again.

"Are you pleased with what you learned?" she asked.

"Very much. Thank you."

"You're welcome to stay and listen more, if you wish. It won't disturb me." She waved her hand over the other 'cordings. "And if you wish to sing more, I'd be pleased to listen. You can stay as long as you wish."

"You are generous with your time and belongings, Cara. I am indebted."

"No. That's something friends do. And I enjoyed it as much as you." She patted his knee, then got up and returned to her quilting.

Rodani sat in her study for the better part of an hour, listening, making notes, and switching out disks. But for whatever reason, he chose not to sing. Cara was disappointed; he had as good a voice as many of the men on her 'cordings. But she kept quiet for fear of making him feel uncomfortable. What they had shared was not something Cara wished to ruin with ill-thought comments. Finally, Rodani turned off the music and came back into her workroom.

"Finished?"

"Yes." With a slight bow, Rodani left his list with her, and headed for the door. He left the room as quietly as he'd entered it.

Cara returned her attention to the quilt in front of her. As she stitched, her mind wandered. Benatacs. Guns. Serano's concoction. Rodani's hug. Singing. Had Hamman heard them? What did she think of the sacrilege? Who did she tell?

That wire. Servants didn't have to tell on them. Not if someone had replaced the wire. They could have done that while fixing the leak in her study!

She began to search the room, going from one item to the other to the next. She stopped at her 'corder, staring at the wires that led from box to speakers. Suspicions tickled the nape of her neck and wound tendrils through her gut. She turned the lanterns on high and stared at the ceiling, following its perimeter through 360°, looking for the wire, and wondering. Rodani had never mentioned it again, and she knew not to ask.

On a whim, Cara knelt under the dinner table and swept its undersurface with her fingers. Nothing unusual intruded. She pulled the pillows and padding off the couch and searched them, pushing and poking for hardness where none should be. The couch upholstery was innocent as well, near as she could tell. She went to the back side of it and pulled it over. Supporting wood slats and screws revealed themselves to her eyes and questing fingers, but nothing else.

"A'Cara, is something wrong?" Hamman's normally placid face was contorted into obvious confusion.

"No, Hamman." Cara returned to the underside of the couch. "Thank you." She got up and, with some difficulty, lifted the couch back on its feet

Hamman left as Cara pulled a ball of fuzz from her eyebrow. She considered the previously guilty bookcase, then went back to the table that held her 'corder. Would she recognize an extra wire? Maybe.

By the time she had memorized its layout, had the whole thing unplugged, on the floor, and separated into components, the rattle of the dinner cart erupted behind her.

"Just lay it out, please, Hamman. I'll be a short while."

"As you wish," said a very masculine, familiar voice.

Cara twisted on the floor. Rodani stood behind the cart.

"Is something wrong with your music player?" he asked.

She turned her back to him. "No."

He pushed the cart over to the dinner table. "And is there something wrong with the table, or chairs?" He swept the room with a professionally critical gaze. "Or the couch?"

Dammit, Hamman. No, that wasn't fair. Cara knew privacy was nonexistent.

"And what of the bookcase?" he continued.

He was taunting her; he must be. "Only an amateur would put another wire in the same place," she said.

"Why do you bother?"

"You never told me what you found out." Checking the 'corder was an exercise in futility. She hooked it back together with some facsimile of expertise and put it on the table as Rodani lay out her dinner.

"Cara, Serano swept your rooms the same evening you showed me the wire. Why do you bother now?"

Over by the fireplace, a bin of logs rested patiently. Cara sat in front of it and pulled them out one by one, ignoring the tall form in black boots that strode to her side. When the bin was empty, she searched it over carefully, then reversed the emptying process. From her place on the floor, she ran her hands over the base of the fireplace and around the smaller stones that framed it. Working her way upward, she inspected the mantle, then worked her way back down the other side.

"Your dinner is cooling rapidly," Rodani told her.

"Yes."

On hands and knees, she crawled past the doorway and dug her fingers into the crack where the walls and floor met. Around the corner, past the dinner table, and down to the far corner. She pulled the vase off the triangular incidental table and inspected the flowers, then turned the table over.

Nothing. Table and flowers returned to their places.

She swept the room with her eyes, giving Rodani short shrift at his perch on the couch arm, and continued down the back wall. Outdoor scents invaded her nose as she neared the window, and shadows made the inspection difficult. But she persevered through sheer human stubbornness, rounding the third corner and completing the last wall.

More nothings. She got up and flexed her knees painfully, then rubbed them.

"Are you finished?"

She gnawed her lip in contemplation, considered her options, and the heights of various pieces of furniture. The dinner table would be best, but Rodani had pre-empted it. One last time, she pulled her 'corder off the end table, pulled the table over to the window, and climbed on it. The intricately carved shutters deserved careful study, inside and out. Rodani padded up behind her and stopped within reaching distance. Cara opened the shutters and bent near them, ran her fingers top to bottom, in and around all the convolutions. Same with the window. She closed the shutters and got down.

Tired, finally admitting foolishness to herself, Cara dragged the table back to the couch and replaced her 'corder, then sat down to dinner.

"Will you eat?" she asked Rodani.

And got the same silent treatment she'd given him.

"Where should I look next?" she said between bites. "My fabric shelves? The bed?" And stared him in the face. "Under my worktable?"

Dark-eyed and harboring an unreadable expression, Rodani remained perched on the side of the couch. His full lips had thinned into a tight line of tension.

"Behind the paintings?" Cara took a sip of tea. "Among the plumbing in the facilities? No? The armoire has dark places. Maybe there."

"Is this a game?"

"You tell me."

"Only Sela knows your mind."

"No. Only I know my mind; and that, only on occasion." Cara concentrated on her meal for a few more bites while Rodani watched, mute. "Did you put that wire in the bookcase, Rodani?"

He not only didn't speak, he didn't move. Selandu stillness put on display at the end of her couch, perfect for a frame and a nail in the wall.

"Where is its replacement?" she asked.

He stood, "Do not waste your time," and walked past her. "You have more important tasks."

SIXTEEN

By the next day, Rodani had filled several pages in his notebook of Cara's translated lyrics. He studied his scribblings before he spoke.

"Do all human have varied interests and talents?"

Cara shifted her position on the floor. "No. One way humans categorize people is by the breadth and depth of their interests. On one side there is Iraimin. She paints. To the exclusion, as far as I have seen, of all else. She's deep." Cara slashed the air with a vertical cut of her hand. "Her mind goes on one track. You and I have many interests." She made a horizontal swipe this time. "We're broad. We ride many paths in life, switching from one to another as we wish, or as the need arises."

Rodani folded and unfolded a translated song in his nimble fingers. "Our culture honors the people who ride one path."

"As does ours, because they're the ones who become the true experts in their fields. But society needs people like us. People who can bring one area of knowledge to bear on another."

"Not Selandu society."

"Then you might be the one to teach them differently," she countered. "Don't denigrate yourself because of your wealth of skills. Our cultures need you."

"Why?"

Cara sighed. "Look at you, Rodani. Sitting, *on the floor*, face-to-face with a human. Singing her songs, of all things, and discussing the relative merits of cultural expectations versus personal abilities. You've not only learned to deal with a human on an everyday basis but have made a friend of one. What else might you do, given the opportunity?"

His pupils grew wide, then refocused on the paper in his hands. It was beginning to look a little tattered.

"I've disturbed you," she said quietly. "I'm sorry."

He tossed the apology. "You are pleasant company. It is your viewpoints that are—occasionally disturbing."

"They're not meant to be."

"I am aware."

"It's difficult to know what's offensive to discuss and what isn't."

A grin appeared on his lips, then disappeared again. "Of that, I am also aware." Cara rocked back with laughter. "But," he continued, "your words give me the courage to ask something else."

She was abruptly quiet. This was an unusual mood for Rodani. He seemed so vulnerable when he requested something of her. As if it weren't allowed. She waited.

"I would wish to learn your language."

Her eyebrows sprung upward, then drew down to meet in the middle. Rodani stopped fidgeting with the paper.

"Why?"

He pursed his lips. "To learn more songs?"

"I can translate more."

Fidgeting erupted. He crinkled the paper, then smoothed it out under his palm. He hesitated, looking out the window into a blue and grey sky. "I am bored, Cara. I am too old for advanced training, and trying would cause unwarranted assumptions in the guild. You are the most interesting occurrence in this manor in ten years."

"Surely no," she joked.

"In my opinion, yes."

"And likely, I'm also the most offensive occurrence in those years. Or more."

"The two are not unrelated."

Rodani's clear gaze settled into her brain. His dry humor tickled. And another layer of her guardian's reserve peeled away.

"Iraimin was correct," she muttered.

His pupils narrowed. "Correct?"

Cara gave a Selandu refusal with the turn of her head. Rodani folded the paper one last time and tucked it into his jacket pocket. "Am I answered?" he asked.

She folded her hands in her lap and thought. "Rodani, it's one thing for others to listen through a wire while you sing. But I don't want them to listen and learn Cene'l while you do."

"There is no wire, now."

Cara's eyes widened. "How do you know?"

"I told you Serano checked your rooms when you were in ours as the leak was being fixed. And," he tilted his head, "Deremic checks again every time you are out."

Eyebrows raised, she stared past him to her workroom. "I'm surprised Kusik let you do that."

"Arimeso has the final say."

"Oh," she said, smiling. "You walked right past him and up to the top."

Teach him Cene'l? It wasn't done without a tribunal meeting and massive amounts of red tape. That was part of the oath all graduates of the CSC took during the ceremony. But she hadn't graduated—was kicked out, actually. Unceremoniously dumped. There was little loyalty left for the tiny institution or its unfounded rules.

"It would take a lot of time and effort to become good at it," she said.

"That is my hope."

"Rodani, if I teach you, if you gain proficiency and teach others, one of those others may be—or become—an enemy of humans. And I'll have hurt my people."

He opened his hands, stretching slim fingers wide. "Then I will never teach."

"On the honor of the guild?" she asked.

Her words brought a stillness to his being. Unwavering violet eyes bored into hers. "On my honor as a guild guardian."

"Likely you will lose what you've learned after I'm sent home."

"Possibly. Letters do cross the hills."

Now that would be pleasant. The possibility of continuing her budding friendships was a thought that hadn't occurred to her. It might even provide a path for her return. *Thank you, Rodani.* "Alright, I'll teach you. Bring me some sheets of heavy paper."

"Yes."

Cara smiled. "The word you want is ^Okay^."

"What is ho-kay?"

The smile went wider. "Your first word. It indicates simple acceptance of a statement or command."

He left on his errand. Cara grabbed her notebook and wandered her rooms, making a hurried list of everyday nouns. At the window, she filled another page. Another half recorded the parts of the body and what clothing they wore. By the time Rodani returned, she'd gotten into verbs, and her hand was getting sore.

He produced his find. Cara took a sheet and held it to the light, then down to her list. "It'll do well, thank you." With Rodani's diligent help, they soon had a stack of blank flash cards. Cara began to write on them. "Pronunciation will probably be the hardest. Cene'l has little to no standardization in that area."

"Why?"

"It's a mix of different languages from all over our homeworld. Some words brought their own pronunciation with them, others were twisted as they were adopted."

"So how do I know the correct pronunciation?"

"Memorization. Or looking it up in a dictionary. It's the same with spelling, as well. Few rules and many exceptions."

He was disconcerted. It was a new look for him. Cara laughed and pointed the blunt end of her pen at the tip of his nose. "You wanted this."

It generated a curve of his lips.

"Reading, of course, will help the spelling."

Rodani finished cutting the last of the cards and laid her scissors on the worktable. "What shall I read?"

She ended the current word and crossed her arms on the table. "The few books I brought will be too difficult for quite a while. Are there children's books we could use?"

"Yes."

"Not borrow. Keep. I'd need to modify them."

"They can be found."

"Then that's your next errand," she suggested. "Begin with those having two- or three-word sentences, then work up from there."

"Ho-kay."

He bent to his task, and she returned to hers. With her list, she made a large stack of common words, then flipped the stack of words over one by one and wrote its translation on the back.

He eyed the tall pile near Cara's elbow. "Should I leave them or take them?"

"If you'll use them other times, other places, take them. If not, you can leave them. But..." she raised a finger. He made careful note of the finger. "Don't let anyone else see them. Obviously, the chain of informers and the taso will know soon. But don't tell anyone else."

He gathered up the ones they'd gone through and pocketed them in various places throughout his jacket. "I have a safe place for them."

SEVENTEEN

The next day, Serano headed down the stairs at a rapid clip and out to the stables. The open area echoed with the stamp of his boots, and the odor of benatac assailed his nostrils. Doors facing each other were adorned with ribbons of various colors and name plaques carved in dark berelwood that had been burnished to a shine. Serano unlocked the seventh door and stepped inside.

"Kibi-kibi-kibi," he nattered to the magnificent beast inside, and withdrew a bowl from his largest pocket, opening the lid. "Are you well, ki'ono?"

The three-year-old female nosed her buttery treat and licked the bowl to a shine within seconds. She snuffled Serano's face as he replaced the bowl in his pocket. He ran his hands down her long neck and across her side, checking the tension in the saddle strap and verifying the fasteners.

"Are you treated with honor?" he whispered. "Does the goddess smile upon you?" He tugged on the straps that were anchored to the bands encircling the benatac's incisors and rubbed one fuzzy ear. Satisfied that the stablehand had saddled her properly, he slipped his foot into the stirrup and pulled himself up, looping his bag onto the hook near his knee.

"Tck, tck."

The benatac nosed her door open and stepped out, claws clattering the stone floor. Serano rocked slightly with her gait, many years used to the motion. It hadn't taken long from guild graduation and entrance into the taso's household for him to make himself known to the stable's unstable beasts. From the time of his small town childhood when stories were told of homeworld exploits and explorations on beast back, Serano had ached for a chance to direct such power and grace.

The benatac made her way out into the sunshine and bent her head to the grass.

"Du." He tapped her with his feet. The mare began to trot. He tapped twice more, and she broke into a gallop, heading across the field on a collision path with a fence. Bent forward, Serano rode with her motion, his own hair a tail of silver flying behind him. She took the approaching turn on high. Serano hung on with every limb and appendage as she shot out of the corner and headed south. He guided her toward a low section of the fence and bent over her neck. She took the jump with practiced ease, flying over the wooden slats as if 300 pounds of Selandu male on her back made not an iota of difference.

The dirt road opened out before them, flat and inviting. The beast's hoofbeats clattered rhythmically. Cool wind and sunshine caressed Serano's face, relaxing the tension that had been gnawing at his innards. Down the road, round the bend that hid him from household eyes, his thoughts as well began to distance themselves from their origins.

Finally, he sat up, signaling to the benatac to slow her pace. They cantered down a path that led to an abandoned field that Arimeso's guild staff had appropriated and turned into another practice ground. Serano hauled on the reins, bringing the mare to a stop. He checked his Dienata and magazines, shook any residual tension from his shoulders, and headed toward the targets littering the field.

Accuracy wasn't easy on beast back. Few even attempted that at which Serano had fought to become proficient. There was no set path. Serano rode where he would over trampled remnants of foliage. He shot at each diamond-shaped target in the nearer section as the benatac cantered by it. After a couple of passes, he sped up and closed in on the next section, attempting each target at least twice as he wound a meandering way around the poles. With more hits than misses so far, Serano prided himself on his skill.

He took a minute's rest and another switch of mags, and a handful of grain to his mount. With a soft "tck-tck" he started her out to the next course, gun ready in his hand. With his body bent forward, he tapped her into high speed. Target after target flicked by at odd angles as he galloped and spun. He fought for each center circle that passed, body shifting from side to side in the twisting ride.

From the road came a clatter and rattle, accompanied by a woman's high-pitched shouting. Another benatac and rider came past the bank of trees in an undisciplined high-speed gallop. The woman was fighting to regain control of the beast, calling commands into unwilling ears. Serano jammed his pistol into its holster and took off toward the pair, anxious to catch them before they got out of sight again. He hurled out onto the path as the woman passed by, gaining the road as she reached the opposite stand of trees. The unruly benatac slowed under his rider's stern hand and sterner words, tossing its head and biting the air. It pawed the road and bucked as Serano reached them, resisting his attempts to grab the reins.

"Do not!" the woman shouted at Serano's well-meaning intrusion. The benatac twisted and skipped sideways. "I can manage! You have alarmed him thoroughly as it is."

Serano straightened in the saddle. "I?"

The woman's eyes flashed oval in the sun. "Were you not the one shooting as if all Temi's demons were after you?"

"I—was practicing."

Her eyes strayed from Serano to the neglected field with its randomly placed target posts, and back to his mare who shied and skittered in reaction to a temperamental male in her presence.

"Your attempt to render aid is appreciated, a'tem. I have no wish to delay your practice any longer." She ducked her chin to look down and away, then lifted her face to the road with a closed-off look to her eyes. She tapped the stallion into a trot.

Befuddled at the events that had gone grievously awry from his intent, Serano delayed for a moment, then rode out after her. He came up behind her and slowly pulled even, grinning at her steadfast refusal to acknowledge his presence.

"I might impart a few tricks on handling an unmanageable beast, a'sel."

Her gaze remained firmly on the road ahead. "He is already manageable, thank you."

"Not if he spooks at the sound of gunfire. He might have thrown you."

"I have been thrown before."

"It is wiser to ride to the side. Those who pass by drive with no thought to obstacles. You might be killed. You are new to the manor, are you not?"

"New to the manor, a'tem, not to the taso."

"Come over to the edge, please, te'ono. The death of an appealing woman such as you would be a great loss."

The look that came his way did nothing to dull his enthusiasm for a fresh game of chase and catch. But there was wisdom in his words; the woman followed him over onto the ground. Their mounts trotted neck and neck over the packed dirt path, the click of claws and tromp of padded feet muted.

"What is your name?" he asked.

No one was obliged to the attentions of a guardian, but propriety was always appropriate. "Larisi."

"I am Serano, Security Sixth."

Larisi turned in her saddle and studied him with a look of mild distaste in her face. "Your reputation seems justified, a'tem."

Serano leaned back in his saddle. "Reputation?"

"It precedes you into ignominy."

Serano beat his fist against his breast. "You wound me, te'ono."

"I am told the physician is available on rest-eves."

"Ah, but this is not a wound of the body, but of the soul," he said dramatically.

"Then I will attempt to procure an audience with the selaso for you."

"You are a priestess?" She wasn't dressed as one; not a bit of gold was to be found in her clothing. But certainly, the self-assurance was there.

"An acolyte. And I have already been warned of you."

"Because?"

"Because you have, by ones and twos, worked your way through virtually every acolyte and priestess in Kimasa's Enclave."

"One who holds the goddess's secrets makes an accomplished partner. Am I to be ashamed of accepting such charity?"

"Most do not call it charity."

"Honor decrees we should search out and assess facts, not decide on hearsay," he said.

"And wisdom teaches us to listen to the experiences of others."

Serano's heart warmed. This would not be effortless, but possibly worth the attempt. Daunted but not disturbed, he slid out of chase mode and into courteous attendance. Side by side, guardian and acolyte rode the dirt track back toward the stable grounds. Migrating birds clustered overhead into groups that formed, parted, and reformed back into clouds of flickering black and grey. Tic'idi serenaded the riders from in front and behind, falling into waves of frightened quiet as the benatacs passed by.

"Have you been an acolyte long, a'Larisi?"

"A short while."

"Most new acolytes have barely reached their majority."

Larisi gave him a withering look. "Neither are you a spring colt, a'tem."

He smiled. "I have no wish to be. Once in a lifetime is often enough to endure guild training. I have earned my status."

"And your notoriety."

They rounded the bend in the road. The stables came into view across the wide training fields. Larisi shouted to her stallion and gave him a mighty kick. He took off down the path toward the gate, powerful legs beating out a rhythmic thumpety-thump on the hard ground, long neck extended with effort.

Caught off guard, Serano pressed hard to catch up, but the stallion outpaced the slower mare. Not to be outdone, Serano angled southward toward the fence and the lowered staves that afforded his favorite jump in a shortcut. The mare bunched the muscles in her hindquarters and pushed outward, stretching with practiced ease to clear the hurdle. She pounded her way toward the stable's entrance as Larisi and stallion rounded the outside corner. It would be close.

They raced toward the entrance, his heart pounding with the thrill of this dual chase—public and private. He guided the mare into the doorway, begetting a chorus of protesting shouts down the corridor. Stablehands flattened themselves against the stalls as guardian and benatac rode full tilt past them, seemingly heedless of consequences. As Larisi rode in the north entrance, Serano hauled heavily on the reins to prevent a collision. The mare came to a stuttering, sliding stop in the rushes and launched into a claw-waving fury at the stallion, voicing her protest to the detriment of everyone's ears. Serano clung to the saddle as she reared up underneath him.

Serano straightened in his saddle and bowed formally to Larisi, then turned the mare and clicked their way back up the corridor to her stall. He dismounted and led her inside, grabbing a towel from the shelf just inside the door. Stablemaster Domendi strode down from his office. All averted their eyes as he passed by them to enter the stall with Serano.

EIGHTEEN

Rodani strolled to the workroom window. An autumnal blue sky and wisps of white clouds greeted him. Birds flocked across the horizon, cawing and twittering to each other, trying to reach a consensus on when to leave. He folded his hands behind his back and stared out at nothing.

"Are you well?" Cara asked him.

He turned away from the outside world to face his adashi. "Yes."

"Do you tire of giving and taking lessons?"

"No."

Cara waved her hand toward the study. "You can sing."

The study was quiet, dark, with the shutters folded to let in the afternoon sunlight. The dining table was pushed into the corner, the tea table empty of items, drinkable or otherwise. The 'corder was silent.

"I have no wish to disturb you further."

"You won't be disturbing me. You sing well."

His attention returned to the window. He placed his hands on the sill and leaned forward, inspecting the frame, the shutters, the wall above and below and to the sides.

"Singing is also a way to release pent-up emotions," she added.

"So I have noticed." Rodani waved to her sewing machine. "If you will continue the work for which the taso is agitating, I will sing."

He was taking an unconscionable lot of her time for personal reasons. Serano had been tracking close behind that one. A little caution was in order. Cara's primary responsibility here at the estate was her own crafting, not keeping a bored guardian from losing his edge, or catering to his eccentricities. Her creative outflow was greater than what Arimeso had expected. If it faltered, the taso would not be pleased. And she would know upon whose shoulders to rest the blame. Rodani's image of that confrontation was not a comfortable one. He tapped the worktable.

"Quilt. That is what you are here for. Not to learn to shoot or throw knives. Or to teach me to sing or speak Cene'l." He headed for the study. "Craft."

He clicked on the 'corder, sat in his favorite spot on the floor, and began to sing. Tentatively at first, he soon moved into a full-throated serenade. One song, two, three songs.

Cara got up and went into the study to sit on the floor in front of him. "May I sing with you?"

Rodani turned his focus on her and glanced at the worktable behind her. "What is your plan when Arimeso is angry at your diminished output?"

"Run?" she joked.

Silence filled the space between them. Rodani's expression fell into astonishment.

Cara leaned away from him. "Did I say something improper?"

"You would run in the face of punishment?"

Cara's face blanched. She looked away. "Earned, no, Rodani. Unearned? Yes. If I couldn't fight."

Rodani relaxed against the front of the couch. "Who decides what is earned and unearned?"

Cara fiddled with the ring on her finger. "We have people who decide on guilt or innocence, and punishment. But everyone is allowed to have an opinion. And there is room to run to other places if one feels unfairly persecuted."

"And how are those who run perceived?"

"It would depend. Some would call them dishonorable, cowards. Others would think them courageous and honorable to flee from unjust treatment."

"There seems to be a great deal of leeway in what is honorable for humans," he offered, staring at the fire. "Have you second thoughts about tonight?"

"Not enough to change my mind."

"Then eat lightly at dinner," he told her, and left the room with his usual dispatch. Cara got up and went back to her quilting.

***

After the rest-eve gathering, Rodani brought her back to the rooms he shared with his partner. Hands behind her for propriety and a show of respect, she wandered over to Rodani's bookshelf of creations. The portrait of a woman stared at her from across many years. Cara bent over to study her. A curve of the jaw, the arc of eyebrows—something clicked in Cara's brain, and she straightened to verify her guess in Rodani's face.

"She's a relative."

No answer is still an answer. Rodani turned his back and went over to the shelves that held the radio, pulling open a tall door.

"Your mother?"

"Yes." He lifted a bottle and glass and brought them over to the table.

"Alive?" she said softly.

"Yes." He poured himself a measure of eisenico.

Cara pulled the painting off the shelf and looked at it more closely. Slender, regal, Rodani's mother had one hand on her hip and the other draped casually down the line of her long skirt, and her head was cocked at an angle. She was staring straight ahead, unsmiling. Cara placed the picture back on the shelf and went over to the table to sit across from Rodani.

"Why that one?"

He took a sip. "You are full of questions tonight."

"The better to understand you, ^my dear^."

The Cene'l term confused him; the reference slid past unseen. "Is it necessary?"

Cara's face fell, as did her jaw.

"I have offended you," he said. "Forgive me."

"Questions and answers are necessary for two to be friends, Rodani."

"It is part of friendship?"

"Yes. Very much so."

A clatter and clink of glassware erupted behind them. There was a scrape and thump of a chair as Serano took his seat.

"Am I forgiven?" Rodani asked.

Cara hesitated. "A friendship develops with sharing of lives and knowledge, Rodani. Closeness doesn't grow without it." Rodani stared into her face, noncommittally. "Does that disturb you?"

He rubbed his hand across the table in a horizontal motion. "Not if I have control over what I share."

"Always, a'tem. I don't steal secrets. I request them boldly," she quipped.

"That you do."

"And part of the fun is wondering which will be revealed and which will not, and guessing at the answers for those withheld. My imagination could ride wild."

His expression set off a spate of laughter in her, extended unduly by a further narrowing of his pupils. Serano turned in his seat to investigate the alien uproar. Cara's arms were crossed over her; Rodani's were the same, but for different reasons. Wordless, the men let her go about her uncontrollable mirth, waiting for some evidence of sanity. Slowly she regained it, punctuated by minor outbursts.

Serano was intent on processing the herb's leaves as he had done the previous two rest-eves. Cara left Rodani to watch him. The accessory table in her guardians' quarters was more cluttered than usual. Her stomach began to roil in anticipation and fear. She had no idea what to expect, even with Rodani's attempt at an explanation of the effects. She knew changing her mind was still an option. Serano had made it clear she was not obliged, despite the fact that last week's tip-of-the-tongue-taste had caused no detrimental reactions. In fact, it had caused no reactions at all that she could tell. But Cara's curiosity had caught her, and her pride wouldn't release her. She swallowed the lump in her throat and waited.

"I can feel your tension from across the room, Cara, not to mention what appears on your face." Rodani took out a pack of cards and began to shuffle them. "If you insist upon standing over my partner's shoulder, you may inadvertently cause him to make a mistake." Serano's grey eyes sent a black look in his direction. "Come game with me," Rodani continued. "We can finish last night's run."

Cara took the hint and left Serano to his solitary task, seating herself opposite Rodani at the table. He dealt out the cards expertly.

"It is well you ate lightly at dinner," he told her. "Although you've felt no nausea so far, this will be a much stronger dose."

Cara picked up the cards and arranged them absentmindedly. "You told me not to, and I agreed. I'm nervous," she admitted. Even Serano seemed quieter than usual at the gathering, not his sociable self. Maybe the second thoughts hovering in the room were his.

Rodani closed his hand of cards, then re-opened and repositioned them with methodical precision. "You may still decline."

"Thank you, no." She drew and discarded. "You'll stay with me, as you said?"

"Yes. For the duration. Serano will stay until after you peak." Rodani drew his first card.

"Peak?"

Rodani held his cards near his chest and drew on the table with a fingertip. "The effect starts slowly, rises in a hill, then falls off again." Cara recognized a bell curve. "The top of the hill is called the peak. The effects are strongest then. The time period and height of the effects depend on the herb and the user."

^Okay,^ she said in her own language.

The play resumed.

Off and on, Serano's customers came by for their evening's entertainment. Cara felt vaguely ill at ease at the activity. Although both guardians had assured her Serano's activities were quite legal, Cara had the irrational fear that the next knock on the door would be the uniformed visage of the Glaniad sheriffs, as if she were at home. Resolutely, she turned her back and concentrated on the card game.

Three more hands went by before Serano was relieved of every dose in this week's batch except the one he'd saved aside for Cara. He took the small vial and walked over to the table in time to see her lose her thirty-second consecutive game.

"Have you changed your mind?"

"No." She took the vial from him. A small measure of translucent liquid resided therein. It was greenish in hue. "Where should I take it?"

"Where are you the most calm?"

Good question. Where she felt most comfortable was her study. She laid the cards on the table in a neat pile, got up, and headed for her rooms. The two men followed. Cara went into the study. "Should I do anything in preparation?"

"Use the facilities," Rodani said, "then relax in a chair or on the couch. Music is acceptable, as is anything else you might wish to do during the journey."

Cara took the advice, then settled onto the couch with a soft pillow and her sketchpad and pencil. Serano handed her the vial and moved one of the dinner chairs to a place opposite the low tea table in front of her. Rodani settled into the comfy chair between them, to her left. Both sets of reflective eyes steadied on her.

Gingerly, she uncapped the bottle and held it up to her nose. It was rank.

"Drink it, do not smell it," Serano said.

She grinned at him, then swallowed the noxious liquid as quickly as she could.

"Ugh. Water, please." She handed the vial back to Serano. He capped it and pocketed it.

Within a few moments, Hamman appeared with water, and Cara rinsed the taste from her mouth. "What now?"

"Wait," Serano replied, "and do what you wish in the meantime."

"Can I have the window open?" she asked.

Before he could answer her, Rodani spoke. "Shutters, yes. Window, no."

Her mouth turned down in frustration, then she reached out for the pad on the table and turned slightly to face Rodani. With practiced ease, she sketched a three-quarter portrait of her guardian. An outline of the head came first. The eyes came next, with particular care. If they're wrong, everything else is as well. The nose, the mobile mouth with the lower lip protruding in a pout. A little more emphasis to the jawline, a hint of hollow beneath the cheekbones, a curve of the swept back ear, a suggestion of the hair pulled back from his forehead, and she was done.

She turned to Serano and outlined the frontal view of his slender face. Looking at her guardians, after being there for months, she wondered why she ever had difficulty telling them apart. Serano's eyes were more closely set, not to mention the color. His lips were a little thinner, the chin more pointed, his head more oval.

As Cara finished the last touches to the sketch, she felt a lassitude wash over her. She had difficulty concentrating. Her hand didn't want to obey fuzzy orders. She flopped the sketchpad on the table and tossed the pencil down after it. The pencil rolled off the tea table and onto the floor. She watched it fall.

Unnoticed, her two guardians exchanged glances.

Disorientation began to overtake her. She tried not to panic, tried to study the effect and her reaction with clinical detachment, instead. Pillow in her lap, she stretched her slippered feet out and put her heels up on the table. Highly improper, but she didn't think they'd chastise her in this frame of mind. She stared at the embroidered slippers, fascinated with the pattern and colors that wove through the fabric. She studied the flow of color in the threads, trying to find rhyme and reason to the choices the crafter had taken. This, she didn't mind.

Mind? Where was her mind? How much time had passed? Seconds or hours? She stared at the pillow in her lap. In front of her eyes, it grew. It ballooned outward as if filled with air; her hands and arms shrank to winter-withered sticks on top of it.

"Cara?"

That was her name. Yes. Funny how it was pronounced. Her family never pronounced it that way. CAH-rah. She smiled at the sound it made in her head. *CAH-rah.*

"Cara?"

Name. Someone called her. Where was the voice? In front. She looked up into a pair of grey eyes that glowed magnificently.

"Where are you, Cara?"

Where. She knew where. Are you? *Yes, I'm Cara. Always have been.*

"Are you well?"

Word by word, Cara translated. She thought it out carefully, then retranslated her answer. "Sai." *Yes.*

"Music, Cara?" Rodani asked.

"Sai."

She watched the man with purple eyes rise from his chair. It took several seconds. Another few seconds, and he was standing by her 'corder. How did he get there? He hadn't crossed in front of her.

He picked a 'cording and pushed it in. Soft instrumentals filled the room. This time, Cara tracked him back to his chair. He waded through the air like it was water. His hair moved independently as if under its own volition.

Cara closed her eyes. Vision faded out and sound focused in. A song she liked. She listened, hearing each note separately in her brain. They mixed into incoherency, then back into order. Every instrument wove a separate path through her consciousness. The bass line throbbed through the floor and into the couch cushions, warming her from below. Her heart beat in time with it.

After a year's contemplation, she decided to get up and go over to the 'corder. She opened her eyes. Another month passed, and she put her fists down by her hips. Push up. On feet. Where were her feet? Somewhere beneath her, maybe. The floor tilted, then leveled again. She walked but didn't know how. The walls in her vision dipped and swayed.

Dark. Too dark. She floated over to the lantern's switch and turned it. Lights flared up, then dimmed. Bruises on her eyelids flared and melted into sparkles.

In unison with the music, the walls rotated back and forth on a vertical axis through the center of the room. The woodgrain pattern on the study door came to life. It spun slowly and undulated like an amoeba, formed a face, then dissolved again into randomness. Back on the couch, Cara sat motionless for an eon or two, fascinated with the ever-changing patterns.

"Eshi'nu atamai colasa, Cara?"

The syllables stretched themselves out into infinity and distorted into a low moan. Frightened, she shook her head to clear it. But there was no recognition. She faced the speaker with the grey eyes. Panic began to fill her mind. *What did he say? Say?* Her eyes widened in fear; her breathing became rapid. Lost. She was lost!

A weight bowed the couch, making her lean toward it.

"Cara?"

Her head spun to face the new sound. Her hands shook; Rodani held them.

"Ti sua ma'in?" he said softly.

No translation. Nothing. She tried to free her hands and stand, but he held tightly. The room spun around her, making her dizzy. Her pulse pounded in her ears. ^What are you saying?^ she asked in Cene'l.

He continued to speak in Selandi, softly, slowly. The words flowed past her, unintelligible. She swallowed convulsively; her eyes blinked rapidly. She shook her head. ^I don't understand you.^

^Okay,^ he said in her language. ^You are okay.^ Carefully, he pulled her into an embrace and held her, whispering to her.

Her skin tingled where Rodani's hands rested. As he drew his hands down her back, chills of pleasure crawled up her spine and tickled her scalp. Her breathing slowed; she closed her eyes. Patterns formed and reformed on the insides of her eyelids in time with the rise and fall of Rodani's caresses. Concentric ovals swelled from a pinpoint and swept out beyond her vision. Lines grew and crisscrossed, then faded out again. With each wave of pleasure up her spine, fireworks exploded in reds, greys, yellows, and whites.

As a favorite song came on, she got up and stood in front of the 'cording player. Eyes closed, she moved with the rhythm while song after song played within her and through her, occasionally distorted as to be almost unrecognizable, sometimes as beautiful as the best symphony.

Cara was totally inward now, unaware of who or what was around her. She sat down next to Rodani's legs, her back against the couch. She closed her eyes again, face serene with visual and aural hallucinations.

In a little while, Cara sagged and lay back on the thin rug. Someone lifted her head to put something soft underneath it. She stretched her legs out and crossed her ankles, then slipped her hair clip out from underneath her neck and fumbled to unroll her hair. Her strongest sense had swelled during this peak time. Every fingertip was alive with sensation. Even as she held them motionless, they tingled. When they touched her hair, she could feel every strand, every curl. Every cell.

Hair clip in one hand, she let the fingers of the other travel across it with infinite slowness. The design that had been carved in the clip expanded into mountains and valleys that her fingers caressed. Later, she would swear that every ridge of skin on her finger held a nerve that lead directly to the pleasure center of her brain. For now, she was content simply to touch. Back and forth, back and forth, so slowly, one could hardly tell she was moving.

Gradually, as the fourth hour turned into a fifth, Cara's sensations traveled from her fingertips to a more sensitive spot further down. She didn't notice it at first, but it soon became difficult to ignore. Cara put the clip aside and began to think.

Think. Yes, it was easier to do that now. She opened her eyes to the world that had slipped away. Mostly it held steady. An occasional odd movement of a piece of furniture or a spot on the wall was all she noticed now. But the warmth in her groin was fast becoming an itch that needed scratching.

She sat up. Rodani, still at her side, wrapped his arms around his knees and watched, waiting. Concentrating, Cara tried to dampen the unexpected desires. But as the minutes passed she began to realize the futility of her efforts.

Still a little unsteady, she climbed to her feet and headed for her bedroom. Rodani followed. She shut the door in his face and locked it. Cara sat on the edge of the bed, arms across her waist. The lock rattled again, and Rodani walked in. She looked up in surprise. "Du!"

"You cannot be by yourself, Cara. Do you understand me?"

"Sai."

"Is there a problem?"

Translations she could do; dredging up the proper words to speak was still beyond her capacity. And the subject matter was pretty much off limits.

"Du. Berai, ashi." *Go, please.*

"Du."

Frustrated by both him and her drug-induced desires, she strode past her earnest guardian and back into the study. She grabbed the quilt off the couch, wrapped it around her, and went to the window. Before she could come to a stop, Rodani was beside her, ready to keep her from opening it. Cara stared into the black night in a vain hope that something would distract her. But when nothing did, she tucked her head to her chest as she fought inner temptations.

Holy space dust, this was insane. She knew her body's own natural desires. But this was a volcano next to a warm cup of tea. Cara was acutely aware of Rodani's tall form next to her and the fact that he was very much male. But fear and her ignorance of Selandu biology kept her wrapped in her fabric shelter. She turned back to the couch and sat down. Rodani took the chair opposite her that Serano had vacated. Both sets of eyes were on her.

A shiver fell down her spine and lodged where she wished it wouldn't. She was not averse to pleasing herself on occasion, but good gods—not in front of an audience. Not of any shape, sex, or species. She lay down on the couch, back to her guardians, still wrapped in the quilt. She covered her head, giving in to the vivid imagination in which she took so much pride. And with drug-enhanced senses, imagination alone was almost enough. But not quite. It left her aching with frustrated desire. There were no more flashes behind her eyes, no more aural distortions. Just an overpowering desire that she couldn't satisfy where she lay. She pulled the quilt more tightly around her.

Rodani watched her intently.

"Remember your honor, tem'u," Serano warned him with narrowed eyes. "And the guild rule."

"I have not forgotten," Rodani said sharply, as Serano exited the room.

She was still on the couch, motionless. Rodani felt some distress for her, knowing the strength of his own desires during his few journeys. But he couldn't leave her alone. He stared out the window into the night sky that had so held Cara's fascination and waited for time to pass.

Finally, the quilt stirred, and Cara sat up. She looked around in some confusion. Rodani leaned forward in the chair.

"Are you well?"

She thought that one through, taking a little longer than normal. "Yes."

She stood up quickly, then lost her balance. In a flash, Rodani was at her side, steadying hand on her arm. He watched her closely, trying to decide whether it was safe to let go or not.

"Sleep," she said.

He released her and trailed her back through her workroom into the bedroom.

The sense of disorientation was still there, a dizziness she couldn't shake loose from her brain. She was tired. Her eyelids felt heavy. "It seems to be over. You can leave if you wish. And thank you."

"Can you sleep?"

"Likely."

"If the herb is still in your system, you cannot. When you go to sleep, I will leave."

Cara fumbled with her slippers. Kicking them off, she reached out to pull the quilts back from her bed. She climbed in, clothes still very much on. Wisely, Rodani made no mention of the fact. Whys and wherefores were unnecessary. He brought a chair around to her bedside.

As the herb left her bloodstream and nervous system, she became more and more sleepy. Occasionally, she closed her eyes to rest. She curled up around her pillow, quilts draped over her. In the middle of the large bed, it made her look even more childlike.

The times when her emotions overflowed and became the driving force behind her actions she seemed only a child in an adult-shaped body. Other times, when she quilted or taught, laughed, sang, or socialized during gatherings, he could see her only as very much an adult. The dichotomy wove a disturbing tapestry in his mind. With some relief, he watched Cara's body relax into slumber. He looked at his 'com. Over seven hours had passed. He waited a little to make sure she remained asleep, then quietly left her rooms to seek his own.

NINETEEN

Bright light hurt her gritty eyes and there were cobwebs in her brain. Cara rolled over and contemplated sitting up. At least she was alone in her room. Her last memory was of Rodani sitting in her chair in the semi-darkness, eyes reflecting softly.

She'd survived. Unreality still clung to her like the spray of an airbrush, coloring the room's furnishings with a shade of abnormality. The door still played a few tricks on her eyes—the patterns shivered playfully in her blurry vision. Strange what a plant could do to the mind and body. She rubbed her fingertips together, but there was nothing out of the ordinary left to her sensations. No glimpses of the goddess. A few new design possibilities, maybe. Nothing much else but an aching body. It confused her for a moment, then she remembered. Remembered the heat that had flooded her, and the social impossibility of responding to it.

Gods of the deep night. Did the herb affect Selandu the same way? If humans got hold of such an aphrodisiac, the whole species would copulate itself into ruination. She shuddered at the thought, and the memory of last night. Of Rodani standing next to her at the window, tall and graceful. It was a good thing he didn't know what was happening to her, and what she was thinking wrapped up in her quilt. Occasionally, it was true; ignorance is bliss. For them both.

She wandered into the workroom. Her current project laid in its frame, supremely uninteresting to her eyes this rest-day. After opening the shutters just enough to allow some sunshine, she pulled the chair back and straddled it, hunkering down near the windowsill. The stone sill was rough, and tiny pebbles littered it. Irritated, she brushed them off onto the floor. Visual disorder didn't bother her. But aural and tactile chaos drove her crazy. The former caused her dislike of angry voices; the latter, a penchant for picking the tiny pills off fabric, splinters off of tables, and rough edges off her fingernails.

She turned at a familiar sound. Rodani stepped out of her bedroom doorway and came over to the window, peering out.

"I thought the window would be open."

"I thought about it. Didn't wish to hear your censure."

"And your safety?"

"Is there a gun that shoots from the forest to my window?"

Rodani declined to answer.

Cara returned to the windowsill, resting her chin on the pillow. The outside world looked inviting, lacking the obvious confrontations that popped up all too often.

"What did you think?" he asked.

"Of the window? The world?"

"Of last night."

"As you said, very interesting. Very confusing. Did I do anything regrettable?"

"No. I would not have allowed it. What do you remember?"

"Patterns. Patterns on the doors, patterns on my eyelids. Time distortions. Aural distortions. Incredible tactile sensations." She smiled out the window. "Incredible."

"Do you remember being frightened?"

"For a minute, yes. Thank you for calming me."

"It seemed appropriate."

She watched a yosi wheel away, flapping its wings in an effort to move north against the wind. Cara felt an overwhelming longing to follow it, flapping her arms in flight like the children of fairy tales.

"What will you do today?"

The deep voice startled Cara out of her reverie. "Mmm. Sit here at the window until I am bored, or until you tell me I have been unsafe long enough." She turned her head to rest her cheek on her hand. "Then read until I am bored with reading. Listen to music until I am bored with listening to music. Pester you to take me outside until I get a yes or you get angry at my disregarding your nos."

Rodani pushed on the shutters, passing them in front of her nose and dislodging the pillow from its place. They clicked shut as Cara retreated from the sill.

"I came to inquire upon your well-being. There are things I have need of doing this morn."

Damn. Two refusals, back to back. She didn't even bother to watch him exit her room. Tired of her, obviously. She didn't own him. She was his job, for all the gods' sake. It was his rest day. He had his own life. Iraimin did, even if Cara didn't know what it was. Falita did. Unfailing in her daytime duties, she was never around in the evenings. Ditto for Hamman, backwards. Serano...well, everyone knew what Serano did in his spare time.

She was stuck in a trap she'd walked herself into. Three months had never seemed long until she'd relinquished her freedom. She retrieved her stationery set and pen from the study and sat back down at the workroom's window. Cara re-opened the shutters (but kept the window closed), pulled out a sheaf of paper, and rested her head on her arm, low profile, writing letters.

When she was done, she relaxed into a drowse, pillow protecting her arms from the stone ledge.

The horizon seemed a million miles away. To the north and west, great tracts of forest formed a fuzzy carpet that faded into the distance. East, the woods thinned to stands of trees erupting in the midst of patchwork quilted fields, beyond which was a low line of cliffs. Directly west was the Tuka estate run by Sagadad, who was Arimeso's nearest neighbor. Allied, luckily. No border skirmishes for this taso.

"Cara?"

The pillow almost fell. She grabbed it and turned. "Iraimin!"

The painter swept into the room with her obligatory long skirts aswirl. "I hoped you would visit. I seem to be the one fated to intrude upon your solitude."

"Please intrude. I have too much solitude. And Rodani is busy elsewhere."

Much more comfortable than in earlier visits, Iraimin eyed Cara with a gleam almost impish in nature. "Busy? Busy arguing, it seems."

"Arguing?" Cara waved Iraimin into the study and turned on the largest lantern. Gossip deserved comfortable accommodations. "With whom?" They sat on opposite ends of the couch.

"An outlier."

"What's an outlier?"

"Someone not residing on the estate."

"Where? How long ago? What were they arguing about?"

"More than an hour, in the lower northeast hallway. I heard little. But there was something said about him not having much time. She seemed quite annoyed."

She? "What did he answer?"

"That he had many duties."

"You heard nothing more?"

"It was not wise to remain in the area," Iraimin admitted. "There was no way to conceal my intentions with other activities. But at the end of the hall, I looked back. The woman was walking away."

"And Rodani?"

"Watching her."

Cara's shoulders drooped, and her eyes went wide. "It's my doing."

"Yours?"

"I asked him to socialize with me. Because I need it, he feels obligated. Now he has even less time of his own."

"The goddess wills, Cara," Iraimin said with conviction.

"Wills my loneliness? Wills his loss of a woman's affection? Why would the goddess do that?"

"He is being tested."

"For what?"

"Sela keeps her secrets."

Falita brought in a tray, then left. Cara regarded the unexpected tea curiously.

"I ordered it as I passed through," Iraimin offered. "Is that improper?"

"No. Thank you." Cara poured two cups and slid the tray nearer to Iraimin, who added sweetener and milk and lifted the cup delicately.

Cara raised hers as well, sweetener only. "Why could the reason not be the vagaries of life?"

"The goddess does not work in that way."

"What if She's not doing it? What if She forms you, then steps back and lets you go your own way?"

"She does not. She gives us our skills and our temperament and guides us along our paths."

"And Rodani's path is filled with thorns and stable sweepings?"

"Possibly. We cannot read the future."

The tea was hot. Almost too hot for Cara to drink, though Iraimin sipped hers with no sign of discomfort. Cara took a careful sip. "Why would She do that to him?"

"To prepare him for other things."

"And if those other things don't appear? If he ends up with his life the same as it is now?"

"Then the goddess will nestle him close when he crosses over."

Cara held her teacup at chin level and stared into the wavering fire. "Forgive me, Iraimin. I wouldn't treat my children so cruelly."

"Comfort for all times in the bosom of the goddess is more comforting than any to be found in life."

"Has anyone returned from the crossing to tell you so?"

Iraimin eyed her levelly. "You are full of heresies."

Cara dropped her gaze to the ornate copper teapot on the tray. A dot of tea lay below the curving spout. "It's not my religion. My people gave up worshipping a goddess."

"Your people could find Her again. Many here would help."

"I don't need Her. Thank you, anyway."

"Then She has not yet tested you."

Cara set the cup back on the tray and glowered at it. "Please don't assume my life has been easy."

Iraimin's eyes widened. "I have offended you. Forgive me."

Cara tossed the apology. "Likely, my patient companion, I've offended you a dozen times over. I should apologize."

"You are alien."

That seemed to sum it all up. Everyone's view of her. Strange. Full of heresies and improprieties. Misunderstandings that must be met with obligatory patience. Or a swift slap. She was thankful again that Serano wasn't her primary guardian. Would she ever be accepted? Three months was not enough time. Not nearly. Especially when she was kept closeted off from all but a few. And fewer than those few dared to look inside her heart and mind.

"So, what does your goddess hold in store for me?" Cara asked.

Iraimin shifted the cup in her hands. "I make no pretense of divining Her plans."

Cara smiled. "An easily defendable position."

"The only position to take."

"And what do you see as your life's path?" Cara asked her.

"To paint. For my good, for the taso's, and for the goddess's."

"And the other areas of your life?" she asked softly. "The less public life?"

Iraimin's expression closed down abruptly. "It remains obscure."

"Isn't everyone's future obscure?"

Iraimin sipped her rapidly cooling tea. "The taso's is not. Nor Kusik's. Nor Kimasa's."

Cara turned toward the center of the couch, bringing one knee up on the cushion. "But are they happy in what they do? Do they wish a change?"

Iraimin's stare was solid, unaccusing, and uncomprehending. "Why would they?"

"An idle question, Iraimin. For idle minds."

"I have never seen your mind idle, Cara. Even when you are quiet, there are questions in your eyes."

Cara laughed. Iraimin even responded with a smile of her own.

"Did you leave a mate behind?" the painter asked.

The question abruptly sobered her. "No." She dug her fingers into the rough weave of the couch's fabric. "I have had no more luck with men than Rodani seems to have with women."

"Why?"

"Eccentricities. No one has found me compatible."

"It is a burden, is it not?" Iraimin said, almost softly.

All of a sudden, the gulf that had seemed uncrossable just got a little narrower. Cara suppressed an urge to hug her. "Yes."

"Someday, I will paint your portrait."

"Mine?"

"Yours. I should not wish to lose the opportunity to paint the only human I have ever met or am likely to meet."

Cara froze. "Arimeso has already decided no one will replace me when I return?" It was another sobering thought.

Iraimin was silent for a moment. "Your mind travels unexpected paths."

"I'm alien."

"And your paths seem to be drawn to the dark."

"To the dark?" Cara asked, eyebrows raised.

"Your assumptions are often unpleasant ones."

"They have a greater chance of being correct."

"The goddess brings light as well as dark."

Cara chuckled dryly. "She had better hurry."

Iraimin pursed her lips and glared at her with steel-grey eyes. "One does not lay orders upon the goddess."

"Forgive me," Cara said with another wave of the hand. "Does She accept petitions?"

"Yes. Shall I take you to the selaso?"

"No," she said, drawing out the word in emphasis.

Iraimin poured another cup of tea and glanced into the workroom. "I saw the new target board next to your door. That is for knife practice. Yes?"

"Yes."

"Yours? Or his?"

"Both."

"Do you practice often?"

"Only with Rodani. He keeps the knives."

"Why?"

"Afraid I will accidentally aim for the servants, or some such," Cara said morosely. "I haven't figured it, yet."

"Guardians have a tendency toward exaggeration of dangers."

"Rodani even chided me for looking out the window this morning."

A look of disbelief crept across Iraimin's face. But there was no such impropriety voiced. "Your life is quite constrained, is it not?"

"On beautiful days such as this, I almost feel like a captive."

Iraimin sat back and regarded Cara calmly. "I am visiting my sisters, today. Would it please you to accompany us?"

The offer stunned her a moment. "I—yes. Yes, it would." Cara stared down at her hands. "Would they accept me?"

"On my word, yes."

"I have to ask Rodani. He'd shoot me if I left without his permission."

"Unlikely."

"Not so unlikely. And even if he doesn't, I wouldn't wish to hear what he had to say to me when I returned. He'd put even more restraints on my life. After he knocked me flat to the floor for my disobedience. I have no wish to endure either headache."

Iraimin rose from the couch. "Then we ask."

But after a quick call from the servants' room, Iraimin headed back down the hallway with an absent-minded thank you to Falita, leaving Cara to trail behind.

"The answer seemed obvious," Cara began as they reseated themselves on the couch. "But what did he say? May I ask?"

Iraimin warmed her tea with another addition and leaned against the corner where back met armrest. "You could not be allowed to go unescorted. We could not protect you," she spoke in a testy, chanting voice. "He does not know my sisters. He would have to accompany you and felt his presence would be an intrusion. You would not be allowed in town. He could not guarantee your safety."

Cara pulled the embroidered pillow into her lap. "This isn't unexpected."

"Do you receive such answers often?"

"No, I've had no opportunity such as you so generously offered. But I've heard enough of guild safety rules to begin to think as he does and anticipate his reactions. I guessed correctly."

"Does it displease you?"

Cara leaned her head against the couch and tucked her legs up. The pillow's soft covering soothed her agitated fingers. "Yes. But I have no wish to be shot by some angry Riverchild while I'm outside the manor."

"You believe that might happen?"

"Might? Yes. Likely? I can only assume the guild knows the possibilities. I don't."

"Rodani has you frightened of our people."

It was an accurate assessment. She thought the fear had come from inside herself, but a look back at her first month reminded her of the lack of fear that had sent her exploring the huge house and its surroundings. "His duties force him into it. I'd never want to be a guardian."

"Nor would I."

"What will you and your sisters do today?" Cara asked.

"Socialize. Eat the dinner our father will be cooking. Discuss who we wish the goddess would remove from the face of the world, and who we wish She would bring into our lives."

"Ask Her to have a handsome, courteous mate waiting for me when I return home, please," Cara said, smiling.

"I will ask," Iraimin responded gravely, as if it were a duty conscientiously accepted.

"I regret not being allowed to go."

"Rodani did say if my sisters visited me here, he would have no objections to allowing them to meet you."

"Kind of him," Cara deadpanned, then added more genuinely, "I'd be pleased."

"My sisters will scandalize him."

A mischievous glint appeared in Cara's eyes. "Then I will as well. He needs scandalizing. He's too…correct. Too proper."

"That is his outer wrapping. He must be proper on the outside because he carries improprieties in his inner nature."

"Do you know him so well?"

"No." Iraimin set her cup down on the tray. "That I have seen, no one but Serano seems to. But the goddess gave me a gift. An ability to see inside people. To decipher some of the puzzle that resides in them. It helps me paint."

***

Rodani stomped down the hall in a foul mood. Fellow Selandu gave him a wide berth at the facial expression he didn't care to hide. It wasn't his fault he had so little spare time. The hallway rejection he'd just faced reminded him all over again that guardians didn't make good life mates.

The keso's office door came into view. He raised his fist to pound out his tempers, then stopped and chided himself for the near mistake. Kusik hadn't sounded in any better mood when he ordered Rodani to report to him. He stood outside the door, just breathing, until his ear tips stopped twitching.

He knocked and entered at the acknowledgment. Serano was already there, standing in front of the desk. Rodani took his place beside him, facing their keso.

"I am displeased," Kusik said, quietly.

Rodani held himself stiff and silent, knowing that his keso's soft voice was no less dangerous than his shouting.

"When I gave you permission to administer the herb to the human, I had hoped for a more," he paused, "useful outcome. One that would damage. One that would maim. One that would send her crawling back across the hills."

"A'Keso," Serano offered, "I did mention that I thought it would be unlikely. Though we could not be sure."

Kusik leaned back in his chair. "You could have given her a stronger dose."

Serano's eyes went wide. "A'Keso," was all he could manage.

Temi's knives! Rodani thought. *Are we to be poisoners?*

"And now," Kusik continued, "have you heard there is another issue?"

The partners glanced at each other. "No," was the dual response.

"There are rumors. Rumors walking the hallways, skulking behind closed doors. Rumors imbibing in the festive room." He laid one hand on the butt of his gun as it rested against his hip. "Rumors that she is somehow dissatisfied in our home."

"Dissatisfied?" Rodani ventured cautiously. "Of...?"

"Nearly everything, a'tem. Her food. Her rooms. Her servants. Her restrictions." Kusik leaned forward. "Her guardians."

"I have heard nothing of the kind, a'Keso," Rodani replied, disturbed at a revelation he didn't trust.

"Maybe someone else wishes her gone, a'tem," Kusik said in a smug undercurrent.

"Who?" Rodani spat. "Someone not on the list?"

"You will speak to her of this, Rodani. You will remind her of agreements. Of promises. Of dangers."

Rodani stared at the far wall, feeling the tempers that rode along his nerves. "A'Keso."

Kusik dismissed them with a wave.

"Tem'u," Serano began, outside the door.

Ignoring him, Rodani headed for the central stairs at a rapid clip that caused heads to turn. Up the stairs, down the hall, and through the door. He came to a dead stop at the sight of the open shutters over Cara's worktable. He slammed them shut, then strode into the study to face two startled women and a spill of tea. "I closed those earlier."

Cara glanced at Iraimin, whose expression was blanked of emotion. "Yes. But the window was closed."

"Would you have gone off with Iraimin and her sisters, also? It may be well I checked."

"No, Rodani," she said, annoyance in her voice. "I would not have. Please place your anger on someone who deserves it, not me." She turned her attention back to Iraimin's revelations. "What else does your gift see inside of him?"

Iraimin's eyes pulsed at the provocation. "Great honor," she said, "and great pain."

Rodani remained rooted to his spot while the two women played a dangerous game. His temper bubbled just beneath the surface.

Cara got up and poked the sleepy fire. "When do you meet your sisters?"

"Soon," Iraimin said.

"I'd be pleased to meet them some day." She dropped the poker and sat back down.

"Yes." Iraimin rose from the couch and excused herself from the room.

Rodani was in no mood to leave. He walked in between the

fireplace and tea table and stopped.

"Forgive me for pulling you away from your rest-day activities, Rodani," Cara said, resting her feet on the table. "That was not my intention."

Rodani studied her expression. *Sincere? Impudent?* He couldn't tell. "I would prefer you apologize for opening the shutters after I closed them."

Cara flung her hands outward. "Rodani, if I can't see and feel the world outside, I'll wither like a potted plant kept indoors too long."

"And if you hang your head out the window for very long, you may lose it. One more time, a'Cara."

"The window was closed!" she retorted. "I had a pillow under my arms. It covered most of my head from those on the ground."

"One more time," he said slowly, "and I will have them bricked up." At his threat, emotions flowed over her face too quickly for Rodani to decipher.

"You were letting me have them open if the window was closed. Why are you changing your mind?" she demanded with a raised voice.

"I have that right."

"And that doesn't answer my question," she retorted.

"The answer is *not* something you need to know. Obedience is my intention. You can never be sure when danger is near." Ice. He put ice in his voice in the hope she was astute enough to hear it.

Cara's jaw dropped, and she looked at him with a side-eye. "You heard something." Into Rodani's silence, she added, "What did you hear?"

He stilled his body, giving her nothing but a cold, predatory gaze. *Heed me. Obey me.*

"Stop staring," she demanded.

Still as stone, he fixed his focus on her, silently willing her into obedience.

"Stop!" she shouted.

He blinked.

Cara shot out of her seat and into the workroom, then slammed on the brakes when she grabbed the bedroom door handle with an attempt to slam it shut.

"It is well you learned that lesson from our fight, Cara."

She trembled in the doorway, but didn't turn to face him, didn't unclench her fists.

"Cara, I have no wish to fight with you again."

She unfroze and faced him. "But you'll frighten me into running from you?"

There was no withdrawal in this confrontation. No backstep in the need for security. "I cannot risk you repeating earlier mistakes. Nor can you."

"I opened the shutters!" She flung her arms out.

"I sense a change in you."

Her angry expression turned to something he thought was puzzlement. Then embarrassment, possibly.

"Maybe you do, Rodani. And maybe you misinterpret. Excuse me." She stepped into the bedroom and shut the door in his face.

He opened it. She spun and took a step back.

Rodani studied her eyes, and the agitation in her body. "Calm yourself."

"You should have taken that advice a few minutes ago, a'tem."

"I have."

"It's extremely improper to open a woman's bedroom door without permission."

"It is also improper to walk out on a discussion before it is resolved."

She turned her back to the wall, her side facing him. Not dismissal, certainly. But not accepting of the situation. "I said all I wished to say until I can calm down."

"Had I said all I needed to say?" he retorted.

She gave no answer.

"Have you calmed?"

She paused. "Not enough."

"Do you need comfort?"

Her eyes widened abruptly, and her mouth turned down. "No. Thank you."

"I will wait."

She grimaced and turned toward the armoire. "I can't calm down when you're hovering."

"I will try not to disturb you."

"Your anger is disturbing me!"

"You are losing your calm."

Cara swore and banged her fist against the armoire with a force that jerked her whole body. She turned around to face him. He was still there. Waiting, as he had said, patiently. "What do you still need to say?"

Jump to the end of the trail, temichi. This path is going nowhere. "Cara, do you wish to return home?"

Her jaw dropped. "Home? Who said? What did they say?"

"That you were dissatisfied with your life here." His pupils narrowed. "That your servants and guardians displease you. That you are not shown the respect you deserve as an artisan and as a guest."

Cara glowered at him, curling her lip. "Lies, Rodani."

"Often it is difficult to discern the liar from the truth teller."

"You call me a liar?" She raised her hands in entreaty. "What do I gain from lying about a desire to go home? If I wanted to go, I'd ask. Where's the sense in lying?"

"Sense is debatable between species."

"What would I gain?"

"Lost status of those who you feel wronged you," Rodani replied heatedly. "Political discord. Trouble for the taso."

She shook her fist in the air. "That's the very last thing I want. I know the consequences. Have I acted as if I want to go home?"

"Not that I have seen."

"Then someone is lying about me."

Rodani thought back to Kusik's meeting. "More than one someone."

"No, Rodani." She raised a finger. "Only one person need lie—the one starting rumors. The others simply have to believe him."

It made sense to him, but... "I should believe you?"

Her eyes went wide. "I've never lied to you."

He studied her for a moment. "I would prefer to believe that."

"Then believe how I act, not what others say."

Back to the beginning, a'tem. "The shutters stay closed unless I am here."

"And you haven't told me why." She shook her hands in agitation.

Rodani stared down at his adashi, sensing anger and frustration in her words, her gestures. His own thoughts swirled uncomfortably in his head. He watched Cara as she meandered the room, remembering his taso's early words: *Keep her content so that she may concentrate on crafting.* "Would it help if we went outside for a time?"

She spun around with a surprised look. "Yes!" Then leaned back, her expression changing to something he wasn't quite sure of. "If we don't argue anymore."

"Are you calm enough?"

She closed her eyes and took in a breath. "I can be, if you are."

He nearly retorted the same statement, but bit it back. He had to keep reminding himself of her labile emotions—while ignoring his own that had just flared—and the fact that her reactions seemed tightly tied to his. "I will."

TWENTY

The road led east. Way southeast, an hour or more. Serano drove the carriage with some temper. Cara put her hands out on the seat on either side of her legs to counteract the pull of his high-speed turns.

"Serano," Rodani said quietly.

There was no answering look from his partner, but the wild weaving diminished. Farmlands gave way to forest. An occasional glimpse through the trees afforded Cara a view of the vertical distance they were climbing. Cara pressed her nose up against the left side window.

The road ended in a rocky clearing. Three forest paths took off from it, east, west, and north. Rodani and Serano climbed out, each pulling a large pack from the back. Cara trailed them, grabbing the food basket from Rodani before he slammed the door shut.

Serano headed north, Cara following.

"Tsss."

Rodani was heading west. Cara changed direction, scurrying to catch up with him before he was lost to sight among the trees. Their path struck a direct course through the undergrowth, giving way only for the massive trunks of the never-die trees. It led to a dead end at the edge of a cliff. With a view and a vertical drop that left her breathless.

Cara dropped the basket and sidled toward an edge unrestricted in its dangerous access. A yard from the drop, she went to hands and knees, then crawled forward to peer over the edge.

Instant vertigo.

It was a sheer drop of a thousand feet to a pebbly shore of house-sized boulders overgrown with trees. Wind caught at her hair and jacket, threatening for a moment to tumble her out where only the yosi thrive. Cara scooted backwards and sat on her heels, looking at the expanse of lowland spread out for a hundred miles to the northwest. A crazy quilt covered the land, brights turning to greys and muted purples as distance stole the intensity from the colors. She drank in the sight, the taste of the air, the scent of the forest. She stripped off her jacket and unclipped her hair.

"I could almost believe in your goddess, Rodani." She turned in his direction. The wind blew strands of hair over her face. He was watching her bemusedly.

"Almost?" He stepped forward and crouched down next to her, leather jacket crinkling as he folded himself into a silver and black ball. Wind whipped the hair that fell down his back in a three-inch-wide waterfall. "It deserves extended contemplation."

"It's beautiful. But why is there no fence?"

"No one comes here except accompanied by guild. As well, a fence would destroy the beauty. Do not," he said, "become accustomed to the edge."

He rose and returned to the pack he had dropped next to the basket, then pulled out a blanket. With a massive flap of his arms, the blanket flew open and landed haphazardly on the ground between them. Almost against her will, Cara turned away from nature's expansive beauty to help her friend. She weighed down the corners with rocks as Rodani dug into the basket. He poured them each a drink before finding a comfortable spot on the blanket. Cara sat near him, both facing the cliff edge.

Wind rattled dry leaves above them, sending an occasional one down within their notice. Rodani sipped his eisenico in a steady, measured rhythm. He stared out into the distance, silent regard matching silent vista. His knees were tucked under his chin, his arms wrapped around his shins.

Cara folded her legs in front of her as she sat, not too close to Rodani but not so far away, either. A flock of fechi, black and white against a blue and white sky, passed by on their way to southern mating grounds. Spring would find them flying back, fledglings trying to keep up.

Ten minutes, fifteen, twenty passed in companionable silence. Then Cara set her drink down on the basket top and crawled to the edge of the cliff. With a side-hand throw, she tossed a stick out into the open air. It arced gracefully and fell from sight within seconds. Cara stared down into the distance. Instinct tickled her scalp. She backed away. "Has anyone ever fallen?"

He turned her way, drink in hand. "A gloomy question."

Cara stared back into his expressionless face. "And what can one say of your thoughts right now, a'tem?"

His gaze lingered on her, his silence filled the air. He took another sip of eisenico. "No one I know of has fallen by accident," he said. "Two have suicided since arrival."

"Gods." She shifted uncomfortably. "Long way to fall with no chance to change your mind."

Rodani continued to nurse his drink as the breezes played games with the tendrils of his hair. Cara's unclipped tresses were already tangling in a free-for-all of knots. She pulled her jacket back on against the cooling temperatures, gripped her glass in both hands and sighed deeply. "Rodani, what's wrong?"

Another sip of his drink. A slow blink into the vastness beyond them.

"You were angry earlier, and seem distracted now, or sad," she told him. "And Serano seems like he would prefer to be anywhere else."

Another blink. Another sip.

"I mean no ill will," she continued. "It is as a *friend* I ask you."

Rodani pursed his lips. "Serano was pulled away from more pleasant activities for duty here."

"And you?"

Another sip. An errant breeze ruffled his feathering hair. The strands sparkled silver in the light. Rodani closed his eyes; kept them closed, long. Then he opened them and stared out again. Pupils constricted in the change of light. "The goddess thwarts me, Cara."

She held her breath.

Silence.

"You have status, skills, respect," she prompted.

He swallowed another taste of eisenico. "A man wishes for more."

There it was. Out on the table. What had it cost him? "As does a woman."

He turned his head so he could see her, arms still tightly wrapped around his legs. "Iraimin spoke to you?"

"I would no more betray another's confidence than I would yours."

His pupils pulsed. "I am reproved. Forgive me."

Into his seriousness, she smiled back, a small smile that curved the ends of her mouth but left the rest untouched. "There's no offense."

Rodani lapsed back into silence, into sips of eisenico that

occurred at regular intervals, as if the rhythm offered comfort. Cara pulled her jacket more tightly around her as the temperature began to drop with the increasingly cloudy sky. Rodani noted the action and took off his own jacket, laying it across her shoulders.

Cara took the edges in cold fingers and drew it close. "You offer me comfort, and you're the one in pain."

Rodani loosened the grip on his legs long enough to toss her observation. Then he took another sip of his drink. A larger one.

"What can a friend offer for comfort?"

"Comfort is unnecessary," he told her.

^Bullshit,^ she said in Cene'l.

Rodani cocked his head to regard her from the corner of his eye. "You have not taught me that word."

She met his cool gaze with a warmer one of her own. "It's a rude term for stable sweepings."

His face held a look of contemplation while another breeze ruffled his thin shirt. "You profess to inform me of my own needs?"

"No. I know that you have strong emotions as well. I've watched Selandu children in the gatherings. They show emotions, and their parents stifle them. I believe you hide your pain because you were taught to, not because it doesn't exist."

"Strong words."

"I stand by them until new evidence changes my mind."

He looked back out over the cliff. "You are stubborn."

"Prove to me I'm wrong."

He closed his eyes again. His face, almost impossibly, went further to mask. There were no more sips. No more words. No expressions. Gingerly, Cara reached over to him and ran her hand up his back underneath his hair, and back down. Up, then down. Rodani bent his head until his forehead touched his knees. Cara set her glass down and knelt next to him. She took his glass from his hand and found a resting place for it, then wrapped one hand around his shoulder. Her other, she curled over his arms. She rested her head next to his.

It was bold. It was unheard of. It was a risk. But her heart could no more ignore his pain than it could ignore her own oft-occurring miseries. Rodani neither accepted nor rejected her offer. He was still, his body warm despite the cold wind that whipped past them.

Under the weight of Cara's arms, Rodani shivered and shivered again. Rhythmic, as his sips had been, it came and went in almost imperceptible spasms. Cara opened her eyes, but from her close proximity, Rodani's face was a shadow. Was he cold? What did he feel? She tightened her grip as a greater shudder overtook him, and his breathing deepened. There they remained, body to body, alien to alien.

Gradually, Rodani's shivers lessened in frequency, then died out into his former stillness. He raised his head to the open expanse of his adoptive world's beauty. His dark eyes blinking erratically, but no tears had fallen. Cara pulled back, putting a hand on his near shoulder and another on his arm. When he didn't acknowledge her presence, she let go and moved back to her seat on the blanket. A long swallow of shigeli relaxed the tension from her muscles. Rodani's gaze was fixed on the horizon and remained there even when bootsteps intruded upon their silence.

If Serano had seen them together, he gave no sign, simply tossed the shoulder-sack on the ground and grabbed a bottled drink from the basket. He took a seat on Rodani's other side. Rodani broke his long silence as Serano settled in.

"All is well?"

"Yes." Serano leaned back on his hands and stretched his legs out toward the edge. "What do you think of the highest cliff in the taso's estate, Cara?"

"Awe-inspiring," she replied, thankful for a respite from strong emotions. "And a little frightening."

"Caution is always in order."

"Rodani said two people have suicided here."

He glanced at Rodani. "My partner is a collector of trivial information."

"Suicide is trivial?"

"No, it is stupid."

"You've never been in great emotional pain?"

He turned to face her. "That is not a logical conclusion."

She backtracked and rethought. "You're correct, Serano. Forgive me." She sipped the shigeli. It warmed her from within as Rodani's jacket warmed her from without. "Suicide is stupid in your opinion?"

"There is always an alternative."

"Even when someone has a painful, incurable disease?"

"He can still allow the goddess to choose the departure time."

"Is suicide always dishonorable?"

"No. It depends upon the reason." Serano took a long drink.

"Suicide to atone for dishonor is honorable. As is fatal illness. I feel it is stupid because I hold out hope for more acceptable circumstances to come from Sela."

"And if they don't?"

"I cannot know *don't* until the time comes. By then, suicide is unnecessary." He crossed his legs at the ankles and stared out over his toes. "What did you think of last night?"

"It was very interesting, thank you. What do I owe you for it?"

"Rodani paid."

She stared at the silent man sitting between them, motionless in his misery. "Thank you."

His eyes flickered in her direction; it was his only response.

"What did you experience?" Serano said.

Cara tilted her head back to face the sky overhead. "Hallucinations. Aural, visual, tactile."

He let the following silence ride a few seconds. "Nothing more?"

"Nothing I wish to discuss. Would you ever try it?"

"No," Serano said.

"Why?"

"As I said before, I have no creativity to enhance."

"You can still enjoy the experience."

"Which part?"

Cara grinned. "All parts of it."

Serano twirled his bottle in his fingers. "For the only reason I would take it, my female companions inform me it is not necessary."

Cara's eyes widened. She broke out in laughter, rocking to the side. Her drink lost some drops as her elbow broke the roll. She righted herself with a push, giggling. "And do they also inform you that you're full to the ears with your own importance?"

He took a swig from his bottle, then resumed its lazy twirling. "Not if they wish to continue the affinity."

"You should still try it."

"No."

What would such desires as she had experienced do to a pleasure-seeker such as Serano? Might it put him over some Selandu edge of control? Maybe his own desires were so strong that an overwhelming experience such as the one she'd had would be a pleasure impossible to deny. She'd seen a couple of her friends sink into the mud-sucking bottoms. It was a danger anyone with a soul full of unresolved pain had to face. The herb Serano distilled didn't seem to Cara to be a killer, but to someone bent on pursuing bodily passions, it could become terribly addictive. Likely, they knew that. Neither guardian was a slouch in the brains department. Probably no one who survived guild training was.

"Are we finished here?" Serano asked.

Rodani drew his eyes away from the horizon long enough to glance at the level in Cara's glass. "When our drinks are empty."

Serano repeated Rodani's action, peering into both glasses. He rose and headed toward the basket. "Then I have time for another."

"No." Rodani didn't even bother to turn and look at his partner standing behind him. "Not until Cara is back in her rooms. Her safety is paramount."

Cara ducked her head. Serano held himself still, arms at his sides, gaze remaining fixed on the jacketless back in front of him. Whatever he may have been thinking remained lodged behind his teeth. He strode back to the cliff edge and tossed the empty bottle with a violent wave of his arm. It sailed into the distance before dropping from sight. He retook his seat.

"We will have a discussion upon our return," Rodani said quietly.

The atmosphere soured. As usual, Cara was the cause of it, directly or indirectly. She could easily think of three possible offenses Serano might have incurred, but she was ignorant of which ones were noticed. It looked to be another rocky ride back.

Cara finished her drink as quickly as she could, given the depleted state of her stomach. Rodani took his time. Deliberately? Best it be him that made Serano wait. She'd managed to avoid giving him any offenses this outing and wanted to keep it that way. Rodani finished his drink with the same steady rhythm of sips with which he'd begun, then took his and Cara's cups back to the basket and wrapped them inside. Cara shooed Serano off the blanket and folded it, then grabbed the basket. They made their way single file back to the carriage, retracing their entrance into the woods.

The trip down was just as beautiful despite the vehicle's chilly contents. Cara felt a pang of regret as they unwound from the last hairpin turn and headed north.

"Rodani," she said, leaning over the seatbacks. He turned so that he could see her. "Can we return another time?"

"Yes."

As quick to affirm as to deny, that was a trait in him Cara

appreciated more and more as their time together increased. She wished she could make him smile. Not one had she seen the whole trip up and back. But she resisted trying. Human humor could be construed as supremely insensitive, if not downright offensive in a different culture. And she had no idea what would truly cheer him up. She consoled herself with his earlier acceptance of her embrace and held the memory of it as a talisman against the silence.

The manor came into view, and the stables before it. Idly, Cara glanced into the training ground and was startled to see a tall form in the center of the ground with a benatac colt on a leash. Cara moved to the window for a closer look.

"Something wrong?" Rodani asked.

"No, the colt is out. Someone has him on a leash."

She watched until they were out of sight of the stables, keeping her wish unvoiced. One outing when Rodani was hurting was more than she had a right to expect.

TWENTY-ONE

As they neared the manor's garage, Cara turned around and watched the stables and surrounding countryside shrink into the distance.

"On what or whom do you linger?" Rodani asked from behind her.

"The world," she replied. "The outside. Sunshine. Fresh air."

"You appreciate the goddess's gifts."

"That's not what I would call them, but yes, I do." Cara turned to face forward, leaning up against the front seats as Serano turned into the garage. "When can we return to the cliff?"

"Winter storms will be starting soon," Rodani told her. "The area can turn treacherous quickly. We must be cautious."

Cara could only hope that didn't mean winter outings would be forbidden to her. She'd never seen more snow than a light coverlet on the ground, except on distant mountaintops. And she couldn't afford to go traipsing off on her own.

They walked the last hall. Rodani opened her door and peered in, listening, then ushered her in. "I will acquire more books as I can," he told her.

"Will you read more now?"

"No. I have crafting to accomplish. I have a commission due."

Cara turned to him in the doorway. "Can you craft here? Any of it?"

Rodani regarded her steadily.

"If you could—you'd be welcome. I can make room…" She faltered in his silence. His eyes roamed the little room.

"I will consider." He pulled the door to its frame, then stopped, reopening it partway. Cara hadn't moved. Their eyes met across the distance of half a room. "On the cliff," he said quietly. "Thank you."

Something uncoiled inside her, and a warmth flowed through. She nodded. It was enough. He closed the door. Cara stared thoughtfully at her worktable and the shuttered window that started the day.

So. He did recognize her attempt to comfort him. Had it helped? At least she'd tried, just as he had tried on occasion, to offer solace to an alien being when understanding was minimal. Possibly, she'd earned a miniscule place in his heart. It was a cheering thought. She wandered into the facilities, stripped, and washed.

Hamman brushed her hair thoroughly and expertly wound it into the traditional bun that unmarried women wore. As a widow, Hamman had a choice of wearing hers up or down. It stayed up.

Cara thanked Hamman and returned to her translations of the children's books, hoping that in another hour or so Rodani would return for her. Without his interruptions, the third book's translation went more quickly. She made a note of likely words to be added to the flash cards. Hopefully, Rodani would find some more level two books for them.

She put the finished translations aside and moved back to her worktable. The room was quiet. No sounds emanated from the servants' corridor. The shutters were closed against nature's noises. She reached for the fabric pieces she'd been working on.

<Click>

Cara looked around the room. Nothing out of the ordinary betrayed its presence. She spread all the assembled pieces outward, the better to lay the rest of them in their places.

Something whispered in the back of her mind. She froze, handful of fabric forgotten. Her heart thumped in her chest. Nothing was amiss, and everything was. Instinct screamed alarms in her head. Eyes roved the room, searching. A flicker of movement drew her gaze toward the door. Her breaths went shallow.

The doorknob was moving.

She backed away, away toward the bedroom and the relative safety of her servants' quarters. She raced through the short hallway, dared a glance into Hamman's bedroom, and into the living area. It was empty.

"Hamman," Cara whispered into the emptiness. "Hamman." She followed the hall and peeked into Falita's room. It was similarly empty.

Trapped. Nowhere to go. She slipped back down the hall toward her bedroom, peering past the doorframe. No one in the bedroom. No one in the workroom. No one in the study that she could see. Absolute silence reigned, broken only by the breaths she tried to stifle. If she were very, very lucky, whoever it was didn't have a key, or didn't know how to pick a lock.

Nothing jumped out at her. Nothing grabbed her from behind. She dared to breathe and blink, moving to a seat on the bed. No phone, no 'com, no gun, no knife, no way to holler a warning. Unarmed and incommunicado. Cara wrapped her arms around her knees and fought an adrenaline rush that she couldn't convince the danger had passed.

Hopefully passed.

She wanted tea. Wanted a drink. Wanted Rodani to return. She sighed and leaned against the bedpost, settling down to wait.

A rattle of keys made her jump, and her heart pump double-time. Not with a handful of books did Rodani return, but with an armload of tools and sundry items instead. He stood in her doorway, waiting for her response, with an uncertain expression on his face. It was a new look for him.

The fact that he'd taken her up on her offer flooded her awareness. In response to his own uncertainty, Cara put hers aside. "What kind of room do you need?" she asked, walking into the workroom.

"A half of a side of your worktable, less when not working. And a chair." He came into the room.

"What side?"

"Here would do well," he said, sweeping a free hand across the near right corner of the table.

She moved her own belongings back from the area to make room for his. "What did you bring?"

"Sandpaper, metal cutters." He emptied the small box. "Files, drafting and designing tools, paper." He headed back to the door. "And a seat." He opened it and rolled in a chair, bringing it over to the worktable next to hers.

"Satisfactory?" he asked, taking his seat.

"Absolutely." A deep breath. "Rodani."

"Yes?"

She stared across the room. "Someone tried to open my door."

His gaze traveled from her face down the line of sight to the door and back. "When?"

"F—five, ten minutes ago."

He sat down and folded his arms on the table, leaning toward her. "Tell me."

There wasn't much to tell.

"And Hamman is elsewhere?" Rodani asked.

"Both of them."

He rose abruptly and strode down the servants' corridor. Muttering came through. In a moment, he was back.

"She is there now. What would you have done if he had come in?" he asked, reseating himself.

Cara picked up a pair of scissors and toyed with them, snipping tiny cuts in the edges of her design spec. "I considered that. Hide under my bed, most likely. Or Hamman's bed, since my life would be in danger."

"You could have run."

"Once he came in, yes. But he didn't or couldn't. So, I couldn't run out."

"Understood."

"Rodani, I need to be able to use the servants' radio. Or have a 'com."

His eyes drifted over the array of tools he'd brought in. "I will consider." One by one he picked up the tools and arranged them around his workspace.

"Or a gun."

He put down the file. <Clink> "No."

"Rodani, I have dangers outside, and now dangers inside. I need the extra safety."

"I am your safety." His voice had gone deep, pupils drew inward, paper thin. "You have told me the rumors of your dissatisfaction are not true. Do you lie?"

Cara blinked stupidly, drawing her mouth downward. "What do rumors have to do with carrying a gun?"

"You imply my skills are inadequate."

Her shoulders slumped in disbelief. "Your skills that I've seen are much more than adequate, Rodani. But you have to be near me to protect me."

Now it was Rodani's turn for incomprehension. His feathery eyebrows drew inward. "That is why we insist on escort outside your rooms."

"I mean danger here, in my rooms! You aren't always here."

"The intruder did not enter."

"What if he did?"

"He could not."

"Keys can be stolen. Locks can be broken."

"I will handle your worries."

"Rodani, I can't just pass them to you and forget about them."

He studied her for a moment, then looked away. "Try." He spun his chair and rattled his hand in the toolbox.

That, obviously, was all the answer she would get on the subject. Her design spec was showing wear and tear. She put the scissors down and tried to relax, tried to pass off her fear. She rubbed her hands across the table, across her pant legs and down over her knees. Her sewing machine waited patiently on a table littered with fabric, rulers, tools, pins, and paper. "Do you often craft on rest-days?"

"Yes," Rodani said. "You and guild matters take up much of my time. If I wish to craft, I fit it in during my own time."

"I'm sorry."

"You have done nothing for which you need apologize."

"Did Arimeso know your duty to my safety would interfere with your crafting?"

"Yes." Rodani picked up a rectangular piece of silver whose edges had been sawed into curlicue shapes. Twice as long as it was wide, it was obviously meant to be a hair clip. "There are other jewelry crafters in the house."

"And no other quilters?"

"Yes."

"And no other guardians capable of putting up with me?"

"No. There are one or two others who might manage the task. But not as well as I." He reached for a pencil-thin file. It was concave on one side, convex on the other—almost like a spoon that had been stretched. He shifted the clip into a comfortable grip in his hand and began to file the edges with short, light snaps of his wrist.

She smiled over his unconscious arrogance, unwilling to argue the point. Maybe the arrogance was taught along side weapons training and field strategy. She pulled the loosely arranged pieces of a quilt block toward her. If Rodani was going to craft, she might as well also. He glanced at her smile with a questioning look.

Maybe he didn't see his arrogance. But no matter. "You're in the room," she said. "May I open the window?"

He considered a moment, eyes flicking around the room and into the study. "Yes."

Before he could change his mind, she slipped off her chair, opened the shutters, and pushed the window outward. Cold wafted in. She pulled the window back closer to the frame, just enough to get the fresh air she craved without freezing her fingers into inactivity.

Rodani worked his way slowly and carefully around the inner and outer curves of the hair clip. Cara took the completed blocks that made up her newest wall hanging and stitched them together on point. Occasionally, her attention would be drawn from her own creative efforts to Rodani's nimble fingers as the rough edges of the clip dissolved into smoother arcs.

As Rodani finished his circuitous route around the perimeter of the clip and reached next for sandpaper, Cara squatted in the open area between table and door, flapped the completed quilt top and laid it on the floor.

It took several minutes to accurately sandwich the quilt top, batting, and backing. Then she sat on it and reached for her needle and thread. Working outward from the center, she basted the layers together with long stitches. She picked it up and flipped it out. As she turned back to the table, she stopped at Rodani's regard.

"Quite a labor-intensive process."

"Not on this size. Try a bed quilt sometime." Around the back of the table, she rolled the sandwich around her frame and found a corner in the center area to begin on.

Familiar with this stage, Rodani went back to his sanding and polishing. The afternoon moved by in snippets of conversation and thread, and a dusting of silver.

Rodani held the clip up in the light. The lines were even, no unsightly bulges or curves where no curves should be. Slowly, he ran his little finger around the edges. There were no rough spots, nothing that could catch on cloth or skin.

Evening darkened the sky behind Cara's head. The clanking dinner cart interrupted their work. Rodani set the clip down and assisted Hamman. Eager to get as much quilting done as she could, Cara joined them at the last moment.

"To what do I owe the pleasure?" she asked him.

He pulled her chair out as Hamman retreated from the repast. "One gives, one receives."

"Always?" She slipped into the chair as he walked around to the other side to do the same.

"As much as possible."

"An admirable philosophy."

"The goddess wills."

She pulled the meat platter toward her. "And if She changes

Her mind?" One slice, then two ended up on her plate.

"She will not." Rodani poured endichu onto his. The pebbly vegetable lent a ginger taste to an otherwise bland meat and gravy mixture. "Her laws were fixed at our creation."

Cara frowned. "Your species evolved, just as ours did, Rodani."

"So the Guild of Scientists tells us."

"You don't believe them?"

"The priestesses say it is false information."

"The priestesses have a vested interest in keeping the information disbelieved."

"Why?"

Cara dug into her fruit with a spoon. "You have a good mind, Rodani. Use it. The priestesses' power comes from people's belief in the goddess. If the beliefs are proved false, the ground on which belief rests becomes unstable. Your goddess might fall from Her high place. The priestesses would fall also, their power gone. They'll prevent the loss of their power and status at any cost. Therefore, they deny the scientists' knowledge."

Rodani chewed on her words. "They have powers the scientists do not."

"Power? Like lighting those candles at the harvest dinner?" she asked, mocking his answer. "That was trickery, Rodani. I know how she did it."

Rodani set his knife down with an audible clink and stared at Cara as if she had just sprouted feathers. "How?"

"When she went among the people, and they bowed over her hands? I bowed, also. Do you remember?"

"Yes."

"What do you do when you bring your face to her hands?"

"Close my eyes," Rodani said. "Receive her blessings from the power she emits. It is only proper."

"I smelled her hands."

Rodani's pupils pulsed. "Smelled?"

"And caught a distinct whiff of ysan."

"It is used as incense."

"Because it burns well," she agreed. "And under proper conditions, it also ignites at or just above room temperature."

Rodani leaned back in his chair and crossed his arms. The look on his face was comical. Cara's grin spread from ear to ear.

"What conditions?"

"Sufficient quantities of the powder, a certain oil, warmth, and a combustible material nearby."

"What oil?"

Cara laughed out loud, a rollicking laugh that brought a frown to Rodani's face. "Questions, a'tem. Such questions. You've been around me too long." She sat her elbows on the table, impropriety when there was still food to be eaten. She didn't care. "I don't know its name. But I'd recognize it if I saw it."

He stood up from the table with a speed that startled her. "Come."

Cara glanced over the still laden table but followed as Rodani headed for the door. He led her across the hall and into Serano's—unoccupied—bedroom. There was a bookcase on the far wall. Rodani ran his finger down the spines, looking for something in particular. He found it, pulled it out, and flopped it on the immaculate bed. Cara looked at the book, and at Rodani, who had re-crossed his arms. *Put up or shut up*, he seemed to be saying.

Cara sat on the bed and flipped through what looked like a botanical encyclopedia. Now she knew why it resided in the room it did. She paged through the detailed color plates, quickly scanning for the leaf and flower geometry she recognized. Rodani waited wordlessly as a third, a half, and then two-thirds of the book went past.

"There." Cara pointed to a blue-green plant, tiny pale-yellow flowers sprouting from each of the six stems that protruded from each parent stem. "Cibain. It's made into an oil."

Rodani pulled out his 'com and flipped the switch. "Six, Five. Six, Five." He waited, eyes on the page, for his partner to answer.

"Six."

"Are you occupied?"

There was a moment's hesitation. "Yes, and no."

"You will run an errand to the botanical pantry."

"For?"

"Cibain oil. Is it carried here?"

Another hesitation came across the wavelengths. "Likely."

"Get it. And some ysan powder. Bring it to Cara's rooms."

"A'tem," came Serano's hesitant reply.

It was a tactful accusation; possibly Rodani's earlier censure on the cliff had not worn off. "If the experiment works, Serano, I will reward you with a truly unusual demonstration, and a piece of knowledge that will shake the complacency out of you. If it does not, Cara will offer you her apologies."

"Rodani!" Cara slapped the book shut. "An experiment was your idea."

He clicked off the 'com and stuffed it in his pocket, pointing to the book and sweeping his hand over to the bookcase. "Dinner is getting cold."

"Yes, it is." She slid it into the open place where it had rested.

Cold indeed. They finished quickly, then retired to the couch with drinks in their hands. The fire burned brightly.

"If I fail, Rodani, it doesn't prove my words false. It only proves I don't know the proper quantities of the elements, or the correct process. You do realize that?"

"How do you know it works?"

"I've seen it done."

There was a knock on the door, quickly followed by a key and a rattling lock. Serano strode into the study, each hand filled with a jar. He gave them to Cara with a look in his eyes that she couldn't interpret. Or wouldn't. "What experiment?" he asked in a peevish voice.

"It was Rodani's idea, Serano, not mine."

"I heard. What experiment?"

She glanced at Rodani, who declined to help. "Enjoy the rest of your evening, Serano, please. If it works, I'll repeat it at a better time for you. If it fails, I'll have embarrassed myself in front of only one person, not two."

Some message must have passed between the two guardians, as Serano turned and headed back to his evening's pleasures with no more words. Rodani retrieved a candle from the mantle and put it on the floor in front of the fireplace, then sat down. Catching the obvious, Cara slid off the couch and joined him. She opened the two jars and placed the lids on the floor. She closed her eyes and thought back ten years to her father's workshop, and the stools she and her brother Davad had perched on while their father showed off his botanical knowledge.

Slowly, Cara put her palms together, then rubbed them vigorously. Nervously, she dug a fingertip into the oil and rubbed it on two fingers, leaving a shine on the skin. Then she pinched a bit of the fine powder and dribbled it on the spot of oil. Fingers pressed together, she held her hand over the candlewick, making sure the wick touched the powder.

Nothing happened.

She spread more of the oil over the rest of her hands and rubbed them together for several seconds. They warmed with the friction. She took another quick pinch of powder and dribbled it, placing her hand over the wick.

The candle remained stubbornly unlit.

Cara stared at the candle in contemplation of past and present. She and her brother had watched in overt fascination as her father went through the same steps she was trying to repeat. It had been daytime. The sun had shone outside the door. Insects had droned in the bright light.

Heat. In her memory, it had been summertime. It was winter, now, and Cara's hands were cold. She leaned toward the fireplace and held her palms out, keeping them near until the skin became hot to the touch. She brought her hands back to the candle, took a larger pinch of powder, and patted a place on her palm. Tiny particles drifted down and settled on her pants. Quickly Cara held her hand over the unlit candle.

<Pfff!>

Rodani's pupils widened into saucers as the wick burst into flame.

As did the rest of the oil on Cara's palm.

She screamed in fright and shook it, then rolled on top of it, gasping as the oil burned away and skin took its place. Rodani charged across the intervening space, knocked the candle over, and pulled her arm out from under her chest. The fire was gone, but her blouse was marred with oil, powder, and char. Rodani pulled her over to the table, where ice that had kept their drinks cold sat melting in a bowl. He held the bowl out for Cara, checking the state of the fallen candle behind her. She slid her hand into the ice water, palm up. Immediately, it went numb. Blessedly numb, then painfully numb. She pulled it back out and studied the damage.

Assessment was difficult given the residue that still clung to her hand. She went to the facilities and washed carefully, one finger at a time, then the palm.

It could've been worse. Much worse. It hurt, but it was manageable.

"There are some raw patches," she said, "but I was lucky. Most of the burning was the oil." She held out the hand for his professional scrutiny.

They went back to the study. Cara slipped her hand back into the bowl of ice water and followed Rodani over to the couch. The offending candle was tipped completely over, its flame extinguished against the cold stone. He righted the candle and put it back on the mantle, then closed up the two jars and placed them on either side of the candleholder. He retrieved his drink and sat back on the couch, nearer Cara than he was wont to sit.

"Forgive me, Cara."

She left off looking at her hand and turned to her guardian. "For what?"

"The experiment. Your hurt."

"I did have the right to decline, didn't I?"

He looked across at the flames contained in the fireplace. "Yes. But I would not have believed you had you not demonstrated it."

"That's the way it should be."

He looked back, an expression of confusion filling his face.

"Your people are used to being expected to believe what they're told by high-status people, are they not?" Cara asked quietly.

"Yes. Yours are not?"

"They are, in some ways. In others, they're taught how to question, how to reason, how to find out for themselves." Cara shifted in her seat, sloshing drops of ice water on her pants. "What did you learn tonight?"

He thought for a moment, fingers running up and down the sides of his eisenico glass. "That experiments can be dangerous."

"Anything else?"

"That Kimasa must get small burns from her trick as well."

"Yes?"

He paused. "That one of my beliefs has been rudely and crudely shattered."

It shocked her into wordlessness for several seconds. "What it teaches you, Rodani," she began, "is that the way to shatter assumptions or beliefs is to experiment. In ways that can be documented and repeated by others." She waved her uninjured hand. "That's the way of science. Your Guild of Scientists has neglected to teach its methodology. It's how we winnow fact from fiction, objective knowledge from belief." She sloshed her hand gently in the water and withdrew it, laying it out on top of her leg. "And it's my turn to offer apologies."

"For what?"

"For rudely and crudely shattering one of your beliefs."

"Was that not your intent?"

It tripped her, this blatant honesty. It forced away what

arrogance was left. "Yes. But I didn't know it would disturb you so."

"Disturbing truths must still be assimilated. A guardian deals with facts whenever they are available. To do otherwise is to court death."

"Speaking of courting death," she said lightheartedly, "May I open these windows, too?"

Rodani rose to unlatch them. Cara followed him over and stood at the sill, looking out into a clear night sky. The blackness was alive with shimmering stars without a greater moon to wash them out. A memory of hallucinations floated across her mind. The room fell into sudden darkness.

"Why turn out the lantern?" she asked, turning to look.

"Security. Backlit, you are an excruciatingly clear target."

"Ah." As usual, her head was in an alternate reality while his was where it should be.

Rodani stepped up behind her and looked out over her head, no difficult feat considering their size difference. The curls on the top of Cara's head fluttered despite the containing bun. Rodani raised his arms and put his hands on the shutters. "And you have tested for the presence of the goddess?"

Ouch. "I don't want to offend you, Rodani."

"I would not ask a question to which I did not wish an answer."

Cara sighed. A shiver ran up her spine.

"Are you cold?" He reached for the edges of the shutters.

"No. Yes. Please don't close them. Hand me the quilt?"

He pulled the quilt off the couch and wrapped it around Cara's shoulders as he had seen her wear it the night before. He tucked it under her hair bun and smoothed it across her shoulders before raising his hands back up to the shutters.

Cara froze at his unexpected touch; the hair on her neck tingled, and her shoulders tensed with the effort to remain facing the window. She became acutely aware of his presence behind her in the darkened room, and desperately fought the urges that overwhelmed her anew, urges brought on not by Serano's biologicals but her own internally generated ones. She pulled the quilt more tightly around her, leaving her burned hand outside in the cold. She could sense, rather than see Rodani lean over her, likely watching the ground below.

"Will you answer my question?" he asked.

Gods. She'd forgotten it in the hormonal rush.

"I haven't tested Sela. I don't need to."

"You fear the answer?"

"No. Science can't test anything outside the natural world."

Behind her, close behind her, Rodani was silent. The wind died and was reborn in gusts that peeled back the sides of the quilt. The stars continued twinkling. Cormoren, the planet nearest their own on the inward track, shone with a steady light above their heads.

"Perhaps it is for the best." He lowered his arms and rested his hands on the windowsill, one on either side of Cara's waist. Surreptitiously, she looked down at them. The strength and nimble creativity in those slender fingers still amazed her. From side to side, the nails curved sharply downward in an inverted U. Grown out, they would turn into a reasonable facsimile of claws. But Selandu prided themselves on their civilization, hiding the animals that shared their ancestry. They kept their nails relatively short, their hair clipped back or spiraled, and their bodies concealed in loose clothing. But their eyes reflected light in the dark, and their movements were reminiscent of the grace of their non-sapient ancestors.

"Do you not miss a goddess watching over you?" he asked.

"If you lived with my mother, Rodani, you wouldn't need to ask that question."

"Why?"

"She was extremely watchful," she explained. "Extremely protective. Quick to confront or attack with words. I struggled under it."

"Your independence has been remarked upon."

"By you most of all, I'm sure. I value my freedom."

"That is your difficulty here?"

Cara glanced over the stars. Worst Luck twinkled in the sky, the first constellation to be named by the first generation. Imagination drew the lines between stars and led her off to Huw's Chair to the southwest.

"Mostly," was her belated answer.

"We cannot allow it."

"I know."

"And what else?"

"Companionship," she said after a moment. "But you and Iraimin have helped a lot in recent weeks." The admittance and the thoughts behind it made her heart thump in her chest, her knees weak. She wanted to turn and face this tall, almost-familiar stranger who hovered so closely. Wanted to run her sensitive hands down that long body to see what happened. Wanted to snuggle into his warmth and to hell with the consequences. Wanted…

Gods of the deep space—what couldn't be! She was a child to him, needing his protective skills. Needing guidance to navigate his culture's minefields without damage. Someone demanding of time and energy he might well resent giving. If he knew what he was doing to her, he was acting supremely ignorant of it. Ignorant of the fact that her body was nearly vibrating with desire. Cravings she couldn't act upon.

Distraction. She needed distraction. Against the cold sill, she leaned out into a twinkling panorama as glorious as the more earthly one she had seen from cliff's edge earlier. Her imagination leapt outward, pretending to be one of her ancestors on shipboard. *What was it like? What did they see?*

"Where are your thoughts, Cara?"

She startled, gripping the quilt tighter in her right hand. The burning in her dominant left came back into focus. "You'd think me foolish."

Rodani shifted behind her. Something jingled, as if he had put his hands in his pockets. "You have taught me something today, ki'ono," he said. "There is more to your foolish ways than what appears on the surface. Test me."

A new, colder breeze blew in. Cara shivered despite the protection the substantial quilt afforded. "My mind was flying between the stars."

"Your mind left your body?" he asked with surprise in his voice. "We have heard of such occurrences in our history."

"Only in imagination."

"Where did your imagination take you?"

"On a distant journey."

The leather of his jacket rustled and rasped behind her head. She imagined him crossing his arms. "Do you wish to leave?" he asked.

She jerked her head sideways, just enough to catch a glimpse of him out of the corner of her eye. She'd imagined his stance correctly. "No." *Didn't you just ask that earlier? Calm, fem.*

"You may visit home for a time, if it would comfort you."

She bent her head. "I'd fear not being allowed to return."

"That is unlikely."

"I don't want to take the chance." Her attention fell back on the starry night sky. "Unless you wish me to leave."

A pause. "Why would I wish that?" His voice held a note of irritation.

"I meant no offense."

"Why would I wish that?"

His repeat of the question forced out her truth. "Because I'm a difficult duty."

"To what or whom do you compare yourself, ki'ono?"

"I—don't know," she ended lamely, her voice low, quiet.

Leather creaked. Pockets jingled in the darkness. "You confuse me anew. Explain. Please," he added.

"I prefer to withdraw the comment, and all that came after."

Rodani leaned over her and rested his hands back on the sill on either side of her. Unwillingly, Cara's eyes were drawn to them. "You are an enigma," he said over her head.

"A problem?"

"A puzzle, ki'ono." He bent his head lower. "To me, Serano, Hamman, Iraimin. Not one of us has yet put your pieces together into a coherent whole."

Cara's pulse rocketed upward as Rodani's deep voice drifted down from too damn close above. Her very private ache became more insistent.

"That may be impossible, Rodani. Likely, some of the pieces have been lost over the years."

"Lost pieces?"

It didn't take much to imagine his warm breath wafting over her face despite the cold air coming in from the out, or his arms coming up from the sides to wrap her in a brazen embrace.

"I must have lost some pieces somewhere, or my needs wouldn't be so high."

"What needs?" he whispered into her hair.

Almost. Almost she turned to him, an offensive maneuver that might ruin all she had gained. She took a last long look at the sky.

"Rodani, please; I'm cold. I need to sit at the fire."

A short silence descended. The touchable hands withdrew along with the too-close presence that had disturbed her so deeply. Regretting her cowardice, she turned in the open space and went over to the fire and knelt in front of it. The shutters clicked behind her.

"How is your hand?" Rodani asked as he sat down beside her.

She studied it in the flickering firelight. "Uncomfortable for another day or so. It'll mend."

Rodani grasped her wrist lightly and pulled it toward him, flexing her fingers downward and shifting it in the light. She drew it back when he let go, and re-wrapped the quilt around her, bending her face to the fire, eyes closed.

"Are you well?"

"Yes. Just tired. Last night was a late night for both of us. It's been an emotional day."

Rodani stood, and looked down at her with firelit eyes, rewarming the heat that had begun to abate. "For you or for me?"

She had to lean back on her hands to look up at him. The injured one complained against the pressure. "Both."

"If you need salve for your hand, Hamman can procure it. Safe night," he said, and walked through the doorway, hand on the frame.

The hand remained. Rodani stuck his head back into the room.

"The shutters remain closed."

TWENTY-TWO

Serano shut the door, leaving the target room to Toranel and Vanu. "Tomorrow is another rest-eve, not today, tem'u. And your mind was not on practice. Your aim was off, your stance awkward, and your vision was elsewhere. This does not bode well for our ranking."

Rodani refused to glance at his partner. "Your imagination flies with the yosi."

Serano's jaw tightened. "No imagination. We have much to lose."

"We will not."

"What I said last spring still faces me."

"As I remember, you had much to say."

"And now she has much to say."

Rodani fingered the grip of his Dienata, settled the pistol further into its holster. "Cara?"

"The rumors, te'oto," Serano explained, stepping up to his partner's side.

"She denies them."

"And you believe her."

"Yes."

"What I believe, Rodani, is that she is a danger to us all. I do not approve of her being here."

Rodani flung his hand in the air. "And this is news?"

"The arguments surrounding her get tiring," Serano complained.

"Then cease repeating them."

Serano took off, Rodani after him. The pair turned the corner, their boots raising an angry ruckus over the stone floors. The dim lights cast shadows before and behind them, silent observers.

"What lies between you two?" Serano asked.

Rodani stopped, stared at his partner's narrowed eyes with a matching expression. "I can only assume she was attempting to comfort me on the cliff."

"You told her?"

Rodani folded his arms across his chest. "No. Iraimin did, though Cara would not admit it."

"Is there a destination to this path you walk with her?"

"No path. Brambles and thorns. Gnarled roots."

"Will you approach her?"

Rodani stilled. "You are intensely premature in your inquiries, as well as your assumptions."

Serano's pupils pulsed. "You will pay."

"As well, I would earn."

"No more than what you would get from one of your own. Would you break guild rules so heedlessly?"

Rodani leaned forward, pupils narrowing into slits. "I break nothing heedlessly."

"Kusik would relish deciding your punishment, and revel in its delivery."

"Which is why I walk on the side of propriety."

"You are stumbling."

Rodani took a step forward. "Each of us stumbles at times."

"On the edge of a cliff?"

"The goddess has given me no signs of a cliff."

"You ever walk your own path, heedless of difficulties. Would you listen if She gave you one?"

Rodani balled his fist, his arm shot upward. The blow caught Serano on the jaw and spun him around to face the wall. When he turned back, Rodani was nose-on to him.

"I will deal with my choices."

Serano leaned back, as if the wall would envelop him. "You are my partner. Your choices affect me."

Rodani glared, jaw outthrust. "You reproach me for something I have not done."

"I see your eyes when you are with her. Does she see?"

Rodani shifted his focus out to the end of the hall. A tall form stood quietly in the crossway, hands behind the back. "I know not," he answered his partner.

Rodani walked past him and headed down the hall at a rapid clip. Serano trotted up behind him. As the guardians neared the cross hall, the form took a step forward, head lowered. Rodani slowed and stopped, stiff with repressed tension. Serano stopped at his side.

"A'tem'ai," the form said.

"Litelon," Serano answered in the face of Rodani's outraged silence.

The stablehand dared a glance in Rodani's direction, then bowed. "I would ask permission, a'tem."

"For?" Rodani asked, the word drawn out with an underlying growl.

Litelon drew a deep breath. "I am one of the best riders in the estate, a'tem. I wish—"

"No."

"Guild accompaniment is acceptable, a'tem."

"No." The voice went a step deeper.

"A'tem, I would let no harm come—"

Rodani tensed into deadly stillness, pupils paper thin. Serano gripped Litelon's arm and pulled him back.

"You have courage, te'oto, but no sense."

Litelon's gaze bounced from a face that sported a reddened jaw to another that broadcast incipient violence, and back again. He bowed deeply.

Rodani shot past the young man and out into the cross-hall. Serano followed, leaving Litelon to be disappointed alone.

"Kusik is already angry, tem'u," Serano whispered loudly as he caught up with Rodani.

"He has spoken to me. When I hear from the taso directly, I will listen." Rodani lowered his voice; stairwells carry sound.

"He will kill us both."

"No."

"On what do you base your surety?"

Ignoring Serano's question, Rodani sped up the steps. Serano followed him to their corridor, then turned into their shared quarters as Rodani turned to Cara's.

***

The window was open, in a manner of degree. The cold air that had blasted Cara was now constrained behind glass pulled down to a horizontal crack. She was content with the whispers that escaped through the opening. It wouldn't do to have cold hands when crafting. Manual dexterity was inversely proportional to temperature, at least in humans. And the fireplace was neither in her sleeping room nor her workroom. If she'd moved here in winter, she'd have made the study her bedroom.

Rodani pushed his chair over to the small vise he had attached to the worktable's edge. He slipped the silver clip into it carefully, positioned it horizontally between the padded jaws of the vise, and tightened it.

"You've had little time to work on it." Cara lined up a ruler to the rough edge of a new piece of fabric.

"Yes." Rodani's head was bent, eyes intent on his business.

"And what else have you been doing this week?"

"Besides guild business, reading to you, singing, weapons training, and keeping the shutters closed and doors locked?"

"I haven't opened any doors in a while. But, yes."

He went back to his silversmithing. Cara grinned at his turned cheek. Her rotary cutter swept smoothly along the edge of the ruler, producing a neat, accurate cut impossible to create with traditional scissors. With deliberate care, she pushed the wide ruler up another measured width and leaned on it with all the strength available to her, cutting another swath. She repeated the steps until a pile of strips lay off to the side and two yards of fabric had been reduced to less than half of that.

"The taso tells me that another of your quilts has sold," Rodani said.

"Really? Who bought it?"

"She did not say."

"So, I suppose I'm not allowed to ask."

He came to a straight line in the design and began to saw vigorously. His silver tail shook against his jacket with the motion of his arms, face tightened in concentration. "You may. Shall I request an audience with the taso?"

"Ah, thank you, no."

"Where is your courage?"

"It flees in the face of deadly authority, Rodani."

The saw stopped. He rested one graceful hand on top of the vise, fingers curved downward in an arc. "As an authority figure, I could be offended. Where is your antipathy for me?"

His pupils remained the oval of calm; there was no anger in his eyes. But they were difficult to face, nonetheless.

"I have none," Cara said.

"Then your statement is incorrect."

"Mmmm, incomplete."

"Please complete it."

She pulled a strip of fabric toward her and measured off the first piece. Authority figures who had other interests at heart? Who were blatantly unfair? With whom one had no recourse? She cut the first piece, then another.

"Do you have antipathy toward the taso?" he continued.

"I'm not so stupid as that, Rodani. It would seem very difficult for her to have an alien in her household. I've been treated well, and honor her highly. But she has the authority to kill me. I fear her, and so feel a great degree of discomfort in her presence, and in Kusik and Timan's."

"That is as it should be."

"To fear her?"

"Always. But not to the extent you cannot bear her presence." The saw resumed its vertical motion. "And what of my abilities?"

"I fear your skills, but they've saved my life. You have the ability to kill, but your authority to use it comes from the taso. Yes?"

Turning a corner with a coping saw takes patience and a certain delicacy. He readjusted his position at the vise before continuing. "Ultimately, yes. But I have some latitude to follow my professional judgment."

"What would it take for you to kill me?"

Rodani hesitated, sending that look her way. "The taso's order, or your immediate threat to her life."

"For what reasons would she have me killed?"

Rodani stood, his chair scraping roughly along the stone. "I will return when you have had time to remember your courtesies."

Cara leaned back in her chair, open-mouthed, as Rodani strode to the door and opened it.

"I have a legitimate need to know," she called out to his departing back.

The door shut with an emphatic click. She stared at his tools and the chair he'd vacated. The previous tensions that had eased between them reared their very unwanted heads. *Blast him!* She should have a right to ask. To have one's life held ransom to rules that hadn't been discussed was dishonorable. But best to tell him that when he calmed. The man was getting as temperamental as a love-lost youngest child. Maybe he'd had another rejection.

Iraimin might know! Cara got up from the worktable. "Hamman?" she called out.

"A'Cara?" The familiar voice wafted through the corridor.

"Would you see if Iraimin is available for tea? Please assure her she's not obliged if she's occupied with something important."

"A'Cara."

Cara returned to her work to await Hamman's answer. She smoothed out the cloth strip and cut two more pieces, mirror images of each other, then lay them aside and repositioned the quilter's square for a different set of cuts.

Hamman reappeared in the doorway. "She has accepted your invitation, a'Cara, and will arrive when she has finished."

"Thank you. Tea, please, when she arrives."

TWENTY-THREE

Cara flipped on the 'corder and slipped in a compendium of soft singables. Joining her voice to the 'cording, she pulled the last strip of fabric over, folded it into fourths, and lay the square down on it. Careful alignment and accurate cutting were the first rules of quilting. Besides patience. And besides quality fabrics and sturdy tools. Cara lay the cut pieces to the side, careful not to pull the edges. She drew another length of fabric from her stash on the shelves and unfolded it.

The click of shoes and a flutter of skirts proclaimed Iraimin's arrival. Cara greeted her warmly and led her into the study where a bright fire burned. Hamman followed them in with a tray of tea and warm biscuits.

"Are you well?" Cara asked.

"I am rarely otherwise," she said.

Cara smothered her humor in a sip of tea. "Rodani was here for a while."

"I saw his tools. Leaving them out is not the guild way."

"We were talking. I asked him a question he thought discourteous, and he left. Would you offer assistance?"

Iraimin looked at Cara from the corner of her eye. "To you or to him?"

Cara coughed up her tea and guffawed. "I assumed I was the discourteous one."

"Possibly, you were. But with you being new to our culture, Rodani should not have withdrawn. He should have corrected you. Since I am here, it is obvious he taught you nothing from the incident."

"True."

"May I ask what was said?"

Cara shifted and tucked an ankle under one knee. "I had mentioned people of authority such as him and the taso. I asked what it would take for him to kill me. He told me. I then asked what it would take for the taso to order me killed. It's a difficult subject, but I thought it was an appropriate question."

"No. It was discourteous. That does not negate his answering discourtesy."

"But I should know, Iraimin. I wish her neither dishonor nor danger. But ignorant, I may make mistakes."

Cara added some sweetener to her tea. Duli tea could be bitter when harvested late.

"It is Rodani's job," Iraimin told her, "to prevent such mistakes. I know neither the taso's mind nor Rodani's. But your unpredictability would be cause for caution."

"If I were told what not to do, I wouldn't do it."

"Or if your honor is not what it seems, you might do exactly what you were told not to. Knowledge is a doubly edged knife." The painter stopped, cup to her lips. "Forgive me. I can read my offense in your face."

Cara shook her head. "You're answering the questions I asked. It would be dishonorable to take offense."

The fireplace flickered, casting chaotic shadows on the wall, the floor, and the two sapient women who shared its warmth. Cara swallowed another sip of tea.

"Such things are not asked so openly in our culture, Cara. An adult has already assimilated the knowledge from childhood experiences."

"But I didn't spend my childhood here."

"And that is what points to Rodani's discourtesy."

Cara rubbed absentmindedly at winter dry skin that was paying the penalty for a cooler climate. "He's been," she hesitated over an incoming indiscretion, "different, of late. Have you noticed?"

"No. I am rarely in his presence more than once a week."

"No rumors?"

"No rumors."

"No more hall sightings?"

A sparkle appeared in the painter's eye. "No."

"Should I talk to Serano?"

Confused, Iraimin tilted her head. "Does Rodani disturb you so much?"

It brought her up short. She opened her mouth to speak, took a deep breath instead, and closed it again. What to say? How much to say? She curled into the intensity of her thoughts and wrapped her arms around herself, trapping the crumbling biscuit between hand and ribs.

"Forgive me," Iraimin spoke up. "I have disturbed you."

"There's no offense."

"There are other guardians."

She dropped her arms at the thought. The crumbling biscuit disintegrated into a mass of brown pebbles on Cara's lap and fell into the cracks between the cushions. "Not necessary. I enjoy his company—when we're not arguing."

"Have you discussed it with him?"

Cara's very human pupils pulsed. "No."

"You should. Just as he should have discussed your unintended discourtesy. That is how problems are solved."

"Yes. It's just difficult." Cara picked up the teapot and held it out, filling Iraimin's cup when she responded.

"How goes your work?" Iraimin asked.

"Well enough. Rodani said I sold another quilt."

Iraimin's eyebrows raised. "The goddess blesses. Good wishes for more."

"Thank you. I hope so. But sometimes, I fear people will lose interest."

"The taso decides what is allowed to be sold. Leave that fear in Rodani's hands."

"I'd rather know who and what to fear," Cara replied.

"I would rather not fear. The goddess protects me."

"Rodani protects me."

"Sela is behind Rodani's protection," Iraimin countered.

"We've had this dialogue before."

"Yes."

The two women smiled at each other. A squeak of wheels erupted from the workroom, along with a clatter of tools. Cara put down her teacup to investigate.

It was Rodani, as she had hoped. She turned back to Iraimin. "Will you sit with us?"

Iraimin waggled her fingers. "For a short time. I have my own work."

"And beautiful work it is." Cara brought the tea tray out and set it on the worktable, then pulled a dining table chair out from the study, placing it opposite Rodani. She sat down at her sewing machine. Iraimin took the chair. Rodani maneuvered the coping saw back into position and began to cut at the first inner piece.

The teacups rattled against the tray.

Cara looked at it, and at Rodani. He glanced at her and resumed his work. The teacups resumed their noisy display. Cara pulled hers off the tray. So did Iraimin.

"You failed to close the shutters after I left." Rodani blew on the silver filings that had accumulated around the saw blade. A cloud erupted and dissipated as it floated downward onto the cluttered table.

"Forgive me. Your leaving distressed me so much that I forgot."

"How many times will you forget?"

"It seems we exchanged discourtesies instead of explanations."

Rodani stared at her from across the corner of the table, then turned his attention to Iraimin. "You counsel her?"

Iraimin lifted her chin. Professional to professional, she refused to be cowed. "When you are disinclined to, a'tem. Or when I am asked."

Rodani bent his head to the vise and the work in progress it held in its jaws. "You overstep your boundaries."

"No," Cara said. "She doesn't. Not in my culture."

"And how many times must you be reminded you are not in your culture?"

Cara stood up, gripped the table, and stared across the intervening space into Rodani's wide eyes. "Iraimin is a *friend*, Rodani, as you are. It angers me that you tell us what we can discuss and what we can't. Unless it's a security matter, I refuse to believe that's your right."

Rodani stood up, gripped the lower handle of the vise and started to turn it, loosening it from the table. "I think I do not belong here."

"No!" Cara leaned across the table and grabbed the vise. They eyed each other, the short and the tall, the disturbed and the confused. "I offered you a place here, and I'm not rescinding it because of senseless arguments. Sit down."

He regarded her intently, as if staring at a new species in the forest. "You are bold."

"I'm being treated unfairly. I'm angry."

Slowly, Rodani sat back down. His eyes didn't leave Cara's face until she, in turn, let go of his vise and sat. "It was not my intent to anger you," he said.

"It was not my intent to make you leave," she countered, as Rodani retightened the grip of the vise with slow deliberateness.

"Do you really feel you can tell Iraimin and me what to talk about?"

"You should not be discussing improprieties."

"Ah." Cara folded her arms on the worktable and angled her body toward him, eyeing Iraimin before speaking. "And you and Serano never discuss improprieties?"

His answer was unspoken, but not unreadable.

"And what improprieties were Iraimin and I discussing?"

Rodani focused his vision on the clamped clip. "The nature and scope of my duty to you."

"Well, when you walk out of the room, it's impossible for me to discuss anything with you. Yes?"

It was Iraimin's turn to stand. "I believe I have nothing to add to the discussion, a'sel'ai. I will return another time."

"Thank you for your visit, Iraimin. It's appreciated, as is your advice."

"I have more if you need it."

Cara grinned. "I may."

Iraimin left with a swirl of skirts, leaving behind two bemused people who had no one to talk to but each other. Cara dove in.

"What's wrong, Rodani?" She put her chin in her hand and waited for a reaction. There was none. "I can understand you still being disturbed by what other people have said about me. But if that's the problem, you're taking it out on the wrong person."

Rodani went back to his coping saw, in what state of mind Cara had no idea. He worked it vigorously. "I ask your forgiveness."

"You have it. Though, I'd rather have an explanation than an apology."

With a tap of his hand and a flip of the wrist, Rodani sent the jaw-lock bar spinning. He held his fingers on either side of the clip, waiting for it to loosen from the vise grip. When it did, he spun it 90° and reset it between the padded metal jaws.

"Was it the candle test last rest-day? The lies about me?"

His shoulders sagged, just a little. He scooted into a different position and resumed work.

Frustrated, Cara went back to cutting fabric pieces. Two complete inner pieces of Rodani's project had been deposited on the table and four of the quilt blocks completed before they headed downstairs.

***

The food line was thankfully short. Cara and Rodani returned to their places in time to see Serano enter, a woman at his side. They walked to the bar. Soon, Serano returned with four glasses. He sat them on the table and turned back to the food table as Iraimin sat her own plate down. She glanced at Cara, who smiled broadly in return. But no words were exchanged on the subject of the painter's earlier visit. Rodani declined to address her.

"My dual portrait begins next week." Iraimin said.

Cara looked up from her plate. "The taso's relatives?"

"Yes."

"Are you excited?"

"Yes." Iraimin cut a piece of a tuber and bit it delicately. "But it means I must hurry to finish my current one."

"Forgive me if I delayed you."

"It was not my intention to censure you. It was only an observation."

Cara took a sip of shigeli and eyed the filling room. More and more she recognized faces, though there were few she could name. Not too far away was Litelon, the stablehand. There was the couple with the baby.

Cara glanced around the table, then felt a presence behind her and turned. She switched mindsets with some difficulty. "Litelon."

"A'Cara." He came around to her side. "Are you well?"

"Yes. How do you fare?"

"Well enough. Ichi's training consumes much time, and I still have other duties."

"Ichi?" she asked, with a touch of forced humor. "He has a name, now?"

Litelon crouched down at her side, the better to look, as well as talk. "The dam's owner names any colts when they begin training."

"What does it mean?"

"Nonsense as best I know. But the owner's ancestors came from a far country in our homeworld. It may mean something to her."

Litelon rested his hand on the back of her chair. Grey eyes swept the tabletop and the nearly full plates. "May I sit at your table?"

"Yes," she replied.

Litelon's pupils pulsed. He looked around for a chair.

The taso's table had no extra, the better to curb unwanted

visitors to high places. Toranel's table, however, did. Out of Cara's earshot, he approached her and bent to ask for the chair.

Serano neared his own seat, hands laden with plates. Rodani motioned to him in code and rose to follow Litelon. He approached the stablehand as Litelon put his hands on the empty chair. Rodani slid his knee onto the seat of it and gripped the chair back between Litelon's two hands. Rodani spoke softly, Litelon stiffened and replied with some heat. Rodani's face held an aura of authority. His leg and hand remained in place as Litelon tugged on the chair and answered. Rodani replied something curt.

Litelon froze in place, his hands clutching the carved arcs that decorated the chair back. He glared with eyes wide and chin jutting, then thrust his face into Rodani's, spewing a stream of low-voiced words. Rodani leaned into the verbal fray with a rejoinder. Litelon waved his hand in furious remonstrance. The hand got too close to Rodani's face.

Rodani grabbed it and thrust it back at Litelon's head. Humiliated, Litelon fought to release himself. Bad went to worse as they struggled momentarily. A hush fell over the gathering room.

"You have no right!" Litelon hissed.

Cara slid to the edge of her seat.

Rodani grabbed Litelon's shoulder and pulled, unbalanced him, and swept his foot out from underneath him. The boy sprawled on the floor, Rodani's hand still gripping his. They stared at each other silently for a space of seconds, then Rodani yanked him to his feet.

Cara got up and took a step.

Serano reached out and grabbed her arm. She struggled for a second, much as Litelon had done, but he stood and pushed her back in her seat, burning her with a glare that threatened dire punishments if she interfered.

Rodani still had hold of Litelon, eye to angry eye. Rodani spat words at him, then thrust him backwards.

Litelon stumbled, spun on his heel, and walked back toward his own place, declining the obligatory courteous bow. Rodani watched him until he had seated himself at his own dinner, then turned to speak a few words to Toranel. She waved her fingers. Rodani returned to his own table with one more glance at Litelon.

The silent spectators refocused on their own business.

As Rodani sat, Serano waved code at him. He answered the same way and took a drink of his eisenico. Cara leaned back in the chair, folded her arms, and glanced at Iraimin before turning to her inscrutable guardian.

"May I ask?" It was polite, considering the circumstances. What in hell had Litelon done that was so wrong? They'd almost had a fist fight, all over a seat at her table.

Rodani returned his attention to his meal. Cara sighed audibly and dropped her chin to her chest, contemplating verbal mayhem. It was like living and working with mimes. Ineffectual mimes, and she couldn't walk away.

On Serano's side, another body approached the table. A woman this time, plate in hand.

"Iraimin, if you would please," Serano said.

The painter looked over her shoulder and scooted her chair and dishes closer to Rodani. The woman laid her tray on the table as Serano pulled Toranel's empty chair around for her.

"She is Larisi."

"A'Larisi," Rodani said, Iraimin following.

"A'Larisi," Cara said after some hesitation. Serano could have a table guest, but she couldn't? Damn this misapplied propriety. She left her arms crossed over her chest, reaching out only to gather up her drink. Rodani tapped her on her foot under the table. Unwilling to provoke another argument, Cara reluctantly sat up and unwrapped her arms.

"I have wished to meet you, a'Cara," Larisi ventured. "Anyone who can create such beauty in a strange land among strange people should be an interesting person."

Surprised, Cara leaned forward and curled her fingers around her glass. She cocked an eyebrow. "Someone else at the table admits to a sense of curiosity."

"Cara." The censure in Rodani's voice was obvious.

Cara opened her palm. "Please forgive my offense, a'Larisi. I meant none. Your words are appreciated, your curiosity welcome."

"I have heard you are a seeker of knowledge."

"Always."

"Then we have something in common."

Cara fingered her glass. "And likely we have something in difference, as well."

Larisi took a drink of water and raised an eyebrow at Cara.

"You receive answers to your questions." She caught Rodani's glance from her peripheral vision and purposefully ignored it. More than guild could play games.

"You do not?" Larisi asked.

"Occasionally, I do."

Rodani clicked his knife against the plate. "A'Cara, you test my temper."

"And you test mine," she said with not a blink against his scowl, ignoring the warning in his formality. "Shall we both apologize?"

Their mutual stares silenced voice and activity at their table, and at a few nearby ones as well. Propriety was not faring well, tonight.

"There are things we must discuss." He returned to his dinner.

Cara interlaced her fingers in front of her plate. "I've been asking you to do exactly that, Rodani."

"What I wish to discuss is not what you would wish."

"You scratch my back, I'll scratch yours."

Four pairs of eyes locked onto her face. She saw only two and grinned. "Forgive me, a'sel'ai. That's a direct translation from my language. What I meant," she said to Rodani, "was if you agree to answer my questions, I'll answer yours. A trade of information."

His look was unforgiving. "I am your guardian."

"And I'm your adashi, a'Rodani, a guest in this house and in this extremely foreign country. I can't learn in a vacuum of knowledge."

"There is knowledge around you. You choose to ignore it."

"I see knowledge of what not to ask. That's not my idea of information."

He sat up straighter, pupils gone to slits. One hand clenched into a tight fist. "Cease baiting me," he said slowly.

Shocked into silence, Cara clamped her teeth together and leaned away.

Good gods. Her best ally was showing ragged holes in his patience. No one spoke. Such an inexcusable public display of their emotions was unheard of, silence the only courtesy. Cara fumbled for her satchel, slid off her seat, and headed for the hall doors.

Rodani shot out of his chair and followed her into the hall.

"Cara, stop." He planted his body in front of her and leaned forward, daring her to walk into him. "Stop." He danced to his left as she tried to pass and trapped her against the wall. She stopped, but her face remained stubbornly averted. "Have I caused this?" he asked.

She sighed deeply in an effort to control out-of-control

emotions and shuddered; it was a reaction surprisingly similar to Rodani's, out on the cliff edge. "Mostly."

"Let us speak those mutual apologies, Cara, and postpone that discussion."

"Please," she said in a dour voice.

Rodani pulled his hands behind his back and straightened his shoulder. "Forgive me for disturbing you so greatly."

"Accepted. And forgive me for baiting you into a display of anger you never would've shown otherwise."

"I accept."

Things felt marginally better, but still she was not ready to meet his eyes. In turn, she waited for him to make a move—either back to the gathering hall, or back to her quarters—where he would undoubtedly drop her off like an unwanted younger sibling.

"Are you calm?" he asked.

She managed a nod.

Rodani stepped to the side and held out a hand for her to precede him back into the gathering. Reluctantly, she obeyed.

Their food was cold. Cara nibbled at it, deeply disinterested in what she'd wanted earlier. Serano and Larisi whispered between themselves.

"Will you have another drink?" Rodani asked.

"Please."

He took his glass and headed for the bar.

"Trouble?" came a terse query from her left.

Cara almost refused the new piece of bait. It hovered in the air with a taint of humor. She glanced at Serano and crossed her arms on the table. "He started it."

"I believe it is a little more complicated than that."

Her head whipped around. "What do you know that I don't?"

Serano lowered his eyes and focused on the nearest hand of his tablemate—and latest lover, if Cara guessed right. She waited for his reply, then turned to Larisi.

"Do you understand my earlier statement, now, a'Larisi?"

"Yes. But I do not understand your great depth of feelings on the matter."

Enough. Tired of questions, tired of fighting for answers, Cara responded with her own refusal of the implicit question. She lifted her glass of watery shigeli and wrapped both hands around it, bringing it to her lips. The glass lingered there, comfort somehow, when nothing else was available. She stared off into the distance and lifted her drink to her forehead, letting the cold glass rest against her skin. She wanted to go back to her rooms, to the dark of the night. To hide.

"You are sleepy, Cara?" Iraimin asked.

"Tired, not sleepy. It's been a difficult day."

As he began to sit down, Rodani looked off to his right. "Serano," he said, his voice a curt warning.

"What?"

Drink in hand, a woman sidled up to the table to stand between Serano and Larisi. Serano looked up.

"Katu." He was courteous, careful.

She lowered the glass to her side. "Serano."

Serano stiffened, expression closed down. "You are well?"

"I will be."

Katu splashed her drink into Serano's dinner. Golden liquid sloshed in the plate and dribbled off the sides onto the table. From there, a steady stream trickled into his lap. Serano's eyes pulsed wide, then narrowed to the merest slits as Katu stalked off past Rodani.

Rodani's face went to mask. And Iraimin's. And most certainly Larisi's. No such possibility for Cara. She slipped her hand over the lower half of her face, as Serano, pants wet, launched out of his seat to follow the spurned woman into the hall.

Cara began to snicker, sputtering behind her hand and rocking to the side in mirth. It was just what she needed to lift her black mood. She dared a glance at Iraimin across from her. The painter caught her look and smiled back, sending Cara into another wave of mirth. She lay her head down on her arms and laughed at the floor.

Rodani glanced at Iraimin and bent over Cara's dark head. "I suggest you gather the remnants of your control before he returns, or you may do permanent damage to his good will for you."

"Good will for me?" She rose up. "He has less for me than for Katu!"

"Do not mistake me, Cara."

She took a deep drink in a concerted effort to control her humor, then met Iraimin's eyes and fell into another paroxysm, sputtering shigeli. In response, Iraimin smiled broadly. Larisi, however, remained still, one hand in her lap, the other on her water glass, eyes on her plate. Cara noticed her and, much too belatedly, began to stifle herself.

"Please forgive me, a'Larisi, for any additional," Cara searched for a word, "discomfort I've caused you."

Larisi glared from the corner of her eyes.

"Are you aware," Cara continued, "that human emotions constantly bubble up from deep inside and roil on the surface? Like a pot of water left too long to boil."

"I have heard such things."

"For ill or good, a'Larisi, it's true." She stared into her drink. "Likely, Serano got what he deserved, but I would never purposely offend *you* because of it. I'm sorry."

For her judgment, she got another tap under the table, but Rodani's eyes were roaming the room.

In a short while, Serano rejoined them. He had changed clothes. The whole table of companions had donated their extra napkins in an effort to ensure the other side of his pants remained dry as well. He swiped them off and retook his seat, settling down to face a mightily cold dinner. But at his presence, Cara began to grin, then to smile. Fortunately, Rodani caught it just before Serano did.

"The shigeli is affecting you, Cara. You should retire," suggested Rodani.

Cara rolled her fingers away from her palm in acceptance and drained her glass, then rose and flipped her satchel over her shoulder. "A'sel'ai," she told the assembled. "It was quite an interesting evening."

The pair beat a hasty retreat before Serano had a chance to get too badly offended. Silently, Cara wished him a very interesting night. Upon leaving the gathering room, Rodani came to a halt in the hallway. Two men stood midway down the corridor, deep in conversation. Rodani grasped her arm and spun her around, then pulled her back into the gathering.

"Go back to the table. Sit." Before she could fumble a query, he had disappeared into the hall.

She wound her way back to her seat.

Serano was staring at her. "Where is Rodani?"

"He sent me back here."

"Why?"

"I don't know."

Serano's pupils narrowed. He leaned to the side. "Toranel." The guardian looked his way. Serano talked with his hands, gave her some kind of command. She got up and walked out.

"Who or what was in the hall?"

Cara closed her eyes in thought. "Two men, standing and talking. One was Litelon."

"The other?"

She leaned back in her chair, eyes still closed, arms crossed. "Someone I've seen before."

"Artisan or staff?"

"Artisan."

"Who?"

"Let me think, Serano." She ran her hand over her face, down her chin, up to rest against her mouth. "The first rest-eve I went to. Do you remember a man who tried to give me a drink from the bar? Rodani intercepted it and chastised him?"

"Yes."

"I believe it was that man."

"Are you certain?"

"Not completely," Cara admitted. "What's his name?"

Serano considered the request. "Garidemu."

"Is he a danger?"

Toranel came back to their table and sat in Rodani's seat, giving her report with rapid flickering fingers. When she was finished, Serano inclined his head in thanks. Toranel returned to her own table.

"Talk, please, Serano," Cara asked.

Oh, he talked.

To Larisi. Low voiced, personal things.

Ignored, Cara bent her head into her hands. Too many things were happening, actions in the background, activities just out of view. Vague rumors and lies, tempers, threats, and that's only what she knew of. She felt left in the dark, swallowing a vacuum of knowledge. It made her want to spew. Or scream. Neither would earn her anything but anger, disgust, and a worse reputation than she was already gaining. Troublemaker.

Even someone as low-key as Rodani, level-headed and patient, was losing it.

"Cara?"

Gods bless the painter. Iraimin hadn't ignored her.

"Are you ill?" she asked.

"No." Cara lifted her face from her hands. "Worried about Rodani. And about whatever is happening."

Her lips curled into a Selandu smile, barely noticeable.

"Guardians are secretive. Have you forgotten?"

"They won't let me."

The smile widened.

Rodani returned. "Come."

Cara took one more look at Iraimin's pleasant face, then followed Rodani back out into the hall. No one took a second glance. No one pulled any knives, pointed any pistols. Cara walked in through her door when Rodani opened it for her. It clicked shut behind her as she headed for the bedroom, but she whirled in surprise when bootsteps followed her across the stone floor. Rodani tucked his hands behind his back and looked elsewhere.

"Don't let me delay you." Declining to get comfortable, she stood in front of Rodani, waiting.

He looked anywhere but her eyes. "I would ask your forgiveness for my tempers."

She studied him; his face, his stance, his demeanor. "You're forgiven, of course. Will it continue?"

"It will not."

"Will you forgive me for mine?"

"Yes. Will it continue?"

Biting her lip, Cara looked away. "I'm in much less control of mine than you are yours, Rodani. But I'll do my best. Your control of your anger will assist me in mine." She plunged ahead. "Why did you humiliate Litelon?"

Rodani crossed behind her and slipped into his chair. "He was improper in his approach to you and became out of control when I confronted him."

Cara's eyebrows shot up. "He was? I thought you were going to hit him."

"It was scarcely necessary."

Rodani looked so…comfortable, she thought, sitting there at her worktable, sitting so casually, legs extended under it, one hand resting languorously on the table. Like it was the most normal thing in the world. Like he belonged there, in her life.

An overwhelming longing flushed through her, threatening improprieties. She turned her back and stuffed her hands in her pockets. There must be a way to get control of her emotional needs. Three years was way too long a time to keep flashing on impossibilities, to keep reining in her impulses. Maybe she could take that vacation back home Rodani had suggested.

Cara took a breath to speak.

Rodani's 'com buzzed. He pulled it out from some pocket or another as she turned to watch.

"Five."

"Office," a deep voice commanded.

Rodani's gaze flicked over to Cara, then went to the door. He rose from the chair, graceful, even at the end of a difficult day.

"About Litelon, the hallway, or me?"

It earned her another one of those damnable looks. Rodani left the room and shut the door behind him.

She slammed her fist on the table, scattering tools.

TWENTY-FOUR

There was honor, there was duty, there was fear.

Shurad sat in front of the fire. Its flames mirrored the heat within him.

He couldn't. But he had no choice. He wanted it to be different. His wants were ignored. He hadn't the skills. It made no matter. He was the only one. The only one in position to carry out this last symbolic act.

And it was symbolic. The actuality had been denied. His parents had failed. Three times was the maximum number of petitions for a single person or group on a single subject.

Now the onus was on him, thrust upon him by obligations not to be denied. He had known for months that it might come to this: honor against honor, culture against culture. It was a painful dichotomy, one his parents' generation could not feel.

The goddess had given no signs. He'd waited, watched, hoped for guidance. There was none available. He thought of the selaso but rejected that option. Her counsel could be conjured in advance.

The flames spat at him, much as his parents had done for all his childhood. He'd left them, hoping to leave their influence behind as well. But the reins of honor they'd attached to him as a small boy still pulled at him, invisible in their strength.

He sighed and rose from the couch. In his bedroom was a locked box. He opened it and pulled out a handful of coins, coins he was saving for when he asked Geseli to be his chosen mate. They jingled and grew warm in his hand. He distributed them equally into four pockets, then closed and locked the box.

In the hallway, neighbors and acquaintances greeted him, two offered to accompany him to the festive room. He turned them down. It was still early; vehicles should be available. He wanted no shared rides into town this day. With a key from the garage wall he drove off, heading northwest.

The Riverfolk deserved better. He believed it. Could believe nothing else.

He wasn't up to the task. Others were more capable. But others lacked the personal interest, the honor, the attachment to the problem and its solution. He was the only logical choice. The alternative was unthinkable: facing his family with a refusal. Better to fail in his task and face the goddess, honor upheld. With effort, he controlled a shudder that threatened his equanimity.

It would take a little time. The skills had lapsed in his household years. Years of writing, years of being sedentary. Quiet years of blessed separation from his people and the event that had nearly destroyed his people. Years to gain some distance from the intensity, the anger his family still carried within them.

He'd begun to consider it a poison, this debilitating emotion. There seemed no purpose in a vendetta when both species shared common problems. Natural disasters or the hidden enemy overhead could wipe out both populations. Surely, the goddess would wish life over the death of the two species on-world. He saw no honor in beginning what could lead to genocide for either or both.

The town of Enidan appeared as a line on the horizon, thickening as he neared, growing into recognizable buildings. The shop was on the far side of town, a five-minute drive from its eastern border. Shurad parked in the dirt in front of it and got out. A few faces peeked out from other doorways. Wind whipped dust and leaves down the road in eddying swirls. Wooden columns held up a canopy. Shurad gripped the doorknob, then felt as well as heard the alarm buzzer his touch had initiated.

Someone stirred inside.

A tall, lanky man in dusty guild colors stood as Shurad opened the door. The man's face was weathered, his hair streaked with black. He inclined his head at his solitary customer and put down the pistol he'd been cleaning, rag hanging dejectedly from the barrel.

"Temi's greetings. What do you need?"

TWENTY-FIVE

Rodani raised his arm and jerked his hand forward. Light glittered off spinning metal.

\<Thunk\>

The point of the knife went into a practice board next to her hallway door. He readied the next knife in his fingers.

Cara stilled the sewing machine treadle to watch him. It was hard to believe he'd let her try throwing his knives. He was calmer today than in previous days, fortunately, at least on the outside. And in turn, so was she. But she was not quite ready to assume tempers were under control. Not quite.

\<Thunk\>

The sleek curving blade protruded from the center circle next to its twin.

"Tea?" she asked, when he took a break.

"Thank you."

Cara went into the bedroom and made the request of Hamman. Rodani was already in his chair when she returned, pencil and sketchbook in hand. Cara walked around and sat next to him, looking past his arm. Minute designs filled the page. Notes were scribbled along the edges. Smudges and erasures could be seen throughout the design work.

"Rodani."

He sketched a curve along one segment of line, mirroring its twin on the other end, then flipped the pencil back and forth between his fingers.

"Yes." Another curve appeared from the center of the last one.

"I'd still like to know why you wouldn't allow Litelon to sit at our table."

"If you are unaware of the nature of the problem, Cara, it is best you remain that way."

"But I saw no problem."

Rodani's pencil scratched curves and arcs across the only

empty corner of the page. "Then you need feel no distress over the problem."

Cara turned in her seat, facing her guardian. "If he's a danger to me, shouldn't I know?"

Hamman entered the room and left the tea tray on the worktable.

"It is my duty to deal with dangers that face you. You know this."

Acutely aware she was treading on risky ground; she took another step. "I saw no danger."

"There are many types."

"What type does he represent?"

Rodani sighed. "He is an ignorant boy with an inappropriate interest in you," he said, pouring her a cup of tea. "He knows nothing of you, your culture, your mind, or security concerns. He is immature and irresponsible. And as I pointed out to him last night, you are many years older than he."

"He—" Cara took the cup he offered and sat back in her chair. Good gods. "But if he just talked to me?"

Rodani poured his own cup and folded his arms across the sketchpad. "Would you wish a chaperone during each and every visit?"

"You don't chaperone Iraimin."

"I researched Iraimin when she first evinced a desire for companionship. I have few worries of her."

Well. He was turning out to be her conscience and arbitrator of her morality as well as guardian. Ok. "What did you tell him?"

"To find attentions elsewhere."

"So, he carries frustrated interest in me and anger at your interference."

Rodani turned back to his sketching. "Appropriate interference is part of my duty."

It was going to be a long three years.

Cara turned on her portable 'corder and picked a song Rodani liked. If he was preventing other friendships, she was going to take advantage of the one she had. She peered over his arm again and pointed to one of the designs. "That one is attractive."

"Why?"

"Its intricacy. The interweaving of the lines. It's delicate."

"It has possibilities."

"For a hairclip?" she asked.

"Or bracelet."

"For whom?"

"No one, yet."

She studied Rodani's designs a while longer before returning to her own work, remembering his earlier words about Arimeso and deadlines. There was plenty left to be done on this one. She put her foot on the treadle and resumed stitching. Pieces of fabric formed and reformed into larger ones as others were added in the configuration the design demanded.

"Will you sing?" Cara asked her silent roommate when one of his favorites began.

"The machine interferes."

She stopped immediately and folded her arms in anticipation, eyes bright. Rodani turned to look at her, uncomprehending of her gesture.

"Sing," she said. "Please."

"Why?"

"I want to hear you."

He tossed the implied compliment but consented to her request. He took a deep breath, then opened his mouth and filled the room with melodious song. Cara listened with rapt attention, hardly believing the beauty the man could create. When the song ended, she sighed, grinning like a fool.

"Another?" she asked.

"Your turn."

Cara switched 'cordings and clicked up to one of her favorites. A happy sounding tune, it had a powerful beat and a truth to its words. Rodani watched, enthralled.

"I request a translation," he said as she finished. "Any song that puts such a smile on your face is one I should understand."

"It's amusing because it's a truth many women have faced about men. While it's occurring, it's no longer so amusing."

"I anticipate the translation with great pleasure."

This, Cara realized, could provoke more than thought. It was a song of a woman's conflict when her lover left her in the morning. Maybe Rodani wouldn't ask again. She replaced the 'cording with another one, cover for her own conflicting feelings. They both joined into their favorite duet that warmed Cara's heart and sent a flush to her cheeks.

"Cara," he began.

"Yes?"

"I would ask a question."

She opened her palm.

"It may be," he paused, "inappropriate knowledge that I request."

"I won't take offense."

Rodani sketched in a few more lines to his current design, then recrossed his legs in the other direction. "What do you do when you close your door in the evenings and turn up your music?"

Hmh. Someone had finally noticed. Hamman, most likely. "Is something wrong?" she asked.

"No. I have heard reports of the movement of furniture. If there is a problem with the room, I should be informed."

She relaxed. "There's no problem."

"Why do you move the furniture?"

"I dance."

Rodani looked into the study. "There is room for the dances Serano taught you."

"Human dancing can take more room."

"Human dancing?"

"We do dance."

Ignoring her smiling censure, Rodani went back to his sketching, aimlessly drawing paths around the various designs. His eyes remained on his work. "May a friend watch?"

Ah. The diffidence she had sensed showed its justification. "Yes."

The pencil continued its rather aimless meandering. "When will you dance next?"

"Would you excuse me for a few minutes?"

Only then did he turn to her. "Yes."

She opened her palm.

He tossed his sketchpad and pencil onto the worktable and rose, leaving her quarters without further discussion. Cara went into the study and moved the couch out of the way, then put in a 'cording and programmed the songs she wanted. She changed clothes and waited for Rodani back in the study.

But the more she sat, the more nervous she became. To forestall an impending case of nerves, Cara limbered up with some spins and stretches. She twisted bare feet on the cold stone floor and took out her hair clip, letting the brown curls fall to her waist. It was well she'd eaten lightly.

An hour's perception later, she heard the door. Taking a deep breath, she stood in front of the fireplace and waited, hands demurely behind her back.

Rodani entered the study and stopped.

Cara's free-flowing skirt fell in waves to her knees and was slit up the thigh. The blouse's V-shaped neckline showed more curves than was typical. Her hair flowed in waves over her shoulders and down her back. Her chest moved with the great breaths she would need to sustain the dance.

"Press the play button, please," she asked. "Then make yourself comfortable." Without a word or a blink, he obeyed, then straddled one of the dinner chairs across from her.

The music started. Cara saw no spectators. The rest of the room didn't exist. Only the music. Only the movement. Only the interplay of muscles in the delight of motion. Spins turned into sways into dips into lay-back bends. Her hair took on a life of its own in delayed reaction to her movements. The swirls of her skirt played peek-a-boo with her legs.

As a faster section began, Cara flexed her knees and highstepped across the floor toward the door, keeping her hands near her sides. A repetitive refrain set her feet into an intricate dance across the floor sideways, hips swaying. On the second repetition, she turned her face to the fire and swayed and stamped back the other way. Her head rocked, her shoulders dipped and oscillated in tandem. A third repetition again brought her face about to her silent audience. Her hands pushed at the folds of her skirt; feet stepped in accurate intricacies. Anything not held down by gravity bounced and swayed. As the tune wound down, she slowed, breaths coming in controlled gasps.

The second song was slow—a love song. It pulled her into a series of spins, arms spiraling up and down, in and back out from her body in waves, imitating the motion of an embrace. She reached out with her arms; her hands gently grasped the air and let go again as they neared her chest. One hand then fell to the foot that she angled gracefully upward, the other reaching for the sky. More spins brought the skirt out into a halo around her thighs. As the notes fell away into heart-wrenching silence, she spun once more and spiraled downward onto the floor, falling into a decorous swoon.

Quiet filled the room. Cara got up and pushed the power button on the 'corder, then turned, finally, to Rodani.

His pupils were wide open, his face a mask. He sat motionless, confounding Cara's desire for a favorable reaction. Her singing skills were adequate, but she knew she could dance. Rodani blinked.

"That is how all humans dance?"

"Few," she said, still breathing heavily with the effort. "Many generations made up these moves. I put them together in the way I wish, to go along with the music." She rested against the arm of the couch.

"Why do you dance without shoes?"

"Traction." She gave in to her curiosity. "Did it please you?"

"It was..." Rodani fumbling for words was a new experience to Cara. "...most intriguing. Our dancing must seem quite tame to you."

"Sometimes. But it's not nearly so draining of energy."

He stood up and unstraddled the chair. "I now know from where you get your exercise. And why you move the furniture."

Cara laughed.

"Thank you for the demonstration." He made an abrupt departure into the workroom on the heels of his words. Cara followed him out. Slowly, Rodani made his way to the worktable, hands clasped behind him. He pulled the sketchbook toward him and reached for the pencil half-heartedly, flipping to the page of designs. Cara closed in on him from the near side and slid into her swivel chair. She curled one bare foot beneath her and let the other swing freely.

"Is there a problem?"

His face relaxed into inscrutability before he glanced at her. "No."

"You're quiet."

"Such a spectacular meal takes time to digest," he admitted.

"Shall I teach you to dance, as well?"

"I would be as clumsy as an inebriated benatac."

The image brought a spate of laughter from Cara. Rodani's grace and economy of motion were the exact antithesis of his excuse. "You might surprise yourself."

Finally, Rodani turned his gaze to her. "With my truth?"

"With your incorrect assessment."

He returned his attention to his sketches, then impatiently flipped to the next empty page. Cara got up and made her way behind him to change clothes again. When she reopened the bedroom door, Rodani was standing at the hall door, hands clasped formally behind him. She stopped in surprise.

"I have duties to attend to, Cara," he said, forestalling any query she might make. "I bid you safe night."

Cara stared open-mouthed as Rodani left the room and locked the door behind him. Twice in two days? Disbelief washed over her—along with a tide of other emotions. She spun with the same force used in her dance. "Hamman!" The servant bustled out of the corridor separating their apartments. "What happened to Rodani?" Cara asked. Frustration spiked her intensity.

Hamman stopped and looked around the room, as if expecting him to pop out of the walls or from behind a table. "I do not know, a'Cara."

Cara started for the door, reaching out for the knob. "If I've offended him that badly, I need to apologize."

"A'Cara," Hamman cautioned against the forbidden action. "If you wish, I can ask."

"Thank you." Cara waited impatiently as Hamman ran her errand. She was back within two very long minutes.

"There is no offense, a'Cara."

"Then what's wrong?"

"He admitted to nothing wrong."

Cara bit her lips in high denial. She turned and muttered an expletive worthy of a fisherman, crossing her arms and staring into the study. What happened? Was her dancing too gross of an exhibition for Selandu sensibilities? And if she had truly offended him, he would've let her know somehow. Of that she was sure.

"Thank you, Hamman."

Hamman took the dismissal for what it was and returned to whatever occupied her hours when Cara had no need of her.

Cara was the one offended. She'd taken vicarious pride in her guardian's ability to find good in the different. And she was baffled. He wasn't offended; she'd bank on that. Maybe he found it humorous. Maybe he couldn't keep his laughter inside anymore. Was he sniggering at her on the other side of the hall? Somehow, she couldn't picture Rodani sniggering. Serano? Yes. Not Rodani. He'd already had too many opportunities to do that and hadn't.

That she was aware of.

Angry. Maybe he was angry? But that went with offense. Maybe he was concerned she'd offend others with such an uncivilized display. But given his reaction, she wasn't about to dance for anyone else on this side of the Himadi Hills. She was disappointed.

Damn the man.

Well, there was nothing for it. She'd find out later, or she wouldn't. Cara returned to her oft-delayed project, determined to make noticeable progress before retiring.

TWENTY-SIX

She'd gone to bed rationalizing and got up rationalizing. Sleep hadn't come easy. It was nearly noon. Cara could hear her stomach rumblings over the music in her headphones.

At least the quilt was nearing the halfway point. Smaller diamonds and triangles had been sewn into larger square blocks that would be joined into a complete pieced top. Sandwiching the batting between the top and back was the easy part on a small wall hanging. The meandering quilting pattern she'd planned would take only a few days by hand. Hopefully, her trail of successful sales would continue. Please the taso above all. Cara couldn't forget the priorities imposed from above. Even Rodani's first priority was his duty to Arimeso.

Maybe that was the cause of last eve's misunderstanding. Maybe it wasn't Rodani's good opinion she'd failed to garner but Arimeso's, as seen through his eyes. If Arimeso would be offended by degenerate dancing, she'd better not perform for anyone else. Oh well. Back to the closed door. She began to put it behind her.

Another singable song began. She joined it, dividing her attention between voice and sewing. Another rumble escaped her stomach. As she joined the female vocalist in the chorus, she shut her eyes and concentrated on her voice in an effort to match the accuracy and resonance of the recorded professional. When she opened her eyes, Rodani was standing in her bedroom doorway.

"Bright morn," she said.

"And to you. Now I know why my knock went unanswered."

"I'm sorry. I didn't mean for my singing to bother you."

Rodani leaned against the door frame. "No apology is necessary."

She held her breath and jumped into the quagmire. "What about my dancing, Rodani? Did it offend you?"

He pulled away from the doorway that had supported him. "No." He walked into the room. "Are you hungry?"

Cara leaned back in her chair and clicked off the 'corder, smiling. "Maybe you heard my stomach's complaints, not my singing."

"Having previously heard both, I have no trouble discriminating."

"And?"

"There are a few favorable outdoor spots for lunch you have yet been shown."

She accepted with a widening smile and an open palm.

"I shall return." Rodani disappeared through the bedroom corridor. Cara made her own quick preparations. When he came back, they made their way to the garage. He unlocked the center door of the dark carriage for her and then surprised her when he climbed into the driver's seat.

"Serano isn't joining us?"

Rodani turned to face her, his expression unreadable. "Do you wish him to?"

"No!" She leaned back. "I wouldn't have patience with his impatience today, and you might have to interrupt another confrontation."

Rodani cocked an eyebrow. "Or referee one." He started the carriage and pulled out, heading northeast.

Trees passed by, their branches waving in the cool fall winds. Half were nearly bare, others wore tatters of color, not yet taking the final plunge of the year.

The road ran on for some miles. Cara began to wonder how secluded this spot was that Rodani had decided on. "Have I been so far, before?"

"Not since the day you arrived."

"Is this still Arimeso's land?"

"Yes."

The travel lulled her. She curled up in the seat and gazed out the side window at the changing landscape. The carriage vibrated a lullaby.

Centripetal force pulled her out of her doze. Rodani was turning onto a side road. Gravel scrunched underneath wheels. They bounced along for several hundred yards before a dirt path appeared on their left. He pulled in and parked. As usual, there was a padlocked chain across the path, which Rodani knew the combination to and a warning sign to keep the curious at bay. She hoped it would. An outing with just the two of them was something she didn't want interrupted.

Once past the chain, Rodani relocked it, making sure the sign was still prominently displayed.

Out of sight of the gate was a standard outdoor table near the edge of a standard woods. Familiar with the next steps in the ballet, Cara helped Rodani unload their lunch. Winter wizened fruit joined the sliced meats, cheeses, and breads that inhabited the picnic basket. They spread out the spread and seated themselves on opposite sides of the table.

"Did you pack this?" Cara asked, smearing slowberry jam on a muffin.

"No."

"Who does?"

"An assistant chef." Rodani speared a few slabs of roast and flopped them on his plate.

"Do you check what she fixes me?"

"He. Before you arrived, he was given the duty of researching human foods and dangers. Only he prepares your food." Rodani picked up a butterscotch-colored bread. "And yes, I check it as well. This soft bread," he said, waving the object of his lecture in front of her nose, "is forbidden to you. It contains both a yeast and a spice that is known to cause unfortunate reactions in humans."

"How do you know?"

"Hadaman. We coordinated closely with them from the moment you accepted the taso's offer."

"Arimeso has truly been cautious and foresighted, hasn't she?"

Rodani regarded her from behind the forbidden bread. "As have I—in every area that concerns you."

Cara swallowed a mouthful of muffin and began to cut at the meat in front of her. "Yes. Sometimes to the point of extreme frustration." The tines of her fork impaled the piece of roast. "Nonetheless, it's very much appreciated." She swallowed a bite. "I'd be lost without you."

The trees danced in the breezes. No four-footed denizens of the woods appeared in the undergrowth despite Rodani's vigilance. Cara finished her lunch without undue procrastination, having learned Rodani preferred not to linger. They folded, closed, stuffed, and packed up, taking the leftovers back to the trunk. Cara waited for him to climb in, but he turned back to the table.

"There is something more I wish to do. Follow me."

Surprised, Cara pulled away from the door and did as he bade, trailing him into the woods. There was no track; Rodani wended his way through the undergrowth. He worked his way inward, looking out and up at the trees as he neared each of them.

"Where are we going?"

"North."

"What are you looking for?"

"A bechiat grove."

"What is a bechiat?"

"A tree."

"What does it look like?"

Rodani continued walking, watching his feet and the surrounding area carefully—even more than he watched the trees overhead.

"Can I help you look?"

"Tsss. I cannot search and listen for danger while you prattle." Rodani continued for a few paces, looking from side to side, then stopped. He turned around, and retraced his steps guardedly, eyes wide. "What has disturbed you?" he asked her.

She clutched a tree branch that shivered with her agitation. "That...was...not...prattle, a'tem."

"The woods are more dangerous than the clearing where we ate," he said, studying her intently. "And I am unpartnered."

"And that makes it your duty to speak to me as if I'm a disobedient child?"

Rodani drew back his shoulders and lifted his chin. "I have offended you. I am sorry."

Cara breathed deeply, then shut her mouth with an audible click of teeth before something flew out that she couldn't take back.

"Cara, may I request a postponement of the discussion until we are safely back at the table?"

She willed her temper underneath the good will she felt for her guardian. A shower of dying leaves rained down on her as the branch she'd been gripping rebounded in release.

"Yes."

He waited before turning his back to her. "Follow closely. It is unsafe to lag behind."

Rodani resumed his slow trek, with Cara dogging his heels. The cool wind pulled at her loose curls, tickling her scalp and sending a chill down her spine.

Rodani's head was on a constant swivel. He stopped next to a tree and rested his hand on the trunk, his other hand on a vine that hung down. His silver hair cascaded down the back of his jacket. Five grey fingers and a scarred thumb gracefully stroked the bark. One long leg held his weight, the other was bent at the knee. The effect was a tilt to the hips that drew Cara's indecent curiosity. Taut fabric teased her eyes and hid muscular curves. She held herself stiffly against an overwhelming urge to make a very personal mistake. The fabric shifted as Rodani moved, a provocative flip of light to dark, taut to slack to taut again. The memory of his strong arms and his hands on her thighs as he carried her across a stream swept through her mind, threatening mayhem.

Take a deep breath, fem. This is no calm lagoon to swim in. This is deep water.

Rodani moved out, more speed in his pace now. Cara hurried to catch up.

"There." A dark grove of trees stood ahead. Rodani headed for it. Cara followed behind, obstinately determined not to say a word until spoken to. Clusters of nuts depended from every branch on the trees. Little clusters, big ones, massive ones, from just outside her reach to as high as her eyes could discern them, they hung ripe for picking.

Rodani fumbled in a deep jacket pocket and brought out four cloth bags. He passed two to Cara, the other two went back in his pocket. He interlocked his fingers into a foothold and held it knee high.

"Climb," he told her.

She slid her shoe into his hands and grabbed his shoulders. With a heave, he lifted her up to the branch with enough height to make the ascent an easy one.

"Pluck the whole cluster," he said, "and stuff it in the bag. When your bags are full, then stop. I will do the same." He chose a branch a little farther around and pulled himself up.

Cara filled her sacks quickly, and the little bags became heavy. They were clumsy to carry from branch to branch; she worried about falling.

She and Rodani finished at the same time. He tied up the bags and jumped down, then put his hands up to catch Cara. She jumped, enjoying his brief touch before it ended.

Back at the table, Rodani sat down across from Cara, opened a bag, and removed a cluster of rattling nuts. He pulled one off and offered it to her. "Have you had them before?"

"Are they safe?"

"I believe they are."

I believe? That wasn't Rodani's usual answer. She stared at the fingertip-sized nut, suspicious of it and of Rodani's choice of words. Dealing with guardians on a daily basis could lead to paranoia.

With a twist of her fingers, Cara sent the nut spinning across the table between them. She grabbed it as it wound down into an erratic wobble and attempted to peel its thick, horny shell.

Rodani reached across, took it from her fingers, and gave it a sharp rap on the edge of the table before passing it back. A portion of it had shattered. Cara broke the rest of the shell and pulled out a nibblet.

"Tasty," she decided, and pulled out another piece.

He took the rest of the cluster in both hands. With a nut between each thumb and forefinger, he forced each off its stem in turn. They rattled and clicked on the table. Within moments, the cluster was shorn of its seeds. He tossed it onto the ground and reached for another one.

Cara pulled a cluster to her and studied his movements, then began her own cleaning process. Nuts rolled and spun over the tabletop, lodging against their clothing and in the cracks in the wood. Ricochet caused others to hare off to far corners, and occasionally off the table. The mound grew quickly.

True to her nature, Cara made a game of it, popping the nuts off in the direction of where Rodani's jacket met the table, then upward toward his pockets. His resulting look provoked a peal of laughter, which in turn prompted him to try his hand.

Kernels shot forward in a rapid staccato, pelting her jacket, then dribbling down into her lap. She retrieved the nuts with both real and feigned embarrassment, tossing them back at him before renewing her own barrage. The game continued, then wound down into congenial silence.

Cara leaned forward for another batch and felt an unusual something where nothing should be. She reached down deep inside her blouse beneath the jacket and retrieved a solitary nut that had nestled into warmth. On impulse, she tossed it at Rodani. He caught it, dropped it into his breast pocket, and returned to the duty at hand without a glance at her.

"Am I forgiven?" Rodani ventured into the silence.

Cara's fingers slowed to a standstill. She massaged the beginnings of a cramp in her thumb. "Yes." She picked up the half empty cluster and turned it over, idly. "I was trying to assist you in your search."

"That is clear, now," he admitted contritely. "I am sorry for my impatience."

"I'm sorry I bothered you when you were worried about our safety."

The quiet deepened. Rodani's face retained its outward, unruffled appearance.

She spoke into the silence. "Who receives your gift?"

Rodani looked across the table in puzzlement. Spreading her fingers, Cara rattled the nuts in front of her. "Serano gave the redfruit he found by the stream to Katu. Who do these go to?"

"Your interrogations have yet to be circumspect."

"We're interested in such things, remember?"

"In your company, I cannot help but remember. Most of this goes to the house. The rest," he said, "goes to my sister in Tendiman."

"Tendiman? She's guild, too?"

"Yes, though there is more in Tendiman than the guild headquarters. And you? Who receives your gift?" His head remained bent over the cluster in his hands.

"Me?"

"Unless there is a ghost standing over your shoulder."

"You believe in ghosts?"

"Having no evidence, I reserve judgment."

"Now you're sounding like me," Cara pointed out, amused.

"Does that disturb you?"

"No. Does it you?"

Rodani tossed the empty twig to the ground and reached for another one. "I am uncertain."

The pile grew ever greater.

"Did you think we could spend all this time together and not influence each other somewhat?" Cara asked.

A cascade of nuts flew from his mobile fingers. "My assumption was that your influence would be minimal."

"Surprise," she replied with a grin.

Their gaze locked momentarily. Rodani was the first to break away.

"You were the one who wished to learn to sing," Cara reminded him. "And to speak Cene'l."

"And you needed *friend*."

She tossed the truth back at him with the gesture. "The friendship has been mutually beneficial."

"To that, I must agree."

Cara sighed and stretched a kink out of her back. "What did you expect when you took this assignment, Rodani?"

"Never having guarded a human before, I kept expectations to a minimum." He rubbed the tips of his fingers together before reaching for another cluster.

"What were those minimum expectations?"

While Rodani considered the question, the pile between them grew larger, as did the one on the ground beside them. "Confusion and improprieties, at first. Then, with Hamman's instruction and mine, I expected you to mold yourself rather seamlessly into our society."

"Hamman's instruction?" Cara quipped. "She hardly says a word to me. And Falita even less. Serano instructs me with the back of his hand. Kusik looks at me as if I am stable sweepings that have been brought in on your boots. And you frightened off the one man who showed any interest in me. I have only you, and Iraimin, when she stops painting long enough to visit me."

Rodani looked up in surprise at the unexpected outpouring. "Hamman is intimidated by your expressive ways, Cara, though she regards you favorably," he said. "Falita will not cross status boundaries. Serano expects you to know instinctively how to act and react as a Selandu. My attempts to dissuade him of his mistaken notion have failed deplorably. Kusik regards you as a danger to the taso. Iraimin is something of an enigma in the house." He reached for another cluster. "Litelon is not much more than the child so many see you to be." More nuts rattled off into the pile in rapid succession. "And I apologize for my inability to meet your needs."

Cara's hands clutched reflexively. A cluster fragmented into broken twigs. "Rodani, I didn't, I don't..." she peered dejectedly into the broken jumble in her hands. "That wasn't what I meant."

His unreadable expression filled her vision and her heart. What had her presence done to his life? He tried. Harder than she knew, probably. Who knew what he thought of his time spent with her, and what he'd rather be doing. What kind of life did he lead? Twenty-five hour duty to her needs and social desires left little time for his own. He might have lost the attentions of one woman on that account, already. Cara took and took and took and gave back so little. The mirror he'd flashed in her face showed a disturbing image. She dropped the cluster and rested her hands on top of his.

"And I'm sorry for what I've done to your life."

He blinked and withdrew his hands. "What have you done?"

"Disrupted it. Taken too much of your time without regard for your own life's needs." The warmth she'd felt from Rodani's skin faded quickly. Her hands felt as empty as her heart. "I'm sorry."

His fingers resumed their motion, this time with an air of agitation. "You have done nothing wrong. The duty is more involved than was originally anticipated. There is no fault in that."

"But it's still disruption. And I'm well aware I can be difficult at times."

"As can I."

Cara tossed her empty cluster and reached for another. Her fingers were becoming sore. She flapped her hands repeatedly before resuming. "Arimeso chose well," she said quietly. It wasn't her place to call judgment upon the taso's decisions. But the tone in Rodani's voice had punctured her defensive walls and left a wound in both of them that needed healing. Even a Selandu guardian should know he is appreciated.

She concentrated on matching the speed of Rodani's stick stripping. Economy of motion, just the right force at just the right angle, and each nut popped off its stem with an audible snap. The first bag was almost full, the second one half empty. Nuts took up less space than spindly sticks that had a tendency to tangle. The pile grew.

"How much do we do, today?" Cara asked finally, shoulders sore and fingers cramping.

"Not much more. We fill the first bag, and let the kitchen staff do the rest," he answered. "Tiring?"

"I'll manage." *Yes*, that meant, in a manner that didn't lose her respect in front of the guild.

"Stop when you require," he told her. "This is neither duty nor punishment, but a favor to others."

She took the opportunity of his consideration to finagle the accumulated nuts into the bag. Only a few escaped into the grass at her feet. "How many of these do we pick up?" She dug at the dry grasses with the toe of her shoe.

"Those that are easily seen."

Thank the gods of space the man was a pragmatist in matters other than security. She didn't relish scrabbling through the dirt for those that didn't want to be found. Live and let live was her motto, and it held for the flora as well as the fauna. At least what didn't attack her.

By the time she was done, Rodani had tested the bag's closure and called a halt to their labors. "Unlock the door?" Rodani asked her, keys held out in one hand. She took them and went around to the back door to open it. Rodani carried the bags to the back and dropped them behind lunch's leavings.

"Ready?" he prompted.

"Actually, I need to," Cara averted her face, "use the goddess's facilities, first." She tilted her head toward the woods. Rodani gestured his understanding and took a properly distant path from hers, then came back and waited a discreet distance away until she finished. They returned to the carriage together. She climbed into the front seat and buckled up, leaning back into relaxation as he spun the wheel and took off.

Cara rubbed at her fingertips absentmindedly while they tooled down the dirt road toward the gate. She dug through her satchel and retrieved a vial, pouring a bit into her palm. Rodani glanced at her as she rubbed it over her sore fingers.

"What is that?"

"Healing lotion. Try it?"

He sniffed the air. "I would be teased for smelling like a girl on her first outing with a boy." He pulled over into the grass by the side of the road. "But...yes."

Cara squeezed a large dollop out into his waiting hand. He rubbed all dozen digits gingerly then pulled back onto the road home.

Rodani turned to her. "Back," he said, nodding at the middle seat.

She curled her lips into a beguiling smile. "Please?"

He remained Selandu still, and expressionless; his gaze shifted away, then back into her face.

No dice.

Cara dropped the attempt at playful coercion and sighed heavily. She grabbed her satchel and wormed her way back through the divided seats into her usual place. Rodani drew his gaze back from the rearview mirror and pulled out onto the country road.

"Thank you for the lunch," Cara said. "It was quite pleasant."

"And for accompanying me," he replied.

"When will you send the bag to your sister?"

"When I return you safely to your rooms."

She didn't want the reminder. This road was becoming a talisman that she held onto during the long days inside. Sky she could see. Wind she could feel. But freedom was denied to her by the man in front of her, and the woman who commanded him.

They headed toward the manor, Cara's arms draped over the seat backs in front of her. She stared past Rodani's shoulder at the ever-winding road as turns came into view, neared, and disappeared under the front hood. Forest was their constant companion. Cara hummed a tune or two. Rodani joined in, then surprised her by starting in on one of their favorites. His deep voice filled the interior. Cara listened raptly, joining him on the choruses, the only part in her range.

A dot appeared on the horizon, resolving itself within moments into the manor at Barridan.

"Did I offend you last night?"

Rodani craned his neck around to stare at her without the distancing of a mirror. "Cara, that is the third time you have asked me that. Will a third *no* be sufficient?"

She swallowed against the renewed hurt that had sent her hollering for Hamman last night. "You left abruptly."

"I had tasks to do."

Cara gritted her teeth in frustration. "I'm beginning to recognize a lie-that-is-courtesy, Rodani." She leaned back in the seat and thrust her fists into the car seat. "Possible scenario one: my dancing was ludicrous, and you left the room to laugh in private. Possible scenario two: you were offended to the point where you needed to leave my presence, but because you had asked me to dance, you couldn't discipline me. Possible scenario three: my dancing took longer than expected, and you left in a hurry to meet Katu, who had asked you to comfort her sorrows after your partner spurned her. Possible scenario four—"

Rodani pulled the carriage onto the shoulder and slowed to a stop. He turned to face her. "Is this a game?"

Cara curled into the seat, upset by his expression and mortified that in her own pain she'd restarted what had erupted between them two days ago. "Rodani—"

"We had agreed not to bait each other." His pupils closed down to irritation width.

She was not going to cry. Was not. But the fields looked watery through the film in her eyes, and pain filled her chest. "You offended me badly last night. I'm still attempting to find out why."

Rodani reached through the steering wheel and punched the button that shut off the power from the batteries. Silence descended. His eyes bore into her face, angry expression dissolving into disbelief, then confusion. "Forgive me. If the words were in your mind, Cara, why did it take you a half day to speak them?"

"I couldn't."

Rodani turned farther in the seat, settling a boot on the floor in front of the passenger seat, a hand draped across the armrest. "I offended you," he began, list-making. "You cannot tell me directly, but you are angry. In your offense, you use words to anger me. I become offended. I offend you again. Then you re-offend. Yes?"

Holy space dust. Her own race's logical insanities thrust in her face. It shamed her. But he was looking at her with those penetrating eyes. Invading eyes. She felt stripped of all the human camouflage that covered wounds and built distance.

"Yes," she admitted, trying to keep from panicking.

"Is there sense to this I cannot see?"

"I'd have to think about it." The corners of her mouth drew downward. "I never made a claim to sensibility. I'm an artist."

Rodani lay his forearm on his thigh and relaxed into the seat, as much as possible for a being his size. "Is it reasonable for me to assume that when you start throwing knives at me, I have offended you?"

Knives. "Word knives?" she guessed. His silence answered for her. "Yes," she admitted.

"I will keep that in my saddlebag," he continued. "But it would be less difficult for us both if you tell me directly when I offend you."

"I'll try," she replied softly.

He looked her over from face to feet. "I have apologized. Yet you are disturbed. You are still offended?"

"No," she answered.

"Then where does your distress lie?"

"Shame," she admitted, slowly. "And old hurts mixed with new. Unhealed wounds that still hurt. Those are not your fault. Forgive me, please."

"Old offenses?"

"Yes."

"Giving offense disturbs," he began. "Receiving offense disturbs. Discipline disturbs. Punishment disturbs. Discussing offenses disturbs. Old offenses disturb." Eyes fixed on her, Rodani rested his cheek on his palm. "Are you ever calm? Do you know peace?"

Cara crumpled in the seat and into a raining upheaval. Rodani closed his eyes, discouraged at his obvious inability to deal properly with such an emotionally unstable sapient. Advance? Retreat? Be silent? Talk? Question? Stay? Return? An array of options appeared in his mind with too little knowledge to prioritize, too little experience to predict. When seconds turned into minutes, he tried the only thing he knew. Twisting in the cramped space, he maneuvered his tall frame into the center area, tugged her upright, and put his arms around her. Soon his shirt was wet, his jacket sleeves crumpled, and his kerchief wadded and soiled.

From last night's dance to this, he felt as if he had been wrenched into a dream, or his adashi had been replaced with a doppelgänger. Extremely disconcerting, this perceptive shift. It left his own emotions unbalanced, his certainty confused, his honor unfocused.

Time passed. Rodani considered climbing back behind the wheel, but Cara's spasms came and went with the gusts of winds, and he was reminded of her cliffside vigil over him. He remained where he was. As one receives, one gives. He slipped his hands under her jacket and began rubbing her back, hesitating in renewed consternation when she began a new bout of grieving.

"Don't stop," she whispered.

He resumed the caresses patiently, rubbing his hands up and down the child-sized back until her spasms stopped and she relaxed against him, clinging to his jacket like an infant to her mother's chest. After some time, he ventured out of the silence.

"Are you well?"

"Better," she replied.

"What does raining do?"

"Releases emotions kept inside too long."

"So," Rodani considered, "if you had told me yesterday I offended you, this might not have happened?"

"Yes and no." She drew her fingers across the leather of his jacket. "Yes, because I wouldn't have spent last night and today being angry at myself and wondering what I'd done wrong. No, because more than yesterday's offense was released."

His hands came to a stop. "From my prior offenses?"

"No. From months and years ago. Before coming here was even a thought."

The hands resumed their motion. "Your people do not apologize?"

"Some do, some don't. My parents rarely did, rarely noticed what they did to their children. They were too busy making sure we had food and education."

Rodani fell into stillness. His chest rose and fell with his breaths, his hands slowed. "May I ask?" he said softly.

"Ask?" she answered into his warmth.

"What they did?"

She waved her fingers against his shirt. "Nothing terrible. Nothing even as physical as what I have felt or seen at the manor. But they have had to work so hard at keeping the new colony going and their children alive that they rode by all our inner needs at racing speed. It left us feeling abandoned, even when our stomachs were full, and our bodies clothed."

"And you still feel that abandonment?"

"Yes." It came out a whisper.

"And the rain?"

"Grief for the losses," she said, wiping the grief from her eyes.

"Does this bear on your responses to Serano's and my reprimands?"

"Yes."

"Does this also bear upon your inability to tell me when you are offended?"

Cara rubbed her cheek against the supple leather jacket. "Yes."

"You were not allowed to confront your offenders?"

"Not if they were our parents, or teachers, or other adults. Not directly. We could only relay our hurt back to them indirectly."

"There is a dawning in the eastern sky," Rodani replied. "And holding you comforts?"

"Yes."

"And when do I let go?"

Now she chuckled. "When you must, Rodani, or when I've received enough for the time, whichever comes first." His arms remained in place, resting heavily but comfortably across her back and shoulders. "There are human women," she continued," who would give much for a man to sit and hold them without complaint. You'd be in great demand among the women of my people."

"And what would the men think?"

His words invoked a scene: family and friends gathered in her parents' sitting room, watching Rodani wrap his arms around her and run his hands up and down her back. The array of imagined expressions ran the gamut from surprise to jealousy to outright disgust. How many would openly confront them? Probably the vocal minority.

"Many would be angry."

"Then it is well there are no human men here. Yes?"

"Yes. However, being a guardian, you'd have nothing to fear from them."

"They would kill me for giving comfort?"

She couldn't see his face, but the incredulity came through. "Highly unlikely, Rodani. But many would be shocked and offended. Some would wish to fight you. Others might dump a drink in your lap."

His hands stopped moving. "But I have done nothing with my lap to deserve that."

Cara pushed up against the resistance of his arms; Rodani released his hold on her. He was grinning. She sat back against the window as a flush rose up from under her jacket and spread across her face. "We'd better return."

TWENTY-SEVEN

Rodani leaned on the wall next to the study's door, arms crossed, relaxed.

Winter morning sun reached tendrils into the increasingly crowded workroom, but its meager warmth failed to alleviate the cold. Cara was double-sweatered and double-socked inside her embroidered house shoes. She retrieved the knife from the stone floor and stepped back to the line Rodani had drawn on the floor. The charcoal was becoming smudged and somewhat difficult to define. She went into her windup and released the knife. It thumped against the target and fell.

"Do not lock your elbow," Rodani said. "You lose control over the throw."

At least the knife was sticking into the practice board occasionally, but accuracy was hard to come by. Throwing wasn't nearly as easy as the Kishata, where point and squeeze was the rule. Involving her whole body in a motion that was supposed to end with a knife tip inside a tiny circle was like diving off the Community Building and landing on a single copper coin. She didn't hold out much hope of proficiency. The next throw landed far and wide.

"The only thing correct in that one was the bend in the elbow." Rodani pulled himself away from the wall and retrieved his knives, passing one back to her. "Concentrate, Cara. Your arm was too low upon release, and it curved downward. Your knife goes where you send it. Do not think of the knife. Think of the throw. Try again."

He leaned back against the wall, carbon copy of his previous stance. Cara threw. The knife clattered uselessly to the floor.

"Too stiff," he said.

Cara shoved her hands deep into the pockets of her pants and turned to her instructor. "If I concentrate on the mechanics of the motion, I lose the feeling. If I concentrate on the body feel, I lose the correct motion. I'm doubly cuffed."

Rodani's lips curled upward. "Where did you learn that one?"

"Iraimin."

He held the other knife out to her, twin to the one on the floor.

Cara took the knife from his fingers and held it in her palm. She settled in behind the line and shook her shoulders to loosen them, then threw as hard as she could. The knife clattered to the floor. Rodani retrieved them and studied her.

"Step back a half pace."

She slid her foot back.

"Throw as hard, but with less tension."

"How?" she asked, hand out in entreaty.

"Keep loose."

"Then I lose control over the throw."

A solid stare was the reply. She took the offered weapon, concentrating on the strange combination of anger and relaxation. Frustration welled upward. She threw.

<Thunk>

The knife stuck a hand's width to the right of the center circle, taunting her with her near miss. Rodani waved the second knife's handle in front of her face. She took it and repeated the throw.

<Thunk>

The second knife stuck lower down; a finger's width closer to that elusive center circle. Rodani slipped the third knife out of his wrist holder and passed it to Cara.

<Thunk>

It landed near the first one, just below it. She crossed her arms and stared at them.

"Enough." Rodani passed in front of her and collected his double-edged blades, slipping each into their sheaths. He called to Hamman for a pot of tea and laid his hand on Cara's shoulder. "My turn."

"Shouldn't I practice more?" She followed him into her study.

"If you were guild," he said, sitting on the couch, "I would agree. But your life does not depend on them. You are throwing and shooting for the same reasons I am singing and learning Cene'l." He reached for the second level primer he was working his way through.

"And that is?"

Rodani turned the pages, scanning. "Curiosity. A chance to do unusual things. A way to relate to someone whom one spends many hours with. It is not surprisingly pleasurable to do something forbidden."

"Do you feel guilt? Or feel wrong inside, dishonored, because of your impropriety?"

Rodani looked at her under lowered brows. "Would you do the forbidden?"

Her eyes widened at the depth in his voice. "It would depend on what it was and what could be gained or lost."

"And have you?"

"To the extent that you have, where no one else in your society will even consider it? No," she told him. "But I've had my share of dishonor."

Rodani leaned forward, the slender book drooping vertically between his knees, thumb in place between the pages. "I believe you have many stories to tell."

Cara leaned forward in imitation. "I believe you have just as many."

Their eyes met across the tea table. Cara lost her nerve first and snuggled back in the chair. "Will you read?"

His gaze remained on her for a moment longer, then he opened the book. Pronunciation was still a problem, but he had a good memory for vocabulary. With great care, he worked his way through twenty or more pages of the second level book. Despite boredom, Cara listened closely and corrected carefully, knowing for a certainty that Rodani was just as bored instructing her on beginning weapons handling. She was reminded of the many required hours spent listening to her younger siblings read from their primers. Rodani began to stumble in his reading, then called a voluntary halt.

"Lunch time. Will you join us?"

Her interest sparked. "Us?"

"Me, Serano, Larisi."

"Yes," she said, eyes bright with anticipation. "Where do we go?"

"A new place." He rose from the couch, hand on the quilt.

Cold weather gear was certainly in order, as even Rodani put on a heavier coat. The temperature dropped a few degrees daily. Already it was colder than anything Cara had ever felt. She pulled the collar up close under her chin as they entered the garage. He took the basket he'd carried out from the kitchens and settled it into the back of the carriage. Cara put the folded quilt next to it, then sat inside. Rodani followed, sitting beside her.

"Where are they?" Cara asked.

Rodani lifted an eyebrow. "Impatient?"

"To get out? Yes. Do you expect any different?" she said, smiling.

"No."

"Where is this new place?"

Rodani's gaze was fixed on the view outside. "Near the cliff, but not so high up." A little amused, he waited for her next questions.

"Will we get to the cliff?"

"Not today."

Through the front windshield were open garage doors, the stables, and a flat expanse of land ending in a grey shadow of trees. Buildings dotted the countryside at intervals.

"Has Serano gotten over his wet pants?"

"Likely, though you would do well to refrain from reminders."

"I will, for Larisi's dignity if not for his."

Rodani tugged on his jacket and twisted in the seat, incidentally brushing his leg against hers. The skin on her thigh tingled. "Serano's dignity matters so little to you?"

"It matters at all only where it affects me, Rodani. His ability to protect me is my only interest in him." Cara stretched her legs out into the empty middle of the seats in front. "I wish him no ill, but he pleases me no more than I please him."

"Does that disturb you?" Rodani asked quietly.

She grinned and nudged his arm with her elbow. "Not when I have you for company."

The warmth gained from close quarters bled through the edges of her garments. The wind whistled and moaned. Some trash eddied around the edges of the walls.

"And if you did not?" he asked into the silence.

Her stomach clenched in sudden anxiety. "Are you leaving?"

"Not that I am aware."

"Why did you ask?"

"Did I anger you?" he asked, instead of answering.

"No. It seemed an unexpected thing to say unless it was possible."

"Anything is possible."

She turned her head to him. A smile on his face was not what she expected. "Now it's you who're confusing."

The smile lingered while his eyes roamed the confines of the garage.

"They're taking their time," she said.

"Yes."

Cara crossed her arms and hunkered down in the seat. "They should do such things after we return, not before."

It took a second for him to react. But Cara saw the look from the corner of her eye as she stared outdoors between the bucket seats in front of her.

"Best you say those things to me rather than Serano," he chided her.

"Did I not?"

Rodani's answering gaze lingered long enough for him to pull his 'com out of an inner pocket. "Six, Five. Six, Five."

"Six."

"Where are you, tem'u? We are exposed for too long."

"In the last hall."

"Ninety-nine."

Soon there was a click and clunk at the back of the carriage. Larisi plopped a basket on the floor and pulled the door shut. The pair got in and exchanged greetings. Serano pressed the button to the battery and drove out.

Larisi turned in her seat as they passed the stables. "How do you fare, a'Cara?"

"I'm well, thank you. And you?"

"Well, thanks to the goddess. What do you think of your stay in the taso's house?"

Cara stared out the side window past Rodani as the trees sped by. "An interesting and frustrating blend of the expected and the unexpected."

"Unexpected?"

"Of the unexpected, I began allowing others to take care of me. At home, I'm very independent. More difficult are the security restrictions, since I can no longer go where I please, when I please. Also difficult is dealing with our different cultural proprieties. But the worst," she paused to reflect, "was my loneliness. Fortunately, Rodani has helped alleviate that with his companionship."

The carriage bounced and swayed as Serano tooled down the south road; its occupants moved in tandem.

"Do you live at the manor?" Cara asked Larisi.

"Yes."

"What do you do?"

Larisi turned sideways to see into the seat behind her. "I am an acolyte of the goddess, training to be a priestess."

Cara's eyes widened. "Why?"

"Cara," Rodani said. "One does not question the Enclave on private matters."

Cara retreated in the face of his censure and Larisi's silence. "Forgive me, please. I meant no offense."

"I take none." Larisi glanced at Serano, then turned to face forward.

It effectively shut off the conversation, at least until Cara could think of something else to discuss. Larisi's relationship with Serano was out of the question, as was her occupation. Cara declined to question after other, less interesting subjects. Serano gathered up Larisi's attentions with a question of his own. Cara fell into reverie and fantasy, imagining herself on a double date and smiling as imagination took her down human tracks, with substitutions in all the appropriate places.

The road was familiar for quite a long way. The jagged line of hills and cliffs became more distinct as they neared. Serano pulled off onto a different road this time, winding his way further east into the forested slopes. Sunlight dappled the carriage, and the road, as it stretched out before and behind them. A darkening forest of trees rose up on either side. Wind brought out driblets of the forest floor and strew them on the road for the tires to crunch and crumble.

The foursome rode their winding way upward, swaying with the turns and the uneven surface. A last turn led them to a path that disappeared northeast among corrugated brown trunks. Serano drove between them a ways, then pulled to a stop.

They unloaded and headed further into the forest in single file. Serano took the lead with Larisi behind him, Cara behind her, and Rodani at rearguard. A short walk led them to a large clearing surrounded by never-die trees. The sound of continuous splashing drew Cara's attention to the south, where behind a handful of trees a waterfall fell five or six times the height of a Selandu. Half obscured by foliage, the water fell straight into splash to form a rocky, foaming pool. The pool fed a stream that broke through its northern boundary.

Cara hurriedly set her burdens down near a blanket Larisi was shaking out and walked to the base of the waterfall. It splashed and spluttered against the rocks, creating a cold mist that settled over all the foliage that drank from it. Cara shivered and pulled her jacket closer.

"In a month, it will be frozen solid." Rodani had walked up behind her, too quietly to hear.

Cara turned around, startled. "You've seen it?"

"Yes," he said.

"You live in a beautiful land. Thank you for bringing me here."

"There is a small price to pay." Rodani's face was solemn, but his pupils were wide ovals.

"Which is?"

"Serano needs more plants."

"Why does that not surprise me?" Cara said with a laugh.

"Are you hungry?"

She glanced over her shoulder at the waterfall. "Will I have a chance to return before we leave?"

"Yes."

"Then I'm hungry."

Rodani held his hand out for her to pass by him and followed her back through the trees to the clearing where Serano sat knee to knee with Larisi. Lunch baskets sat haphazardly near them, on the blanket. He looked up at their approach.

"Do all humans disappear before their tasks are completed?" Serano asked her.

"No. You could have left it for me to finish when I returned."

Trust Serano to spoil a mood, an outing, or a day. Cara wanted to ask Larisi what she saw in him. Instead, she settled down on the near end of the blanket, and not incidentally, away from them. Serano reset his attention on Larisi, relieving Cara of the burden of overtly ignoring him. Rodani folded his long body down across from her and reached for the food basket. Cara got up on hands and knees and brought the insulated ice basket over and poured them both a drink.

Rodani arranged the food on the blanket then took the heavy-bottomed glass from her outstretched hand. "Thank you."

"My pleasure."

There was a hesitation before he took a sip. "Is that a Cene'l reply?"

"Yes." She took a brown biscuit from the tin that held them. They wouldn't stay warm long.

"Are you going to share?" came a sarcastic voice from her right.

Cara didn't even glance up, just kept her eyes on her plate.

"Are you going to sit with us," Rodani asked, "or play guessing games with each other's pupils?"

Larisi's gaze flicked from one guardian to another as Serano gave his partner a dark look. He lifted the other basket and brought it over, Larisi trailing him.

Cara scooted around to Rodani's side to make room for the pair. "How likely is it for animals to be nearby who'll threaten us, like the benatac did?"

"Not likely," Rodani answered easily. "Most are underground for the winter, including the toracs. And we will be gone before the rest start to hunt."

"The benatac?" Larisi asked. "May I ask?"

"One got loose when I was playing with her colt," Cara told her. "We got chased."

"And?"

Cara scooped a spoonful of stew. "Rodani saved my life. I owe him an unpayable debt." She smiled up at him warmly.

"You are my duty. Litelon, however, owes you a repayable debt," Rodani continued.

His gaze pushed Cara's warmth a few degrees upward. "Meaning?"

"He should have been beaten for the lapse in attention that put our lives in danger."

"How do you know he wasn't?"

"Guild may inquire."

Cara swirled the drink in her glass. Its blue depths reminded her of the cove her grandparents went fishing in before the last night-bug outbreak brought their deaths. "Possibly, that was the subject on his mind when he approached our table."

"No. I know what he was attempting."

The glass went from knee to ground. Cara's grip never left the broad base. "Would that be so terrible?"

"To some, yes. To others, no. Do you desire him?"

This was not a comfortable turn of conversation. Especially in front of Serano and the unknown Larisi. Cara swallowed heavily and cradled her plate in her lap. "No, nor do I not," she said slowly. "I know little of him."

"Must a human know another for there to be desire?" Serano asked.

"No. There's physical desire for a body one sees, and there's emotional desire, which requires some knowledge of the other person to believe it can be met. The best mates meet both needs."

"He is too young," Rodani said.

"I didn't say he interested me. But age matters much less than how one is treated."

Larisi leaned forward. "That is a trait we have in common."

"It's good to find something the two sides of the hills can agree on," Cara told her wistfully.

The level of lunch in the baskets lowered as the foursome took second helpings. Winter denizens became musical accompaniments to their meal as Serano regaled the party with his insect lore. Larisi listened raptly—or pretended to. Cara listened less raptly, aching to explore the waterfall instead of waiting for Rodani to finish his drink. She began staring in the direction of the falls, hoping to catch his attention without imposing on his relaxation time. When that didn't seem to work, she took to surreptitious visual lingering on his physical attributes. They were, after all, more interesting than a stand of never-die trees.

His beautiful eyes were focused somewhere out past Larisi's head. His slightly flattened nose and sharp nostrils caught the afternoon light with a line of shine and shadows. Full lips rested lightly against each other, parting slightly for a swallow of his drink. A black leather jacket followed the line of his chest from neck to waist. A triangle of fabric revealed the shirt he had chosen today, a silky grey. His pants, loose when standing, clung tightly to his folded legs in a way that allowed Cara an almost indecent line of sight for her imagination. Cara let her gaze roam in indelicate appreciation until she looked once more at Rodani's face.

He was watching her.

Cara looked away and raised her glass to her lips to hide the deep embarrassment that flooded her face and soul. "Forgive me," she whispered.

"For what?"

When he heard naught but silence, Rodani rose and shook out the legs of his pants. "I have a task. Does anyone need aught?"

Serano glanced up at his partner. "No."

"No," Larisi said.

"No. May I join you?" Cara asked.

Rodani hesitated.

Across from her, Serano burst out laughing. Larisi's eyes were wide.

Rodani's eyes flicked back and forth between them. His pupils relaxed into the ovals of calm as Cara drew up her knees and buried her head in the soft cloth of her pants, face flushed for the second time in as many minutes.

"Not this time," he said. "Guild reasons." He turned toward the path. In moments he was gone.

Cara was left alone with the two whispering lovers—sharing a joke, almost certainly, at her expense. She tightened her grip on her pants, hoping body tension would drive her most recent gaff from her mind. But her head remained stubbornly filled with the echoes of Serano's laughter, and Larisi's aghast expression.

Cara wanted her guardian. Wanted the patient, handsome, immensely dangerous man who walked through her days, to face that unpredictable one who muttered and whispered to his bedmate a few feet beyond her. Wanted Rodani's quiet strength, his shadow-hugging presence that didn't ruffle her feathers every time he drew breath. Wanted his comforting arms.

It wasn't like her to be so needy. Something had happened in these four months. Some deep hole in her soul had slid back its cover and revealed its cold emptiness to her conscious mind. Circumstances, decidedly abnormal ones, were the problem. Watched, waited on, curtailed, chastised, hit, and frightened out of her hard-earned rationality, she felt her reservoir of self-healing salve reduced with each unexpected incident. She was running low and had no one around to draw upon for replenishment.

Except Rodani.

It was no wonder she clung to him when he wrapped his arms around her. He was a rock to a drowning victim. Calm, contemplative, he handed her his stability as an anchor with which to weather her storms.

"Cara, get me a drink from the ice basket."

Disdain crawled over her nerves and settled into her gut. Cara went to the nearby basket and scrabbled around inside it. She fished out a drink, then walked over and handed it to Serano. He took it without comment and passed it to Larisi. Cara returned to the far end of the blanket.

The ice basket sat closer to them now. Grandstanding, he was. Putting on a show. Maybe they weren't lovers yet. Maybe he was displaying his power for Larisi's benefit, hoping to draw her to him. It wasn't a comforting thought. Cara would spit in the face of any man who treated another woman so contemptuously, especially for the benefit of wooing.

She sat facing the path, facing the direction from which Rodani would return. Soon, she hoped. The cold wind whipped over her curls and down into the V of her jacket, ruffling the edges of the blanket and sending the near corner folding back over itself. She grabbed a quilt to wrap around her.

"The nibble tin, Cara."

Oh, goody. First it was a drink for his lady friend, now it was dessert. Cara clenched her jaw and stood, dropping the quilt behind her. She walked to the food basket, grabbed the handle, and dragged it over to where Serano sat, watching with narrowed pupils. Straight-backed, Larisi stared into her lap.

Cara dropped the basket within Serano's reach. "If this is some kind of game you're playing for a'Larisi, please have the courtesy to deal me out." Quickly she headed back to her corner of the blanket.

Serano shot upward, grabbed her arm and spun her around, then slapped her to the ground. Dazed, Cara shifted her weight off of the same angry shoulder. Her cheek stung. She rose up on one arm and shook her head. A slow burn crawled up her spine and brought her to a stand against her tormenter.

"I am not your servant, Serano."

Eyes blazing, he fetched her another blow that sent her reeling and back down onto the blanket. She crawled to her knees and up to her feet, then stepped back a pace.

Cara rose again. "I am a guest in your taso's house!" She wasn't backing down on this one until she was unconscious, or dead.

Another slap.

She greyed out upon landing, bouncing against the ground with the force of his blow. Slowly, she struggled to stand. Larisi was at Serano's side by this time, pupils glowing orbs. Cara breathed deeply to regain the air knocked out of her.

Serano unclasped his belt buckle and whisked the belt from around his waist. "Stand."

"Serano," Larisi cautioned.

Cara scooted backward; eyes wide. As adrenaline flooded her body, her hand brushed against something rough. She glanced quickly and reached for it, then spun to her feet. A dead branch half her height now saluted Serano from her wavering hands. She shuffled her feet. If she were going down, he was going with her.

"You dare?" He raised his arm. The belt swayed with the motion.

"Yes, I dare!"

"Serano! Cara!"

The two froze. Serano glanced over her head. Cara didn't take her eyes off the enemy in front, not even to look at her rescuer behind. Rodani strode into the clearing, clearly furious.

"Cease this! I am gone fifteen minutes, and you are at each other's throats."

Larisi sidled backwards. Serano pulled his hands around to his back, the belt barely visible behind his legs.

Rodani walked up to them. His pupils were slitted, lips parted over a line of white teeth. He fetched his partner a blow to the jaw. Serano jerked and stumbled.

"Put. Up. Your. Belt."

Serano obeyed, fumbling with the belt loops.

Rodani turned to Cara and tore the branch from her hands. Bark ripped across her palms. Cara gasped, then brought her arms up against his oncoming slap. Bone jarred against bone. She staggered and cried out. Rodani swept her arms aside and finished the task with a backhand swipe. It landed in the same sore spot Serano had created.

Her eyes watered as she stumbled into an explanation.

"Du!"

She turned her back on the tall trio, stuffing her hands in her pockets. Her chin dropped, and her gut burned.

Rodani stepped between the warring parties, his face frozen in cold fire. "Sit down," he said.

Cara walked over and sat as far from Serano as she thought she could get away with. Rodani positioned himself equally between the two and folded downward onto the blanket.

"Start at the beginning," Rodani said to no one in particular.

"Typically," Serano folded his arms in disgust, "she was being offensive."

Cara stiffened. "That is not the beginning!"

Rodani turned to her. "Where is the beginning?"

"The beginning is when I misspoke several minutes ago," she said. "Serano laughed. I was ashamed, knowing I had said something very wrong but not knowing what."

"You also have offended with your laughter," Rodani reminded her.

"Yes, but I try not to add more offense on top of it." Cara stopped, as if finished or unwilling to go forward in the face of opposition.

"Continue."

"He kept asking me to bring over the food and drink items so that he didn't have to leave Larisi's side."

Serano leaned in. "You were closer. I was angry at your sneaking away in the beginning, like a child too lazy to do his chores."

Cara sat up straighter and looked Serano in the eyes. "Yes. Tell him what my chores were, *a'tem*," she said scathingly. "To wait on you like a servant. I'm not a servant, Serano."

"If you interpreted my words to be those of a master to a servant, that is your assumption, human, none of mine."

Cara's eyes widened. She rocked forward on her hips and put her hands in front of her legs. "And you are rude and ignorant, Selandu!"

Like a sword of Damocles, Rodani swung his arm down between them. He fixed an angry gaze on each of them in turn. "Cease. You were both playing taso games," Rodani told them.

"Taso games?" Cara asked.

"Testing one another's power."

She grimaced and turned away, muttering "What power?"

Slowly, Rodani withdrew his arm. "Serano."

"I asked Cara to bring Larisi a drink from the ice basket," his partner said.

"Ordered, not asked," Cara interjected.

Rodani hissed a warning to her. "Did she?" he asked Serano.

"Yes. Then, some minutes later, I asked her to bring us the nibble tin. But instead of that, she brought the whole basket and tossed it down at my side and walked away. I decided then to discipline her. But each time I did, she added another offense, until the point where you stepped in."

Cara hit the blanket with her fist. "You started the offenses, and never stopped them, Serano. I am not your servant, and I don't deserve to be hit for being offended by it."

"Why do you feel you were being treated as a servant?" Rodani asked.

"Because there was not one drop of courtesy in his voice or actions, and he was either as close or closer to the baskets than I. He could just as easily have gotten them himself. Taso games?" Cara spat out her words. "Serano was playing games with me to impress Larisi. And all three of us know it."

Rodani refused to look at their innocent observer or draw her into the argument. "A'sel'ai," he said quietly, "the offenses are tumbling over one another like a rockslide. Certainly, Cara has ended on the bottom." He turned to his partner. "Serano, you deserve to be disciplined for pushing her over the edge. I will refrain this time. But this is the last time I will overlook your impatience in the matter of these misunderstandings. If you do not stay your hand from Cara, you will receive mine. Do you see my track?"

"I am weary," Serano said, "of offenses and rumors that are never admitted to."

Cara pounded her knee with a fist. "Ask me what I'm weary of!"

"Cara," Rodani chided her. "Do you see my track, Serano?"

"Yes, a'tem."

"Then that is my expectation. Do not fail it."

Rodani turned to Cara. She wrapped the quilt more tightly around her and refused everyone's gaze. "And you, a'ki'tana," Rodani continued, "your inability to calmly face your offenders and speak to their offenses is causing problems with all of us. I strongly suggest you acquire the ability."

He looked over each of the three of them, slowly. "Are we ready to search?"

"Yes," Serano said.

He led them back to the stream and gave each of them a small bag. He searched the ground around his feet and plucked something.

"This is what I need," he told the two women, Rodani already being acquainted with it. In his hand was a thin-stemmed plant about four inches high, with alternating branches. At the ends of each branch were tiny bud-like objects, probably flowers whose petals had dropped. Cara thought the thing looked familiar.

"Find as many as you can of any size. They have already seeded, so there is no risk to next season's crop." He passed it to Larisi, then turned and continued down the stream bank.

Rodani led Cara back to a place where they could cross the water and motioned her across. They passed over the stream and started up the other side, Rodani to the outside between Cara and the winter forest. Cara squatted, picking flowers, until her knees began to give out from the awkward forward motion.

"Do not be cautious of stains, Cara," Rodani said next to her.

"We will all have them."

Cara made no comment, preferring to keep to herself in the aftermath of his unexpectedly physical censure. It had been weeks since he'd hit her. Granted, the blow hadn't been up to Serano's standards. It had hurt her heart more than her face. Every time she thought they'd gotten beyond such things, he proved her wrong. And her responding despondency proved how closely she'd let her emotional state be tied to him. She could put on a Selandu cultural cloak, but she was still an emotional human peering out from under the upturned collar, seeing the world around her through human eyes, and judging with a human heart. And her heart was aching for a compassion that didn't seem to be common in any form she recognized. It hurt.

She stopped for a moment to rest, shaking out her fingers and twisting her neck. Rodani remained crouched at her side, watching and picking. She continued on, plucking not only those plants she was sure of, but some of which she was not so sure. Several yards later, Rodani closed up his bag and put the next handful into Cara's.

"Thank you," she said, eyes to the ground.

Between the two of them, the last of her bag was stuffed to the brim in short order. Serano and Larisi passed by them on the other side. Rodani held out a hand for Cara, but she pretended not to see it and rose with her back to him. They walked unspeaking up the stream, across it, and into the clearing. Cara handed her bag to Larisi, then walked back toward the waterfall. Rodani turned to watch.

Serano double-checked the plants, then tied the bags together. "You will not stop her?"

"I did not bring her here to constrain her unnecessarily," he replied. "At times, she feels truly caged."

Cara passed between the first two trees, waiting for a verbal reprimand. There was none. The thundering waterfall called to her. Not so wide, but it was taller than any she'd ever seen in the flatlands around her childhood home. The water's constant pounding overflowed her hearing and drummed into the nerves in her skin. Cold mist enveloped her; the droplets that bounced against the boulders and rocks sprayed a continuous rain on anyone who came near.

"Cara."

That voice could still send tingles down her spine, even in the midst of anger. Cara pulled the quilt more tightly around her, turning her head only enough to acknowledge Rodani's presence.

"Are you well?"

"Yes and no."

Rodani came up behind her shoulder. "What is yes, what is no?"

The stream sputtered and frothed at her feet; cold chaos that threatened to engulf anything smaller than her hand. "I'm bruised but otherwise unhurt. I'll heal."

"Why are you still angry?"

"Why did you hit me?"

"I had no choice," he explained. "You both were offending the other, and each ready to do violence for something unworthy of the effort."

Finally, Cara turned to face him. "You offended me."

Rodani knelt, one knee on a patch of moist moss, head on a level with hers. "I am aware. I would accept a similar punishment in return."

Eyes wide, Cara shuffled back from Rodani's offer, from his unruffled expression and calm regard. "No."

He laid his hands over his thigh, resting one set of fingers gracefully atop the other. "Why? You were ready to put a lump on Serano's head, but you will not punish me for my own offense to you?"

Cara gazed into the beautiful eyes in front of her. "He was going to beat me, Rodani. I was defending my safety, not my honor. It's dishonorable to me to exchange pain for pain except in self-defense."

"Why?"

"Because otherwise it does nothing but increase the pain of the world. That's wrong."

"There is always pain in the world," Rodani said.

"And I won't add to it except to protect myself, or another innocent. To do else gains me nothing, and costs others."

"It does not regain your honor?"

Cara dug her cold hands into her pockets and lifted her chin. "In some humans, yes. Not me. I hold to a higher honor."

Rodani regarded her eye to eye for a few moments longer, then rose to stand tall, but not so imposing as before. "Am I forgiven?"

"Yes. Will you promise not to hit me again?"

"No. If I had hit Serano and not you, I would have offended him."

"Then next time, don't hit either of us."

Rodani's pupils pulsed as if he'd been caught off guard. "He would think me weak."

"There is more than one kind of strength."

"Physical strength."

Cara shook her head emphatically. "No. The strength to resist. Or the strength to do right when all around you are doing wrong. The strength to continue when your mind says give up."

"The strength to pursue improprieties?"

"Yes. Sometimes," she amended. She shuffled her feet amongst the dry leaves and incidentals that occupied the forest floor. "What did I say to you that Serano found so humorous?"

Rodani hesitated. "I would not embarrass you again."

Cara saw no hint of anger surface from the dark depths of his eyes. The pupils were relaxed ovals. "The CSC will need the explanation so no one else will make the same mistake."

"If you are certain." Rodani leaned up against a tree and pulled his hands behind him, relaxing his shoulders. "You asked me to gift you my attentions."

"Attentions?"

"Sexual attentions."

Cara flinched and clenched her eyes shut. "I meant no such offense."

"Why do you think it an offense?"

She opened her eyes to face his neutral expression. "I'm alien."

"Did Litelon's interest offend you?"

"No."

"Be chary with your assumptions, Cara, as we must."

They lapsed into silence. Cara turned and walked along the stream toward the falls. Rodani trailed behind. The nearer rocks were slippery with underwater moss that undulated in the flow like the tail of a swimming fish. Cara continued on to the falls, working her way toward the base of it. Ice water peppered her face and left sparkling beads on her hair, skin, and clothing. The thunder of falling water rolled over and through her, filling her with its power. Foam curled around the rocks at her feet, attaching portions of itself to the dried grass that hung over the edge of the stream. Humbled, she turned and made her way back to the bank.

"Can we get up there?" She pointed to the top of the waterfall.

"Yes."

Rodani led her back behind the leafless trees and bushes that framed the falls with stark beauty. Black, brown, and green surrounded them, the colors of snowless winter. At the beginning of an inclined path, Rodani motioned her to climb. Gnarled roots stuck up to trip them. Weather worn rocks tried to get them to slip. Branches lent them helping hands as they crawled upward toward the source of Cara's curiosity. Near the top of the path, Rodani boosted her onto the ground above. She crawled away as he heaved himself up and over behind her. She turned to make sure he made it, then walked the short distance to the head of the falls.

The stream flowed by her, disappearing over the lip of the cliff. Gingerly, she crawled forward onto a piece of slate that edged the cliff. It was half her height in width, cracked, but attached three-sided to its surroundings. A medium-sized tree jutted out from the cliff wall about three feet down from the top, its branches curving upward in a vain attempt to right itself. On all fours, Cara peered carefully over the lip and down into the foaming froth below.

If the view from below mesmerized her, the view from above left her awestruck. The stream wanted to take her, suck her down into the maelstrom of falling water to be dashed upon the rocks below. Cara shifted in her crouch, disquieted by so much natural power but caught in its siren's cry.

As she moved, her foot slipped on a patch of mud. Her leg slid forward. The other foot slipped, and the rock beneath her shifted. She turned over to clutch at rock and grass. With nightmarish slowness, she slid into open air. She screamed in terror. Only one chance lent itself as she went over the edge.

Her jacketed arm caught on the rough bark of the tree and held. Small rocks splattered at the base of the falls, the sound almost eclipsed by the thundering in her ears. She swung on the full weight of her body and cried out at the wrench of her shoulder.

"Find a foothold!" Rodani shouted from above. His head and shoulders hung over the edge; reaching down to grab her jacket.

Desperate to prevent a fatal fall, Cara dug at the cliffside with the toes of her shoes. Fabric tore. She dangled in the air. She pushed against the cold and gravity, then could go no farther. Icy water dripped into her eyes. Her ears were becoming immune to the thunder. Rodani's voice seemed to come from far away.

"Again!" Rodani yelled.

There. The foothold lifted her another bit. She rested some weight on the trunk. She shivered. Her hands didn't want to move.

Rodani reached for a second hold on her jacket. "Get ready to grab!"

With a massive heave, Rodani lifted Cara onto the tree trunk. She wrapped both arms around it. With clothing soaked, her legs felt like lead weights.

He pulled harder, lifting her up.

She brought a knee up. The bark dug into her shin, and her hands clasped spasmodically. She couldn't feel her fingers. Her limbs shook with fatigue. Cold. She was so cold.

"Cara," he shouted above her. "Come to me!"

That voice. Rodani. Cara gave one last heave. Her other leg came up on the trunk. She cried out with a loss of balance. *No!*

Rodani jerked her to her knees. She fell against the wet wall of rock. He pulled again, face taut with the concerted effort to snatch a third of his weight. He grabbed her waistband, bringing her upward. Her body rubbed roughly against the cliff as Rodani pulled her those last few feet to safety. He turned, assessing his options.

Larisi was crouched behind him, eyes wide and anxious to help where there had been no way to do so.

"Quilt," he ordered the acolyte, pointing. "Spread it out."

Semiconscious, Cara lay where Rodani left her. "Dry," she whispered.

Startled, Rodani bent down to her face. "Again."

"Dry. Warm. Warm water."

Quickly, Rodani stripped her of all but her inner clothing, then laid her on the quilt. He rolled her up in it as Serano jogged over to them.

"What did she do now?"

Rodani slid his arms under Cara's body. "Go back and start a fire. Warm the drinking water." He turned back to Larisi as Serano took the command to task. "Get her clothes."

Rodani picked up the burden of his duty and trotted over to the path. Balancing Cara on one shoulder, he used his other hand to steady himself as he slid down the steep path. As it leveled out, Rodani broke into a run. Past the trees, past Serano crouched next to the picnic blanket, out on the path to the carriage. Cara's slight body bounced against the bones in his shoulder. She remained motionless, cocooned. Rodani unlocked the passenger door and laid her on the seat, then ran to the other side. He climbed in and started the vehicle, turning the heater on high.

Cara lay limp. Only the top of her head and face were exposed to the outside. Her eyes were closed, mouth slack. Now he had time to be frightened. Now he had time to feel the dishonor that rode roughshod over his emotions. It had been only seconds. Seconds that had almost lost him the life of his adashi, and his honor and status along with it.

The laxity. Carelessness. It would cost him. He looked over at the bundle of stillness. Cost more, possibly, than he wished to pay.

"Cara," he whispered, fearing no reply. With a relief he would never admit, she opened her eyes and focused on him. "How do you fare?"

Wet hair lay limp against her neck. The bun was coming unraveled, sending brown icicles down her back. "Cold." Fitfully, she pushed against the quilt. "Unwrap me. Please."

Rodani hesitated only a second, pupils dilated. Then he reached out and tugged at the quilt, pulling it out from underneath her when she lifted herself from the seat. They struggled together until the last layer still covered her.

"Stop," she told him.

Rodani leaned back in the driver's seat, watching from the corner of his eye.

Cara lifted her hips and yanked the quilt into a more evenly divided covering, then leaned forward with it, arms outstretched toward the flow of heat in a way that tried to hide what needed to be hidden. She leaned into the vents and let the hot air blow over her face and chest, resting her forehead on the dash.

It had come so close. Never before had she faced death so immediately or been so relieved to cheat it. The pounding waterfall still echoed in her head. The glimpse of the fall's distant base haunted her, flashing itself behind her eyes. Not the epitaph she wanted, death by gravity. Death by stupidity. She sat back and brought the edges of the quilt over her, took a deep breath, and shivered again.

"Please excuse me, Rodani. I need to remove the rest of my clothes."

He thought for a moment. "I will turn my back." Rodani shifted in the seat and turned his upper body to the window, looking out into the forest.

Cara stripped off her sodden underthings then rewrapped the quilt, laying her halter and underwear where the warmth would reach them. "Thank you," she told him. As Rodani turned back to face her, she leaned forward again into the vehicle's heating vents, using the sides of the quilt as blinders for her body.

"Rodani, again, I owe you my life." Her voice sounded muffled to her ears, constrained by airflow and fabric.

Beside her, he stirred and laid his forearms across the top of the steering wheel, facing forward. "A'Cara, I must admit what I have no wish to admit."

The formality brought her up out of her wind tunnel and back against the seat, eyes wide. She huddled in the quilt wrap, wondering what her idiocy had brought her to. Was he resigning his duty? Had she given him one too many reasons?

"I failed in my duty to you."

Her jaw dropped. "Failed? You saved me!"

Rodani turned back to her, harboring a look she'd never seen before. Something haunted his eyes. "I was too far away when you fell. You were nearing the edge of a cliff, and I turned my back on you." He looked out the front windshield again, away from her questioning face. "It was an inexcusable lapse, and it almost cost you your life." Momentarily he was silent. "I am dishonored."

She swallowed heavily. "What will that mean?"

"I will make a report to Kusik, and face punishment."

"No!" she said, appalled. Then idea arose. "Do I have a say in the matter?"

"If you wish. You may write a report as well."

"Does Serano know what happened?"

"Not yet. He will ask." Rodani's hands gripped the wheel. He stared outward.

"If only you and I know," she said cautiously, "why report it?"

His head rotated slowly, eyes fixing a stare on her face. "Would you add dishonor to dishonor?"

"No." She turned in her seat. "But look at you, Rodani. Listen to yourself. Picture in your mind what almost happened."

His eyes widened in response to her unexpected challenge.

"You're punishing yourself already. Why have someone else add to it?"

He turned away. "To prevent a recurrence."

"Would you do it again?"

"No." His hands tightened on the steering wheel, but his voice remained neutral.

"Then a recurrence is already prevented. Yes?"

"It is not the same. I must regain my honor."

"If you must," she said, frustrated. She looked into the back seat. "Can you reach my satchel?"

As Rodani reached for it, a shadow appeared at the window. Serano handed a canteen to Rodani, who passed it across to Cara.

"Is she well?" Serano asked.

"We may assume."

"Larisi and I are ready." Serano glanced at Cara. "We can leave."

Rodani glared. "She was ice cold, Serano. Hypothermia kills humans faster than it kills us. Curb your impatience. The night will wait for you." He turned back to Cara and helped her uncap the canteen. She brought it up to her lips and took a long swallow of warmth. Fear had dried her mouth.

Serano left.

"Thank you," Cara called out the window as Rodani closed it. There was no acknowledgment. After putting the cap back on the canteen, Cara pulled a brush from her satchel and laid it in her lap. She fumbled one-handed with her hair clip before giving up.

"Will you take the clip out, please?"

He considered a moment, then reached out and undid the clasp, using both hands to untangle it from the wet strands of hair.

"Thank you."

Cara ran her fingers through the tangles, then brushed her hair. The job really needed two hands. Every time she let go of her wrappings to deal with the bedraggled mess, the quilt began to fall from her shoulders. Rodani watched, seemingly distant from inadvertently revealing antics.

"Do you need a shirt?" he asked finally.

"Yes, please."

She'd never seen any extra clothing in the carriage's storage area, though stranger things had appeared from the back. But to her amazement, Rodani took off his jacket and laid it between the seats, then removed his silken shirt. It was all Cara could do to keep her mouth shut at the sight.

Muscles rippled under pale grey skin that was, as near as she could tell, perfectly hairless. No nipples marred the line of chest that started broad and narrowed down to his waist. Light and shadows moved over his body as he worked his shirt off in the confines of the vehicle. A spattering of scars appeared down his back, then were hidden as he rested against the seat back. Rodani passed the shirt to her, then reached for his jacket.

"Thank you," Cara said at the unexpected gift, not quite sure what to make of it and the exhibition its removal had given her. She clutched it in her hands.

Rodani shrugged into his jacket and buttoned it over his bare chest. He looked at her. Mouth curling, he turned his back to her.

Cara dropped the quilt to her hips and slipped into the shirt. The fabric was slick, silken. She buttoned the shirt slowly. It was almost like wearing him, wearing his embrace. An intimate touch, and she wanted more. Wanted him to take his jacket off so she could run her hands over that smooth chest. Wanted—*gods*. Wanted him not to be alien.

She reached across the intervening space, toward the back of his jacket. Her hand rested in the open air for a fraction of eternity, then she leaned toward him, took his hand, squeezed it, and let go. "Thank you."

Rodani looked up from the hand she had held, then over to her, his pupils round. But he said nothing.

After another drink of warm water, she attacked her hair with a vengeance, two-handed this time. The tangles gave way reluctantly. Rodani's gaze never left the sight.

Cara grabbed the far edge of the quilt and rubbed downward through her hair several times, then leaned forward into the hot air and brushed out the rest. Gradually the curl came back, the bounce returned.

Rodani was leaning against the door, half turned toward her, arm resting over top the dash.

"I'm sorry," she said.

He didn't move. "For?"

She dropped her hands to her lap, brush still clenched. "For the dishonor you feel."

He pursed his lips in dissent. "Do not distress yourself on my behalf, Cara. You have faced enough today. My dishonor is mine to face."

"I'll decide what to be distressed about, Rodani." She shook her brush in the air. "But you face it because I did something stupid."

"No. Because I did."

"I was stupid first."

"It would not have been stupid had you not slipped."

Cara began the arduous task of spiraling her hair back into a presentable bun. One strand slipped out. Then another. She let her hair drop and gathered it up again for another try. Waist-long hair is heavy, and Cara didn't have much strength to spare. When it fell again, she let go, bowing her shoulders in frustration. "It'll have to wait for Hamman."

"May a friend help?" Rodani's face was impassive, his hands lay loosely over the steering wheel. She passed the brush to him and turned her back.

He began to brush her hair, drawing the brush downward in long, slow strokes. With each brushstroke, the fingers of his other hand drew down in tandem above the brush. Section by section, he worked his way from one temple to the other, fingertips grazing her neck and moving down her back. Cara's skin tingled. She pulled her arms across her chest as waves of pleasure traveled up and down her spine.

"You're playing," she said lightly.

The motion stopped. "Playing?"

"Playing with my hair."

Rodani let go. "Forgive me."

"You didn't offend me. Under the circumstances, there's nothing to forgive."

"Circumstances?"

"I—you have…" She ran her hands over the sleeves of the shirt, pleasuring her fingers. The collar tickled her neck. And a deep breath failed to release the tension in her body. "You mean a great deal to me, Rodani. It doesn't offend me if you choose to explore my hair."

Silence filled the space behind her, as if she were suddenly alone. She clenched her eyes shut, anticipating rejection. But Rodani began stroking her hair again, running the brush down all the waves. He spun her hair firmly and began to wind it at the base of her neck. "Why did you have such different reactions to Serano's censure and mine?" he asked.

"The easy answer is that Serano means nothing to me," Cara told him. "You do."

"That makes the difference?" The winding continued, becoming both less and more difficult as the bun grew, and the length shortened.

"Because I value you, your anger hurts me more. I expected you to be angry with Serano. But when you turned your anger on me as well, I felt shocked and betrayed."

Rodani's hands stopped their motion, his palms rested against the bun. "Betrayed?" he said slowly.

"Not my safety. I didn't mean that," she said. "I saw you as my protector against Serano. When I heard your voice behind me, I felt you had come back to rescue me. But you were angry with me, too. I was afraid you'd ask for reassignment, and again I'd feel abandoned."

"I have explained why I can or cannot interfere with your interactions with Serano, Cara. I cannot always rescue you from him." He slipped the clip through her hair and fastened it. It hung together properly. He slipped his fingers under the bun and drew them across her neck. Cara hunched her shoulders in response.

She turned to face front again, needing a respite from Rodani's touch. In the confines of the carriage, it felt intimate. "If my Selandu enemies don't kill me," she said, "the plants and animals may. If they don't, the earth may. I think you'll need all of your skills to keep me alive, Rodani."

"You will have my best." He reached over and tucked a strand of hair back into the bun.

"And you're greatly appreciated," she replied.

"My skills," he verified against her odd form of reply.

"You. Your skills. Your consideration for my needs. Your socializing. Your patience. Your curiosity. Your creativity. You."

Rodani returned his hands to the top of the steering wheel, out of the way. "Are all humans so free with compliments?"

"No. And I'm not free with them. I pay them out when earned."

Rodani stared at the forest, his face a mask. "Cara, why did you keep contesting Serano in the face of his punishments?"

She stretched her bare feet out to the lower vents, without bother for the uncovered shins. "Self-respect. I refused to bow to his offenses. Refused to accept the punishment as rightful."

"He would have hurt you badly."

"He would not have taken my pride."

Rodani blinked, a look of confusion on his face. He was silent for several moments. "How do you fare?"

"Well enough."

"We should go." He 'commed to his partner. Cara moved to the back seat, taking her underthings with her.

***

Safely back in her rooms, Cara crawled into bed. She snuggled into the covers and rubbed her cheek on the soft pillowcase, relaxing as only the truly weary can do. Rodani's voice faded into the distance, into the servants' adjacent quarters. Soft murmuring lulled her. Cara's close brush with death was fading into unreality, the mind's survival mechanisms turning it into a movie that played through her memories. That same body heaviness that had dragged at her as she hung from the tree washed through her now. The deadly cold was a bad dream that receded upon warmth.

But what floated into her mind now—and refused to leave—were the intimate moments she and Rodani had shared in the carriage. As her fear faded, less appropriate feelings arose.

TWENTY-EIGHT

It was too much.

Too much danger, too much temper, too much desire.

Long past breakfast, Cara remained in bed. Falita's solicitous query on her health was well-meant but did nothing but rankle. She curled into her pillows and clenched her eyes tight against unwelcome knowledge. Her body ached from both the falls and Serano's temper, not to mention her reawakening desires.

Frustrated, Cara smacked the mattress with her fist.

He was alien. Different. Not what she grew up with, not what she'd imprinted on. Strange. Difficult.

She tried to bite back the tears that threatened to fall.

Beautiful. Intelligent. Creative. Exotic, like a wild animal. And deadly.

Melancholy welled up with the tears. Did he feel what she felt? How could he? She wanted to crawl into his arms. Wanted to find out what was under those clothes. Wanted his hands on her, wanted his lips. Wanted him to ride her to the stars.

And didn't know if he even could.

Gods, stop it.

Loss or gain, if she approached him? The loss she couldn't bear—desolation in an alien land. Who would replace him? Who would fill her hours, her heart? A stablehand? Crafting? Serano?

Stop!

But his shirt still smelled faintly of his scent. She clutched it to her chin as she sobbed.

Nothing made sense. Nothing about this was right. It wouldn't work. He'd laugh. Reject her. Take back his friendship. Refuse her his time, her meager place in his life. And she'd have no one to blame but herself.

In between sobs, she heard footsteps. Quiet ones, slow and heavy.

Oh, gods, not now. Please.

"Cara?"

His deep voice shook her to the marrow and set off another flow of tears. Couldn't stop. Couldn't. Too much tension, ignorance, frustration. Lonely longing. Fear...of failure...of success. Of loss. Of gain she couldn't handle.

A weight settled on the edge of her bed, near her knees.

"Cara?"

Another weight pressed down behind her back. It unsettled her balance. She curled inward against it, against her wet pillow.

"What has caused this?" he asked softly.

Her mouth wouldn't work, her tongue was paralyzed. She was grieving—for all she had lost, all she had never held long enough to feel it was really hers. All she needed, and never had.

A cloth dabbed at her eyes, gentle and amateurish. She grabbed it from him and held it over her face. Hide. Hide the shame, the weakness, the fear.

Warm fingers pulled back the curls from her face. "Are you in pain?"

Gripping, tearing pain. She shook her head. Could he understand what flooded her heart and wracked her body?

"Cara, forgive me."

It was all she could do to form the word. "Wha'?"

He hesitated. "The taso commands our presence."

Nausea enveloped her. She opened her eyes. Rodani's pupils were wide, his mouth pursed. Fear?

"Now?"

"Yes."

She sat up, Rodani's soggy kerchief held in a death grip. Tears trailed down her cheeks. Her nose ran. "I can't."

"You must."

"Like this?" She waved her hand over her face and chest.

Rodani's gaze slid from her face to his wrinkled, tear-stained shirt, and back up to her mussed and falling hair. "I will ask for a short delay." He stood and pulled out his pocket-com.

"One, Five. One, Five."

The 'com sputtered. "One."

"A'Keso, I request a delay of the meeting."

"Denied."

"A'Keso, Cara is temporarily indisposed."

She flinched under his accurate appraisal, blew her nose, and hiccupped.

"She is your duty. Manage her," Kusik demanded.

Rodani took a deep breath. "A'Keso—"

"Obey your orders, a'tem."

"Yes, a'Keso," he said hurriedly. "But I would speak with the taso, if it would not offend."

Silence. Cara caught the look her guardian tossed at her.

"Rodani." Arimeso's voice was soft, controlled. It always was, it seemed, regardless of her mood.

"A'Taso, I beg an hour, a half-hour."

"What is wrong?"

"She is—, now is—," he glanced at Cara, then looked away, "not an acceptable time to hold a discussion with her."

"Why?"

Desperate to keep quiet, Cara clenched her hands together, cold soggy kerchief still between.

Rodani's ears twitched. "She is in some distress, a'Taso."

"Because of your errors?"

His pupils pulsed, wide and dark. "I do not know, a'Taso."

<Click>

He turned aside, but not before Cara caught his expression. She threw herself on the bed and cried more.

Now it was guilt. She'd gotten him in trouble with her impatience, her curiosity, her idiotic daring. And it was her fault. She hadn't even written the note absolving him of wrongdoing, because she couldn't find the words. Now he would pay. Echoes of a leather belt hitting bare skin shot through her head. Was that how he got his scars?

"Cara." He shook her shoulder. "Cara."

"I'm sorry, Rodani."

"Get up. Get dressed."

She crawled to the edge of the bed, her eyes streaming. "Washrag. Cold, wet." He headed for the facilities. "Please," she called after him.

He brought the cloth to her and sat down in the chair next to her bed. She slapped it against her face, breathed in the cold, let it drain the heat from her skin and eyes. It brought her a measure of control.

After a short time, he asked, "Are you calmed?"

"Yes."

"Dress." He tugged at his shirt where it lay against her arm, cuffs rolled up past her wrists. "Get out of this."

She straightened and looked at him fully for the first time since he entered her bedroom. Whatever he felt, he was in control again. It was almost a reprimand, that he could face his taso's displeasure with such restraint while Cara fell to pieces for nothing more than a lonely heart. "Forgive me, please," she said.

"Dress." He got up to leave her some privacy.

The workroom door rattled. Kusik stomped in. Cara startled, and Rodani moved nearer her. The security first held the door for Arimeso. She glided in, cool and remote. Rodani stiffened. Cara withered under that cold stare, and the hot one that followed behind. Rodani yanked on her arm. Belatedly, she stood, still covered in nothing but his oversized shirt that fell to her knees.

"A'Taso," Rodani said. Cara echoed the greeting.

Arimeso invaded the bedroom, filled it with her aura, her power. Kusik stood a pace behind her right elbow, brooding, darkly dangerous.

"Where is this distress, a'tem?" Arimeso asked.

"Written in the colors of her face, a'Taso," Rodani said, "and in her swollen eyes."

Cara flushed as the taso raked her up and down with a forbidding gaze, a frown at the edges of her mouth.

"There are things that require discussing, a'Cara," she said. "Are you capable?"

Another flush. What they must think of her—red-faced, childish in unrestrained emotion. "I believe so."

"Whose shirt do you wear?" Kusik demanded.

Surprised, she plucked at the rolled sleeves, at the buttons that ran diagonally across her body, fearing an answer, fearing no answer. Sick of being fearful.

"It is—" Rodani began.

"She can speak."

Cara took a shuddering breath, bereft of the assistance Rodani tried to give. "I would not offend, a'Keso."

"You already offend," he snapped.

She raised her shoulders, then dropped them and pursed her lips, false courage, treading the emotional line. "It's Rodani's."

Kusik turned to his subordinate, his pupils telling the angry tale. "Why do you offer her your clothing?"

Rodani didn't hesitate. "She needed it, a'Keso."

"Still?"

"Hamman was prepared to take it from her last night, but Cara wished to sleep instead. We saw no harm in her actions."

Kusik turned his deadly heat on Cara. "And why do you wear it?"

Her eyes began to water. Damn, and double damn. Where was her composure? "My clothes were wet, yesterday. I…he…"

"Are they wet now?"

"No, but—"

"Then why do your wear your guardian's clothing?"

A surge of anger rode up her spine, overflowing before she could resist. "If you would stop interrupting, I could answer!"

Kusik's expression flared to life: rage, offense. Two steps. A hand raised.

Rodani interposed his body. "A'Keso, I suggested to the taso this was not an appropriate time." His words spilled out at a rapid clip. "Cara is distraught. Her temper flares easily at such moments. I ask forgiveness for her."

Arimeso hissed softly. Cara peered out from behind Rodani. Kusik retreated.

Rodani moved aside. False security gone, she felt stripped by the exposure. "Forgive me, please, a'Taso, a'Keso. I—"

Rodani waited, unmoving now. Cara tried to imitate him, but didn't know where to put her hands, hold her arms, how to stand, where to look. Embarrassed and feeling fragile, she was naked under the shirt and couldn't even cross her arms. And she was getting cold.

"A'Cara, why were you distressed?" Arimeso asked.

Gods, no. Not here, not now. "A'Taso, I can't say."

Kusik glowered at her.

"It is customary among the Selandu to speak of problems, of offenses," Arimeso continued. "To speak to the ones responsible, or to the taso. You are aware of this?"

"Yes, a'Taso."

"Then speak."

Arimeso's expression was blank, unreadable. Cara had been given an order. An order she didn't know what to do with. She opened her mouth without words to say, shut it, opened it and took a breath, closed it again. Rodani looked out past Kusik, eyes narrowed in thought.

"A'Cara," Arimeso reprimanded her.

It wasn't wise to be a fish out of water in front of a taso. But Cara's mind had shut off for the umpteenth time in an hour. She pinched herself to get it restarted. It remained mute.

"A'Cara." The command came out ice cold.

"A'Taso, I don't know what to say."

Stone-faced, Arimeso regarded her. "A'Cara, rumors abound of your dissatisfaction with my household. Yesterday, you suffered under mistakes by both your guardians. Today, you are distressed to the point that Rodani must postpone our meeting, you insult my first in wrath, and you can hardly converse with me." She leaned forward, pupils narrowing. "It is difficult to believe you cannot say why."

Her eyes filled with tears. What bad timing, that Arimeso would force a confrontation now. "A'Taso, I'm not dissatisfied. I am not."

Arimeso didn't look convinced. Kusik looked ready to hit someone.

"Rodani told me of rumors," Cara continued. "I denied them, and I still do. My rooms are fine. My food is tasty. My servants are courteous. Rodani is helpful." She folded her arms across her chest despite the cold. Silky fabric rubbed against her, reminding her that she wore nothing but what seemed to be forbidden to her. "I have no complaints that have not already been addressed or explained."

"Do you wish Rodani punished for his mistakes?" Arimeso asked.

"No! He saved my life!"

"Then whence the rumors?"

Tenacious as a bedamned guardian. "I don't know, a'Taso. Have you tracked them? Followed them to their source?"

"The source is nebulous."

Cara lifted her chin and stood away from the wall, adamant. "The source is not me."

"Your opinion of the source?"

"Those who wish me dead, a'Taso, or gone. What safer way than to sow dissent between us?"

Kusik slipped one hand onto his weapons belt. "What safer way to be sent home without dishonor than to paint blame on the taso?"

"I would never!"

"I am unconvinced," Kusik replied with a growl.

"I don't want to go home."

Kusik waved his hand over the crumpled quilts. "Then why do you lie abed in upheavals instead of crafting?"

She was on the verge of another one. Taking several deep breaths, she began. "I...just have strong feelings at times, a'Taso, and it doesn't mean someone did something wrong. I wish I could stay as calm as others here, but...I just don't work that way." She hung her head. "I'm very sorry."

"So," Arimeso said, not unkindly, "yesterday's errors are not the fault of this?"

She shook her head. "They're not."

"Do you wish a new guardian?"

Cara gasped. "No!"

"This makes no sense, a'Cara."

"I'm sorry, a'Taso."

"I have heard enough sorrys. I would prefer answers."

"I have none, a'Taso." She dared to stand straighter, to look around. Rodani hadn't moved. Kusik was no closer, Arimeso no more happy.

"You are walking me in circles, a'Cara. I am not pleased."

Cara rubbed the streams from her face and created another blot on the shirtsleeve. "I have no wish to anger or offend you, a'Taso. I'm human. Some things are discussable, some are not."

"Apparently." Arimeso walked up to Kusik's side. "On your honor, a'Cara, you are not responsible for the rumors?"

"On my honor," she said, emphasis with voice and gestures. "I'm not."

"On your honor, a'Cara, you have no outstanding complaints against me or my house?"

"On my honor, a'Taso."

Arimeso came a step closer, stared down at her. "You will send a message to your see-ess-see, confirming this fact."

The ambassadors. What was happening back home? What had they been told? "Yes," was all she managed.

Arimeso walked out. Kusik left her with a menacing stare.

Cara collapsed against the wall, snared in another tangled web, one not of her own making. Her unknown enemy's treachery boiled through her; self-pity battled a growing rage. She pounded her fist on the headboard.

"I don't deserve this, Rodani!" The headboard thumped and rattled under the force of her anger. "Nor do you! Nor does Arimeso!"

As the wind-up clock toppled onto the bed, Rodani grabbed her arm. "Cara, stop."

She shook it, trying to free herself. "Why can't he be found? Why can't he be stopped?"

"Anyone can start rumors," he reminded her. "Not only someone who wishes you dead."

She froze, eyes on the workroom door. "Serano."

Rodani glanced over his shoulder, into the empty room. "No." He let go of her arm.

"Why not? He abhors me. And guarding me could get him killed."

"As it could me."

She didn't want the reminder. Not after a morning like this one.

"It is part of a guardian's duty to take that risk," he said. "Serano would not harm you in such a way."

"Why?"

"Because he is guild," Rodani said. "If he were caught, not only would Arimeso punish him, but so would Kusik, and so would I." He headed for the door. "I will arrange the call to the see-ess-see."

***

Shurad strolled into the festive room. It was noisy for an off night. He walked past a membetati game in the near corner. Its ziggurat board rose from a square base; tiny figures dotted the steps, red soldiers, black guardians, gold priestesses. No one had yet reached the top.

The far left corner was currently inhabited by two bare-chested men, wrestling with each other within the outlines of a rectangle taped to the floor. The manor's pre-eminent potter was taking wagers.

"Sel'u." Shurad took a seat at one of the central tables, his back to the door. Garidemu spared him a glance and went back to counting coins.

In the right corner, Litelon sat across from an acolyte. She muttered and made hand gestures while staring into his eyes. He leaned forward in an attempt to hear her more clearly.

In the last corner were two drummers, a man and a woman finger-drumming on the taut skins of dub'ai. The ki'duba, a smaller drum, rested between the knees of the man. The taller bo'duba sat on the floor at the woman's feet. Strips of leather hung from the drumhead in an encompassing circle. A tiny bell hung from each strip and tinkled lightly with any sharp rap of the woman's hand against the drum. The drummers' eyes were narrowed, their bodies tense in concentration of the intricate rhythms they were weaving. A young girl danced in front of them, inaccurate and exuberant steps proclaiming both her amateur status and her possible dancing career. Arimeso's cadre of musicians and dancers were well regarded, and in great demand at the other manors.

Mutters and smiles came from the wrestling corner as one man was hurled out of the rectangle by the other. Garidemu passed small coins to several bettors; others went away with lighter purses. He slid into a chair next to Shurad. "Where have you been?"

Shurad glanced over his shoulder to the stone cooler resting against the wall. "Drink?"

Garidemu rolled his fingers open.

Shurad retrieved two dripping bottles and sat them on the table. "Family matters."

"I heard news of the denial."

Shurad ran his finger through a drip at the bottom of the bottle, then gripped it fiercely.

"My sympathies," the potter continued.

"It should have been an obvious judgment, sel'u," Shurad complained.

"Nothing that comes from Hadaman is obvious."

"Including honor."

"Is your honor not also torn?" Garidemu asked. "Wishes notwithstanding, we do share this planet."

"Since when do you side with the humans?"

"Never. You know my opinions."

Shurad took a deep swig of his drink. "They should all perish in a plague."

"Would that we could conjure one."

"Petition Kimasa."

Garidemu's pupils widened. "I will leave that task in your hands."

Shurad pounded his fist on the table. The bottles danced. "Does no one see this truth that I see?"

Heads turned around to face him. He met the gaze of those nearest before refocusing on his tablemate. "It should be obvious," he continued more quietly, "that we must not share it."

"Then we should leave," said a voice behind Garidemu.

"Because they were here first."

Slowly, Shurad raised his eyes to Litelon, who had heard all the fortunes his pocket could afford.

"And what wisdom, ki'oto, do you bring to this discussion that is none of yours?"

Litelon ignored the insulting appellative. "The wisdom I have gained from talking with Cara, and with Rodani."

"Rodani." Shurad leaned back in his chair to eye the young man. "Rodani the strange."

"Rodani the desperate," Garidemu added, his mouth turned up in a sharp grin.

Litelon took an uninvited seat at the table and tilted his chair back on two legs. "Do you so readily offend guild?"

"When they are so readily offendable."

"I wonder," Garidemu said, "what skills the taso sees in him."

Soft laughter blossomed around them.

"Why do you detest humans?" Litelon asked the writer.

Shurad sat the bottle down at his elbow and stared, pupils slitted. "Can you be so ignorant?"

Litelon turned his gaze aside and made a vertical cutting motion with his hand. "I meant those humans who are innocent. All those who did nothing to your family."

"If they had any honor they would make restitution."

"That will not bring back lives."

"I am not stupid, stablehand," Shurad told him. "Restitution is not about lives. It is about payment. Labor. Goods. Repairs. Restorations. Apologies and facing discipline." Shurad picked up his bottle and swung it through an arc. "The humans will do none of these things."

"They must have good reasons."

Garidemu broke into laughter. Shurad only stared as Litelon's shoulders drooped. They were gathering a crowd. Whispers became the backdrop. The scent of a variety of inebriants clouded the air.

Shurad opened his hand, palm facing upward, and rested his fingers in the air right in front of Litelon's chin. "Next time you see this human guest of our taso's, te'oto, ask her these good reasons."

Litelon eyed the fingers, pupils wide. "I will endeavor, a'sel."

"Do so. I will add it to my book."

"I am going to learn to speak their language, and teach their children about us," said a young voice.

A boy, sprinting toward manhood, stood half hidden in the

crowd. His nearest neighbors stepped aside.

Garidemu took a sip of his drink. "And who are you?"

The boy's eyes widened as all attention focused on his unintended audacity. "I am Emisu. Sehi's son."

"And why do you wish to teach our enemies?"

Litelon and Emisu spoke simultaneously. "They are not enemies."

The whispering stopped. Garidemu set his bottle down with a careful clink and turned to Shurad. "So speaks the youth of our people."

"They are good people, as we are," Litelon said.

"And we can teach them better," Emisu added.

Shurad balled his fist, pupils closing down.

Garidemu leaned toward Emisu. "Can you?"

The boy took a step back. Into his retreat, Litelon opened his palm. "Rodani is teaching Cara."

"And what is he teaching her?" Garidemu asked, his voice full of scorn.

"Honor. Proprieties."

"Treacheries?" Suspicion narrowed the potter's pupils.

"He is guild," Litelon said with a huffy finality.

"And that says all?"

"To everyone but you."

Garidemu rested his chin in his hand. "You should be a priestess, te'oto. You already read others' minds so well."

"At least I have talked with Cara. Neither of you have."

"Cara," Garidemu said softly, "will not long be here."

Litelon's chair went back on all four legs with an emphatic clunk. "Meaning what?"

"Her problems are not for your ears."

"What problems? She is well."

Garidemu took a swig of his drink. "You know so much, te'oto, and so little."

"At least she will talk to me," Litelon spat back.

"For all the good it does us."

"I am going to take her for a benatac ride."

Garidemu and Shurad exchanged looks. "Be sure to ride her too fast and break her neck for us."

Litelon fell quiet as laughter surrounded the table. He paled. Pupils pulsed. He stood in all the indignation an offended virgin possessed and slapped the potter.

The crowd scattered in a sparkle of silver and brights as Garidemu launched himself at the stablehand. They met with a thump and a tangle of arms and legs. Fists found purchase where knees could not, grunts and scuffling took over where drumming stopped.

Young Emisu ran for the two-way radio. Someone was already on it, eyeing tumbling chairs and bodies. Thwarted in more ways than one, Emisu headed out, silver tail flying behind him.

Shurad took his drink and Garidemu's in hand against the possibility that the fight would move back to its origins.

Bets were muttered, taken, or refused. The mayhem shifted from one side of the room to the other. The fighters traded blows—hands, feet, knees, anything and everything that was available. More than one table overturned. Older and more experienced, Garidemu tossed Litelon against the wall, then pulled him over his shoulder and threw him on the floor. Litelon lay in a heap as he had fallen, the potter standing over him, panting.

Security Eighth Pavanec walked through the doorway and into the aftermath. He took Litelon by the arm and helped him up, then escorted both fighters out of the room.

Shurad downed his drink, stared at Garidemu's, then finished it as well. He sighed. Conflicts. Unwanted duties. He wandered out of the room as a duo of servants came in to clean. He trotted down the central staircase and out toward the security office. At the entrance, a guardian looked up from the desk.

"A'sel?" the man greeted him.

"A'tem. Did a'Pavanec bring two men through here a few minutes ago?"

"Yes. Do you wish to speak on their behalf?"

"Thank you, no. I will wait." Shurad settled into a chair. Before too long, his vigil was rewarded as Garidemu and Litelon came out of the door, the latter looking somewhat the worse for honor.

Shurad rose and muttered to his companion, then turned. "Litelon?"

Litelon stopped and faced the writer, expression not quite properly closed off.

"I would speak to you," Shurad continued as Garidemu left.

"As you please." The stablehand held himself stiffly, waiting.

Shurad strolled out of the security room. "I need your help."

"My help?" He followed the other man through the doorway.

"Yours. My latest manuscript is nearly completed, but it lacks something."

Litelon caught up with him. "Lacks what?"

"Immediacy. I wish to talk to Cara."

"Then talk to Rodani," Litelon replied. "And you will need the goddess's help to sway him."

"I can predict his answer without thought, Litelon. I need to talk to her, not him."

"Why come to me?"

"I judge you more flexible than Iraimin." Shurad waved away his mention of Cara's companion.

"I have tried, Shurad. Even to the point of knocking on Cara's door."

Shurad stopped in his tracks. "And?"

Litelon attempted to mask his embarrassment, and the anger he still felt. "She refused me entrance. Told me to seek out Rodani."

Shurad pursed his lips into a thoughtful line and stared down the hallway, seeing but not noticing the other people who walked by. "If I engender a plan, will you help me?"

Litelon swallowed, his expression wary. "The guild has a heavy hand. What do I gain?"

"A chance to talk with her. Alone, if you wish." He raised an eyebrow. "A chance to consolidate her interest. Between her insistence and yours, Rodani may not stand in your way any longer."

Litelon straightened his shoulders, pupils narrowing. "I will consider."

TWENTY-NINE

Another quilt was finished, another was in the making. Cara thanked the lucky star gods that her life had calmed, that her own mind wasn't craving impossible things from her guardian. Now, if only people would stop talking behind her back, twisting her doorknob, and pressing her emotional buttons, life in Barridan might feel somewhat normal.

Another type of interruption came with a knock on the door in five-count cadence.

"Come in, Rodani."

Her back cricked as she straightened up from her cramped position on the stone floor. Hands and knees on a stone floor was not a posture conducive to comfort. The door opened with a click and jingle of keys. Rodani stepped into the room, then was forced to a stop by a floor full of fabric pieces arranged haphazardly.

"You will have Falita in a quandary if she attempts to clean, Cara." Rodani's voice was tinged with amusement.

She sat back on her heels and surveyed the chaos. "I've warned her not to, at least in this room."

Rodani retrieved a silver clip from his work box and sat on the floor across from her, dividing his attention between her creative processes and his as he carefully polished the clip. At one time or another, one of them would sing along with her music; occasionally they'd sing together, mezzo-soprano and beautiful baritone. Cara fretted over the color options in front of her.

Nope. Another rearrangement of the pieces. Nope. She tried another variation. Nope. She sighed, and leaned back against the bookcase that held her fabric stash.

"Try this." Rodani put the clip on the floor by his knee. He took two of the pieces in hand and switched them, took three more and did a round robin switch, then sat back and studied it. So did she.

"For all the demons of the deep. Here," Cara said, pretending to rise. "You sit here, and I'll polish that silver."

Rodani eyed her with just a hint of humor and picked up the clip and polish rag. "You are where you belong."

Cara switched the pieces in the other blocks to match Rodani's change. The pattern began to look right. She picked up the pieces of the corner block and sat down at the sewing machine. Rodani moved to the seat next to her.

"How do you fare?" he asked.

"Well enough," she said with a smile. "We seem to have weathered each other's emotional storms since last week."

"Let us hope the weather stays clear."

Cara glared at him under lowered brows. "On both sides of the hills."

He smiled in return, one of those nice ones she loved to see. "I hoped you might join me in the target room today. I have another request of you."

She stared down at her work, work for which the keso had berated her upsets. But a break and a different activity would be just what her muscles needed.

^Okay.^

"Wear a sweater. Housekeeping is airing some of the rooms in that area today."

Cara pushed away from the worktable. "Is it still cold out?"

"Colder than last time. You do not pay attention to the weather?"

"I'm an artist, Rodani. We pay it no mind until discomfort sets in, then we curse it." She retrieved a sweater, then tiptoed carefully between the cut shapes of her current quilt and out the door that Rodani held open for her.

The target room stood as it always did, but cold. Instead of Rodani going right toward the supply cabinet that held the ammunition, he went left to the accordioned wall. At the top, middle, and bottom, he unlatched the catches that Cara hadn't noticed on earlier visits. As he pushed it open, it emitted an auditory protest of squeals and rattles. Beyond it lay walls.

A score of walls, forming a maze. Rodani walked past her to the cabinet. "Study it," he told her.

She began to get a glimmer of the nature of this practice as she wound her way through the convoluted array of blocks. Some shorter, some taller, some straight, others bent on a vertical axis at angles. It would take a ladder to truly see the layout of the walls, or a blueprint. She was unsure of how strictly to interpret Rodani's command to "study it."

"Make sure you have the practice ones, a'tem," she called out.

He answered with a rather wicked grin that made her spine tingle. "I will ignore that offense." He handed her a jacket adorned with vibrant splashes of color. When she put it on, he adjusted the fit for her, then put a hand on each of her shoulders and looking her up and down. "It will do. Stay down nearer the floor. That will make it more difficult for me to target you." He waved a hand. "Go."

She went.

Before reaching the first break, she heard a shot and felt a bullet thump into the back of her jacket. She sped off, head ducked, and knees bent. Turning left, she heard the massive boom of his gun, and felt a thump, this time in her side. But she kept going, left and forward through another gap, trying to put her pursuer off his stride.

No such luck.

<Boom>

Grinning ruefully, Cara stopped to gather her bearings. She dashed off—

<Boom>

—and peered around the corner she'd just come past. Rodani was crouched not five feet away.

Cara took off again, angling back and forth between the gaps in the walls.

<Boom>

Back and forth,

<Boom>

ever forward,

<Boom>

she wove her way through the walls.

<Boom-splat>

"Ow!"

Cara fell to her knees and put her hand on the seat of her pants. She stared at the paint on her palm, then spun around, crawled back to the opening, and stuck her head into the gap.

"I thought you aimed before shooting, Rodani!"

"Always." His face broke into a sly smile. "I can aim only at what I see."

She frowned at the invasion of her dignity and privacy, then began to laugh as she realized how little of either there was in such a chase to begin with.

Rodani relaxed in the face of her mirth. His left knee and fingertips touched the floor, right elbow rested on his right knee, pistol hung loosely in his grip. His silver hair fell over his shoulder, its feathery ends brushing the floor.

"I will return the indignity, my friend," she said. "You may be sure." A pregnant pause emphasized her threat. She spun off between the next line of walls.

<Boom>

Another dodge.

<Boom><Boom>

They worked their way to the far end of the maze, then stopped and stood. Cara tucked her falling hair into the bun. "You missed once."

"I was exchanging mags."

She lifted her eyebrows, teasing. "You're certain?"

Another stern look met her eyes. Cara took off back the way they'd come, feeling every shot that hit the jacket. Her ribs were going to be sore; so would be the middle of her back. Rodani's aim was too accurate. She dipped and dodged, bumping a shoulder on one of the walls <Boom>. She staggered, then went on.

Two more rows. <Boom>

One more. <Boom>

She rounded the last corner and felt one more shot hit her. Panting from exertion, she peered around the forward corner, back to where she thought Rodani had stopped.

He was in a crouch on the balls of his feet, checking his weapon.

Bent almost double, Cara darted around the corner and ran at him as fast as she could go, forearms up protectively. Rodani spun her way in surprise and blasted a shot into her chest. His eyes widened as she hit him, his feet slipped out and arms flew sideways. He landed with a thump on his shoulder and hip, Cara on top of him.

The force of her tackle stunned them both momentarily. Cara rolled away and sat back against the wall opposite him. Rodani's eyes were twin moons on full. He propped himself up on one elbow as she convulsed in laughter.

"Why did you do that?" he asked.

It took a moment for her to find a breath. "To repay you for shooting me in the rear. Why else?" She grinned like a toothy three-toed rahkti eyeing its dinner. With some effort, he sat up.

"You should have seen your eyes, Rodani." She held her fingers and thumbs in circles. "They were this big!"

Rodani composed his face, pulling his jacket back into place and adjusting his hair. Dignity back intact with his clothing, he returned his attention to Cara.

In the midst of walls, paint splotches, and ankle-turning bullet casings, they stared at each other. Rodani's pupils were wide ovals. Silence filled the room—until, with the creak of his jacket, Rodani reached out and drew a finger down her cheek. When he pulled his hand back, Cara caught his fingers in hers. They sat frozen in the moment, then Cara dropped her arm.

Rodani stood up and held out his hand for her to rise, and unlike at the base of the falls, she took it, and let him pull her up.

Cara handed the jacket over, and Rodani switched back to live cartridges. He slid his gun into the holster at his hip. They headed back. Rodani let Cara into her workroom and followed her in.

"Dinner?" he asked.

She turned. Rodani's face held only bland propriety. She didn't know whether to be pleased or disquieted. "Yes, thank you." She changed into something less inappropriate and followed him across the hall.

The state of the room was immaculate, as usual. Fresh flowers from the hothouse clustered together in a vase on the table next to the couch. She smiled and sat next to them. Rodani fixed two drinks, gave one to her, and sat down. He angled his body to face her and took a sip of his drink.

She studied the one in her hand. "Where is Serano?"

He waved his hand airily. "Out and about."

"With Larisi?"

"Possibly."

"You don't know?"

"Despite what it seems, Cara, we do not tell each other everything. He has his secrets," he said, looking toward the fire. "As I have mine."

"What secrets?"

An eyebrow lifted at her temerity. "If you wish to learn them, you must earn them."

"How?"

Instead of answering, Rodani opened the door. A servant set

their table, then headed back out. Rodani followed him, speaking softly in the hallway, then returned to the room. They sat down, concentrating on the food.

Cara took a thick slice of meat from the platter. "So why did you so improperly shoot me?"

Rodani glanced over at her. "I must aim somewhere. It was the only thing in my sights."

"Couldn't you have refrained? Waited until a different piece of anatomy came into view?"

"It is as valid an area as any to score a hit." A mound of vegetables rolled off the serving spoon and onto his plate. "Were you hurt?"

"Only my dignity." She smiled. "Maybe a small bruise. I hope the shot helps you fight," she continued. "At least it will have served a useful purpose."

"If the memory does not arise unbidden and break my concentration." He took a mouthful of meat and cut another slice. "How painful is that bruise?"

Cara tossed the question, Selandu-style. "Some. I'll live."

He cocked an eyebrow. "Does it need tending?"

"Uhh... No. Thank you." She grinned in return.

A tap on the door interrupted the heat that had blossomed. Cara puffed out a sigh, but there wasn't much relief at the end of it. Her stomach, once empty, was tied in knots. *Oh, boy!*

He closed the door and laid two small plates on the table. A pastry sat on each, covered with curlicued shavings.

"What is it?" she asked him.

"A confection. Something one of the chefs makes for special occasions," he replied, sitting back down.

Cara took a nibble of the shavings and rolled them around in her mouth. Then her eyes went wide. "Chocolate?"

"I passed the last bar you gave me on to the chef. I thought you might approve."

Her heart melted a bit along with the chocolate in her mouth. Embarrassed, she looked down at the gift. "I'm not sure what to say, except—thank you." She raised her eyes to his face, and saw his pupils narrow and widen. His smile had reformed into a tight grin with his lower lip in a pout.

After they'd finished, Rodani pushed the dishes aside and folded his hands near the center of the table. When Cara mimicked him, leaning forward and pressing her intertwined fingers against his, he teased them apart and held them, then began running his thumbs over her palms. It was not too different from what she'd done to his hand after she'd bit him. He looked over at her.

A smile was playing across her face, and her eyes held steady to his. He wanted to say something, anything. But his heart was hammering, and his tongue was tied.

In much too soon of a time, Cara squeezed his hands and pulled away, excusing herself with an aversion of the eyes and a gesture that meant personal business.

Rodani gestured toward the door of his bedroom, beyond which lay the facilities. He watched her through the doorway, noting the sway of her hips and the momentary pause and glance at his bed. What thoughts were running through her head? What was she feeling? His desire to know was second only to his desire to touch.

He moved to the arm of the couch. When she came back out, she stopped a few feet away and looked him over.

Rodani took a sip of his drink and placed the glass on the couch at his hip, wrapped in his hand. His legs were spread into a V shape. "Did you find something of interest in my room?"

She crossed her arms over her chest and averted her eyes. "Forgive me. That was impolite."

"I was not offended. What are you curious about?"

She shrugged, "I...don't know."

"Do you not?" he teased her. The smile was back. "You are facile with words." When she didn't answer, he continued. "Come closer and tell me."

She let out a puff of air. "This is...not easy."

"There is no harm here," he replied softly.

Cara decided she could believe that one. She took two slow steps forward. "Why do you want to know?" she asked.

His gaze never wavered. "To better tend to your needs."

She stood in silence, digesting his explanation. At her next step forward, he pulled his feet back to the couch and parted his knees farther, allowing her closer access. His hands rested on the couch arm on either side of him, drink still in one.

"I can tell you you're a pleasure to look at," she said, and took a small step.

Reflective eyes narrowed in thought. "In what way?"

Quiet. He was very quiet, and still. She took one more step.

"The way you sit, the way you stand, the way you move.

Graceful. Fascinating." She was close enough to kiss him, if she wanted. And she wanted. "Do I disturb you?" she whispered.

His eyelids closed and blinked rapidly, then steadied again. "Yes."

Little but breath was between them. Violet locked onto blue. Grey faced ivory.

With a tap and a clink, the lock turned, and the door opened. Serano stepped into the room and stopped at the unexpected tableau. "Forgive me."

Cara looked away from one pair of cat eyes into another a more comfortable distance across the room. "There's no problem, Serano," she said firmly, retreating to the bookcase, unnerved by her own audacity. "We were just playing a game."

Serano's gaze shifted from his seated partner's back over to Cara, with his own expression of suspicion. "Who won?"

"Unknown," she said airily. The door looked inviting. The atmosphere in the room was thick with emotion. Cara left the bookcase, and the still seated Rodani, and walked toward the door. "But I think the games are over for the night." She passed by Serano on her way out. "Safe night, a'tem'ai."

Serano caught the door Cara had begun to close, then watched her safely into her room. The silence behind him was deafening. He shut the door and walked past Rodani's seated form, turning to stand in front of him as a parent to a child in need of a stern lecture.

"*That* looked like attentions in progress."

Rodani refused to meet his partner's penetrating stare. Though outwardly calm, his nerves were vibrating. It was easier to keep in control when he could look down on Cara from his great height or comfort her childish upsets; but facing her eye to level eye had sent his hormones through dips and spirals he'd rarely felt since his adolescent days. Their strength made his head spin.

"I will walk outside." He arose abruptly from his seat on the couch arm, still avoiding Serano's gaze. He headed for the door, grabbing his jacket along the way.

"You are going to dishonor yourself."

Rodani turned and opened his mouth to say something, shot him a look instead, then left.

The early winter wind tempered his emotions, relaxed the muscles that had tensed when Cara approached him. He strode briskly down the north side of the manor wall in an effort to calm himself, to push the memory of her proximity from his mind. He needed no handlight. Temi's crescent moon gave him all the light that Selandu eyesight needed. His booted feet whispered though the dry grass. The wind whipped the length of his hair against his jacket and tickled the sensitive tips of his ears. As he turned the corner, his clip shone in the moonlight with the same intensity as his eyes.

Honor was an anchor to his storm-tossed emotions, Cara, a wild bird. Approach too quickly, and she would flutter away. Frighten her, and she would scream and caw. Hurt her? Rodani flinched, then sighed, drawing patience from his inner strength. He glanced up at the windows as he passed by, refreshing his memory with who lived where in an effort to get his mind onto a different track.

A pale face looked out from the second story.

Coincidence? Possibly. Security risk? Absolutely. He pulled even with her line of sight and stopped. Backlit, wrapped in a quilt and leaning against the window frame, she looked out into the night. Suddenly, as if she felt eyes upon her, Cara glanced down. Again, they played their game, eyes locked, both faces expressionless. Seconds lengthened to long moments. There was no movement, no visual cues as to the communication taking place. Rodani's heart thudded in his chest. His vision narrowed. Nothing existed in his world except the window, and the silhouette inside it. With a quick spin, he started back the way he came, his stride purposeful.

The bottom dropped out of Cara's stomach as Rodani disappeared into the darkness. She retreated to her study, acutely affected by the evening's confrontational games. Tension enveloped her as she waited for the knock that she knew was coming. She knew now what he wanted. And she wanted it, too. But the looming unknowns threatened to overwhelm her before its direct presence even made itself seen. Her body vibrated with a heady mixture of caution and desire. What had she done?

Cara jumped at the knock on the door. "Come in."

The broad-shouldered shadow filled her doorway. She retreated to the study, leaving him to lock the door and follow if he wished. She leaned back against the wall next to the fireplace, facing the couch. Rodani closed the workroom shutters, then came in and straddled the arm of the couch, waiting out the long silence while she stared at his boots. She kept the quilt wrapped tightly around her, armor against the strong emotions already filling the little room.

"It seems we have a matter between us, kia," he said softly.

She puzzled out the word. Something diminutive, converted to intimate mode. Her heart filled her throat. "Yes."

"What are your thoughts?"

Cara shuddered. He seemed so cool, so collected. His earlier admission that she'd disturbed him seemed a lie, now. "Confusion. Reservations."

"Where were your reservations earlier?" Amusement came though his voice.

"I was caught up in your game. But this is no game, is it?"

"It is not," he said. "But you are the guest. I will follow your lead in this matter. Where is your will?"

She swallowed heavily, her fists tense on the quilt. "Where is wisdom in this, Rodani?"

He rubbed his palms on his pant legs. "I make no claims to wisdom. Only reason, and patience."

The fire flickered in point-counterpoint to Cara's conflicting thoughts. Before her sat an alien man harboring alien expectations of a highly personal nature.

Rodani's expression softened, his eyes were wide. Innocent looking, if she didn't know better. "Do you fear me, kia?" he asked.

"When you're angry."

The corners of his mouth turned up. "Have you seen me angry when you are obeying my security orders?"

"Once or twice."

"Only when you bait me. I will not hurt you. This is a time for goodwill."

That was an understatement of universal proportions. "You're so calm," she said. "I'm shaking."

Rodani intertwined his fingers and rested his hands in his lap. "I am not as calm as I look."

"I don't even know if we can—accomplish this. Do you?" she asked plaintively.

He grinned. "That answer is easily discovered."

She had to laugh. The tension was so thick they could swim in it.

"And," he continued, "word has filtered through from Hadaman that the possibility is there."

Good gods and Temi's demons.

Her body said, *Yes*, but her mind wasn't at all convinced this was a good idea. He was asking her to trust him—with her innermost privacies. She glanced over at Rodani. His face held patience and expectations. His eyes were riveted on her.

Trust? She already trusted him. With her life, for all the gods' sakes. Was this so unreasonable? Or nothing but rationalizing? She was going in circles.

"Kia," he said. "Where is the woman who fought me two months ago?" Reminding her, he was. Of her strengths. Of her force of will.

"She's here."

"Where is the woman who sat me on the floor and taught me to make music with my voice?"

Cara looked down at her feet, the edge of the quilt hiding her mouth. "She's here, also."

"And where is the woman who fights so strongly to save her own life?" he continued.

She raised her head and looked into violet. "Here."

He held out a hand in invitation; his mouth broke into the widest, most beautiful smile she'd ever seen. "Prove it."

Gods he was gorgeous. Overwhelming desire and fear of the unknown swirled in her mind, making her dizzy with apprehension.

Rodani withdrew his hand, interlaced his fingers, and rested them in his lap. "I will not dishonor you."

Was he reading her mind? "Honor is different between us, Rodani."

His eyes widened, his face fell. He turned away. "Forgive me, Cara. I am a fool." He got up and headed for the door. "I had forgotten."

She stood dazed at the abrupt turn of events, jaw slack. "Forgotten what?"

A look of dismay covered his face. "That you cannot tell me when I offend you."

Cara's gaze roamed the room, alighting unseen and unthinking on ordinary objects in the dim flickering light. *Holy hell. Don't make me a party to this decision. Don't make me say I want you. I can't.*

Cara bent her head and stared at her slippers. "I'll tell you."

He took a few steps back, angled around to face her. "You are certain?"

She muttered a very unladylike curse. "Yes." It came out in a whisper.

Rodani sat back down on the arm of the couch and turned his

palms upward on his thighs, his gaze unwavering, pupils reflecting the firelight. The smile was gone, but his intensity burned into her, fanning the flames that licked at her groin.

Cara pulled her body away from the wall and walked slowly toward him. This time, she took that last step to close the gap between them. Taking a deep breath, she let go her useless fabric armor. It dropped behind her. She drew her fingers upward along Rodani's thighs, then laid her hands on his shoulders.

And kissed him. His lips were warm, soft. Not much alien about them.

Rodani put his hands on her waist. She moved her mouth to his smooth cheek, his jaw, the hollow of his neck. She inhaled his slightly spicy scent, then returned her attention to his lips. His hands traveled up her back, his arms encircled her and pulled her against him. She rested her cheek next to his and wrapped her arms around his neck. There they stayed, unmoving, for a lifetime of seconds.

She reached for the clip that held his hair in place. "May I?"

They were eye to eye.

"Yes."

Cara removed the clip and tossed it on the side table. She touched his silver mane, brought strands of it over his shoulders. It was soft, silky. She ran her hands through it and wrapped locks of it around her fingers. "You'll never know how much I have wished to play in your hair."

"You will never know," he repeated softly, "what was in my mind when you allowed me to brush yours."

"Maybe I'll learn," she whispered. Rodani moved his hands over her back and around to cup her face in his palms. "Your eyes," she said. "They're dancing."

His black pupils pulsed, their reflective glow alternately dimmed and brightened. Rodani rubbed his hands over her head, then down to her neck and unclipped her hair. It unrolled and fell to her waist. He ran his fingers through the soft waves, then let his hands drift around down to the top of her blouse, to the first button.

She put her hands on his, bringing questions to his eyes. She stepped back. As she took his hand, he rose from the couch. With a grab at his clip, he followed her into the bedroom. She let go his hand, headed for the far door, and shut it with a quiet click before turning back to him. He took care of the door behind him, then leaned up against it.

"Privacy is relative, kia. Soon Arimeso will know that you have shut the door—and that I am still in the room."

Cara walked forward and touched him on the arm. "Does that disturb you?"

"No."

His shirt was soft under her fingers, the arm beneath, hard with muscle. He was fever warm.

Rodani moved to the edge of the bed and sat down. Cara stood in front of him. He returned to the task postponed in the study, button by button, then slid the blouse off her arms and let it fall to the floor. Cara turned and felt him puzzle out the halter top he had glimpsed at the waterfall. With an undoing of knots, one more article of clothing lay on the floor. Rodani ran his hands up her back and turned her, studied her, then leaned forward slowly. Cara put her hands on the back of his head, coaxing him into explorations he might not know were allowed. He complied with little hesitation.

She tugged at his shirt and pulled it over his head. The expanse of grey skin under her hands was warm and soft. The scars on his back shifted under her fingers. The muscles underneath flexed as he tucked his fingers in her waistband and ran them full circle around her. Soon the last two articles of her clothing were cast aside, and Cara stood before him, ivory and alien.

He ran his hands over her bared skin and cautiously explored her dark triangle. Hands wrapped in his hair, Cara held herself relaxed and still, declining what might have made explorations easier. Soon enough for that. Rodani leaned forward and laid his cheek against her breasts, bringing his hands around behind her.

She tugged gently at the waist of his pants and waited for the cooperation needed to satisfy the rest of her curiosity. He assisted, and one more piece of clothing was tossed.

The rumors were true. He was not quite the same, but not so different.

Rodani renewed his own explorations, which slowed when Cara took him in hand, caressing his intimate skin. He drew a deep breath. His dark eyes focused tightly on her face, pupils pulsing rhythmically. He wrapped his arms around her and pulled her close, nestling his face in the strands of her hair, breathing audibly. Cara parted his legs farther. She stepped inward, tucked his turgid organ between her thighs, and began to rock gently. Silent, he gripped her more tightly. She varied her motions, then slowed, stopped, and clasped her arms around his neck.

He sighed, then glanced down between them. "This is the proper place?"

She dare not laugh. Their mutual ignorance could fill a small valley.

"No," Cara said quietly. "It's a starting place." She released him, then climbed on the bed and pulled him onto it after her. He lay down beside her and rested his head below her breasts, hand searching. As curiosity led him to her most sensitive areas, she shifted her legs to accommodate his touch. With guidance, his explorations narrowed in focus, as did her sensations.

"There," she whispered, when he reached the place where his greatest interest lay. He spent a most pleasant minute exploring, then brought his hand up and rested it on her nether curls, lifting his upper body to face her.

"In the name of the goddess, will you honor me?" His eyes reflected the dim light of the bedroom, pupils wide.

She hesitated. "Meaning, will I join with you?"

"Yes."

She smiled sweetly. "I've not come so far to say no."

His pupils spasmed, wide and round. "I will honor your gift."

Cara pulled his head down to hers and kissed him again. Rodani rolled over, put his knees between her legs, and lowered his hips. He probed gently, then pushed.

Gods.

All her attention focused on that one small area. Heat radiated between them as he continued to push. She held her breath.

Oh, gods.

She let it out, ever so slowly.

They began to move, together in rhythm, the ancient rhythm she knew so well. Cool sheets cupped her from below; Rodani warmed her from above. He whispered to her, words she didn't know. His hands made forays into various places, the movement of his hips brought glorious sensations, his pupils pulsed with passion. She drew her hands up his back and through his hair, then down to what had so tantalized her in the forest. His muscles bunched and rippled under her hands.

They were lost, lost in a haze of pleasure. The outside world went away for a time. Thought shut down. All that existed was physical, was here and now.

They varied their motion—now slow, now fast, learning what pleased, and what pleased more. Eternity passed, and no time passed at all. They spoke, fell into silence, gasped, and fought their way into feverish intensity. Rodani's breathing deepened and became syncopated. He stiffened above her, growled, cried out, then shuddered and shouted, shuddered and shouted, gradually quieting.

She held him tightly until he calmed, until he came to his senses. Above her, weight on his elbows, he began to breathe normally. He flexed his fingers in her hair, disengaged from her and turned onto his side, then pulled her into an embrace. His eyes opened, half-mast. She caressed his face and smiled. His alien scent still filled her nose, his breath warmed her face in the cool air. Silver hair tickled her skin.

Rodani reached behind their heads and slid open a door, revealing a clean, empty storage area. "You were quiet," he ventured, returning his attention to her. "Was there pleasure?"

"Much," she said. "With practice there'll be more. What do you call that explosion of the senses?"

He paled and glanced away. "A crest. We crest the hill." Six-fingered hands explored the curls that cascaded out in front of him. "Do humans crest?"

"Yes. Often with a great deal of noise."

"I heard no noise."

"There was no crest. Even for humans it's a learning process to please a woman."

"Show me."

She smiled. "There's something you may try, if you wish."

Rodani opened his palm.

Cara took his hand and moved it downward, guiding it, explaining. He listened, then made a concerted effort. It didn't take long. Pleasure played across her features as he worked, came through her voice, sounds that increased as she crested, and faded away as she placed her hand on his to stop the exquisite stimulation. She opened her eyes to face a soft expression, and a view of her future she never thought to see this side of the Hills of Himadi.

"This bears explaining," he said.

She blushed, hesitated, then spoke. Rodani listened with all the gravity of a guild student in front of a master.

"If you will teach me, I will learn." He nuzzled her, then sat up, reached down, and brought his shirt into his lap. Surprised, Cara put her hand on his arm.

"Is there somewhere you need to be, soon?"

The shirt stayed in his lap. "No."

She tossed the shirt on the floor and pulled on his arm. He acquiesced to her gentle insistence and fell back onto the mattress. She put her finger on the tip of his nose.

"It's considered very offensive to make haste at such times." She relaxed and curled into his warmth, coaxing his arms back around her.

"You are cold?"

"No."

"You are in need of comfort?" A tinge of concern crept into Rodani's voice.

"Emotional pleasantries, Rodani. A necessary courtesy for human females."

"Why?"

"A swift leave-taking after joining is nearly always offensive. And your embrace encourages bonding."

He bent his head down into her curls. "I mean no offense."

She hugged him close, wishing she could join his mind as she had joined his body. "Nor do I. Are there courtesies I should observe?"

Rodani ran his fingers up her neck and into her hair. "Silence, kia," he said gently. "Anyone who does not yet know should not know." One finger explored the convolutions of her ear.

"Even Iraimin?" His smooth chest muffled her words.

"I will consider. Still, details should be kept to a minimum."

"You are aware of the type of talk women share?"

"Generally."

"You ask much. You'll allow me the same courtesy of silence?"

"I already have."

She lifted her chin and met his eyes. "Serano."

"Yes."

Cara shoved impatient partners from her mind and snuggled back into place, unwilling to leave her newfound haven. Months of solitude had left an ache of unrealized depth. Rodani's steady breathing comforted her. He evinced no impatience to be on his way, accepting her silence with the same equanimity with which he accepted her questions. She explored him, visually and tactilely. The silver hair that fell in rivulets held her attention with the same evident fascination that her curls held for him. No stare-down interrupted her meanderings. No menacing glowers provoked anxious reactions. Just the gentle regard of two disparate sapients who had crossed a wide gulf and founded an unexpected bond.

"You're beautiful, Rodani."

"No."

She almost didn't hear it, so soft had been the reply.

"Yes."

But he closed his eyes against her, preferring, for a moment, touch instead of the clarity of sight. His hands drifted from her neckline down to the bountiful softness not found on the more slender women of his own species. He curled downward, nuzzled and kneaded, and reinspected what the goddess had given the generative gender. A suckling babe would not be more intent. The inward curving waistline and outward flare of her hips attracted his further attention. When he crawled back up her curvaceous frame, his eyes pulsed. She pulled him to her and parted her legs.

Rodani wasted no time accepting her triple embrace as she wrapped her arms and legs around him. He shuddered, a soft growl escaping his throat. Unexpected urgency overtook him. He rode with it, bucked against it, vocalized it, crested it, and shivered as it faded away.

His fingers untangled themselves from the mass of curls under his chin. "Are you well?" he asked the soft form beneath him.

"Yes." She put her hands against his chest and pushed. "I do, however, need to breathe."

He boosted himself onto his elbows and murmured an apology, then broke into a smile. It was, after all, a wondrously ridiculous situation for them to have gotten into: child-sized and giant, aliens in sex and culture, an abyss deep enough to swallow them whole and take the peace of their two species with them. In his few lucid moments since dinner, Rodani wondered into what insanity they had tripped. And if it came to naught, or worse, to death, he had only himself to blame. It was his land, his culture, his adashi, his honor. The guild had its rules; and he had broken one. Had every intention of breaking it often. But for now, there was comfort, of a kind Rodani hadn't felt in years. A peace of the heart as well as body, a peace in the place where the goddess dwells.

Cool temperatures came back to their bodies as they parted. Rodani reached for her soft folds a second time, but she stopped him with a touch and a word. He gathered her into his arms. Comprehension eluded him, but he did not doubt her veracity. He would give her what he could, of all that she could express, regardless of whether it made sense or not. It was his duty. One did not receive without giving. It was one of the goddess's most basic teachings, and unlike Serano, Rodani's childhood had burned it into his honor.

Cara sighed and accepted his embrace with undiluted pleasure. No sound emanated from the adjacent suite. Possibly Rodani had asked for a temporary vacate. The servants took his orders. She learned that the day they'd fought. There were definite advantages to bedding house guild.

"Rodani."

"Yes." Rumbles traveled from his chest to her ear.

"I know now where your heart is."

The silence lasted long enough for her to wonder if that was a mistake. Then he took a breath.

"I have decided it no longer matters."

His words healed something. Something she hadn't known was wounded. "I never want to hurt you."

He pulled a wayward strand of hair away from her eyes. "It is not your intentions that concern us, kia. It is accidents born of your inexperience. Ambassador Second Andreh' assured us of your good will before you arrived. Nothing I have seen has changed that assessment. But your naivete surprised us all."

"As did my non-stop questions?"

One of those looks came her way. "Did?"

She chuckled. "Rodani, you said the people in Hadaman knew that this was possible. How did they know?"

"Such things are noticed, kia, just as Hamman and Falita noted your differences," he said. "If a human man has an appurtenance similar to a Selandu man, then it is assumed a human woman has a place to receive it. I felt it was only a matter of search and occupy."

The terminology jolted her sense of humor. "And I'm part of guild strategy? Something discussed, diagrammed, and assailed in a concerted invasion?"

"No." He leaned over her. "Private plotting and solitary execution with due caution for unknown hazards."

Laughter bubbled to the surface. "And was your mission a success, oh great guild fifth?"

"Preliminary analysis shows a high probability, but further training is necessary."

"And when will this training commence?"

"I wait to be informed."

The bubbles broke into vocal bits of delight that floated between two smiling faces.

"When will you dance for me again?" Rodani whispered.

Blank incomprehension washed across her face. "Dance?"

He waited.

"It—it offended you."

"For the fourth time, I contradict you, kia."

"But you left. You left so abruptly!"

Warm, grey fingers trailed her cheek and rested under her chin. "Ask me why."

"Why?"

He swallowed heavily, as if the memory itself caused the disturbance she'd seen in his face that night. "If I had stayed in your presence, I would have laid hands on you. I could not risk offending you with such base improprieties."

She stared. "It was desire?"

He paled and pursed his lips.

"Gods." She rolled back into his arms. The scent of his skin crawled into her synapses, lodged there, taking root. "Of all the things that walked my mind, Rodani, that one never crossed."

"That was my intention."

"If only you knew how I fumed and fussed."

"Hamman told me. Forgive me, kia. I saw no choice but to offend you by withdrawing or offend in a way that would destroy my chance at earning your attentions."

The comfort of unraveled misunderstandings fell over them. They settled under the covers, sharing warmth and intimacies. Eventually they slept.

Cara woke, feeling unaccustomed movement at her side, a rising of the mattress. It was dark.

"Rodani?"

"Yes?" He sat on the bed and reached for his clothes that had been dropped on the floor earlier in the night.

"You're leaving?"

"I should not be found in your room come dawn." He slipped on his pants.

"Why, if Arimeso already knows—or will know?"

"Propriety. Appearances," he said, reaching for his shirt. "It is one thing to develop a private affinity with you, another to flaunt it."

This was unexpected. "Please stay."

"No." He finished dressing, all except his boots and weapons belt.

"At least lay with me a few minutes more."

He hesitated, then lay down and held her. She curled into his protective embrace with obvious pleasure and shut her eyes, hoping he would do the same. Within a few minutes, Rodani stirred. "You are as transparent as glass, kia."

She reopened her eyes to a grin on his face. "I had hoped you would fall back asleep."

"No."

She tightened her grip around his waist and curled her bare legs around his. "If you go, it'll be under protest."

He arched an eyebrow in response, then dug his fingertips into her ribs. With a convulsive shout, she let go, and he slipped out of bed.

"Unfair! Foul!"

He leaned down and nuzzled her, then grabbed his boots and left the room.

THIRTY

A click of the lock heralded Rodani's return. He walked in, past Serano's bedroom door, past the bookcase that held his crafting. His flowing hair fell to his waist. Behind him, fabric rustled. He put his weapons belt on his bedroom nightstand before turning to face the owner of the familiar footsteps.

Serano, hands in his robe pockets, leaned against the doorway with an angry expression plastered across his face. "You will face censure."

Rodani pulled his hair clip from a pocket and laid it next to his weapons. "I will meet it when it comes."

"Was it worth it?"

Rodani laid down on his bed. "Yes."

"Good timing, that you catch her when she is receptive. So, she is not so different?"

He put his hands behind his head. "If you wish a lesson in comparative anatomy, tem'u, you must research it yourself."

"That may not be so difficult."

"You still seek impossibilities."

Serano crossed his arms, inflated ego full on display. "Whose bed is filled every night he wishes it?"

"With Selandu women."

"Shall we wager?"

The security room barked a command through the radio.

Across the hall, Cara gave up on going back to sleep, but it was too soon to get up. She snuggled under the covers for warmth, hugging the memories of last night to herself, not quite believing, in the dawn of today, that it really happened. But the faint scent of Rodani's body clung to the sheets, and the pillow next to her still held the indentation from where his head had lain. She pulled the pillow to her side and tucked it under her arm.

It could've been a disaster. It could've been a comedy. But it wasn't. Wonder of wonders, it had worked. The future had a sunnier look.

Unless it was a one-nighter.

Surely not.

Please, not.

She couldn't judge him by human standards. Couldn't assume too much. But she couldn't manage to assume too little of him, either. He was too honorable, too steady, too duty-bound to play painful games with her affections.

Then she thought of Serano.

Damn.

She had wanted to ask, last night in her study. But there had been too much that warranted discussing, and not enough reasoning power within two desire-fogged minds to do so. She was lucky to have gotten what explanations she did. Wait-and-see was the only option. She rolled out and padded toward the facilities, wrapping a quilt around her in place of the robe.

She wondered what the day would be like, and how Rodani would act. With a start, she realized she was facing almost as many unknowns today as last night. The image of her mother's face appeared in Cara's mind. She painted it with an expression of horror at the knowledge of what her baby was up to and laughed.

Cara exited the facilities and found Falita waiting for her, as was usual. "Shower, a'Cara?"

"Yes."

Definitely desired after the night's activities. She wondered if Falita knew. Hamman took care of her in the evenings. Falita wasn't usually around. Cara watched her servant for some reaction, but there was none she recognized.

By the time Cara had dried her hair, breakfast was on her study table. She swallowed the fruit and fresh muffin with dispatch. She was anxious to get back to her current creation, and it would take her mind off Rodani.

His switch of her pattern pieces yesterday afternoon had renewed her enthusiasm for the project. Funny how a piece of art or craft could go from terrible to wonderful, and occasionally back to terrible, just by a single event. It drove artists crazy. With objectionable frequency, projects ended up UFOs, UnFinished Objects left in out-of-the-way corners or closets where they never again saw the light of day. She'd left a half-dozen of them back home in her parents' house. She wondered if Rodani faced the same frustrations.

Then she wondered how soon he'd put in an appearance.

This was going to be a flimsy day. Her mind didn't want to stay in any one track but wobbled around like a drunk. Cara sat down at her sewing machine and ordered her day's work, laying out the pieces that would be sewn together first, then second, then third. With her portable 'corder on the sewing table and earphones on her ears, she spun off into the inner world of creativity.

It was a place where every artist wished to be. Some called it a trance; some called it flow. Rodani dwelt there at times. She'd seen it when he sang, or worked his designs on her drawing table, or crafted. Those were virtually the only times she saw him as anything other than a guardian. Until last night.

She smiled, wide and bright.

Time flew by with the speed of the machine's needle. Little pieces became bigger pieces, unfolded and pressed open, repositioned with others, and sewn into even bigger ones. This was her favorite part of the quilting process. The part where nothing turned into something. Her body moved with the twin rhythms of music and sewing, her voice matching the one in her ears, at least in tone if not quality. A backache brought her out of her inner world, and into the outer. She stood and stretched, wondering if it was time for lunch. But a glance toward her bedroom found not Falita with a food cart, but Rodani, arms folded and leaning against the door.

Cara's heart surged upward into her throat. "How long have you been there?"

"Not long."

"Bright morn."

"Afternoon," he said. They smiled companionably at his penchant for accuracy. By now it was an in-joke.

"How was your morning?"

He tossed the question and came over to her side. "Yours?"

"Productive."

He sat down and looked at the pattern she was building. "You kept the change I made."

"Yes."

"Why?"

"It was the right one."

Rodani glanced away in courteous acceptance of the compliment, then back to Cara. He fixed his eyes on her face. It was a new form of the stare-down, and it warmed her from within.

She leaned toward him, arms on the table. "If there are ways in which a man and a woman communicate certain things, Rodani, I wasn't taught them. You must."

"I would be pleased."

"Did Serano say anything this morning?"

"Enough."

She grinned at his admission. "May I ask?"

Silence.

Well, she didn't really expect anything different. "What does your day bring?"

"A meeting. A jewelry commission. Practice."

"Outdoors?"

"Possibly."

"It's been some days since I've seen the sun."

His eyes went dark, his face tensed. "Break no promises, kia."

She sat back abruptly. Was he angry? Why? "What did I do?"

"Nothing." Rodani stepped away from the worktable. "Please continue such nothings." He headed toward the door.

"Rodani," she called after him, plaintive.

He came back and nuzzled her hair at the nape. "I have a meeting."

Befuddled, Cara watched him go.

***

Down the wide stairs, far beyond Rodani's destination, was a room. Hesitant, Shurad stepped in. The room was dim, smoky, small. No windows relieved the dark. Tapestries hung on the walls, with deep subjects woven in deep colors. A table, waist high, sat against the wall. An array of fine powders lay on it, held in precisely arranged silver bowls. Along the far wall was a low altar. Pillows lined the floor in front of it. Balanced on top was a stylized carving of the sun, its golden rays arcing out from the center disk in spontaneous profusion. Higher behind the disk, half hidden, was a circle of silver. A total of seven lit candles spread out in front of the gold disk, each of a different color. Powder ringed their holders.

Shurad took a bowl from the incense table. Cradling it in his hand, he approached the altar and knelt on one of the pillows. The tapestries muffled the sound of his rapid breathing. His gaze lingered on the unadorned icon that represented his faith. His fingers rubbed the bowl absentmindedly, searching for a comfort he had yet to find. The fabric of his pants pulled against his knees, and a twitch of his ankle brought an answering rasp of leather against stone. Back straight, bowl and hands in his lap, Shurad closed his eyes and attempted an expression of calm contemplation. Cold seeped in from the wintry outside. The silence of the season was pervasive, disquieting.

Strengthen me, o Sela, for the task ahead. Steady my hand, Great Mother, calm my throbbing heart. Guide my aim with Your all-seeing eyes. Help me defend my honor, and the honor of my family, and protect me from retribution. If this be wrong, Great Goddess, tell me now. Give me a sign before signs are too late. Smother my fears. Take them from me before they rob me of my courage. Help me.

Shurad lifted the bowl of incense reverently, took a pinch of the aromatic powder, and sprinkled it over the black candle. Sparkling, the flame wavered and spat. An odor of seghai wood wafted upward and merged with the older scents that clung to tapestry and stone.

A deep, shuddering breath was not enough to calm him. He felt bereft of support, empty, as if the goddess had turned Her back. The thin line he'd been walking narrowed. Dishonor, possibly death, threatened on either side. Shurad bent his head to the tabletop.

"Goddess," he whispered.

There was no answer. No voice in his head. No sign.

A picture formed in his mind. Long slender legs outlined by cool sheets, warm grey eyes in a triangular face. Fingertips that fluttered the sensitive hairs at the tips of his ears.

"Geseli, this is not what I wished for us."

He rose, replaced the bowl on the incense table, and left the room.

Neither did his own quarters afford any comfort. They were nearly empty of his meager belongings, which were stored in Garidemu's rooms in the hope he survived. His people would take him back. Shurad walked past the desk. A piece of paper stared up at him, the last one of his book. He sat down in the worn seat.

> As in all life, there are no absolutes. One can only gather facts, discourse on their meanings, judge, and honor the decisions based on them. In the end, honor is all we have.

The box was in the corner.

The box that haunted him over unfulfilled oaths, over a split and shattered honor, over a destiny he never wanted, never earned except by accident of birth. The pall of an uncaring universe fell over him as he lifted the lid and put his hand on the cold heavy metal that lay inside. He tucked it in his waistband under the jacket.

* * *

Cara lifted the presser foot and spun the fabric 90°, then let it back down for another line of stitching. The fabric moved over the throat plate and out the other side. She clipped it loose and spread it out. When the seams didn't match in the center, she shook her head in frustration and scrabbled at the edge of the machine for the seam ripper.

Someone knocked on the door.

Cara waited, tense. Serano? No, if Rodani was in a meeting, likely so was his partner. The knock repeated itself.

"Who is there?"

"Litelon, a'Cara. I would talk to you."

Her shoulders sagged in relief. This, she had dealt with. "Talk to Rodani, Litelon."

"I have. He knows my errand and said you may see me."

Cara leaned back and folded her arms across her chest. Truth? What were the chances? "He said nothing to me," she replied.

"He did not have time, a'Cara. He was on his way to a meeting."

True enough. Had he really talked to Rodani? Surely an overly cautious guardian would have made some arrangement besides this.

"A'Cara." Litelon's voice dropped a notch in volume. "I have a gift for you." The doorknob spun slowly, then went back to its original position. "Please."

Cara breathed deeply of it. "Forgive my stubbornness, Litelon, but I can't." She sat back down and waited.

"A'Cara, please."

The voice was plaintive, and it hurt. It hurt the very young, eager woman she used to be, and still reverted to on occasions. Occasions when she was heart-deep in something. Cara interlaced her fingers and squeezed, external pain to block what churned inside. Patches of white appeared between pale knuckles.

"I can't." Elbows on the table, she leaned her head on her fists. "If you haven't faced Rodani's anger over security concerns, I have. It's not something I want to repeat."

Fabric rustled outside the door. "Forgive me, te'ono." Footsteps moved away, back down the hall.

The unexpected *young woman* term took her by surprise. Insult? Or daring compliment? Litelon was getting bolder. Another run-in with Rodani might have caused it. Or Rodani might have encouraged it. Surely not, after last night. She smiled as she began to break the incorrect stitches. Last night—

A crash echoed through the maids' corridor. Cara gasped. The seam ripper flew one direction, fabric another. A woman cried out.

"Falita?"

Someone tromped into the corridor, heavy of step. Cara slid off her chair and crouched near the table edge. A broad form darkened her bedroom. Falita shouted something incoherent.

Cara's heart beat painfully in her chest. Blood roared in her ears. Her hands trembled. Instinct made her duck.

Gunshots thundered from the doorway. A man stepped in; pistol held at his waist. Cara jerked sideways as another bullet blew past and buried itself in the wall.

The man took another step and shifted the gun. Cara gripped the edges of the quilt frame, with nowhere to go.

Falita ran through the doorway with an iron poker. She drew her arms back and swung for his skull. He jerked and raised his arm, then grunted as the metal struck.

Cara dumped the quilt frame onto its end and heaved it toward the fight, then darted forward, fists clenched. The man bashed the frame away. It clattered against the door.

"Run!" Falita shouted.

Cara took off for her bedroom and the dark corridor behind. Another shot blasted the stone next to her shoulder, creating a hail of pebbles. She ran into the servants' living room, arms outstretched for the doorknob.

Litelon lay unmoving on the floor, his back to her.

Cara yanked the door open. A shot burst through wood where her head had been, showering splinters. The door banged against the wall. Footsteps followed her. Gasping, legs pumping, Cara headed full tilt for the main staircase, weaving a little. Somewhere, sometime, Rodani had told her it was harder to hit a moving target.

She could hope.

Her slippers rasped against stone. She jerked to the right as the stairs came into view. An explosion deafened her. Heat flew by, fluttering her sleeve.

Rodani!

Cara pounded down the extra wide steps a dizzying two at a time, her arm on the railing. The man entered the stairwell behind her before she reached the first landing. She danced erratically across the landing's flat space. Two more bullets shattered the smooth wall beyond her. Stone fragments peppered her head and chest. Her ears rang.

From the bottom of her gut, she screamed. "Rodani!"

Terror wrenched her insides. Desperate, she searched for safety. At the bottom of the stairs, the wide, open hallway gaped at her. She was dead.

Six steps.

Another shot blew by her. Weave and duck.

Eyes wide, a few strangers stood beyond her. They scattered.

"Rodani!" His name echoed through the halls.

Another boom of death.

Three steps. Another blast. Fire burned through her arm. Her hand went numb. Shock stole her balance and her grip on the rail. She stumbled and fell to the cold floor, rolling onto her back.

A few steps up, her attacker stopped, and sighted.

***

"That was the last item on the list." Kusik looked around the security room table at his assembled crew. "Others?"

No response.

"Disperse," he told them. There was a general scraping of chairs and rustling of paper, then a mass exodus of bodies for the doors.

"Rodani."

Rodani turned, blocking those behind him. They bunched up, then began a workaround.

"Wait," Kusik said.

Rodani made his way back to the table near his keso. He fixed his attention on the wall and drew his hands behind him. Timan walked up from the far end of the table to stand near his side.

Kusik shuffled his papers into order and slipped them into a worn leather folder. He flipped it over and pushed the tongue through its strap. "What are you doing?" he barked.

Rodani hesitated, with a question in the movement of his head. "A'Keso?"

Kusik rotated to face him; a whole body turn that cranked Rodani's instincts up to high.

"Has she destroyed your reason?"

"No, a'Keso."

Kusik's eyes narrowed. His fist shot upward and connected with Rodani's cheek. Rodani staggered, then caught his balance. The walls undulated in his vision.

"You have broken a guild rule."

Rodani blinked and took a deep breath. "There are exceptions to the rule, a'Keso."

Kusik bared his teeth. "My place is the only exception. You know this." He leaned forward. "I am discussing your dishonor with Arimeso. I will see you censured if I can."

"I claim extenuating circumstances, a'Keso."

"You claim nothing but air."

Kusik circled Rodani, looking him up and down like a piece of sculpture, judging its worth. The only sound in the room was the scuff of his boots on stone. Rodani stood glued in place, every muscle frozen, every sense attuned to his superior's movements—prey and predator. Kusik pursed his lips. His jaw tightened. He clenched his fist and belted Rodani in the stomach.

He bent and retched. Slowly he straightened upright, his breathing audible in all ears.

Kusik's pupils were slits, face a cold mask. "The thought of what you have done makes me ill."

"A'Keso—," Rodani sputtered. "A'Keso, she is a child of the goddess. She can give comfort and pleasure as well—"

Kusik swung. The blow to his carapace dropped Rodani to his knees and sucked the breath from his chest. "Cease your disgusting explanations!"

Thunder rumbled in the background, indoors where no thunder should be.

As his superior circled, Rodani rose—stood aching, stood and faced a peril no more earned than unexpected. Kusik was blind. Blind as Serano, but infinitely more dangerous. Only Arimeso carried both the tolerance and the wisdom to glimpse what Rodani saw.

The sound of distant shots invaded his head. He drew in an audible breath and tensed. Kusik's pupils pulsed.

A gun blast and the ghost of a scream crawled under the edge of the door, a scream that carried his name. Instincts surged in him. Protect. Kill. He glanced at Kusik's wrathful face. The keso looked away, waved his hand in dismissal.

No thought. No time.

Ahead of Timan, Rodani charged out, weapon already drawn, filled with dread at the sound of more shots. He raced to the end of the hall and skidded to a stop—pistol raised.

***

The man shifted his footing. His gun wavered, then steadied.

Cara laid gasping, head pounding from her fall. Her eyes refused to focus. Anticipation of agony filled her mind as explosions filled her ears.

The man's chest blossomed in red. His limbs jerked, skull pieces parted ways with the rest of him. He crumpled and fell. The pistol clattered on the steps. Three hundred pounds landed on top of her, flaccid, crushing the breath from her lungs. Red spattered her. Waste organs voided their contents. Empty eyes stared. Grey matter leaked onto her neck and dribbled down into her collar. Cara screamed and pushed at the lifeless, bloody body that lay on her with the closeness of a lover. A sickly odor overpowered her. Warm blood soaked her blouse. The body jerked. She screamed again.

A hand raised it up and pulled it off. The head bobbed, spilling pieces of brain onto her chest. Shrieking, Cara dug her fingers into its essence, frantically pushing it off. It clung to her hands, and to her blouse. She wiped her palms together. Another scream tore through her throat.

"Cara!"

Abject horror crept through her, primeval disgust. She squeezed her eyes shut and shook her arms frantically.

"Cara!" Hands gripped her wrists.

Several feet tapped and turned around her. Some stood in place as if conferring together. Voices muttered above her.

"Where are you hurt?" Rodani's face appeared in her vision. Someone was touching her body.

^No,^ she whispered in Cene'l. ^No. Go 'way. Go away,^ she pleaded to no one, fighting Rodani's grip.

"She is elsewhere," Rodani said.

She retched and turned on her side. Rodani lifted her up as she splattered the stone with the contents of her stomach. When she was empty, Rodani carried her into Baldar's clinic, laid her on one of the beds, then was politely but firmly ushered out of the room. He pulled out his 'com with an impatient jerk of his arm. "Six, Five. Six, Five."

"Six."

"Where in Temi's name are you?"

"Hamman's living room," Serano told him. "Cara?"

"Physically, she seems little hurt. But her sanity—" Rodani twisted his head around as the sound of muffled pain escaped through the door. "Talk to me, tem'u."

A pause in the reply did nothing for his equanimity. "Litelon lies on the floor," his partner said, "and Falita admitted to letting him in, not knowing Shurad was behind."

Rage flooded him. "Who is with you?"

"The keso."

"Take my place in the clinic. *Now.*" Rodani jammed his thumb against the switch and stuffed the 'com away. He paced the floor. It took all his guild training to hold a rising temper in check. He saw nothing in the room. Heard nothing now but silence beyond the inner door. Shivers ran through him, threatening to burst forth in destruction. He ran from the room and passed by his partner on the way.

"Stay with her."

Rodani sped full tilt down the hall, past blood, gore, and guild, and took the steps three at a time. Through the cross hall, into the corridor, past the splintered door, and right up against his punitive superior. Kusik eyed him coldly.

Litelon was sprawled on his side. Reserved, still, Falita refused to meet Rodani's hot gaze. He stooped and ran his hands over Litelon's body. He felt for a pulse at the top of the carapace where it met the shoulder plates. Before Rodani could ask, a physician's assistant arrived on the scene, and replaced him at Litelon's side. She examined the boy and rolled him on his back, then called for a stretcher. Rodani planted himself in front of the servant.

Falita froze into immobility, face devoid of expression.

"What did you do?" he demanded.

"Someone knocked on the door, a'tem," she said, her eyes wide and staring into nothing. "I inquired. It was Litelon, bearing a gift for a'Cara. He said he had spoken to you in the hall." Falita's jaw worked nervously. "He said you told him to give the gift to me, to hold it until you got there. I—"

"You believed him!" Rodani radiated fury. His pupils were merest slits, one fist clenched and unclenched rhythmically.

"It seemed reasonable, a'tem."

"Reasonable?" he shouted into her face. "Commands are not countermanded by reason!" He took a rigid step back. "Speak your orders," he said in formal mode.

Falita's ears twitched, her lips pulled into a thin line. "To care for a'Cara's body, belongings, and rooms. To be aware at all times of the need for security and precaution. To allow no one entrance to her rooms. To conduct myself at all times as if she were in danger or were a danger to others."

"And what did you do?"

Falita raised her chin. "Opened the door—to a companion."

Enraged beyond belief, Rodani slapped her, hard. "No companion! An underage and ill-thinking suitor who wouldn't recognize danger any better than you did." He leaned into her face. "I told Ulina in the beginning you were too young for this duty."

Falita's pulsing pupils reflected her emotions. "I fought for her life, a'tem."

"As you should have," he spat.

"She would not have gotten out alive had I not!"

"And her life would not have been endangered had you thought before you acted!" he retorted.

Falita turned her head aside. Kusik remained a step behind, silent.

Rodani fell into deadly stillness. "Continue."

"Shurad pushed Litelon inward," the young woman said, "and hit him on the head, then shoved me away. I grabbed a poker from the fireplace. He went through the corridor and shot at a'Cara, twice. I attempted to hit him from behind. Cara threw the quilt frame at him. In the commotion, she escaped. He threw me against the wall. I fell. He ran after her."

"That is all?"

"All I know, except that Shurad is dead at the bottom of the stairs, a'tem, and Cara alive."

"Why did you not give the alarm?"

Her pupils widened. "I—I was more concerned with—"

He struck again.

Falita's legs buckled. She fell into a huddled heap at his feet.

"Stand to me."

Shaky, she rose.

Rodani's fury bore into her face, burned a hole in her honor, and stripped her of pride. "You are dismissed from this duty," he shouted, struggling against the violence he wished to commit. "Gather your possessions."

A groan interrupted the tension. Rodani turned to the body on the floor.

"I will appeal," Falita said.

Rodani spun. "And I will meet that appeal with the facts." He aimed a long finger toward her room. She walked around the outthrust appendage in overt avoidance and turned her back to it all.

Rodani glanced at Kusik, who had remained silent throughout the censure, then at the doorway, as two men came in bearing a carry board from the clinic.

"A'Cara?" The voice from the floor drifted weakly upward.

Rodani stomped over to him. "What did you do, te'oto? Use another to get her killed?"

Litelon pressed his forearms to his temples. "No. No." He rolled away from the guardians, and from the healers. "She cannot be. No."

"She—" one healer began.

Rodani slashed the air with his hand, terminating the offer of information. "If she is, Litelon, it is your doing as much as Falita's."

Litelon remained wrapped in his pain, arms tightly pressed to his skull. "I would not. Would never. No." His face held horror and remorse.

Rodani bent over the distraught young man. "What did Shurad tell you? What were you about?" He stepped closer, edging between the healers. "Did you know he was behind you? What of this was planned?"

Litelon curled against the barrage of angry accusations.

"A'tem," the other healer said. "Questions may be asked later." He stepped between accuser and accused. "Please."

Rodani let out a gust of breath he didn't know he was holding and turned for the corridor that led to Cara's bedroom. Bullets had shattered the stone and littered the floor with lumps that put a stagger in his walk.

"Litelon?" said a voice. A high voice with an accent.

Rodani jerked to a stop, then ran back.

Wan and shaking, Cara stood next to the carry board, Serano behind her. She was staring at her adolescent suitor as baldly as he was staring back.

"A'Cara," he whispered.

Rodani pulled her away from the board as the healers moved to carry Litelon out. The boy's hand waved aimlessly in the air. "A'Cara."

Rodani kept a possessive grip on her arm and glared over the top of her head as she watched them leave. "I told you to stay with her, Serano," he said, voice regaining the heat that had not quite left him.

"Baldar sent her to her rooms, tem'u." Serano's expression was carefully calm in the face of his partner's agitation, his voice modulated into forced normalcy. "She wished to find you, first."

Rodani clamped the lid on his temper and tugged on Cara's unbandaged arm to turn her.

"What did Baldar tell you?"

Cara craned her neck to look up at him, then over to the doorway where Litelon had been carried. "Minor wound." She turned back and reeled with a loss of balance. "What happened?"

"Serano." Rodani gripped her arm more tightly and led her back to her own rooms, Serano following.

"Did you call for repairers?" Rodani asked his partner.

"Yes."

"Close the door. What type?"

Serano pushed the bedroom door shut. "Wood and stone. Dare I ask of Kusik?"

"He was free with his displeasure." Rodani left Cara standing and went into the workroom.

"Regrets?" Serano continued.

"Not for myself. But I am not finished chewing on some ears." Bullet holes greeted him from across the room. "And as usual your conversational timing is faultlessly flawed."

"I may hope I have no regrets," Serano said.

"It is my choice, not yours."

"What you do affects me."

Rodani shifted to gauge the angle of fire. "Do not repeat nursery lessons." He righted the quilt frame and pushed it back to its place by the window, then picked up the poker. He studied it and passed it to Serano, then walked back into the bedroom as Cara came out of the facilities.

"He stood at the fabric shelves?" he asked her.

Cara lowered herself into the overstuffed chair and pulled her feet underneath her. "Yes."

"What was your frame doing by the door?"

"I threw it at him while Falita was wrestling with him. Who was he?"

"How did you get away?"

Cara closed her eyes. A look of pain crossed over her face.

Serano came in and leaned against the wall. Rodani went to her, bent to look at the bandage on her upper arm. "How much are you hurting?"

"Some."

"How did you get away?"

She sighed. "Falita hit him with a poker. I tossed the frame and came toward him, intending to—to help disarm him."

Serano stirred, raised an incredulous eyebrow. "Disarm him?"

Cara turned her face aside. "Falita told me to run. I decided she was right. I ran out through the door," she cocked her head, "and down the stairs. Who was he?"

"Shurad."

"An artisan?"

"Yes, a writer."

"Why try to kill me?"

"The only answer I have is that he was born on the river."

Eyes wide, Cara leaned back into the corner of the chair. "Gods and demons, Rodani. No one told me there was a Riverchild in the house." She rubbed her shoulders across the chair back and winced. "Why now?"

"I do not know. Yet." The finality in his voice did not bode well for those concerned.

"He was an amateur," Cara told him, adjusting her arm. "It's the only reason I'm alive. I did what I could," she continued. "I'm not a guardian. You said it yourself."

"No one is blaming you for Shurad's treachery."

"If you could ask him, he'd claim honor not treachery."

"He went against his taso's orders. That takes precedence over ancestry."

"Did you kill him?"

Rodani hesitated. Why did it matter? She was safe, and her attacker was crossing over into Sela's arms. But he owed her a courtesy for the danger she'd faced in his absence. "Timan took the chest shot, I, the head."

"What did Litelon do?" she asked. "Did he know?"

"I have not talked with him, kia."

At the private name, her gaze flicked from him to his partner behind him, and back.

"Serano knows," he reminded her.

"I was right not to let him in."

Rodani glanced back at Serano, suddenly alert. "Let who in?"

"Litelon. He came to my door. I refused him." Carefully, Cara placed her hand over the bandage. "He must have tried Falita next," she added, exhaustion softening her tone.

Images of his worst nightmares flooded Rodani's mind. His disobedient adashi murdered, bedmate torn from him a day after their first joining. Honor lost, rank and status stripped from him. Angry humans demanding retribution. He knew what promises Arimeso had made. Rodani slumped onto the bed. "Goddess grant us gifts."

"What do you mean?" she whispered through the pain.

Rodani stared at her intently. "You obeyed me." It was a message he had to get across. Across a gap of culture and temperament that had tripped them more times than he wanted to count. He willed her to listen, to think, to contemplate what had almost occurred. She only blinked at him, body curled, and face folded into pain and fatigue.

"How did you know? To come?" she asked.

"I heard you scream. I heard the shots."

"I couldn't have outrun him much longer. Falita slowed him down."

Rodani's pupils went to slits, his mouth a tense line. "She let him in."

Surprise overrode her other expressions, prompting another flickering gaze between the two guardians. "On purpose?"

"Yes," Serano answered her. "Though likely she did not know there was danger."

"That does not matter," Rodani said. "She will not repeat the mistake."

"She wouldn't," Cara said.

"She will not have the opportunity. I dismissed her."

Cara's pupils widened. The movement made her seem less alien to him. She glanced toward the corridor. "Why?"

Rodani leaned back against the bedpost and regarded his bedmate incredulously. That couldn't be a well-thought question. Was the pain affecting her mind? He had fenced against her in too many conversations to think her so dull-witted. But her axioms were truly alien. And he was guild, owing no one but his superiors an explanation for his decision. He looked away in courteous refusal.

In his silence, Cara pulled the quilt off the bed and attempted to cover herself one-handed.

"You are cold?" he asked.

"Hurting. Tired."

Rodani rose from the bed and yanked the covers down in one massive pull. Cara tossed the quilt onto the bed in a heap, kicked her shoes off, and crawled in one-armed. Rodani pulled the quilt over her and motioned to Serano.

Serano walked out, hand on the doorknob to close it. But another tall form appeared in the doorway, obtrusive presence preventing him from giving the pair the privacy they obviously needed. He stepped back against the door in deference. Kusik filled the room with his anger. Rodani straightened but left a hand on Cara's shoulder—warning.

"Rodani." Kusik tilted his chin toward the door.

Rodani's ears twitched. He bent down, biting back on muscle complaints. Cara's eyes were riveted on the security first, her breathing heavy. "Stay in bed." He went around the end of the bed and passed by both partner and First on his way into the hallway. Serano followed them, shutting the doors. The servants' living area was empty of people, hurt or otherwise. The shutters were open, the room was light and quiet, watchful.

Rodani stood stiffly in the middle of the room, as much from the bodily aches he already carried as from propriety. His chest radiated pain, his cheek carried a dull throb from eye to ear. It hurt to breathe.

As the door to the corridor opened, Kusik sidled up to him—snake in the glade. His pupils went to mere slits. A line of teeth shone between parted lips. He raised his arm.

Rodani saw it coming and tensed. The slap rocked his head to the side, landing where the previous one had. He willed the tension from his body and opened his eyes to the sight of Arimeso and

Timan. The room was suddenly crowded.

Kusik thrust his face into Rodani's. His breath was sour, and hot.

"Your personal pleasures have interfered with your duties. Dare you tell me you could not have predicted this attack?"

The door to Cara's room opened. Heads turned. Shuffling slippers scratched their way into the hallway.

Rodani hissed at Serano, who trotted into the dark hall at a rapid clip. Whispers worked tendrils into the room, then a clear high voice followed. "Who is hitting whom?"

"Tsss."

"Roda—"

The voice cut off. Scuffling erupted, then a click, and silence.

Rodani focused on the far wall, on the door that boasted a hole in it, human head high. "I have read the reports, a'Keso, as everyone else has. I cannot follow every person with anti-human sentiments as they go about their days. Duties preclude it."

"Duties," Kusik drawled. An undercurrent of threat deepened his voice, turned it into a low growl. He clenched his fist and rammed it up under Rodani's chin.

His head rocked back. He stumbled and tasted the bitter tang of salt where teeth met tongue.

"And do your duties include geimach with your adashi?"

It was a crude term, one Rodani had never heard his first use. He swallowed the blood that pooled around his tongue and took a deep breath, glancing toward Arimeso. "A'Taso, I request a hearing."

"Denied," she said.

The next blow went low. Rodani grunted and folded downward.

"Cease." Arimeso walked into the confrontation. "This is personal, not professional, Kusik."

Kusik stood at attention in the face of his taso's judgment. Rodani pushed upward, shaky, abdomen awash with misery.

Arimeso turned to him. "If you choose to continue your present course, you will reap the consequences, as well as any rewards you may find."

Some private message passed from her to Kusik, for he bowed and opened the door for her. Relief mixed with dread filled Rodani's mind as the trio left him alone, a tall, solitary figure in black, in a room of ghosts and sunlight.

His foolishness was coming home to haunt him.

The door to Cara's bedroom was still shut, and surprising silence lay beyond it. Mindful of his aches, Rodani walked down the dim corridor and opened the door. Serano stood with his back to the armoire, facing a seated Cara, who had curled into a ball on the edge of the bed.

"It begins," Serano said, voice low and heated.

Rodani came to a halt in front of him. "Do not walk this trail, tem'u."

Cara lifted her head and stared at the two men, eyes wide and face strained in pain.

"You have set my feet upon it. I see no choice."

"Not now."

Serano shifted against the carved wooden door, and brought his hands forward, near the edge of his jacket. His pupils went to slits. "Now."

Rodani took a deep breath. It caught against the wall of burning in his chest. He stepped back and nodded toward Hamman's living room, but his attention never left his partner. They walked out.

The room was no more comforting to his mind or his body than before. One more confrontation, one more contest to his private decision. His face ached, his stomach knotted.

"Why now?" he said. "Why not last night, or this morning?"

Serano strode to the window and back. "You satisfied your desire and our curiosity on the subject. I did not seriously consider it was more for you than that."

"What I feel for her is my responsibility."

Serano waved his arm in a wide arc. "You have other responsibilities."

Rodani bared his teeth. "She is my adashi. You know the priorities."

"And she is proscribed."

"I have made my decision."

"And dragged me into a fight where I am both blameless and impotent," Serano said, voice rising as he leaned into his partner.

Rodani stood his ground. "You carry no bruises."

"Do not play ignorant with me, Rodani." He shook his fist near Rodani's chin and shouted. "We are partners!"

Too close, and too far over the line. Rodani clouted him with a blow to the temple. Serano replied with a fist to Rodani's sore midriff, and a blow to the jaw as he doubled over. Rodani fell, sprawling. Serano dived for him. Rodani grabbed the leg of a side table and bashed it into Serano's shoulder as the vase that had rested on it shattered on the floor.

The door to the corridor banged open, and a small shape entered his peripheral vision. "Stop it! Stop!"

Rodani ignored her in favor of fending off Serano's attack with fists and knees. They rolled toward the couch, trading grunts and blows.

"Stop, please!" she shouted.

As they hit the couch, Rodani landed on top and put his arm to bear against Serano's throat. Serano brought his knee up in a vicious blow at the pelvis. Rodani bellowed in agony and rolled off. Serano jumped on him and put him in a stranglehold, then tucked his head into Rodani's chest, face avoiding his numbing blows.

Gasping, Rodani bucked and rolled in an attempt to get Serano off of him before he passed out. His vision began to grey and tunnel inward, his strength weakening.

Something overshadowed him.

"Get off him, damn you!"

Serano lifted his head and roared in outrage, eyes wide and burning. He let go of Rodani and turned. Rodani heaved a deep breath and focused outward, just in time to see Cara release her fierce grip on Serano's hair. Serano lunged for her as she dodged out of reach.

"Stop it, you two!" she screamed.

Serano shot to his feet. Rodani rolled and kicked them out from under him before he could reach her.

"Leave!" he shouted to her. *Obey me. Goddess above. Get out!*

Serano rose up on all fours as Rodani scrambled toward them. "Run!"

He was too far. Too late. Serano reached out.

Cara grabbed a lamp off the tea table and swung it in an arc, hitting him in a heavy blow to the head. He collapsed. Rodani yanked his cuffs from his belt and slapped them over Serano's wrists, then sat back on his heels and stared at Cara, his sides heaving.

"Why did you interfere?"

Cara gaped at him and put her hand over her bandaged arm. "He was choking you. He could have killed you!"

Goddess help the ignorant. He thought he'd taught her most

of the things she needed to know. One more mistake to his credit. "Kia, this was not a fight to the death, or even to great harm." He leaned his weight onto his knees and put a hand on the tea table as a prop to rise.

"Then what was it?" she asked, confusion and pain on her face.

She didn't believe him. That was obvious in her expression. He stood on the other side of Serano, shaky from the emotions, and the punishments he'd had to swallow. Anger and pride, both feelings fought within him as he faced Cara. Where was the right? Where was propriety?

"It was a fight for status. For position in the partnership and security staff." He dusted off his pants and straightened with a grimace for abused muscles. "You interfered."

"You were losing."

Between them, on the floor, Serano groaned and turned over, cuffed hands underneath him.

"That negates nothing," Rodani said. "I accepted the challenge."

Cara squeezed her eyes shut and looked away, then back at him. "He was hurting you."

Did she not understand? His words were plain. "I—"

From the floor, Serano lashed out with a foot sweep. Rodani collapsed and fell against the edge of the tea table with a heavy thump. He groaned.

"I claim victory," Serano said. "You were wrongly aided."

"Claim this," Cara shouted, and slammed her foot into his side.

Rodani jerked forward. "Cara, no!"

Serano gasped, curled over, and tried to shift his legs toward her.

Dizzy, back muscles spasming, Rodani pulled a knife and lunged at Serano, reaching for the nearest appropriate spot. Serano froze and glared down his body at Rodani, and at the knife held at his crotch.

"Her interference was not my doing," Rodani said. He crawled forward and fumbled one-handed at Serano's belt for the keychain all guild carried, then stood away from him. He sheathed his knife and pulled off the keys for both Cara's and Hamman's doors. Pocketing the keys, Rodani pulled Serano to his feet and led him out the door. He unlocked the cuffs, gave his partner a parting shove, and tossed his keys on the corridor floor before shutting the door.

Rodani leaned his forehead against the door and sighed heavily, trusting his irate partner not to shoot him from the other side. He hurt in a dozen places and would hurt in a dozen more come morning. It was a tangle of universal proportions he faced, brought on by his own personal failings, by needs better kept to himself, to his own species.

But...

He turned to Cara, and there was a look in her eyes he'd never seen on any other woman. Child-sized, she had run from an enemy bound to kill her, and wounded, fought for him against an opponent who could break her in half.

Temi guard us.

Rodani leaned up against the door, wincing. She meant too much to him to hide his pain from her, but her reactions were already suspect. He relaxed his facial muscles and looked at her. Her eyes were wide, pupils nearly as large as the blue that surrounded them.

"You have done as much harm as good, Cara. Go back."

Her eyes began to shine with excess water.

Inwardly he cringed. "Kia." One more crisis was two more than he could face right now. "Forgive me for whatever offended you and go to bed. Please."

The water meandered down her cheeks. She turned toward the corridor.

"Kia."

She looked back.

"If it would please you, I will lay down with you."

Cara raised her hand, held it out to him.

Rodani managed a wry smile for her open invitation in the midst of an upheaval. "Soon."

THIRTY-ONE

She hadn't quite obeyed him, no surprise. There seemed to be something in her alien nature that prevented her from completely following orders. Instead, she was curled up in the chair. Rodani shut the door behind him and swept his hand over the rumpled covers.

"Bed. Please," he added belatedly.

Cara crawled off the chair and onto the mattress. Rodani covered her, then slipped off his boots and weapons belt, tucked his pistol into his waistband, and scooted under the covers. Gently he maneuvered himself in behind her, cautious with the bandaged arm that rested along her side, and cautious as well, of his own bruises and aches.

"Pillow for your arm?" he asked, remembering her penchant for a folded shelf in front of her.

"Please."

He pulled an extra one from behind his head, folded it, and tucked it underneath the quilts next to her chest. Slowly she moved her arm across the pillow, hand curled against her chin. Rodani flipped the quilts over them both, then laid his arm over her waist and worked his hand up between her sweater and the pillow, hoping she wouldn't find offense in the touch. He rested his chin among the curls on top of her head, his chest against her back.

"I'm sorry, Rodani."

"For what?"

"For so many things."

"What manys?"

She was silent for a moment. He shut his eyes against the pain in his throbbing temple and waited.

"I know Kusik hit you," she said. Her voice was quiet, much more so than usual. What did that mean? Did it go with sorry?

"That was no surprise, kia."

"Was he angry about us, or Shurad?"

"Both."

Again, she paused, as if digesting his admittance, then, "Keep talking. Please."

"There is nothing more to say."

"^Bullshit.^ Did you know last night he would be angry?"

"Yes, though I could not predict his exact reaction."

"Will he," she paused, "do it again?"

"Possibly, but Arimeso stopped him this time. She may take exception to him repeating his actions."

Cara tucked her head, chin toward her chest. The curls under his jaw tickled his skin, and a medicinal soap scent wafted upward. Baldar and staff had done more than stitch her arm in the short time she'd been in his clinic.

"I don't want you hurt, Rodani."

"Leave that worry with me, kia."

"I can't help but worry," she chided him.

Au. "Kia, I am much more aware than you of what is trouble among my people, and what is not. My honor is strong, my awareness high." He caressed her with the hand hidden in warmth. "You do neither of us a worthy duty by concern with what you cannot help."

"And Serano? He fought you."

"You did not cause it, kia. My differences with my partner over you began before you ever arrived. But you should never have interfered in guild matters."

"I thought it was personal, not guild."

"No. That was guild. Kusik's censure was personal."

"Is the partnership over?"

It took some getting used to, this jumping from one subject matter to the next, and back again. "No."

"How can you work together after fighting like that?"

"It is who we are. The bond. The need to be a part of something larger than us. It is the same thing that holds us to a taso."

"What would Serano have done to me?"

"Knocked you senseless."

"But he is supposed to protect me, not hurt me. Arimeso said not to hit."

"And you are a guest here and should not be pulling his hair or bashing him with a lamp."

She huffed. Her soft mounds moved under his hand,

temporarily wiping his hurts from the forefront of his mind.

"By my honor, I had reason."

"And by his honor," Rodani replied, "he could retaliate."

Cara lay quiescent under his arm. He wondered for how long the silence would last. It seemed to be her way not to let a subject die until it was tamed and controlled with a rein of answers.

"And what of Shurad?" she asked.

Not long enough. "What of him?"

"I never wanted anyone to die on my account."

He ran his lips across her curls. "Shurad brought his own death."

"I thought he brought mine."

"I feared not to get to you in time."

"But you did," she reminded him. "Again."

"The goddess watches over you."

"Rodani watches over me."

"I am not Iraimin."

"If you were, you wouldn't be in my bed."

Rodani smiled, inhaling the scent of her hair, her body. With honor and adashi intact, he calmed himself and closed his eyes. Now he had time to feel his own hurts.

Beyond the closed shutters, the sun fell to the west. The room dimmed in the fading light.

"Will I be sent home?" she asked.

"I believe not."

Cara flexed the fingers of her bandaged arm. "Is that a certainty or an assurance?"

"Nothing is certain, kia."

"Come over to my other side?" She patted the mattress.

"Why?"

She sighed. "So I can look at you, not at the armoire."

Slowly he crawled over her, crab-like, cautious against jarring her arm, then settled down on the other side of the folded pillow. One six-fingered hand rested on her hip, the other he curled under his head.

"Oh, my gods, your face," Cara said. Hints and splotches of red and purple over top the grey, an ugly and painful contrast to the beauty of his eyes. She reached out to touch his high cheekbone with a feather light finger. "You need an ice bag. You're hurt worse than me."

"No. I will heal."

"That has to hurt," she said. His face was impassive, despite the damage. "Kusik did all that with two hits?"

He pursed his lips. They curled upward, and just as quickly flattened out as the muscles around his eyes tightened. "You counted?"

"I could do nothing *but* count, Rodani. Serano had me trapped, and I couldn't bear to cover my ears. I had to know—whatever I could."

"That makes no sense. What you do not know, you do not feel. And you feel too much as it is."

"But there are two sides to feeling too much. And there's no such thing as too much happiness, or pleasure."

"That is debatable."

"Not now."

Despite the bruises, her guardian's presence radiated a peace and security that wrapped her in an invisible quilt. Never did she dream he would be sharing her bed, not that day he met her at the boat, not the day they fought with hands and teeth, not the day she'd held him at the cliff. She smiled.

"What do you find so humorous?" he asked.

"Remember when I bit your thumb?"

He pursed his lips, blinked slowly. "I still have the scar."

Cara glanced at the bandage that covered her thumping wound. "I'll have one, also."

"If that is your only one, kia, the goddess truly smiles on you."

"I would rather have you at my side than an invisible goddess."

"At your side," he mused, running his hand down her thigh and back up. "That position may be problematic." He leaned his head toward hers. "I will consider it at my leisure while we heal."

Cara tapped him lightly on his arm for his salacious banter.

The sun and the moon. Goddess and consort. The light and the dark. All decisions had it. He'd incited painful rages in his first and his partner, and possibly provoked dilemmas of honor and politics in his taso that he could barely comprehend. But—make her welcome, Arimeso had said. See that she adapts as much as possible. Do for her what you can, that this venture be a success.

Honor-bound, Rodani had done his duty. He was, after all, the best for the job.

The End

Look for the exciting sequel...

The Fabric of Strife
Available November 2024

Cara stepped through the doorway. The room was bare of anything but a chair and a high window.

With bars.

Vertical bars. Cara stopped and stared open-mouthed at the sight. The door shut behind her. She turned back and grabbed the door handle. It was locked. She banged on the door and cursed the empty room, pacing its narrow width.

No Rodani. No answers. No knowledge.

An illicit love affair.

A locked cell.

Priestesses with a mandate to enforce their goddess's whims.

Cara's fingers began to tingle, and her knees felt weak. Winter sun shone through the barred window, casting striped shadows on the bare floor. A cold breeze came with it. Wisps of clouds floated high in the sky, flying in the freedom she dearly needed.

A Selandu-sized chair sat in the middle of the floor. Cara stared at it.

And back at the window.

And at the chair.

She put her weight against it and tipped the chair on one leg, then swung it around onto a second leg. Little by little she walked the chair until it rested against the wall underneath the window. She climbed on top of the chair back and gripped the bars as high up as she could reach. With a massive pull she got her feet on the windowsill. She tested the space between the bars with her head. They were close enough to keep in a Selandu, but not a human. Twists and turns got her through the gap.

With a last look down, she dropped onto the dry winter grass, ignoring the aching arm that Kusik had gripped.

With her back against the stone, the manor's west wall ran distant to her left, windowless for the first few hundred feet south and interrupted by the water wheel. To her right was a short bit of wall, also windowless, then a corner. She sidled up to the corner and peered around. Along the eastbound north wall were a trio of Selandu, conferring near the garden. Cara could only hope they didn't notice her.

She had to try to find Rodani. Had to see him. Had to know. Along the wall were two windows, then another stretch of unrelieved stone. She tiptoed to the first window. It was barred, and the room was empty. Frustrated, she yanked on the bars. But they remained solidly in place.

Where was he? Arimeso's quarters? She'd never find him there, not without being caught. She went on to the next one, which was lower down and unbarred. Slowly, slowly, she approached the window. The flash of an enclave gold robe passed by. She ducked back and held her breath. *Was Rodani in there? Were they questioning him? Hurting him?*

Cara knelt and crawled under the window, then leaned against the stone. Mutters were all that came to her ears. Female voices only, no beloved baritone. The cold wind threaded its way through the gaps in her jacket and blouse, and bleeding through the loose weave of her pants. Hands and knees in the grass, Cara trembled in agitation.

Where was he? What did they do with him? What was going on? She couldn't peek through every window, and she was bound to be missed. Well, they wouldn't take her if she could help it.

Full of fear, Cara crawled backwards until she was away from the window, ran around the corner, and headed south across the grassy field between wall and woods.

GLOSSARY

Bolded names and terms are the more important ones.

Cara MacLennan	crafter, dancer, independent, opinionated, emotional	
Rodani	Security Fifth: Cara's guardian (m): crafter, eccentric, protective	row-DON-ee
'ai	suffix: plural of a noun: ex: a'tem'ai: a'sel'ai	aye
'com	pocket communication device, brought down from shipboard and run by small atomic battery and carried by all guardians, and occasionally by others	
'corder	music playing device brought down from shipboard	
a'	prefix: honorific: formal courtesy of address	ah
a'em	honorific form of addressing a temichi directly	ah-TEM, as in "temp"
a'sel	honorific form of addressing any regular Selandu person	a-SELL
a'selaso	honorific form of addressing a high priestess	ah-sell-AH-so
a'taso	honorific form of addressing a taso directly	ah-TAH-so
a'temaso	honorific form of addressing the head of guild guardians	ah-tem-AH-so
adashi	one who is guarded from others by a guardian	ah-DASH-ee
affinity	love/sex relationship, usually	

	long-term	
ama	Cara's name for her mother	AH-mah
Andrew Lieu	Ambassador Second: pronounced Andreh' by Selandu	Lee-ooh
Arimeso Osanin	taso: leader of Barridan (f)	Air-ih-MAY-so oh-SAH-nin
Baldar	physician: master healer (m)	BALL-dar as in "dart"
Barridan	name of both the estate that Arimeso rules, and the manor house where the crafters and artists live	BEAR-ih-dahn
bedmate	lover: no formal declaration	
benatac	large horse-like animal: toes and sharp teeth: irascible	BEN-ah-tack
biso	Security Second: partner to Security First	BEE-so
Cene'l	human language: based on Welsh language but intermixed with English and common words from other languages.	ken-EL
Chendal	head of guild guardians: the temaso (m)	CHEN-dahl
CSC	Cultural Studies Center: small group of humans formally studying with Selandu, and two ambassadors working in Hadaman.	
dae	Cara's name for her father	day
Davad	Cara's next younger sibling: (m): same father	DAH-vahd
Dienata	Rodani's gun	dee-en-AH-tah

372

Domendi	stablemaster (m)	doh-MEN-dee
du	no	dthoo: short sound! don't extend the "oo."
eisenico	Rodani's drink, amber in color, full-bodied	aye-sen-EE-ko
Enclave	both the area in the manor where the priestesses live and work, and the name of the group of priestesses themselves.	AHN-clayve
Falita	Cara's junior servant (f)	fa-LEET-uh
festive room	indoor recreation area: drinking, dancing, music, wrestling, betting.	
Garidemu	potter (m): hates humans	gare-ih-DEY-moo rhymes with "dare"
gathering room	for large dinners, celebrations, punishments	
Glaniad	larger human town, government center: (in Welsh, it means landing or touchdown)	GLAHN-yadth
Hadaman	capital city: north and somewhat east of Barridan	HAH-dah-mahn
Hamman	Cara's senior servant (f)	HAH-mun
Himadi Hills	low hills separating Selandan (north) and Newydd Cenedyl (south)	hih-MAH-dee
Himadi House	manor under construction on the Himadi Plateau: Selandu and humans are to live there and work together for the betterment of both species.	same

Himadi Plateau	flatlands north of the hills	same
Imal	Security Third (m)	IH-mul
Iraimin	painter: mirrored: friend to Cara (f)	ih-RAI-min as in "rye"
Katu	Serano's lover at the time the story starts (f): crafter	CAT-oo
keso	Security First: often mate to the taso	KAY-so
ki'oto: ki'ono	little man, male child: little woman, female child: can be used respectfully or insultingly	kee-oto: kee-ono
ki'tana	Little whirlwind	kee-TAH-nah
kia	Little one (intimate usage)	KEE-uh
Kimasa	head of the Enclave of priestesses: the selaso (f)	kih-MAH-sah
Kishata	aun that Rodani lets Cara use (smaller)	kish-AH-tah
Kusik	the keso—Security First: Arimeso's husband	KOO-sick
Lanata	Security Fourth (f)	lah-NAH-tah
Larisi	Serano's next lover (f): new acolyte of the Enclave	lah-REE-zee
Liam	cara's father	
lie-that-is-courtesy	An obvious prevarication for courtesy's sake and should not remark upon it.	
Litelon	stablehand (m): good with the animals. Mid-adolescent. Crush on Cara	lih-TELL-on

mate: bonded mate	spouse: formal declaration of joining lives	
Menachem Mboto	Ambassador First: pronounced Mena'hem by Selandu	men-AH-(flegm) mm-BOH-toh as in "boat" and "tote"
Misheiki	Security Seventh (m)	mish-AY-kee as in the letter "a"
Newydd Cenedyl	land south of the hills: human lands (means "new nation")	Welsh: NEY-width KAN-a-dill
ninety-nine	sign-off on a given command or exchange over 'com	
River Samida	river where the battle was fought: also name of the battle	sah-MEAD-ah
sai	yes	sigh: short sound
sel'u	informal name for Selandu companion ("friend")	SELL-oo
Sela	goddess of the Selandu	SELL-uh
Selandu	species' name	seh-LAN-doo the "a" as in "land"
selaso	head of the Enclave: high priestess	seh-LAH-so
Serano	Security Sixth: Rodani's guild partner (m): womanizer, impatient	seh-RON-oh
shigeli	Cara's alcoholic drink, sky blue in color, semi-sweet	shih-GAY-lee
Shurad	Riverchild: writer	SURE-add

Soldan	ocean-side town where boats from Newydd Cenedyl dock	SOLE-dahn
taso	head of a manor house and all its inhabitants.	TAH-so
tasos and temichin	card game	
te'oto: te'ono	young man, male youth: young woman, female youth	teh-oto: teh-ono
tem'u	informal name for guild partner: close companionship	TEM-oo, as in "temp"
temaso	head of the Guild of Guardians (only three people in guild council are higher)	teh-MAH-so
Temi	consort to the goddess: worshipped by guardians	TEM-ee as in "temp"
temichi	Selandu name for guardian	teh-MEE-chee
temichin	plural of temichi	teh-MEE-chin
Tendiman	town holding the guild training center: west of Barridan	TEN-dih-mahn
Timan	the biso—Security Second: Kusik's guild partner (m)	TEE-mun
Ushando	taso in the westernmost town/manor: hates humans	oo-SHAN-doe

TASOS AND TEMICHIN
a card game by J.A. Komorita

Instructions:

The setup.
1) Two players.
2) Shuffle a standard 52-card deck. Shuffler fans out the cards face down in one hand. Each player chooses one card.
3) The player with the highest card (Aces high) chooses their suit first (explained in step 5). If the cards match, keep trying until they are different.
4) Replace the two cards and shuffle again. Deal out 9 cards each.
5) From the cards in your hand, pick a suit that gives you the most top cards.
   a. Winner of step 2 goes first in choosing which suit they will play. The other player chooses one of the 3 other suits.
6) The Ace of your chosen suit is your Temichi. The other Ace of the same color is your Ally Temichi.
   a. Example: If your chosen suit is Diamonds, the Ace of Hearts is your Ally Temichi.
7) If you are male, the King of your chosen suit is the Taso, and the other King of the same color is your Ally Taso.
8) If you are female, the Queen of your chosen suit is the Taso, and the other Queen of the same color is your Ally Taso. (Optional: choose the card that best represents you.)

The Play
1) The person who lost in Step 2 (above) goes first, for the **first** hand. Alternate in further hands.
2) Players take turns. They can draw one card from the deck, **or** the opponent's hand, **or** the discard pile.
3) You want to try to get and keep (in equal importance) your own Taso and Temichi (in the suit you chose), and secondarily, your Ally Taso and Temichi.
4) It also helps a great deal to get and hold your opponent's Temichi, because it lowers the chance of them winning the hand (meaning they would only win by having both their Ally Taso and Ally Temichin if they drew your Taso).
5) Optional: If you draw your opponent's Temichi, call out

"Temichi capture" (or "Guardian Capture") and lay the card down in front of you. This option **must** be decided before the game begins.
6) With all other cards you may draw, hold the cards with the highest point values and discard the lower ones.
7) To win the hand, you must be the first to have in your cards:
    a. Your Temichi (Ace of your chosen suit) **and** your opponent's Taso (King or Queen of their suit); or
    b. Your Ally Temichi **and** your Ally Taso, **and** your opponent's Taso.
8) First player to hold the necessary cards in steps 7a or 7b calls out "Kill," and lays down their cards.

Scorekeeping:
1) Decide before play begins what score you must reach to win the game. Ex: 100, 200, or 500 points.
2) Temichi of your suit = 15 points
3) Taso of your suit = 14 points
4) Ally Temichi = 13 points
5) Ally Taso = 12 points
6) Jacks = 11 points
7) For all others use face value
8) Winner of the hand gets an extra 50 points.

Notes:
1. You cannot change your chosen suit after the hand begins.
2. For simplicity's sake you both can decide to keep the same suit throughout the whole game, as switching with each subsequent hand can get confusing. Or, you can choose a new suit with each hand. This **must** be decided before the game begins.
3. If you run out of cards in the deck before someone wins, the hand is a draw. Count your cards, but no one gets the extra points for winning.
4. You must discard at the end of each turn, including at the end.

AUTHOR'S BIOGRAPHY

J.A. Komorita is a born and raised Hoosier, who moved to Texas in her late twenties. Within two weeks, she met the man who would become her husband. They raised twin sons and a daughter. They live in a very crowded home with two cats, 900+ books of nearly every genre, and more art and craft supplies, completed and unfinished projects, notes, designs, and ideas than she will ever use in three lifetimes.

She would like to borrow and modify a quote from the esteemed SF author Anne McCaffrey: "My eyes are blue, my hair is grey, the rest is subject to change without notice."